A Little Learning

ALSO BY CARO FRASER

The Pupil
The Trustees
Judicial Whispers
An Inheritance
An Immoral Code
Beyond Forgiveness
A Hallowed Place

A Little Learning

CARO FRASER

MICHAEL JOSEPH
LONDON

MICHAEL JOSEPH

Published by the Penguin Group

Penguin Books Ltd, 27 Wrights Lane, London W8 5TZ, England

Penguin Putnam Inc., 375 Hudson Street, New York, New York 10014, USA

Penguin Books Australia Ltd, Ringwood, Victoria, Australia

Penguin Books Canada Ltd, 10 Alcorn Avenue, Toronto, Ontario, Canada M4V 3B2

Penguin Books (NZ) Ltd, Cnr Rosedale and Airborne Roads,

Albany, Auckland, New Zealand

Penguin Books (South Africa) (Pty) Ltd, 5 Watkins Street,

Denver Ext 4, Johannesburg 2094, South Africa

Penguin Books India (P) Ltd, 11, Community Centre,

Panchsheel Park, New Delhi - 110 017, India

Penguin Books Ltd, Registered Offices: Harmondsworth, Middlesex, England

First published 2001

Published simultaneously in Penguin Books

1

Set in 12.5/14.75 pt Garamond
Typeset by Rowland Phototypesetting Ltd,
Bury St Edmunds, Suffolk
Printed in England by Clays Ltd, St Ives plc

A CIP catalogue record for this book is available from the British Library

ISBN 0-718-14493-7

To Liz and Robin Sutton,
with thanks and much love.

I

Carla Tradescant sat in her kimono of dark-blue sprigged silk, drinking coffee. She drank it from a big, hand-painted earthenware cup brought back from a Tuscan holiday five years ago. Her slender hands embraced its warmth as she watched her husband get ready for work. She observed him with an air of detachment which seemed to comprehend every visible difference between the two of them, like a silent commentary. At Carla's end of the long, oval-shaped kitchen table lay a basket containing two warm croissants, a pot of cherry jam, a white napkin, a plate which matched the coffee bowl, and a copy of *The Times*. At the other end lay a sheaf of messy papers, a plate of toast crusts, and a small, brass ashtray in which a cigarette smouldered. Alan Tradescant sat poring over the papers, sighing occasionally as he tried to put them in some order. His tatty leather briefcase, with its sad straps and worn buckles, sat on the floor next to him. Carla glanced away from her husband to the front page of *The Times*, then broke off a piece of buttery croissant and ate it slowly. After a few moments she stood up and took her coffee cup over to where the pot stood on one of the stainless-steel work surfaces. She poured another cup, fresh and hot.

'More coffee?' she asked her husband.

Alan Tradescant glanced at his watch. 'Just a spot, thanks.'

She filled his mug, which was tartan in design and slightly chipped. His secretary had given it to him one Christmas, and he was fond of it. He always said he couldn't drink from those big Italian things Carla used. They made the coffee spill into his moustache.

She had never said so, but Carla hated her husband's tartan mug.

She took the coffee pot back and sat down again, the hem of her kimono grazing the tiled floor. She was a tall, graceful woman of forty-two. Her dark, silky hair, still untouched by grey, hung a couple of inches above her shoulders, the sides brushing her strong jawline, cut in a fringe above her blue eyes. She had worn her hair thus since the early seventies – which, to Carla, didn't feel like so very long ago. Someone had once told her, back then, that she looked a bit like Sandie Shaw. Alan Tradescant was roughly the same height as his wife, but his once spare figure had thickened to plumpness over the years, which made him appear smaller. He wore thick, frameless glasses, and what was left of his hair, which had once been dark and curling, was greying and fluffy. He had a moustache, very full and thick, whose luxuriance seemed to be an attempt to compensate for his receding hairline. The moustache was something Alan Tradescant had grown back in the late sixties – which sometimes seemed to him a very long time ago. No one knew what his upper lip looked like, not even Carla.

Carla had lately grown to loathe his moustache. Its texture and snuffling touch was the most ultimately repulsive thing to her about their intimate moments.

'Right.' Alan swept the heap of papers from the table

and into his briefcase. He stood up, glanced out of the window at the September rain, and went into the hall, where he examined his reflection anxiously in the hall mirror. He felt a shudder of nervousness run through his bowels at the prospect of this first day of a new term. Each year his position as headmaster of Taft's School seemed more and more onerous, the endless days filled with obstacles and problems, all sent by God to prevent his smooth running of the school. He had a recurring dream, one in which he was trying to grapple with a large, unwieldy burden held together with a variety of differently sized ropes and cords. In the dream he would try to grab hold of these to keep the load together as it pressed against his chest, but always he felt it falling asunder, the contents spilling out as the whole thing gave way. He hadn't had that dream all summer, all blessed summer – during which the worst events connected with Taft's had been tyre marks on the cricket pitch and a smashed window in the pavilion – but he knew it would come. In a matter of days it would come.

He sighed inwardly as he thought of his relatively untroubled days as a mere teacher, the freedom he had enjoyed under that mild oppression of being an ordinary, put-upon member of staff. There had been camaraderie then, of a sort – the odd free period in the staffroom, cups of tea, a snatched fag, common grievances to air – a bit like being a pupil, in fact. Now he was splendid in his isolation as headmaster. He took his tea alone in his room, for there was no time to sit around chatting. Endless paperwork, incessant administration, constant anxiety. And with whom to chat? He was the head, the feared, the respected. That was the worst. With the job came status, but even that was bogus. What he saw in the eyes of his staff was not respect, but marginal contempt. Only Mrs Prosser, his secretary, regarded him with true awe, but that was because she wasn't very bright, and she behaved as she did out of deference to his position and in tribute to her own loyalty, which she imagined was valued.

He shrugged into the jacket of his suit, which felt a little tight under the arms. He had put weight on over the summer. He should try to sort out a fitness regime, if only he could find the time. That was another thing, having to wear a suit and tie. A headmaster had to look the part. As a teacher, even as a deputy head, he'd been able to wear much what he pleased, as long as he looked halfway presentable. The only time he'd ever had to put on a suit was on parents' evenings.

He straightened his tie and turned from the mirror. Carla was standing in the doorway of the kitchen.

'Right. Back to the grindstone. Better get in early and try to keep ahead of the game. Not that there's much hope of that.' He took his raincoat from the coat rack, picked up his briefcase and went to kiss his wife. Carla stood silent, stoic, flinching inwardly as his moist lips touched hers, the hairs of his moustache brushing her skin. His large brown eyes looked anxiously into hers. 'What are you doing with your day?'

'The usual,' replied Carla. 'I'm having lunch with Maeve. And I thought I might take my car into Webb's to have the exhaust looked at.'

'Well, if you're in town, would you mind popping into Austin Reed's and having a quick look at the suits, see if

4

there's anything still in the summer sale? I think I'm growing out of this one. More like a forty-two these days. If there's anything you like, I can go in at the weekend and try it on.'

She nodded. The idea that she should *like* anything to do with his clothing, or with his person, seemed extraordinary. That he should assume it was both touching and sordid. She knew that there had once been a time when she had chosen shirts for him, smiled at the thought of how he would look in this or that, but she could not recall it, not with her senses or emotions. She had no idea how anybody travelled from a state of love to one of mild affection, then further to tolerance, to indifference, and in the end to a kind of guilty loathing. No idea. She only knew that it was a long and treacherous process. The best that could be said for it was that it took so long that one had plenty of time to acquire, first by intent and then by custom, the habits of affection, the guise of contentment. She had hoped, when she had first experienced the appalled realization of just how she truly felt about Alan after fifteen years of marriage, that this would be enough, that if she could maintain the appearance of love and intimacy, these things would reinforce themselves, and keep the show together. Each long day of this past summer had taught her, however, the hopelessness of this.

She nodded. 'I'll see what they've got.'

He left, closing the door behind her, and got into the car to drive the mile and a half to school for the first day of term.

Carla went into the drawing room and stood by the

window, watching him, thinking that if she were Alan she would walk the mile and a half, despite the rain.

Alan put the key in the ignition. As he turned to reach for his seat belt he caught sight of Carla at the window. She didn't usually watch him leave. He took it as a token of unspoken affection. He caught such gestures sometimes – smiles, little interested enquiries, an affectionate passing pat on his shoulder – and they helped to reassure him against the puzzling, troubling notion he often had that there was some kind of distance between them these days. He gave a little wave. Carla, after a few seconds, raised a slow hand in return.

When the car had disappeared from sight she went back into the kitchen and sat down again with her coffee and the paper. She read the home news with her customary distraction, her mind still preoccupied with Alan, his face, his body, his mannerisms. It seemed to her bizarre that he should occupy her thoughts in a way in which he never had when she had first been in love with him. In an endless pattern of disquiet, her mind dwelt on him, and on the impossibility of her situation. These thoughts were without resolution, did not even form themselves to any point of decision-making. They just existed.

Turning the page, she came across an article by Erica Jong. To Carla, for whom the passage of years was unmarked either by children or the accumulation of something which could properly be called a career, it seemed that Erica Jong and *Fear of Flying* were still part of the unending present. She was therefore a little startled to see the accompanying picture of a woman whose face, though still lovely and intelligent, was very much that of someone in their fifties. She hadn't thought it possible that Erica Jong could grow old. Nor Germaine Greer. That had been a shock, almost a sinful betrayal. Her eyes dwelt thoughtfully on the photo for a few seconds, and then she turned her attention to the article. It was entitled *The Perfect Man*. She read it as she now read all such things, with Alan at the forefront of her mind.

Knowing full well that life is too rich and strange for love to come in the form of a prearranged, predictable, prefabricated model, I still feel tempted to compile a composite of the perfect man. He's beautiful, but not without imperfection: a broken nose, crooked teeth. He's intelligent, never pedantic. Most important is his sense of humour. He can laugh in bed.

Carla sipped her coffee, which by now was lukewarm, and thought about this. Alan had his imperfections. He was balding and overweight – though somehow these imperfections seemed to fall into a less attractive league than crooked teeth or a broken nose. He was intelligent, too – but he had definitely become pedantic. She couldn't imagine a headmaster who wasn't. It was part of the job, pedantry. As for laughing in bed . . . well, you had to *want* to be in bed with that person, you had to have tenderness and desire, for anything to begin to be funny. Without those things, there was nothing funny about it at all. She began to read the quotes Erica Jong had culled from other women on the properties of perfect men.

'If I had to single out one quality,' said the singer-songwriter Carly Simon, 'it is a sense of joy.'

What on earth was that? She tried to imagine a joyful Alan. All she could picture was him at Maeve and George's dinner-table when he'd had too much to drink, red-faced and trying to remember old pop lyrics. That wasn't the kind of sense of joy that Carly Simon was talking about. Being Carly Simon probably meant that you got to have young, exuberant, gently spiritual lovers who didn't fart furtively under the duvet or obsess about school league tables, or scrape dirt from under their fingernails with the ends of spent matches.

'The perfect man is someone you love who also loves you,' said the psychologist Mildred Newman.

How true, how heart-rendingly true, and how bloody obvious, thought Carla. It sounded so simple. They love you, you love them back. It had been that easy once with Alan. Now *there* was a Carly Simon lyric. *It was so easy once, so easy holding hands . . .* She couldn't remember the rest of it, but there was a line in it she'd always liked, one Carly Simon sang in that raw, ballsy way you could really identify with: *Love can drive a normal woman to extremes.* What about the other extremes, the ones you felt driven to by a lack of love? Dear God, she didn't like to contemplate those. Carla folded up the paper and rose, taking her cup and plate to the sink.

Standing there, she made a decision. All of this was no use. For months she had dwelt upon the falling away of feeling for Alan, but she had no idea where it was taking her. She must face it now. She must explore it and examine it, and in the light of what she found, she must decide what to do. She was forty-two, and when she thought of the thirty or so years which might stretch ahead of her, alone with Alan, the depression which she felt pressed upon her like a stone. But it had not been always so. She would start at the very beginning, go back to the days when they had just met for the first time, and try to chart the progress of their relationship. Maybe along the way she would find the key, the missing link, the vital element, the thing which she could do to change her feelings back to the way they had once been.

She went upstairs and into the room which she and Alan called the study, where they kept the computer and, in various boxes and cupboards, all the accumulated debris of their past life together. She rummaged through the boxes until she found what she wanted.

Katie Rayment lay in bed, listening to the sounds of the house. Her mother opening and closing the cutlery drawer in the kitchen. The distant hiss of a tap running, the kettle being filled. Her father taking his shower. Sam's feet thumping on the stairs as he went down to breakfast. Max's voice yelping 'Sam! Stop it!' as Sam passed his younger brother, probably clipping his head with his hand or pulling his hair.

She'd get up in a little while. Just five minutes more. Her gaze travelled despondently round the room, taking in the painted chest of drawers, the muddled bookshelves, the Westlife posters, the dusty row of cacti on the window-sill. She'd really meant to do her room out before this term, change everything, ready for the reinvention of herself for the new school year. But she hadn't got round to it. Even though the holidays had seemed long and mostly boring, there had never seemed to be quite enough time. All those animal pictures she'd cut out a few years ago, when she'd still thought hamsters and kittens were adorable, and horses and ponies the most thrilling things in the world ... they were embarrassing now. What if Russell Tucker were to see her room? The possibility of Russell Tucker, prefect, captain of the debating team and flying scrum half, ever entering the precincts of Katie's bedroom, except in Katie's private fantasies, was admittedly remote. Still, Katie cringed as she imagined his critical eye ranging over the bookcase, catching sight of *Black Beauty* and the entire Borrowers oeuvre, glimpsing the china ballerina figures her gran had given her each birthday, year after year, even when she'd grown out of things like that. It was awful, completely unsophisticated. But what was the point of trying to change things when she'd still be stuck with that white-painted chest of drawers with the rose garlands stencilled on it, and those curtains? She'd loved it all when she was ten, but she was fifteen now, and past all that kind of thing.

She closed her eyes, replacing the vision of Russell Tucker sneering at her possessions with one where she was watching him play rugby, standing on the touchline, slimmer, her hair a lot longer, and he was hers, all hers, they were going out together, it was an accepted fact, loads of girls envied her, and then after, when he had showered and changed, he came out of the pavilion with his friends, his sports bag hefted on to his shoulder, and put a casual, proprietary arm around her, and then they sauntered off together ...

'Katie!' The sound of her mother's voice yelling from downstairs shattered the fantasy. Katie opened her eyes and got out of bed, calling down that she was coming, all right? She went along the landing and knocked on the bathroom door.

'Out in a moment,' called her father. She heard the tap running and the sound of him splashing water round the basin after his shave. Sometimes he didn't wash away all the little speckles of dark bristle and they'd still be there on the side of the basin when she went in. Gross. And the way Max, even though he was eleven, still forgot to flush the loo after he'd been. Horrible family.

After a few seconds her father emerged from the bathroom. Katie went in and locked the door. In front of the mirror she lifted her brown hair from the sides of her face and stared. It was still there. Right between her eyebrows, red and angry, with a yellow head. She fetched a piece of loo paper, pinched the spot between her fingers and squeezed. Pain and a small amount of pus. She blinked her eyes and inspected the site. Oozing now. It didn't look any better. She dabbed it with the tissue for a while until the little spots of blood dwindled to a pinprick. When it had dried she could dab some foundation on it. There was one coming up at the side of her nose, too. No amount of Biactol seemed to make any difference. She splashed water on her face and dried it, then smiled into the mirror. When she smiled she didn't look so much like a hamster. Quite pretty, in fact. But you couldn't go round grinning all the time just to make your face look thinner. She stopped smiling and sucked her cheeks in a little. Better, but just as hard to keep up. She relaxed, sighed, went back to her room and dressed. Even though she loathed her school uniform, with its blue, box-pleated skirt and money belt, and white shirt and cardigan, she still hadn't lost that childhood thrill of putting new stuff on for a new school year. That tearing crispness of the new cotton of her blouse, the unsnagged smoothness of her tights . . . and her new shoes. She'd managed to persuade her mum to let her have some Dr Martens this term, on the basis that she'd get a lot of wear out of them.

After she'd rearranged her duvet by way of making her bed, Katie caught sight of her diary lying on the shelf above, the little tasselled pen next to it. She took it down and re-read quickly what she'd written the night before.

MONDAY

I resolve that this is going to be a better year. I'm a new person. I'm going to be confident and organized, and I'm going to make Georgina see that she's not that important to me. Even though she is my best friend, she can't go on treating me like an inferior. O K, she's pretty and clever, but that doesn't amount to everything in this life, and everyone's going to see a new me. Including Russell. Oh, Russell . . . N O. I'm not going to go mooning around over him this term. I can see now it was a mistake to tell Georgina just how I feel about him. She never shuts up about it now. It's like she's taken something private, invaded me. Even though she is my best friend, I sometimes wonder if she really wants me to be happy. It's funny, trusting your friends. Or not trusting them. Still, there's no one else I'd really want to hang around with. But she's going to have to see that I'm someone in my own right, that I don't depend on her for popularity. God, I wish I weren't so insecure. When will my life ever be right? Maybe this term it will be different. Please let me be the person I want to be.

She sighed and put the diary back on the shelf. Then she stood in the middle of the room and closed her eyes. Right, she told herself. This is it. Like a film, with the credits rolling. My life starts . . . now.

She went downstairs and into the kitchen. Jenny Rayment was making up packed lunches for the boys and eating her own breakfast of toast and coffee at the same time. She was a plump, pretty woman in her early forties, somewhat dishevelled and flustered at the best of times, but especially so first thing in the morning.

'Weetabix?' she asked Katie.

'Thanks. But no sugar.'

'Katie, you can't eat it without a bit of sugar. It won't taste very nice.'

'Tastes like dog's crap, anyway,' said Max.

'Max!'

Katie sighed. 'All right. Just a bit, though. I'm really going to lose some weight this term.'

'You shouldn't be worrying about your weight at your age. It's not healthy. You used to love your food.'

Jenny put a bowl of two generously sugared Weetabix on the table. Katie poured milk carefully around them and began to eat, watching her mother move about the kitchen. All very well for her not to worry about being overweight. What was the point when you were forty-three? No one was looking at you. Mind you, she wished her mother would take a bit more care over her appearance. Look at her this morning, in that horrible old sweater with the paint stain on the sleeve, and those M&S leggings. It wouldn't be so bad if she didn't have such a big bottom. She knew from photos how lovely her mother had been when she was younger, but now all her prettiness was swallowed up by fat and tiredness. Georgina's mum was the same age, but she had a figure like someone of twenty. Georgina's mother always looked like she'd spent three hours getting ready just to run Georgina to school, proper make-up, her blonde hair sort of scruffy, but carefully scruffy, like the clothes she wore first thing in the morning – track-suit bottoms and trainers, a pastel-coloured sweat-shirt with a hood, like she was going straight off to do a workout. Even casually dressed she looked amazing. Then again, she was divorced. She had to make the effort, presumably, to find another man.

Katie glanced up as her father came into the kitchen, doing up his tie, his thick red hair combed back sleek against his head, still wet from the shower. Mike Rayment was four years older than his wife, and all Katie's friends agreed that he still looked amazing. Georgina said she fancied him, loved it when he came up behind her in art lessons and put his hand on her shoulder, or had to put his fingers over hers to help her with her brush strokes. Katie's father was the head of art at Taft's, and Katie often thought there was nothing worse in the world than being a pupil at the school where your father taught. She tried to ignore the stuff she heard about him, the reputation he had, like the rumour which had gone around last term about her father and the photography assistant. And there had been that time she'd heard some gossip about her father and a girl in the lower sixth, and it had made her head go hot and horrid, like it was going to burst. She hated it most for Mummy, because it must be awful to know your husband went after other women, and she felt protective of her mother. If she would just lose a bit of weight and try harder, like Georgina's mum, then maybe her father would stop messing around.

Beatrice, her seventeen-year-old sister, followed her father into the kitchen. She was tall, like Mike, and very pretty, with her mother's clear, soft-blue eyes, and long, rippling hair that was an extraordinary shade of reddish gold. Why was it, Katie wondered, that Bea had inherited all the best genes, the willowy, beautiful ones, and she, Katie, had got her grandmother's boring brown hair and her mother's tendency to plumpness? She liked her sister, was inordinately proud of how beautiful she was, but when Bea was around Katie automatically felt like a member of some inferior species. She watched as Bea sliced up an apple, a banana and some celery and chucked it all into the blender. Maybe if she could be bothered to eat as carefully as Bea, she would get thinner, too. But she couldn't eat the muck that Bea did.

Her reverie was broken by the disgusting sound of Max chewing toast with his mouth open while he watched *The Big Breakfast*. Katie stared at him with distaste. 'God, close your mouth when you're eating. You're repulsive.'

'Not as repulsive as you, spotty. Russell Tucker's hardly likely to fancy you with that huge spot in the middle of your face, is he?' He laughed unpleasantly and left the table.

Thirteen-year-old Sam glanced at his sister. 'Russell Tucker?' He gave a brief guffaw and turned back to the television. Katie decided that having two brothers at the same school was probably even worse than having your father there. I hate them, thought Katie, resisting the urge to put a testing finger up to the spot. She took her bowl to the sink, where her mother was rinsing milk bottles.

'Is my sports gear in my bag?'

'Not unless you put it there. I've got too much to do to be looking after all your things for school. Your netball things and your track suit are all clean and put away in your drawers. It won't take you a couple of minutes to find them. Start taking responsibility for your own life.'

'Oh, here we go.'

'Katie, this is your GCSE year. You have to become more organized, get a bit of discipline. And that's another thing. I want you straight home after school this term. No more hanging around at Georgina's house.'

'Mummy, we do our homework. We don't hang around.'

'So you say. Now, go and get your games kit. It's nearly ten past.'

Mike drained his coffee and went into the hall to put on his jacket, roaring at the children to get into the car or they'd all be late.

Ignoring him, Katie went upstairs at a leisurely pace to her room and fished out her sports clothes. Poised in the doorway on the way out, she suddenly remembered that the last ten minutes were meant to be on film, with her as the heroine. Cut. Start again. She composed her features. The film began here. With a half smile on her lips she went gracefully downstairs to begin her perfect day in her new incarnation.

*

Taft's was a co-educational independent school, with some eight hundred pupils, set in spacious grounds on the edge of the town of Huntsbridge, fifty-three miles from London. Established in the late eighteenth century as a school for the sons of local merchants by Sir Josiah Taft, woollen merchant and philanthropist, the original school building was a handsome manor house, which had been embellished down the years by the addition of a library wing, a science block, a sports hall and swimming pool, each in the architectural style of the prevailing time. It was flanked on one side by a busy main road, and on the other by the sports fields, bordered by a line of fine poplars.

As he parked his car in the staff car park next to Olive Draycott's Fiat Punto (trust Olive to be there before him), Alan recalled his emotions that first day, four years ago, when he had entered the portals of the school as its new headmaster. He had taken over the headship from an elderly classicist, under whose reign the school had reached a respectable but staid level of academic achievement. Alan had hoped to bring a fresh, progressive outlook, with ambitions for expanding the IT department and introducing an exciting new variety of GCSE and A-level options. His enthusiasm had flagged after the first two years, partly through a lack of funds, but mainly due to the pedestrian attitude of most of the parents, who couldn't see a need for GCSE Mandarin or A-level Russian. They were more interested in Oxbridge entries and Taft's position in the league table. Alan had tried to deliver, but under his headship the school had recently begun to slip in the league tables. Just eighteen months ago a dynamic new headmistress had been appointed to the local state school, and was already succeeding in turning it around in a fashion which Alan could only envy. He could see the day looming when Taft's would no longer be the only safe option for the ambitious middle classes of Huntsbridge.

Alan sighed as he locked his car and gazed up at the school building. All the vigour and ebullience which he had felt as a young teacher in the state system had deserted him, his enthusiasm stifled by the middle-class expectations and attitudes of those around him, and by the constant stream of paperwork and financial worries.

He went through the swing doors and into the familiar smells and sounds of the school. The sensation was not unlike that of diving into a pool, the waters of this other life closing instantly and gently around him. Even as he mounted the flight of stone steps which led to the corridor and to his office the feeling was one of descent. The place was still deserted at eight o'clock. He went into his office and decanted the papers from his briefcase. The room smelled of polish and disuse. His desk was touchingly neat and uncluttered. How soon that would change. He dumped the papers down on its surface and hung up his raincoat on the peg behind the door.

For twenty minutes he sorted through paperwork, while the clamour of the school grew up around him, a lone pair of feet in the corridor changing to the clatter and tramp of many, single voices rising to the conversational racket of starlings.

Olive Draycott, the deputy head and head of English, came into his room at half past. She was a friendly, plain woman in her late forties, unmarried, somewhat bohemian in appearance, excellent at her job, and fond of Alan. She sympathized with him over his many problems, but since she was something of a traditionalist and lacked any talent for public relations, she hadn't been much help to Alan in creating a dynamic new identity for Taft's. She was, however, very good at the day-to-day running of the school's more mundane affairs, and for this Alan was very grateful.

'Good news or bad news first?' she asked.

Alan gazed dispiritedly at her. 'Let's have the bad,' he sighed.

'Apparently we have a leaking roof, and with all the rain we've had this past week it's rather a mess. Mike Rayment has had to clear all the equipment out of the dark room, and he says two of the art rooms are unusable. So we'll have to find him some space elsewhere.'

'Is that possible?' Of course, it had to happen to Mike Rayment, the bane of Alan's life. If there had to be a leak, why could it not drip instead into one of the language labs, and on to the head of unassuming, accommodating Mr Jellicoe? Mike Rayment took every possible opportunity to bring his sardonic, belligerent person into conflict with Alan's, and here was a heaven-sent one. How much trouble could he possibly make out of the relocation of half of his art department? A good deal, probably.

'Not really. I mean, we're bursting at the seams. But you know the kind of fuss Mike's going to make unless we find him somewhere.'

'Well, we can't sort that out now. It's something we'll have to deal with later in the day, when we see where everyone is. Tell Fiona Mather to apply her mind to it. She does all that curriculum development and timetabling stuff, so this sort of logistical problem should be just up her street. Please let's just find a solution before Rayment starts writing me letters. I can do without that. Have we got someone coming in to look at the roof?'

'I rang the roofers up first thing.'

'Right. Now, what's the good news?'

'I haven't finished with the bad.'

Alan sighed again.

'Julian Sweeney had some sort of nervous collapse over the holidays. Apparently he's in hospital. So that makes us one short in the English department.'

'Wonderful. Why does nobody tell us these things until the first day of term?' Alan drummed his fingers on the desk. 'Hospital? What kind of hospital?'

'Psychiatric. I got a phone call over the holidays, but you were away, and then when you came back I was off. Anyway, there should be a letter.'

'Somewhere amongst this lot, no doubt,' sighed Alan, poking at the half-opened pile of post. 'I always thought Julian looked like he was ready to go over the edge. How long's he going to be away?'

'From what I was told, I don't think he's going to be back this year. It may be even longer.'

'We'd better advertise a temporary position, in that case. I suppose we'll just have to muddle through until we find someone. We'll have a talk about it after assembly.' He glanced at his watch and saw that it was ten to nine. 'Time to address the huddled masses.' Again he felt that nervous rumble in his belly at the thought of facing the assembled school on the first day. Why couldn't he feel confident, assertive, all the things a headmaster should be, bursting with leadership and initiative? 'Give me some good news. I can't just welcome them all back with news of a leaky roof and a defective English department.'

Olive glanced down at the paper in her hand. 'Apparently the Sixth Form Outward Bound Youth Guidance Initiative to Patagonia was a tremendous success, and the PTA raised a total of two thousand and eighty-seven pounds towards astro-turfing the hockey pitches.'

Alan rose from his desk. 'Good. That'll do to be going on with.'

Carla laid the photographs out in a row on the carpet and studied them one by one, picking up each in turn. The first was of herself and some friends at university, sitting at a table in the student-union bar. Her hair had been longer then. How fresh and pretty she looked, eager and unspoilt. That was when she had first met Alan. She had been in her second year, studying English and Theatre Studies at King's College, London, and he had arrived as a new young lecturer. Everyone had fancied him. He was twenty-nine, with dark, curling hair worn quite long, and a moustache, and he wore flared jeans and boots, and shirts with long collars and no tie. His glasses were the trendy granny type, as worn by John Lennon. He was radically different from the rest of the teaching staff, who were all older and a good deal more conservative. It gave Alan a dangerous edge. That, and the precious bit of distance which came with being a teacher, a person in authority. She remembered the way her heart would tighten when she saw him walking from the car park to his room in his long army coat, that big scarf wound round his neck, bell-bottoms flapping over his square-toed shoes. The epitome of the trendy seventies academic.

She picked up the next photograph. Again it was one of herself and a group of other university friends, taken on a trip to Paris in 1977. She studied the group. There was Alan at the back, his hand resting on some girl's shoulder. Carla remembered the girl, a third-year student. She couldn't recall her name. Alan had probably been sleeping with her. Everyone slept with everyone else in those days, the wonderful post-Pill pre-Aids era. Or so it had seemed. Not Carla, though. She had still been a virgin when she met Alan. Looking back, Carla could see that, beneath the hipster jeans and psychedelic shirts, she'd really been very young and reactionary, and had been quite shocked to discover that Alan, a lecturer, was indulging in the forbidden practice of consorting with his students. That initial disapproval had quickly given way to jealousy and curiosity. How could anyone dare to go out with someone ten years older than them, especially a member of the university staff? At nineteen, she still viewed her teachers, including Alan Tradescant, with awe. Was it that awe which had been her undoing? Carla looked up to where the rain still pattered against the window, and made a mental note to consider this question more fully at a later date. Perhaps the key lay there.

Carla looked back at the picture, tracing one of the faces with her finger. Lawrence. He had been her boyfriend, sort of. She'd thought him handsome back then, though now he looked rather geeky, with his shoulder-length hair parted in the middle, and those long sideburns. He'd played the drums in a rock band. Poor old Lawrence. The night of that party when Alan had made his move, Lawrence hadn't had a look in.

Carla sat back on her heels, the photograph in her hand, recalling that party. How nervous she'd felt when Alan had come across the room towards her, cigarette in one hand, drink in another, scrutinizing her through those pebbly glasses of his that she'd found so wildly attractive. She'd felt horribly unsophisticated, terrified of what he would say to her, how she would respond. God, thought Carla, shutting her eyes. To think that that same man, who'd made her heart beat like a trip hammer, whose skinny, tank-topped body she had longed to embrace, was the same portly person who'd left the house an hour ago, wearing a shabby raincoat and carrying a briefcase.

In her recollection, Alan was always taller than she was. At first, at least. Maybe the boots he wore then had had heels. Had they? She tried to remember, and failed. She could recall some of his clothes, particularly the ones which had lain discarded on the floor of her room at the hall of residence that first time they'd made love. Jeans threaded at the waist by a very broad leather belt with a butterfly buckle. A lilac shirt with those massive tab collars and sweat rings under the armpits. She hadn't minded his sweat then; had liked it, and the feel of his moustache against her face. But no boots. Boots did not come into the recollection. That first time had had an awful seediness about it, even then. The middle of the afternoon. She'd been so afraid of someone coming in and finding her in bed with a man, and a lecturer of all people. And Alan's urgency had been flattering at first, and then a little frightening. His reaction to the blood on the sheets, finding out she was a virgin, hadn't helped. She remembered sharing a cigarette with him afterwards. Not that she smoked a lot, but it seemed a very cool thing to be doing, sitting in bed with your lover, smoking.

He'd left her alone for a couple of bewildering months after that.

Then when he had eventually taken her to bed a second time, she'd been so grateful after the weeks of aching misery and anxiety that she'd actually willed herself into enjoying it. That was how sex had been between them after that. She adopted a particular state of mind which told her that it was wonderful, and that she was mad about the way Alan made love to her, and it had been fine for as long as she revered and adored him. Amazing how far one could go to deceive oneself. Then again, she'd had no one to compare him with.

Carla dropped the photograph and picked up the next. It was of herself and Alan at some pop festival – Glastonbury? No, the Isle of Wight. There she sat amid a crowd of other people, Alan sprawled behind her, both arms protectively around her neck, drawing her close to him. An amazing summer. She'd been in love. So had Alan. She studied her own smiling face intently. It was crowned with a wreath of daisies woven by Alan, picked from the grass outside their tent. Was it the fact that they had smoked a lot of dope in those days which made the recollection of life then rather indistinct? She had been happy, that much she could remember. She'd learned to cook chilli con carne and spaghetti bolognese, even a lot of macrobiotic food and brown rice, and how to behave and talk when she was with Alan's friends. They seemed to expect Alan's women to be cool and knowing, assured and self-effacing at the same time. So she'd drifted round his flat in her bare feet, cooking for them, squatting cross-legged to engage in their conversations, learning to belong to Alan Tradescant. How proud she had been of that belonging.

Carla picked up the packet from which she'd taken this particular photograph and flicked through the rest. No, of course there wouldn't be any pictures of Daniel, or that French guy she'd met when hitchhiking with Samantha. Only legitimate liaisons were dignified by photographs. She and Alan had been together for a year, and then he'd started seeing someone else, and there had been rows and recriminations, and they'd split up. She'd left university and gone travelling for a year, meeting other men, learning a little more about life. But Alan had always been lurking at the edges of her consciousness, like a part of her she could not shake off. There had been something paternal and safe about him – maybe that had all been to do with his position of authority. Anyway, that first real relationship was bound to imprint itself indelibly on one's soul. Little wonder that she'd been drawn back to it. When she'd returned to London to do her teacher training at Goldsmith's, Alan had heard through friends that she was back, and he'd called her. Carla saw now that the whole thing had had a kind of inevitability about it. Of course they had got back together.

Carla pulled another photograph from the pack. This one was taken on the back steps of the house in

Kennington, where they'd lived with some other people. A great time. She stared at the picture, at the forgotten faces. It was summer, and they were all in the garden. She and Alan were at the front, holding one another in a relaxed kind of way, her head on his shoulder. The relationship had changed, she had felt more like an equal, but she had still regarded Alan as the person who knew all the answers. Say what you like about the sixties and seventies, thought Carla, adding the photograph to the pile, we girls still liked to look up to our men. Maybe girls still did.

Then there was the picture of their wedding. Impossible clothes. Those huge lapels, Alan's hair and droopy moustache, her white satin dress with the short skirt and that self-consciously held bunch of freesias. That had spelt an end to their carefree Kennington days. They had got a little flat in Dulwich, tarted it out in Laura Ashley browns and pinks, sanded the floors and become serious people. They gave dinner parties, shopped at Habitat, stayed in bed with the Sunday papers and waited for the babies to come. Carla had carried on with her job teaching English and Drama at a girls' school in Herne Hill, and to the surprise of all their friends, Alan had switched from lecturing and got a job in the English Department at a sprawling state school in Plumstead. It had been practically unheard of then, to give up university lecturing for a job in teaching. But that had been radical Alan for you, wanting to be on the front line, meeting the job head-on. Carla gave a wry smile. How things changed.

Carla's mind suddenly felt weary with reminiscence. This business of retracing steps was more emotionally arduous than she had expected. She picked up the photographs and slipped them back in the box, which she shoved on to a shelf. She already had more than enough to look back upon and mull over. The next stage of her past could wait for another day. She stood up and went to the bathroom to shower, to make herself ready for some odds and ends of shopping and lunch with Maeve.

2

On the third day back at school, Katie, coming out of the locker rooms after retrieving a forgotten leotard, almost collided with Russell Tucker. He and some friends were on their way to play basketball, stripped down to shorts and T-shirts. Russell Tucker's nonchalant 'sorry' was swallowed up in the rumble of adolescent male voices as they swept past Katie, ignoring her. This sudden contact with her god, almost flesh on flesh, left her weak and exhilarated. Their eyes had met for the briefest second, his arm had bumped against hers. His suntanned, muscular, eighteen-year-old arm. He must have been abroad for his holidays. She watched as he disappeared through the swing doors, caught sight of his slightly sun-bleached brown hair. He was perfection.

She grabbed Georgina on her way into the cafeteria. 'I just saw Russell Tucker going into the gym. He's really suntanned. And he looked straight at me. Oh God, he's divine,' she breathed.

Georgina flicked her blonde hair back over her shoulders and surveyed the choices for lunch. 'You're not still going on about him, are you?' She picked up a plate of spongey-looking quiche with limp salad on the side, watching out of the corner of her eye as Katie helped herself to chicken and mashed potato. 'I'm more interested in real men these days.'

'Aren't you having the chicken? I thought it was your favourite. You never have quiche.'

'Well, I do now. I'm a vegetarian. I decided over summer. I'm not prepared to sanction modern farming methods. They're appallingly cruel, but most people just turn a blind eye to it. That chicken –' she gestured disdainfully at Katie's plate, '– probably had no beak, lost most of its feathers through stress, and had a short and horrible life.' Georgina picked up her tray and Katie followed her. They found an empty table and sat down.

'Maybe it's free range,' said Katie.

'Free-range chicken in a school lunch? Do me a favour.'

Katie said nothing for a moment, wondering how it was that Georgina always managed to find the moral high ground. Sometimes Katie thought she did these things on purpose, just striking poses to make other people feel inferior. She sprinkled salt on her chicken and watched as Georgina began to eat her quiche. It looked disgusting. She probably would have preferred the chicken. Comforted by this thought, Katie said, 'What were you going on about a minute ago, talking about real men?'

'I just realized over the holidays that people like Russell Tucker and his crowd are babies, really. Schoolboys. They're a waste of time, compared to someone mature.'

'What do you mean, over the holidays? What did you get up to?' Katie felt a familiar twinge of anxiety, the sense that Georgina was one up on her.

Georgina gave a small, mysterious smile. 'Nothing much. Not around here, anyway – you know that.'

'Come on. Something happened when you were away. Tell me.'

'OK.' She felt she had tantalized Katie sufficiently. 'It was when Mum and I went to stay with my aunt in Bromley right at the end of the holidays. My cousin Lauren took me out with her a few times. She's seventeen, and she gets to do pretty well whatever she wants. Anyway, I met her friends, went out to a couple of clubs, that kind of thing. Stayed out really late.'

'Didn't your Mum mind?'

Georgina shrugged. 'I suppose she thought it was all right if I was with Lauren. Anyway, the guys she hangs out with are all in their twenties, not sad schoolboys. I got off with one of them, a guy called Ryan. And let me tell you, there's a whole world of difference between someone who's twenty-one and the average sixteen-year-old scruffs we have to put up with round here.'

'So what did he look like?'

'Ryan? Gorgeous. Not very tall – you know I don't like really tall men – but with this black, soft hair and amazing eyes. Come-to-bed eyes.'

'You didn't, did you?' Katie gazed at Georgina, trying to detect a switch to some new level of worldliness.

'No, of course not. I'd only known him for a few days. We just had a good time. It got pretty heavy, though. If we'd stayed another week, I might have.'

Katie considered this. The closest she had come to sex was Liam Crooks trying to put his hand inside her bra. That and snogging, which was about the most anyone in their year got up to. There were rumours about some girls who were said to have gone all the way with certain boys, but they were girls on the fringes of Katie's acquaintance, and she knew only the whispers. And there had been

Karen Walsh, who'd suddenly been absent from school for two weeks, and when she came back the word was that she'd had an abortion. Not that anyone really knew, but it had been funny the way Karen never said anything about why she'd been off. She'd been really quiet for a while, too. Katie felt a small pang of envy at the thought of Georgina's holiday exploits. Of course older guys would fancy her. She looked a lot older than fifteen, especially if she was wearing make-up, and there was something about long blonde hair that seemed to act like a magnet on boys. Georgina, too, would know how to handle someone of twenty-one. Katie knew she wouldn't have a clue. And the idea of sex – the real thing, going all the way – was something that vaguely alarmed her. It was still an act which belonged to the confines of a few sex-education films and PHSE discussions, not a thing she thought about in relation to herself. Even in her fantasies about Russell Tucker, nothing ever progressed to any distinct physical conclusion. But Georgina had clearly got pretty close.

'So, if you didn't sleep with him, what did you actually do? I mean, you said it got pretty heavy . . .'

Georgina, who had left most of her quiche and was busy finishing a pot of apricot yoghurt, glanced at Katie and gave her that knowing, aloof look which Katie found so galling. 'If you don't know, I can hardly tell you, can I?'

'Why not? I'm your best friend.' Katie waited, but Georgina carried on calmly eating. When she had finished she shoved the empty pot to one side and got up. 'Come on. Let's go and have a quick smoke before afternoon lessons.'

Round the back of the science labs lay an area of scrubby garden, roughly divided into plots and irregularly tended by the younger pupils, screened from the staff car park by a row of trees. Here Katie and Georgina smoked their illicit fag. Katie didn't really enjoy it as such, and she suspected that Georgina didn't either, but she was getting used to it. The taste was familiar now and oddly comforting, as was the small badge of defiance which she felt she wore each time she smoked. Mellowed, Georgina confided in Katie just how far she had been prepared to go with Ryan. As she listened avidly, Katie was mildly surprised by the little stirrings of excitement she felt, and wondered what it would be like to do that with Russell Tucker.

At the sound of the bell, Katie chucked her half-smoked cigarette into the bushes with something like relief. 'Come on. We've got Droopy Draycott for double English.'

'You're up to speed on your timetable, aren't you? That old cow can just wait until I've finished.' Georgina leaned against a tree and drew on her cigarette, while Katie stood obediently and patiently by.

They collected their books from their lockers and went upstairs. On their way they passed a tumult of sixth-formers milling around outside the two art studios which hadn't been damaged by the ingress of rain, while two art teachers tried to sort out the disorganization.

'What's that all about?' asked Katie.

'God knows,' said Georgina. Both girls caught sight of Katie's father, in a ferment of ill temper, coming along the corridor from the opposite direction, and scuttled into Miss Draycott's lesson.

Mike Rayment pushed his way into the crowd of students. 'What the hell is happening here?' he demanded. At six feet four, he stood well above the heads of the pupils and the two members of his staff, Verity Roberts and Nigel Sproke. He had the build of an ageing rugby player, a languid but remarkably carrying voice, and an ebullient manner. He wore his mane of red hair rather long, and swept it back at regular intervals with one hand. 'Why are all this lot here?'

'It's the lower-sixth intake. Thirty-six of them,' replied Nigel nervously.

'Impossible. We can't possibly have that many. Our maximum is twenty-five.'

'They're all timetabled for A-level art,' said Verity.

'Typical! The timetabling this term is an utter shambles. That woman Mather has made a complete arse of everything. See if you can sort this lot out,' he said to Nigel, 'while I have a word with the head.'

Mrs Prosser was sitting before her computer, her glasses dangling on the end of a chain, while she sipped her tea. When she saw Mike Rayment, she instinctively raised a protective mental barrier. She didn't like Mr Rayment. He was sarcastic, he wrote too many letters complaining about all manner of things, and he seemed to delight in giving poor Mr Tradescant a hard time. Apart from which, there had been that incident three years ago when a new young science teacher, a very nice young woman to Mrs Prosser's way of thinking, had been forced to leave in unhappy circumstances. And Mike Rayment had been to blame. Mr Tradescant had had his chance then, he could have got rid of him and spared himself a multitude of troubles. But

Mike Rayment was too valuable. He was head of the most successful department in the school. All his A-level students got As, and it was this fact that kept up Taft's local popularity with parents despite the recent general slipping in the league tables.

'If you want to see the headmaster, Mr Rayment, I have to tell you that he's very busy just now.'

'I don't care, Mrs Prosser. I need to speak to him.' He planted both hands at either corner of her desk and leaned towards her as he said this. Unnecessarily theatrical, thought Mrs Prosser.

She sighed and rose from her desk, and went into Alan's room.

'Headmaster, Mr Rayment's outside. He'd like a word.'

'Oh, would he?' Alan's heart sank. He thought he had resolved the temporary problem of the water-logged art studios through Olive's brilliant suggestion that the art department could use the theatre workshop space until the roof was mended. What fresh grievance had Rayment decided to air now? 'I suppose you'd better show him in.'

Alan knew better than to ask Mike to sit down. Over the course of many interviews he had learned that Mike preferred to range around the room like some irate lion, using his height to his full advantage, taking in Alan from every angle as he held forth on the latest deficiencies in the running of the school, while Alan swivelled in his chair, hands clasped beneath his chin, listening with an air of benign concern.

'I take it there's a problem, Mike?' he asked, trying to make himself sound brisk, cheerful and authoritative all at the same time. Like his attempts to get Mike to sit and

34

speak to him at the same level, Alan's efforts to take command of these interviews invariably failed. The authority which Alan so longed to transmit, Mike Rayment had in spades – a natural, unforced authority born of arrogance, terrific self-belief, and a disdain for others. Besides, Alan had to sit there behind his desk looking up at Mike, making him feel unpleasantly like a small, trapped animal in the presence of a larger one.

'Of course there's a bloody problem. When isn't there, Alan?'

Alan particularly disliked the way Mike Rayment used his name. It was perfectly natural that a head of department should be on first-name terms with his headmaster, but the antagonism which characterized their relations infused Mike Rayment's use of his name with faint contempt. He did not speak it in a matey fashion, as Jeff Perkins, head of PE, did, or in a pleasantly deferential way, like Olive. Mike Rayment spoke it with a nasty, aggressive emphasis.

'I want to know,' went on Mike, 'why I appear to have thirty-six lower-sixth pupils when we agreed a maximum of ten per group. They're milling around the corridor like bloody lemmings.'

Alan coughed. 'Well, yours is a very popular subject. I have to admit there was considerable pressure on us to accept more students than we normally would –'

'Pressure? Come off it, you're talking about money. That's what it's all about. Making more money, piling students into my department to keep the parents happy and the funds healthy. Why was I not consulted about this?' Mike was pacing round the room now. It occurred to Alan not to do his usual swivelling act, which was only a polite way of trying to show he was following the argument, but to sit still and keep his eyes fixed on his desk. No, that would look abject. So he sat back in his chair, clasped his hands, and began to swivel. 'I particularly like to keep the numbers to a manageable size, and over my head you do this.'

'Mike, you must be aware of the problems –'

'No, no. My department does not exist to solve the school's financial problems. How am I supposed to cope with that number of students? Not only do I have to try to run half my department in a shed at the back of the theatre, but I have to take on more A-level students than my staff can adequately deal with.' Alan opened his mouth to reassure Mike that the rain-damaged studios would be fit for human habitation by the middle of next week, but Mike Rayment was unstoppable. 'Added to which, if I was not very much mistaken, I noticed the face of Philip Ferris amongst the crowd in the corridor. I particularly didn't want that boy.'

'Mike, his father is very high up in the Foreign Office, and he is especially keen that Philip takes Art A-level. It's very hard to raise an objection.'

'I don't care if his father's the Ambassador to France. The fact is, Philip Ferris is rude, disruptive, a complete yob, and I don't want him in my A-level year.'

It was the point of conflict which they invariably reached, and Alan sometimes wondered why Mike didn't see it coming and just back off. However much Mike might rant and rave, Alan's word was final, and the law.

'Well, I'm afraid you've got him.'

Mike Rayment let out a sighing roar of exasperation.

'It's all about money, isn't it? And kow-towing to the right kind of parents. Of course, Alan, I quite understand. Your priorities are rather different from mine. But let me make it clear that I have no intention of trying to teach that number of students without extra staff.'

'That's out of the question. We're financially stretched as it is. We can't afford to increase staffing levels.'

'Well, if you increase the pupil levels, that's exactly what you're going to have to do, I'm afraid. And this is by no means my last word on the matter.'

He strode from the room. Alan sat forward in his chair and planted his chin on his hands. Dear God, that last threat probably meant more letters. As though he didn't have enough to worry about without Rayment demanding extra staff.

Carla Tradescant and Maeve Porter always played two sets of tennis on Thursday afternoons. In spring and summer they played on the outdoor courts, and in winter on the indoor. Afterwards they would shower and change and have fruit juice in the sports club's bright and empty bar. Carla stood in the ladies' changing room before the mirror. She lifted her arm to apply her deodorant, and thoughtfully touched the slightly slack skin beneath her upper arm. Old age, she thought, creeping up on me. She leaned towards the mirror and examined her neck, noticing the fine crepiness. Soon it will be too late, she thought, and felt one of those agonizing jolts of mortal fear. All summer long this thing seemed to have been mounting, like a slow panic. The idea that soon her chances of love would be lost, that true, romantic love, and the delirious satisfaction of mutual sexual craving would be denied her. Who would want her at fifty? She would be locked out of that world for ever.

Maeve padded out of the shower, a towel round her plump little body.

'My neck,' said Carla. 'It's getting scrawny, like a chicken's.'

'Looks all right to me.' Maeve dried herself and slipped on her underwear, peach-coloured satin edged with lace. Carla, who had never worn anything but clinical white underwear, occasionally wondered whether she should start wearing that kind of thing. The trouble was, it might just encourage Alan, which was the last thing she wanted.

They dressed and went down to the bar. Over their fruit juice, Carla surprised Maeve by suddenly asking her, 'Tell me – do you still fancy George?' Although Maeve and Carla were fairly close friends, intimate subjects like sex had never much come under discussion. Maeve would happily have talked about it for hours, but Carla had a natural reserve which was not encouraging. Besides, Carla had no children, and so she and Maeve had never indulged in those cosy, in-depth, technicolor conversations about childbirth and episiotomies and cracked nipples which so naturally progressed to matters of sex.

'*Fancy* him?' Maeve considered this. 'No, of course not. Not like you might fancy George Clooney, or the odd builder. No, I've known him too long. Why do you ask?'

'Well . . .' Carla hesitated. Maeve was the closest of her female friends. They never talked about these things, but today it seemed of paramount importance that she should find out certain things. She felt rudderless, confused. 'What about sex, then?'

Maeve shrugged. 'That's different. I mean, you come to regard it as a separate thing, something you do, something you like because of the way you've got used to one another.'

Carla nodded. She felt more lost than ever. She had once felt that way about sex with Alan, but it seemed like a long time ago. She couldn't even remember now if she ever had actually wanted him. But she must have. Or was it always just the being he represented? Had she spent the whole of the last twenty years under some illusion?

There was silence for a moment, then Carla said suddenly, her voice wild and wistful, 'But what about love?'

'How do you mean?'

'I mean *being in love*. Feeling exhilarated, passionate, totally bound up in someone, wanting them completely. Not just the tired, safe, mechanical business of being married. I'm forty-two, Maeve, and there are times when the idea of never being in love again seems unbearable. Don't you ever feel that way?'

Maeve let out a reflective sigh. 'I suppose I know what you mean. But then, I'm forever falling in love. I fall in love with someone new every month. At the moment it's the delivery bloke from the Wine Society.'

'That's not what I mean. Not those little fantasies. They're not enough. The soul has to have something more to nourish it. Something deeper, something with real meaning.'

'How poetic,' remarked Maeve. 'I suspect what you're talking about would involve having an affair. That's where things get a little tricky and dangerous. Had you anyone particular in mind?'

Carla gave a wry smile. 'No. The thing's theoretical. Anyway, I don't know that I am talking about an affair. I don't think I can explain . . .' She realized that it would be impossible to describe to Maeve the isolation she felt, the fear that there was no love left in her life, when this life was all there was.

That evening at supper Alan talked about his problems at work and Carla listened, or appeared to. She watched as Alan wiped crumbs of garlic mash from his moustache. He has more of a marriage with that school, she thought. Was that the key – had the falling-apart begun on the day he had accepted the job at Taft's and they had left Dulwich for the leafy fringes of Surrey? She hadn't minded at the time. She'd been relieved to give up her job. Furnishing and decorating the house which came with Alan's new position as headmaster had been more fun than slogging in and out of school each day, spending all her evenings marking and writing reports. She hadn't had to find another job. They had enough money, and besides, the headmaster's wife wasn't supposed to work. Not full-time. She'd been happy enough for the past three years, employed by Taft's to tutor the A-level Theatre Studies students three times a week with their monologues and duologues, so that she kept her hand in but was spared the arduousness of full-time work. She sat on the committees of two local charities, sang in the PTA choir and occasionally drove one of the school minibuses to various venues. She was in charge of the flower arrangements in the school chapel, and was expected to be in attendance with Alan at the numerous school functions throughout the year. It was a busy but undemanding life, one that befitted the wife of a headmaster, and one that was probably driving her slowly out of her mind.

When they'd left London it had been something of a relief to leave behind their tired old social life. Their friends had all consisted of other teachers, it seemed, and conversations were always about work and pupils. No one had enough money, and everything was vaguely left-wing and make-do-and-mend, and Carla, from her comfortable middle-class childhood, had ambitions for something more than that. She'd known she would miss her closest girlfriends, of course, but since Huntsbridge was only forty minutes away on the train, she'd imagined she'd often be popping up to London to see them, and vice versa. It hadn't worked out that way. She'd made new friends, people like Maeve and Jenny Rayment, but it wasn't quite the same. They were women whose lives were already wedded together by a shared history of children and past experiences. Carla still felt somewhat on the margins. And when she was with them she occasionally felt stiff and humourless, because when you came to friendships in your late thirties it was difficult to create the kind of warmth and silly intimacy that you could in your twenties.

'We've advertised for someone, but it may take weeks to find the right person. It's not exactly the best time of year to be looking for staff. Poor Olive will just have to make the best of it.'

'What?'

Alan realized that Carla, although she had been gazing at him with an expression of apparent interest and concern, hadn't been listening to a word he'd been saying. That happened a lot these days. When he was talking, she'd make noises like 'quite' and 'really?' at appropriate pauses, but sometimes the noises would be the wrong ones. Not that he much minded – he did it himself, and anyway, often one talked just to get something off one's chest, so to speak. Still, it was irritating to think that he might be becoming boring.

'You haven't really been listening to what I've been saying, have you?' asked Alan, with more curiosity than rancour.

'Sorry. Yes, I was listening. I got the bit about Mike Rayment, and then my mind wandered off. Sorry. Tell me again.'

Alan considered not telling her again, but there wasn't much point in being huffy with Carla these days. She simply didn't notice.

'I was talking about Julian Sweeney.'

'Oh, yes. The nutter in the English Department. Haven't you advertised for a replacement?'

'That's what I was saying. We have, but it leaves a gap until we find someone suitable. Poor old Olive's in a bit of a dither.'

In a bit of a dither? Carla gave a small smile of astonishment. Five, ten years ago such an expression simply wouldn't have been in Alan's vocabulary.

In her exasperation, suddenly conscious of her own ennui, she said, 'Why don't I fill in?'

Alan looked at her in surprise. 'Well, it's a thought. But are you sure you'd want to? Julian wasn't just teaching the sixth form, you know. He was teaching all the years. It wouldn't just be part-time.'

'It would only be for a couple of weeks until you find someone. Anyway, stops me from getting rusty. I'd like to do it.'

'Well, if you're quite sure . . .' said Alan slowly. 'I know Olive would be glad of the help.'

It was true, she would, thought Alan. But would he be happy with Carla as a full-time presence in the school, even for a few weeks? Over the years she'd acquired a tendency to treat him in rather an offhand manner. Life at Taft's was difficult enough without Carla behaving like that in staff meetings, or in front of the pupils.

As though reading his thoughts, Carla said, 'Don't worry. I'd keep a low profile.' Then she smiled, to make it sound like a mild joke.

After supper, Alan went upstairs to the study to read through some papers. Clearing some things from the desk on to the shelf, he noticed the box of photographs which Carla had left there. He opened it, pulled out a couple of wallets of photographs, glancing with curiosity at their contents. As he leafed through the photos he began to smile. How young we were then, he thought, how beautiful Carla was. Still was. He'd noticed her from the very first, when he'd started lecturing at the university. He'd held her in reserve, something for a rainy day. That was the way things were in those days. His whole life taken up with scoring chicks. It had been so easy, a young teacher in a university full of nubile young things. There hadn't really been anyone serious, not until Carla. He remembered the expression on her face that evening he'd come over to her at that party. Anxious, grateful. She'd been such a girl.

As he gazed at the photos, Alan suddenly realized that there was something elusive and disconcerting about them. What was it, this quality which he could not identify? Slowly, he sat down and began to go through the pictures again.

Outside, the sky darkened, and the street lamps glimmered. Alan switched on the desk lamp, his papers lying forgotten next to him.

Gradually understanding came to him, like a rock rising from a receding tide. In all the early pictures of them together, she seemed to be leaning into him, against him, and his arms and hands were always about her in a protective fashion. That was the way it had been in the beginning. She had looked up to him, taken his lead. She had always had a kind of inner strength – that was one of the things that had drawn him to her, in a way no one else could – but still he had been the dominant one. How that balance had shifted. Yet it had been imperceptible. Not even the discovery that his low sperm count was the reason why they couldn't – didn't – have children had made a significant difference. Not at the time. Yet he could see now that it must have. The illusion of him as the great virile lover, all the years of careful precautions. How wryly Carla must have looked back over those. It must have tipped the scales, weakened her perception of him. Carla hadn't been the kind of woman for whom having children was central to her very being. She had been almost fatalistic about it when they found out. He had been the anxious one, filled with guilt, insisting that they explore the issue, find out how it affected their relationship. Carla always said it made no difference. Not true. Those long conversations, carefully conducted without censure or judgment, his tentative suggestions about artificial insemination, adoption, they had all done their work of diminishing him. His own sense of failure as a man must have transmitted itself to her. He could see it now, contrasting the atmosphere of those photographs to the way things were between them now.

He looked up, gazing at the dark translucence of the window. Yet they were still quite happy, he thought. Since they had moved to Huntsbridge she seemed to enjoy her life. They still made love now and again, and he liked it as much as he ever had. Did she? She seemed to. He glanced back down at the photo in his hand. It had been taken at the house in Kennington. The expression on Carla's face was open and utterly unclouded. People changed, time made a difference, disappointments, whatever. He studied his own likeness. Moustaches and granny specs had been sexy in those days. Just as his being ten years older than her had been. She'd liked that. It had been part of his attraction. An older man. How different moustaches and glasses and ten years' seniority were when one was middle-aged. God, to retrieve just some of his old swagger and sexual self-confidence. If some woman were to want him as much as they had all wanted him back then. . . .

He heard Carla's footsteps on the stairs. She passed the doorway and looked in. The sight of Alan sitting there, with the old photographs in his hand, gave her a sudden pang.

'I came across those the other day when I was looking for something,' she lied. 'They're funny, some of them, aren't they?'

'I was just thinking how good we looked together.' His voice was sentimental, and he stretched out a hand towards her. 'Come here.'

Entirely masking her unwillingness, she went towards him, and he held her, his head pressed against her stomach. 'You sound sad,' said Carla, and was instantly sorry she had spoken. She didn't want to know about whatever springs of emotion the photographs had touched in him.

'I was wondering . . . We haven't talked about it for a long time –'

'What?' She was curious now.

'Do you never wish we'd explored it all a bit more, gone into it more thoroughly – having children, I mean?'

If any ripple of stifled regret or resentment touched her, it was tiny. Too tiny to matter now. 'No,' she answered. Without wanting to, and out of habit, she stroked her hand over his thinning hair, touching the hot, glossy skin of his baldness with her fingers. It was probably a good thing that it was just her and Alan. No untidiness, no third parties made miserable, if everything fell apart. It felt to her as though that was what was happening, each day another little piece of her breaking away from this thing they had built, this marriage. Why did he not seem to see it, or feel it, too? She felt his hands move slowly over her hips and buttocks. She knew this would end in sex, and tried, as she had so often tried over the past year, to resolve her contradictory feelings of revulsion and sad affection. If only he would do something to make her hate him, something mean or deceitful, or behave unpleasantly and coldly, then she could cease to feel this guilt, and her feelings could find some justification. As it was, she had to face the fact that Alan was a very nice man, one she had long since ceased to be in love with. She wondered, with an ache of despair, whether she would ever feel anything like desire in her life again.

3

'Oh, this is so helpful of you, Carla. We put an ad in the *TES* last week, but no response up to now.' Olive Draycott fumbled amongst the papers on her desk. 'Now, what I propose is this. It seems silly for you to have to acquaint yourself with all the syllabuses for such a short space of time – at least, I'm hoping it will be short – so I've rearranged things so that you will be teaching years seven and eight and the A-level years, upper and lower. You're going to be tutoring the upper sixth on their Shakespearean monologues anyway, so that ties in nicely, and it leaves me free to concentrate on the GCSE pupils. They're a mixed bunch this year, and they need to be properly grounded. Let's see, A-level syllabus where are you . . . Ah, yes, Paper Two, let's see what we've got . . . *A Room with a View*, Forster. Fine. And what else? *The Wife's Tale*, that's the Chaucer, and . . . oh yes, *A Doll's House*, Ibsen.'

Carla wondered whether Olive Draycott actually thought it necessary to remind Carla of who wrote what. She sighed inwardly as she watched Olive poring over her bits of paper. It was interesting to observe how people were like the rooms they occupied. Olive's room was old-fashioned, cluttered. She had inhabited it for all the fourteen years she had been teaching at Taft's, and its contents were an accumulation of the functional and eccentric, the shelves stuffed with books, the walls decorated with prints and pictures from her excursions abroad. Olive's person, too, was a bizarre combination of the utilitarian and ornamental. Her clothes were what Carla always thought of as the 'here-we-go-gathering-nuts-in-May' type, long skirts of sprigged or Liberty print, badly ironed blouses with Peter Pan collars worn under long, sloppy cardigans in pastel shades. Her hands and feet were large, and she strode around in open-toed sandals in summer and flat-heeled pumps in all other weathers. Carla had no idea of her real age, but she guessed Olive to be in her late forties, though her fussy mannerisms and vague responses seemed to belong to a woman ten years older. Her hair, which had once been soft and silky brown, was now greying, worn in a practical but unbecoming pudding-basin cut. Her skin, like the expression in her eyes, was still marvellously soft and clear. She was not pretty, with her long face and bony nose, but the humanity and intelligence of her face made her quite attractive. In her aspect she reminded Carla a little of Joyce Grenfell, with her mixture of enthusiasm and girlishness. This last was reflected in her little vanity of wearing a good deal of jewellery, which, like the rest of her, was an odd combination of the old-fashioned and the youthful – a multitude of silver rings, long necklaces, and dangling earrings.

'Paper One – well, of course, you know all that – unseen prac. crit., unseen poetry and prose . . . I think that about covers it. Have you a copy of the timetable? Good.' She clasped her hands and smiled at Carla. 'Again, I can't tell you how good it is of you to help tide us over. And very nice to have the headmaster's wife in the school full-time.'

Carla had never quite got used to the sycophancy with which the staff treated her, simply because she was Alan's wife. 'Happy to help,' she said. She scanned the timetable. 'So my first class is at eleven?'

'That's right. They're a terribly nice bunch, this year's A-level group. A lot of the faces you'll already know, obviously. You'll see from the timetable that they're in C20. I'll pop along and introduce you at the start of the lesson.'

'Fine. Alan gave me a copy of the syllabus, and I spent most of the weekend going over the texts. I'll go and spend the next hour in the library with Ibsen.'

'Lovely. And thanks again.'

Carla headed for the library, where she took out her battered and heavily annotated copy of *A Doll's House* and settled herself in a sunny corner of the library to read.

Mike Rayment, who was searching in the Art section for a particular volume on textiles, glanced up in surprise at the sight of Carla Tradescant. He watched her for a moment over the tops of his half-moon spectacles, pondering. Had she seen him? The way she sat down, crossing her legs like that, suggested she had but was simply ignoring him. She had always tended to ignore him. Which simply convinced him even more that she was attracted to him. Mike's vanity had endowed him with an uncanny facility for interpreting every discouragement from the opposite sex as a sign of interest. The fact was that most women, on meeting him, did find him attractive. He had the unmistakable aura of the successful sexual predator, handsome, brutal and charming. Women either became rabbit-like beneath his leonine gaze, or else, in the case of a tiny minority (whose existence would have astonished Mike), found him intensely unlikeable. Carla belonged to that minority.

When he had found his book, Mike wandered round to the shelves housing the books on architecture, putting himself more clearly in Carla's view. Still she did not glance in his direction. He pretended to scan the shelves, then, after a few moments, pocketed his spectacles and wandered over to where she sat in the sunshine. He loomed over her.

'Mrs Tradescant. We don't normally expect to see you in here.' He spoke in this ironic, mock-formal manner as an unconscious means of protection against the cool reserve with which Carla generally behaved on the various occasions when he had tried to flirt with her at school functions.

She looked up. 'I'm reading,' she replied, then looked back at the book.

'So I see.' Mike sat down in a chair opposite, as much at his ease as if she had smiled invitingly at him and closed her book. 'Ibsen, eh? *A Doll's House*. I think Bea's studying that this year.' Beatrice was Mike Rayment's daughter, whom Carla had known since she was thirteen, and of whom she was quite fond. She was looking forward to having her as one of her students.

'That's right,' murmured Carla. 'I'll be teaching her. For a while, at any rate. I'm filling in until Olive finds someone to take Julian Sweeney's place.'

'Really? Well, it's always a pleasure to have the headmaster's wife around the place. As you can imagine.'

He smiled at her, thinking how good she was to look

at, that face, those long legs. What did she and Tradescant get up to in bed? He'd love to know. He couldn't imagine that ineffectual joke of a headmaster was particularly exciting. When he thought of what he would like to do to her . . . probably could, if he played his cards right. That chilly little stare was such a come-on.

Carla had been prepared to deliver some crushing little retort, but the look in his eyes suddenly transfixed her. The slanting sunlight lit up the gold of his hair and caught the strong planes of his face. He was lounging in his chair, large legs apart, body at ease, staring at her with naked interest. She had always been aware of his good looks, viewed them with the same dispassion with which she observed his astonishing vanity and listened to his insinuating, egotistical conversation. But never, until this moment, had she felt the slightest attraction. It hit her suddenly, making her body tingle, her stomach dissolve in heat. She looked away quickly. How could she feel such sudden desire for someone whom she had always detested? It must be to do with the confusion and emptiness of the past few months. Maybe it was the onset of the menopause, her hormones getting messed up. Or perhaps if anyone looked at you in that way, it would have the same effect. No, she was used to that practised, suggestive gaze. Oh, God forbid that she should start wanting the likes of Mike Rayment.

Mike sat for a few seconds longer. Had he caught a hint of interest? He thought he had. Something in her eyes. Still, she was pretending to be immersed in that damn book. He could take a hint. Not that he wasn't utterly confident that he would have her at some time, some lazy afternoon when Alan was busy with his report to the governors, or OFSTED appraisals. They all came round in the end. Even old Olive had been more than willing, when he had first arrived at Taft's. God, he looked at her now and wondered how he could possibly have done that. What a difference ten years made. The period bell sounded and he eased himself out of his chair.

'My summons to year eight,' he said. 'See you in the staff room.'

Carla nodded without looking up, and he left. Her eyes were fastened on the book, but she wasn't reading. In spite of herself, she had begun to wonder whether it would be possible to have an affair with someone you disliked, just for the sex, just for the relief of it. She thrust the thought from her mind. There must be something far wrong with her if she could begin to think in such a way of that man. The small, heated stirrings had still not subsided. She closed her eyes and let out a little sigh, as though in pain.

Alan sat at his desk contemplating the memorandum headed 'Art' which Mrs Prosser had just printed out. How explosive could such an innocent-looking document be? Mike Rayment was bound to resist its contents, but really, given the problems with budgeting, there was no other choice. Space was at a premium. There was simply no way that they could continue to run a GCSE Photography course. He sighed. Flak from Mike would be bad enough, and there were bound to be ructions with the parents. It couldn't be helped. He read through the points again, hoping the tone of the memo wasn't too antagonistic.

Though Rayment was inclined to find antagonism where there wasn't any, anyway.

1. *We shall have to limit Art to 5 rooms and 3 teachers (or equivalent). We cannot promise to change this in 2001/2 either. The situation in Art and in all subjects will be constantly reviewed, especially in the light of future school finances, requirements, plans, etc.*
2. *In 2001/2 D14 will cease to be an area for photography alone. With the expected demand for 5 GCSE Art sets in Years 10 and 11, and 3 A-level ones for years 12 and 13, in 2001/2 the school must prioritize the location of resources to this demand.*
3. *We cannot end up in the position of turning down pupils who want to take Art, which is of course a National Curriculum subject, by committing ourselves to Photography.*
4. *Much as I wish to, for I admire her ability and personal qualities very much, we can only employ PK if she can teach in more than one medium across years 7–11 in 2001/2.*
5. *We cannot afford to run a new separate GCSE Photography option for 2001/2.*

Alan scribbled his initials at the bottom and sighed. That last justification was the one Mike Rayment most despised. But what was he to do? The bottom line was money, or the lack of it. As for the fourth point, he suspected that one of the reasons Mike would stoutly defend the retention of GCSE Photography was because he was knocking off the girl who taught it, Paula Kennedy. But she'd have to go, since she couldn't teach any other subject. No doubt Mike would find someone new to amuse himself with. It was quite amazing how, at forty-seven, Rayment still behaved as he probably had at twenty-seven – as Alan himself had – shagging everything that moved. Looking back, Alan knew that he hadn't really been that much of a Jack-the-lad at heart, not like Rayment. It had just been the thing to do. Then Carla had come along, and he hadn't had to bother any more. No, he didn't much envy Rayment his conquests, but he did wonder where he got the energy.

He stood up and walked to the window, where he stared out across the playing fields. God, he could do with a cigarette. He envied the lab technicians in their furtive little huddle near the staff car park, puffing away. In these days of political correctness, he couldn't even smoke in his own office, given the non-smoking policy of the school. At Plumstead Comp. they'd had a smoking room. Even becoming deputy head there hadn't excluded him from the happy, smoke-filled enclave. There were days when he looked back wistfully to life in London. OK, a head-mastership had been an obvious step up the ladder, but some people were cut out for leadership, and others weren't. After four years, Alan wasn't certain that he was. This constant battle to keep morale up, to stop the fatal slipping in the league tables. Thank God for Rayment's consistently brilliant results. Say what one liked about the man, he was a good teacher.

The period bell rang and Alan returned to his desk with a sigh to tackle the next wearisome issue – that of the forthcoming governors' meeting, and the question of what he could say to convince them that things at Taft's were going to improve.

Carla's eight A-level students were already standing in a lounging line outside room C20 when she arrived with

Olive Draycott. Each gave her a curious, appraising glance as they filed into the room. Beatrice Rayment smiled at her shyly, tentatively.

When everyone was seated, Olive began her little speech. 'Good morning, all. I'd like to introduce Mrs Tradescant to you. A few of you know her already. Mrs Tradescant has very kindly agreed to fill in until we find a new teacher to take over while Mr Sweeney is away. She's fully conversant with all that you've been studying over the last year, and I'm sure you'll all get on very well.' She smiled at Carla. 'Right, I'll leave you to it.'

Carla took the register, fixing names to faces. Some she already knew from her tutorial sessions, others were new. In each face she could read a slight anxiety. This final A-level year was a critical one for them, and Carla could sense that Mr Sweeney's disappearance and the sight of a new face was unsettling. She only hoped she could keep them calm and confident. She began by discussing the year's syllabus.

'Now, this lesson each week is going to be devoted to work on Paper One – the unseen practical criticism, and unseen poetry and prose, but I'd just like to say a couple of words about your Paper Two texts. Apart from *Hamlet* and Chaucer, we're going to be studying *A Doll's House* and *A Room with a View*. On Monday I want to start discussing *A Doll's House*, so I'd like you all to have read the text by then. It's not very long, so you should be able to manage that. OK? Fine. Now, let's have a shot at some unseen poetry . . .'

Alan arrived home late that evening from a meeting with the heads of department, followed by a lengthy wrangle with Mike Rayment over the contents of the memo about GCSE photography. He found Carla lying on the sofa in her silk dressing-gown, fresh from the bath, leafing through her copy of *A Doll's House*. He sat down at the other end of the sofa and absently stroked her toes. Carla allowed this for several long seconds, then, moving casually so as to suggest she wasn't thinking about it, rearranged her position so that her feet were no longer within Alan's touching distance.

'I've already eaten, I'm afraid,' she said, putting down her book. 'My first day's teaching made me ravenous. I'll cook you something if you like.'

Alan shook his head. 'I'll make myself something later. I'm not hungry right now. I need a drink. You?'

Carla nodded. Alan went through to the kitchen and opened a bottle of wine, then brought through two glasses. He handed one to Carla and she sat up.

'So, how was your day?' Alan sat down next to her and stroked her damp hair.

'Good. It went very well. I think I'm going to enjoy the A-level group. They're a decent bunch – enthusiastic, intelligent.'

'Of course they are. They've got it made. Nice, middle-class children with their bright futures mapped out for them.' Alan gave a cavernous yawn and took off his spectacles to rub at his eyes.

It seemed to have set in rather earlier this year, Carla noted. Alan's disillusion with the private sector was something which surfaced now and again, a throwback to his radical days as a young lecturer. Of course, he'd had to put all his left-wing principles to one side when he'd joined

Taft's. That was what happened when money and comfort became the overriding considerations. Carla sipped her wine and reflected. Was that the key? Had things changed because Alan had turned into a fake establishment type, the respectable head of a safe little independent, in late middle age? Since coming here he'd lost his hard edge, his cynicism had turned into weary resignation. She liked it when she could see a flicker of the old Alan, having a go at elitism, railing against privilege and the class system. But unfortunately, now that he had bought into the private sector and all it stood for, his tirades sounded like mere petulance. Which was what they were, in fact, for he only talked like this when he was tired.

'Well, I'd sooner have them than a bunch of disaffected, gum-chewing inner-city kids.' Carla tucked her feet up beneath her and drank her wine greedily. She had discovered that a couple of glasses each evening made things more tolerable. The alcohol relaxed something within her, so that she could be kind to Alan, maintain a semblance of affection and interest. 'Beatrice Rayment has turned into something of a beauty,' observed Carla after a moment. 'She has her father's looks without any of his horrible personality. I like her.'

Alan had noticed that these were two things which Carla never failed to mention when talking of Mike Rayment – his good looks, and how much she disliked him. He had often wondered whether this was a smokescreen. Rayment had flirted with Carla from the very beginning, and there had been a time, one of stress and anxiety and horrible lack of self-belief two years ago, when Alan had begun to suspect that she might be having an affair with him. But that had passed. In his heart he didn't believe Carla had the temperament for adulterous liaisons. However much she might have changed in other ways, he didn't think that her values, her sense of loyalty and decency, had altered. Basically she was still the nice, middle-class girl he had seduced all those years ago. Besides, he knew that she didn't approve of adultery, and particularly Mike Rayment's intensive brand of it. He had often heard her lamenting poor Jenny Rayment's lot. Still, there was something about the way Carla's manner had altered over summer that made him wonder whether he could still read her in the same way. That new air of detachment. Anything could be possible.

'Yes, she's a nice girl,' he agreed, as these thoughts passed through his mind.

'Quite nervy, though. She strikes me as the kind that might work herself into a bit of a state about things.'

'Like her bloody father,' observed Alan. 'I'm not sure it's healthy for all the Rayment offspring to be under the same roof as their father day and night. Max and Sam Rayment seem to think that their father being a head of department gives them licence to act as if they own the place, whereas Katie Rayment looks as though she wants to crawl away and die of embarrassment half the time.'

'It's because of the concession on the fees. Mike and Jenny couldn't afford to educate them privately otherwise.'

'I suppose not.' Alan glanced at Carla's book lying next to him on the sofa and picked it up. 'This one of the A-level texts?'

'Yes. I've just been going through it, annotating it.' She

drained her glass. One more, and she might be able to loosen this feeling of rigid distaste which had taken hold of her when he'd sat down and touched her. That lingering touch of his, that assumption of possession. It appalled and saddened her that she should feel so towards him, that she should manage to conceal it so well that he had not the least idea. His innocent ignorance added to her guilt.

'God, I hate Ibsen,' sighed Alan, leafing through it. 'And this play in particular. Bloody Nora.' The aptness of this surprised him and he laughed at his unintentional joke. Carla got up from the sofa and went through to the kitchen. She brought the bottle back through with her and curled up on the sofa once more. 'I mean,' went on Alan. 'why do they make these poor kids study his plays? Where's the connection? All the issues are dead and gone, all the moral messages stale and irrelevant. I'll bet most seventeen-year-olds don't know what he's banging on about.'

'That's ridiculous,' said Carla. She refilled their glasses. 'Nora's predicament is just as real today as when Ibsen first wrote the play. It's about a woman living a lie. Lots of women still do that.' Carla sipped her wine. 'Until something happens to wake them up to the fact and make them see things and people as they really are.'

'You really think that Nora is happier at the end of the play than she was at the beginning? I like her at the beginning. She's a good wife, a good mother, contented. By the end she's as bad as that mate of hers – what's her name? The one who marries the clerk.'

'Kristina. Mrs Linde.'

'That's the one. And at the end she walks out on them all, probably going off to lead a miserable, lonely life.'

'How can you say that? The point of the play is the way that she finally discovers herself. She sees her husband for what he really is, realizes the sham her life has been, and is able to begin again without him. She starts off as a child and ends up as a woman.'

Alan closed the book and chucked it aside. 'Maybe so, but she was a damned sight happier in the first place, before her eyes were opened, that's all I'm saying. Still, you're teaching the thing, so it's just as well you like it.' He stood up, loosening his tie. 'Is there any of that ham left over from yesterday?'

'Yes. It's on a plate in the fridge.' Carla poured some more wine and lay back on the sofa, waiting for it to dissolve the little knots of tension that sprang up in her whenever Alan and she were alone.

Katie lay on her bed, clutching a hot-water bottle to her stomach. It didn't matter what she took for period pains, they were always agony, a dull ache throughout her lower back and abdomen, blackening everything. She glanced at her diary lying on the bedside table next to her. She couldn't even be bothered to write in it tonight. She didn't want to have to face her thoughts and feelings in black and white, to read them back to herself and see the awful hopelessness of it all. Nothing had gone right since the start of term. Every resolution seemed to have crumbled to dust in the space of just two weeks. She had meant to work really hard for her GCSEs, but already she was falling behind in her course work. It all seemed so boring, so pointless. English was her worst subject, and the syllabus this year didn't help. *Macbeth* was deadly. And the diet she'd been meaning to follow – how could she, when her mother bought all the wrong things? Anyway, it took ages, trying to work out how many calories were in everything. Maybe she should just give up food altogether. It would probably serve them all right if she became anorexic, though that seemed unlikely. She couldn't imagine not eating. That was the problem. Maybe she should have a shot at bulimia. But the idea of sticking your fingers down your throat after every meal seemed pointless. You might as well not eat. Which brought her back to square one.

Georgina, for some unfathomable reason, had been horrible to her all day and had sat with Hannah Keys at lunchtime. Katie really couldn't stand Hannah, but she knew Georgina liked her because she had so much money and bought loads of designer stuff and could afford all the latest CDs. Katie stared at the ceiling. It wasn't the first time Georgina had done this. It sometimes seemed to Katie like she wanted to show Katie that she was the powerful one in their relationship. Katie knew that she could lie here and make all kinds of resolutions about breaking off her friendship with Georgina, but tomorrow Georgina would no doubt be as nice as pie, and Katie's resolve would crumble.

The worst thing of all was that Russell Tucker had taken Rosie Dobson out – twice. She and Rosie were in the same class. How galling that he should ask out someone younger than himself, and pick Rosie. The thought of it made her heart ache, quite literally – she could feel it. A hopeless kind of empty pain. Oh, Russell . . . she shifted the hot-water bottle up a bit. Maybe she *would* write in her diary in a while, a whole load of stuff about Russell. She could write about him forever. And think about him. Maybe she should take some comfort from the fact that he was prepared to go out with girls younger than himself. There was hope for her yet.

If only she could feel better about herself, then life might improve. But everything and everyone around her seemed determined to undermine her. Mummy got at her all the time. She complained about the clothes and make-up she wore at the weekends, and nagged her about her homework when the exams were absolutely ages away. She had come into the café at the shopping centre last weekend and caught her smoking, and had made her feel really small in front of Georgina and her other friends. Then there had been an almighty row about it at home, and she'd been grounded that evening and so couldn't go to Karen French's party, which everyone said had been completely wicked. There were rows all the time these days over just about everything. Bea and Mummy never seemed to argue. They were always chatting, laughing about stuff. Bea got to do pretty much what she wanted. OK, Bea was older, but Katie couldn't remember their mother going on and on at Bea when *she* was fifteen. Katie sometimes felt as though Jenny loved Bea more than her. The constant criticism, getting at her about her work, about being round at Georgina's all the time. It wasn't as though she was there *all* the time, though no one could blame her if she was. The atmosphere there was better.

At least Georgina's mother didn't get at her constantly. In fact, she seemed to let Georgina do pretty well what she liked.

The hot-water bottle had grown tepid. Katie dropped it on the floor, turned over and buried her face in the pillow. She could hear her mother in Max and Sam's room, talking about something, then laughing. It seemed to Katie that she never did that kind of thing with her. All she did was put her head round the door and say things like, 'I want that light off in ten minutes.' And she probably wouldn't even do that tonight, not after the argument they'd had downstairs. When she'd stomped off upstairs Mum had said, in that sort of exasperated way, 'I'll come up and see you later.' But Katie had told her not to bother, so she probably wouldn't now. She simply had to face the fact that her mother didn't really love her.

The tears came easily, and Katie cried into her pillow for her mother for a good five minutes. Then she got up, listened at the door to make sure her mother had gone back downstairs, fished a packet of ten Silk Cut from beneath a pile of knickers in her underwear drawer, and went to the window. She opened it and smoked into the night air for a while, waiting for it to make her feel better and take her up above her problems, into a place where things went right and she worked hard and looked prettier and didn't need Georgina and she and Mummy got on. But it didn't happen. The cigarette made her feel slightly sick, and she crushed out the remaining half and watched the stub roll down to the gutter. Then she closed the window and got back into bed, picked up her diary and began to write about how unfair it was that her parents wouldn't let her have her own television in her bedroom, when just about everyone else she knew did. She would save Russell till the very end.

4

The weeks went by, September faded to October, the nights drew in and the weather began to turn chilly. The term progressed in its familiar cycle. Taft's played a variety of schools at rugby and netball with mixed success, the swimming gala came and went, Rt Hon the Lord Comber addressed the sixth-form society on European integration, and letters from Mike Rayment concerning the demise of GCSE Photography and the need for an increase in staffing fell on Alan Tradescant's desk like so many autumn leaves. A meeting of the school governors took place at which Alan gave assurances that a development plan was in hand to target areas of performance throughout the years, including monitoring the performance of all departments, holding heads of departments accountable for results, assessing teaching methods, resources, schemes of work and lesson plans. He referred to the need for a culture of excellence, streamlining responsibilities, pioneering innovative practices, sustaining levels of confidence, and achieving significant year-on-year improvements and realistic performance thresholds. Thanks to prior consultation with Verity Roberts, he was able to make use of words such as 'targeting', 'benchmarks', 'fast-track', 'focus' and 'consultation'. All this seemed to go down very well with the governors, and although Alan congratulated himself at the time on having given a very positive, resolute performance, he found himself wondering later whether he had in fact said anything of any substance at all.

Carla remained mired in her state of marital confusion, grateful for the distraction of her daily teaching. She had abandoned the process of working back through her relationship with Alan for clues as to why it seemed to have foundered, and concentrated instead on trying to manufacture kind feelings towards him, in the hope that she might, by sheer effort, overcome her lack of love or desire. It didn't work. Mike Rayment's constant proximity in the staffroom, in meetings and in assembly was disturbing, and although every contact with him only increased her dislike of him, she found her dreams were often sensuously troubled by vague images of him. Each day she woke and wondered when a solution would present itself, or whether she was destined to continue in her emotional limbo forever.

In the week before half-term, Olive Draycott told Carla that they had found a new teacher to take over Julian Sweeney's post.

'His name is Peter Barrett, a very nice young man. He has a degree from Bristol, taught in a school there for three years, and then went abroad to teach English at a school in Rome. Since it looks doubtful if Julian will be coming back to full-time teaching, Mr Barrett will be taking over his classes permanently.'

Carla's own disquiet at this news took her by surprise. Of course she had known they would find someone, but she had begun to find the pattern of classes and the preoccupations of her students soothing. The thought of reverting to idle days filled with unnecessary housework, reading and tennis was dispiriting. She suddenly saw her life as a void, loveless, pointless, and wished for a brief, panicky moment that she had applied to take over Julian's job permanently. Too late now.

'. . . So it would obviously be a good idea if you could meet him over the half-term holiday and have a chat about the syllabus and the classes you've been teaching. That will help him find his feet. As I said, he is *very* young.'

Olive spoke wistfully as she said this, but with a secret joy. The moment young Mr Barrett had walked into the interview room three weeks ago, she had felt that some new inspiration had entered her life. Never had she set eyes on someone so magically, youthfully perfect. Behind the façade of her businesslike questions at the interview she had gazed on him with the eyes of a sixteen-year-old, intoxicated by his manner and looks. For someone of twenty-seven, he had an artlessness, a smiling candour that quite captivated her. He reminded her of one lost love, whose memory was misted over now with sentiment and time, and of many, many loves ungained. To Olive, he was the essence of young manhood. As the interview had progressed, she had found herself hoping ardently that Mr Tradescant would like him, would want to employ him. To have this young man in her department would bring a new dimension to her existence. The intoxication of seeing him each day, of talking with him, getting to know him and sharing fragments of her life in exchange for some of his . . . Infatuation had struck Olive hard and fast. Yet she was a woman of pragmatism, one whose expectations had been dulled by disappointment and experience. If, of the four candidates for the job, he had been one of the unsuccessful three, she would have accepted it as fate, and would have closed the suddenly opened door to her heart and looked elsewhere for her crumbs of romance. But the others on the interview panel had liked him just as well as she, if not in the same degree, and young Mr Barrett had been offered the job.

'Why don't I invite him to lunch?' suggested Carla. 'Perhaps you could come, too, Olive.'

'What a good idea,' said Olive. 'I'll get in touch with him and see what day would suit him.' How happy she was.

'Guess what?' Georgina's face was pink, her eyes alive with excitement.

'What?' asked Katie. It was very rarely that Georgina allowed herself to lose her cool and appear animated about anything.

'Ryan rang me. He's coming down to Huntsbridge.'

'To see you?' Katie pushed through the swing doors to the cloakroom.

'Sort of. Yes. He's got some friends living on the edge of town, and he says he thought he'd come and stay with them for a bit. Oh, I can't wait to see him . . . You'll like him, he's so gorgeous . . .'

Katie hung up her coat thoughtfully, testing her feelings at this news. So long as Ryan had remained on the edges of her imagination as Georgina's nebulous holiday romance, he existed within acceptable dimensions. But the idea of his real, twenty-one-year-old presence as an entity in Georgina's day-to-day life was a troubling one. She was used to being a unit with Georgina, going to classes with her, hanging out with her at weekends and going to parties together, talking about the same subjects, the same boys. This Ryan creature would annex Georgina, marginalize Katie. She saw herself alone, abandoned, while Georgina's time was totally taken up with the sophisticated Ryan.

'What's he going to do while he's here?'

'I don't know.' Georgina shrugged. 'Maybe he's got a job. He just said he would be coming down this weekend. He's going to ring me when he gets here.'

'We were meant to be going to the cinema on Saturday,' Katie reminded her.

'Yeah, well . . . I might have to skip that, I'm afraid. It depends on Ryan.'

Katie said nothing. Here was something to make her life even more miserable and insecure. Not even the sight of Russell Tucker putting his books into the locker at the end of the corridor could cheer her up.

'I thought I might ask this new English teacher to lunch next Tuesday. It was Olive's suggestion. Give him the low-down on the classes I've been teaching.' Carla was sitting at the kitchen table marking a pile of year-nine essays while Alan cooked supper.

'Young Mr Barrett?' Alan gave a short sigh and poked at the pieces of chicken he was frying. 'I'm just hoping he's not going to cause too much consternation amongst the girls. I think Olive's pretty well smitten already. She was backing him from the word go. Not,' added Alan, emptying the chicken on to plates, 'that he wasn't the best candidate by a long shot. I'd just prefer it if he weren't quite so young and good-looking. Yes, by all means have him round to lunch. I'm afraid I can't be there, though. I've got that two-day conference in Nottingham.'

He fished cutlery from a drawer, poured sauce over the chicken and took dishes from the oven. Carla cleared away the pile of essays and glanced in irritation at the cigarette which smouldered by the sink, wishing Alan wouldn't smoke while he cooked. It was quite disgusting, really, but it was something he'd always done. She actually felt a faint tremble of anger run through her. Why hadn't it bothered her for all the years they'd been together, why only recently? Because everything about him bothered her these days. Even the inflection in his voice when he said certain familiar things, his habit of stroking his moustache when he considered something, the way the light glinted on his glasses, the sound of his step on the stair, the splash of his urine in the toilet bowl, the way he parked the car exactly between the lamp-post and the end of the wall, the sight of his coat on the hall stand . . . Jesus.

She clenched her fists, the familiar fear rising, curdling her stomach. Only it wasn't so much fear these days, it was a panic amounting to terror. Only a small terror, yet enough, a secret, explosive thing lodged within her. She watched as Alan brought the plates to the table, mechanically following his movements. Her mind flew back to the article she had come across while idly flipping through an abandoned Sunday colour supplement in the staffroom, an account of the breakdown of a marriage. Carla had read it from start to finish with the avidity with which she read all such things, as if in desperate hope of enlightenment, seeking a sign that her feelings were not unique, and she not alone. She recalled what the author, a man, an American man, had said about those words 'irretrievable breakdown of a marriage', how passive and deceptive they were, suggesting that marriage was something with an independent organic existence. *It exonerates us by portraying us as merely the clinicians pronouncing the body dead.* She remembered thinking how true that was, how perfectly expressed.

Alan sat down, pushing the dish of new potatoes a little way towards her. 'Help yourself.' Then he remembered the wine and got up again. Carla spooned two potatoes on to her plate. Alan fetched the wine and a couple of glasses.

The author had described the very moment when his wife suggested a separation, the clarity of it, how it focused everything, brought it all to a head. *At what precise point does the breakdown of a marriage become irretrievable? The moment we declare it so, and no sooner.*

Alan poured some wine carefully into Carla's glass and handed it to her. He was smiling, not consciously, not broadly, just the small, accustomed smile of a person at home and at peace with himself, thoughtlessly, moderately content. She watched as he ate some of his food, then drank a mouthful of the wine. He gave a little nod, indicating the bottle.

'That's from the Wine Society's mixed case. Not bad at all. Very good value. I keep telling Jeff Perkins he should join . . .'

Carla sat, letting the words roll over her. The familiar

words. Everything he said seemed to be a rehash of things he had said before, the same words spoken in a different order. She stared at him, watching as he spoke how his moustache moved with a life of its own, like a hairy caterpillar. Perhaps now was the moment. Perhaps she should say something now, just let the words cut across, clear and sharp and final. But she didn't even know what those words were. What had the wife of the man who wrote the article said? *'We have to separate.'* She tried to imagine herself articulating those same words, Alan with his fork halfway to his mouth, astonished, time frozen in that moment.

'Aren't you going to eat anything? This chicken's quite good, if I say so myself.' Alan drank some more wine and regarded his wife. 'Carla? You look as though you're in another world.'

It was as though some resolution which had been forming, crystallizing, suddenly shivered into soundless fragments which melted away around her. Her senses swam back to reality.

'Sorry.' She picked up her fork and began to eat. Then she took two large gulps of wine and felt the warmth spreading through her. If she could just keep the panic down, she would be all right. This would pass. It might even just be the time of year, an autumn depression. Why did she let herself get things so much out of proportion? This was just eating supper, they were all right. Everyone got tired of their marriage, but it didn't mean they had to abandon everything. No, things might be bad at the moment, but she'd probably felt this way before. After she found out that they probably wouldn't ever have children? Yes. She must have felt all these things then, too. It would pass.

Alan began to talk again, something about school, but Carla was hardly listening. She was trying to imagine, appalled, what would have happened if she had said those words, if she had set in motion a thing which would have to then be explained and carried through. This home, all the things in it, the lovely kitchen, the tastefully decorated, cosy rooms, the garden which gave her such pleasure every summer, would have to be left behind. This was Alan's house, part of the headmaster's job. If she separated herself from him, she would be the one to leave. Her mind leapt ahead to a vision of herself alone in a rented flat, working each day in some comprehensive, the weeks and months and years of middle age settling around her like a shroud. But perhaps it wouldn't have to be like that. Perhaps there would be someone – someone who would fill her up with the kind of love she needed before it was too late.

'. . . and he was saying that they found a very good hotel on the other side of the New Forest. Very reasonable, and the food was excellent. So I thought, with half-term coming up, why don't we get away for a few days and try this place?'

Carla caught enough of this to comprehend what Alan had been saying. He was talking about going away for the weekend. She tried to meet this idea in a flat, matter-of-fact manner, without any acicular feelings. With a swift mental shift of gear she replied, 'Why not? It would be a nice change. Find out the name and number of the hotel and I'll ring them up.' The words and manner were those of a contented, untroubled woman. She took another long drink of wine and refilled her glass, and began to eat again. There, that hadn't been too difficult. It was just a question of practice, really. If she adopted the right frame of mind she could behave as normally as the next married woman.

'I thought you were going out with Georgina to the pictures?' Jenny Rayment looked up from her ironing to where Katie lay curled up on the sofa, watching MTV.

'We changed our minds. There's nothing good on.'

Jenny flipped over the pillowcase she was ironing. She didn't believe her daughter for a moment. If Katie and Georgina didn't have anywhere to go on a Saturday night, Georgina either came here, or they were both round at Georgina's. Usually the latter. There was something unhealthy about the way those two hung around together all the time. Not that she had anything against Georgina, but she did wish that Katie had a wider circle of friends. She wasn't sure about Judith Lister, Georgina's mother. She was always too carefully made up, and Jenny suspected that she didn't keep as careful an eye on her daughter as she ought to. Still, you had to admire the fact that she always looked marvellous, as pretty as Georgina. She slid the nose of the iron thoughtfully into the sleeve of one of Mike's shirts. Perhaps Georgina had a boyfriend, and Katie felt cut out. Jenny felt a surge of sympathy for her, recalling her own youth and long hours spent moping around, worrying about chocolate and spots and imagining the rest of the world, happy and slim, having a wonderful time every Saturday night. This momentary empathy translated itself into a mild, protective fearfulness as she glanced at Katie, slumped in an unattractive heap on the sofa. No mother wanted her daughter to feel plain, rejected. Not that Katie was plain. She was very pretty, really, but she was a little overweight, and she lacked confidence. She seemed to rely on the golden Georgina for assurance, for validation of her own precarious tastes, desires and ambitions. Jenny sighed inwardly. She shouldn't worry too much. There was nothing really wrong with Katie. She was just a normal, anxious, difficult teenager, hard to reach and impossible to reason with, who was feeling bored and glum on a Saturday night. Jenny tried to cast her mind back to when Bea had been this age. She couldn't recall Bea moping around like this, nor could she remember Bea being sulky and belligerent, like Katie. Bea had always been so easy – cheerful, quiet, independent, but never any trouble. But then, if you looked the way Bea did, maybe it was easy to sail through life on a tide of happy self-assurance. It couldn't be easy for Katie, having an older sister like Bea.

'Surely you've got other friends besides Georgina,' remarked Jenny, tipping more water into the steam iron.

'What do you mean?' Katie gave her mother a resentful stare.

'Well, just because Georgina's doing other things doesn't mean that you have to stay in, does it? There must be lots you could be doing with other people.'

As usual, a couple of innocuous remarks seemed to be Katie's cue to go ballistic. 'Who said anything about Georgina doing other things? I told you, there weren't any films on that we wanted to see! OK? God, I really wish you'd get off my case!' Katie flung herself at the television, switched it off, and stormed out of the room and upstairs.

There was a time, a year or so ago, when Jenny would have followed Katie, shouted at her to get back down here this instant, how dare she take that kind of tone, she would apologize right now or be grounded for a fortnight. But now she had learned to leave well alone. She remained at the ironing board, spraying a little more starch on a shirt sleeve. She felt for Katie, but at least, at the end of all this teenage turmoil, she had her life before her. She had the certain hope of love, excitement, freedom of choice. Katie might bewail her lot, but at least life was still full of chances, of possibilities. Jenny had given up on those long ago. Sometimes she blamed herself. If she did as Carla and Maeve did, went to the gym, played tennis, counted calories, then perhaps she would still be slim and pretty, as once she had been, and Mike would want her, and wouldn't need to have all those wretched little affairs, the ones that had turned him into a defensive, blustering liar, and her into a self-disgusted coward. But with four children, where was the time? And what was the point? He would probably do it anyway. Sometimes she blamed him entirely, and told herself that life still had something to offer, that she should get out before all the chances vanished, that there was someone out there who might love a fat, middle-aged woman with the remains of a sense of humour, who had once been someone quite different ... But she loved Mike. No matter how bad it got, she could not escape that fact.

Finishing the shirt, she hung it neatly on a hanger, buttoning every other button, and picked up another from the basket. She laid it out on the ironing board and sprayed

77

a fine mist of starch over the back. Mike said he liked his shirts so stiffly starched that he could feel the cotton of the sleeves crisply parting as he put them on in the mornings. Jenny suddenly stopped and stared at the shirt. What was she doing? Here she was, carefully laundering and starching and ironing his wretched shirts, just so that he might enjoy the sensual pleasure they gave him, so that each day he could put one on, admire himself, filled with the hope that some new woman, some fresh hope of sexual adventure, would come his way. She felt like weeping. But she did not weep. She did not give way. She stood at the ironing board with her head lowered for a little while, then eventually she picked up the iron and carried on.

Katie lay on her bed. The worst of it was that her mother was right. She should have other people to go out with, not just Georgina. But she and Georgina had been a twosome for too long, other people in their year at school had formed themselves into different, impenetrable groups who went everywhere and did everything together. Yeah, they were her friends, individually, but she didn't feel she could attach herself to them socially. She was an outsider. She stared at the ceiling, half-listening to her Britney Spears CD, and wondered if Georgina would feel the same if it had been Katie who had found a boyfriend. No, of course not. Anyway, she would never have let it happen. Somehow, whenever Katie had been getting friendly with a boy, Georgina would wear her down, bad-mouthing him, annexing her. Why? Katie had often pondered the dynamics of her friendship with Georgina but had never quite been able to fathom them. She failed to understand, for instance, why Georgina wasn't part of the larger cliques at school, why she preferred the singularity of hanging around with just her. Sometimes, like this evening, for instance, she resolved to break away, to let the thing cool off and form other friendships, maybe make a real effort to get in with the bigger crowd in her year. She would probably have more fun. But putting this resolve into action was actually much more complex and difficult than its mere formulation. She didn't know where to start, really. How could she go about marginalizing Georgina when she wasn't around to be marginalized? And there was the problem of trying to make headway with a new circle of friends. That was harder than people thought. You were always reading stuff like that in problem pages. 'Find yourself a new set of friends. Join a club, take up a hobby . . .' It didn't work like that at all.

Sam put his head round her bedroom door. 'Do you want a game of Monopoly?'

Katie considered this. She actually loved Monopoly.

'All right. I want to be the boot.' And for the rest of the evening she left her solitary, troubled world and returned to the warm family familiarity which could still claim her, if she let it.

The next day, Katie waited throughout the morning for Georgina to ring, but she didn't. At noon Katie could wait no longer, and rang her. Judith, Georgina's mother, answered the phone. She said that Georgina wasn't up yet, so far as she knew. There was a clunk as she put the phone down, and Katie could hear her calling up to Georgina. After a few seconds there was a click on the line as Georgina picked up her extension. That was another thing Katie was mildly jealous about. Georgina had a phone in her room *and* a television. No way Katie's parents were ever going to allow that.

'Hello?' said Georgina, her voice sleepy.

Katie hesitated, then heard the click on the line that meant Mrs Lister had put the phone down. 'How was last night?' she asked. 'I'm dying to hear about it. I thought you might ring.'

'I've only just woken up.' Katie could hear Georgina yawning.

'So how was it?'

'Oh, we went to his place and just hung out, you know.' Georgina's tone was distant, almost bored.

'You must have got in really late, to sleep in till now.'

'About one.'

Katie marvelled. If she got in any later than eleven, her mum would hit the roof. Past midnight and her Dad would be out in the car, combing the streets of Huntsbridge. 'Where's he living?' Katie asked.

'He's sharing a big flat with some other blokes out near the Superbowl. It's a bit of a dump, but the other guys are really nice. We had a good laugh. Actually, when I've got a bit of my course work done, I'm going across there this afternoon. D'you want to come?'

Katie felt the cold prickle of fear and excitement. No way would her mother approve of her going with Georgina to the flat of a load of twenty-something men she'd never met. But it was too tantalizing and frustrating to have Georgina being part of something that she couldn't share. It wouldn't do any harm. If she caught up on some of the maths she'd been neglecting, she could go off with a clear conscience, tell her mum she was going round to Georgina's. She quite often did that on tedious Sunday afternoons. 'OK,' said Katie.

She worked industriously throughout the afternoon, little flutters of apprehension growing in her stomach as four o'clock approached. What was it going to be like, this place? What if there were drugs, that kind of thing? From what Georgina had told her of Ryan, he didn't seem to be that kind of person, but you never knew. He and his friends were so much older than the boys she usually met. Grown up, in fact. Men. The word held a kind of threat, a dark reality that she wasn't yet ready for. Was this a completely daft idea? Maybe she should just forget it, stay safe at home, let Georgina get up to whatever she wanted. Hadn't she told herself – and her diary – time and time again that she wasn't just going to be Georgina's shadow, doing everything that she did? But she was curious to see this Ryan person, and his friends. If she didn't go this afternoon, it would become Georgina's thing completely, and she would be shut out. So she put on a minimal amount of make-up, brushed her hair, and put on her trainers and coat. On the stairs she met her father coming down from his studio, in the long, paint-splattered shirt he always wore when he was working at home. He gave her a close glance.

'Where are you off to?'

'Georgina's.'

'Have you finished your homework?'

Katie nodded.

'OK. Be back by seven.'

Mike went into the kitchen, thinking about Georgina Lister. She was quite the little flirt, Mike had noticed recently. One of the ones who always stood that little bit closer to you when you were going over their work with them. The mother wasn't bad either. Vaguely tarty, but definitely someone to put by for a rainy day. She'd been at great pains on the last parents' evening to let him know that she was divorced. Nice to think there was always something new in the offing.

By the time Katie and Georgina got off the bus by the Superbowl, dusk was falling.

'How many people share the flat?' asked Katie.

'Three. Apart from Ryan, I mean. Phil and Des and Andy. You'll like them. They're a laugh.'

They walked past a shuttered parade of shops, the wind whipping leaves and litter round their ankles. It was a seedy part of Huntsbridge, mainly off-licences, kebab shops, bookies and run-down corner-shops, and the air of Sunday melancholy made it even more drab than usual. Despite her excitement, Katie was conscious of being slightly miserable. Maybe it was just guilt. What if her mother found out? She might be ringing Georgina's mother right now. Too late to change her mind. What would Georgina think of her if she turned round now?

'Here it is.' The block of flats was next to a Chinese takeaway. They climbed the steps to the first floor, and Georgina rang the bell. After a few moments they could hear feet, and the door was opened by a dark-haired youth, barefoot, wearing jeans and a sloppy jumper. He smiled when he saw Georgina; a nice smile, Katie thought.

'Hi.' He kissed Georgina swiftly and self-consciously.

'This is my mate, Katie,' said Georgina.

Ryan smiled at Katie. 'Come on in.'

The girls followed him through to a large, shabby room, where several young men were lying around on a battered sofa, watching television. At least it seemed like several to Katie. After she had sat down on a bean bag which Ryan pulled out from a corner for her, she realized there were only three of them. They all glanced at her and said hi, then returned to their film. They were watching *Zulu*. Ryan and Georgina were sitting on the other side of the room in an armchair, Georgina on Ryan's knee. They began a muted conversation. Katie sat on her bean bag and stared at the television, trying to look absorbed. She stole furtive glances at the men on the sofa. Men was what they definitely were. Young men, not boys. Way out of her sphere. She knew that she was a schoolgirl, she felt like one, and she had no doubt that they regarded her as one. They were drinking lager from cans.

One of the men got up from the sofa. 'Hey, Phil, get us a can,' said Ryan.

Phil nodded. He glanced at Katie. 'Like a drink?'

Katie shook her head. 'No thanks.'

Phil came back from the kitchen with some cans and handed them round. Ryan cracked his and Katie watched as Georgina took a sip. Georgina hadn't paid any attention to her at all since they came in. Now she looked across at Katie and giggled.

'You've still got your coat on.' Katie felt herself blush and tried to get up to take her jacket off. It wasn't easy to rise elegantly from a bean bag, but none of the men was watching her. They were glued to the screen. 'Make yourself a cup of tea if you want,' added Georgina proprietorially.

Katie struggled up from the bean bag once more and went through to the kitchen. It was large, dilapidated and dirty. The sink and draining board were a clutter of dishes and old curry cartons, and a black bin bag full of dirty laundry was propped next to the fridge. The vinyl flooring was holed in places, curling up near the door, and the window was grimy and uncurtained. Through it Katie could see the rooftops of the line of shops and the grey October sky. She tested her feelings for the melancholy which had beset her on the way here, but found it had gone. What she felt now was interest. This adventure was new and not exactly pleasant, but at least she wasn't bored. She found the kettle, filled it and plugged it in, then spent a few minutes going through the cupboards looking for tea and a mug, and inspecting the young men's provisions. They seemed to be odd and very basic, a lot of pot noodles, tins and packets of biscuits. The contents of the fridge, when she went to find milk, were equally scant, mainly cans of lager, plus a brown paper bag of tomatoes, some cheese developing a blue mould, and a withered half lemon.

Katie made her tea and took it back through. She settled down on her bean bag and watched as hordes of Zulus swept down on Michael Caine and James Booth and the rest of the beleaguered garrison.

When the film was over, two of the men on the sofa, whom Katie had worked out must be Des and Andy, began a discussion with Ryan about whether to go out or not. Phil glanced in a bemused way at Katie and asked her a few questions about herself, about school and where she lived. Katie was conscious that the enquiries were made in a kindly, distant fashion, adult to child, but decided that she didn't mind. She wasn't here in the same capacity as Georgina. She had no pretensions, expected and wanted nothing from the situation.

'What do you do?' she asked Phil.

Phil clasped his very muscular arms behind his head and thought. 'I don't really do anything. Well, I play a bit of music down the pub on Fridays and Saturdays. The Imperial. D'you know it?'

She shook her head. 'I don't go to pubs.'

'No, right.'

'What do you play?'

'The accordion.'

Katie laughed.

'What's funny about that?'

'Nothing. Well, a bit. It's a weird kind of thing to play. I thought you meant like a guitar or saxophone, something like that, in a band.'

'I'm in a band. But we do a lot of Chas and Dave kind of thing, so the accordion's really good. It was my uncle's. He taught me.' He got up. 'Come on, I'll show it to you.'

Katie followed Phil into his bedroom. It was a pit. She had never seen anything so shambolic, bags of stuff everywhere, piles of books and music, the bed unmade, the sheets grey. Phil didn't seem to notice. He pulled out his accordion from a space between the bed and the battered wardrobe and showed it to Katie, explaining it all to her. She watched and listened. What would her mum think if she knew she was sitting on some strange man's bed on a Sunday evening? But it was nothing like that at all. Nothing.

When Phil had finished explaining, and let her have a shot at it, they went back through. It seemed that a decision had been reached between Des and Andy and Ryan, that they would go out to the local greasy spoon and have something to eat.

'You girls coming?' Ryan asked Georgina and Katie.

'Yeah, we'll come. Won't we, Katie?'

'No,' said Katie. 'I'm going home.'

Georgina looked at her for a moment. 'Oh, come on.'

'I'm going for the bus. You stay if you like.'

Georgina wasn't quite prepared for this. She hesitated for a moment and then said, 'No, I'd better come with you.' She turned to give Ryan a kiss and whisper something to him, so Katie put on her jacket and headed for the stairs.

On the bus Katie listened while Georgina talked about Ryan. She said nothing. After a while Georgina said, 'You're very quiet. You're not jealous, are you?'

'Don't be stupid,' said Katie.

Georgina was mildly surprised. This was not the kind of thing Katie generally said to her, at any rate not in that flat, dismissive tone. There was a pause. 'Anyway, what were you and Phil doing in his bedroom?'

Katie turned to look at her friend. 'He's got an accordion. He plays it in a pub at the weekends. He was showing me. It's very heavy.'

'Right.' The bus rumbled past the empty park. It was

nearly dark. 'So, d'you fancy going round there another time?'

'I might. I don't know.' Katie gazed at her shadowy reflection in the bus window, thinking of the tranquillity of the last two hours, and the lovely isolation of being somewhere which had nothing to do with the rest of her life.

5

On Monday of the half-term week, Carla spent the morning planning the menu for Mr Barrett's inaugural lunch and then went into town to do the shopping. As she foraged amongst the bagged salads in the supermarket and waited in line at the fishmonger's, she felt an odd sense of detachment, as though she were some distant eye watching herself, observing her remarkably convincing portrayal of an ordinary, sane human being going about her everyday chores. Inside she felt leaden. Her problem, which had so far been an emotional and intellectual one, seemed over the weekend to have developed a corporeal aspect. While unhappiness might be a frame of mind, despair was physical, despair clutched at your insides and wouldn't let go. And fear. Fear was like a weight, dragging you down.

The weekend had been unremarkable. Alan would probably count it a success. They had stayed at a pleasant hotel near the New Forest, one which boasted a golf course, a gym and a swimming pool. They arrived too late on Friday for dinner, but had steak sandwiches and drinks in their room. After breakfast on Saturday, Carla had gone to the gym, while Alan sat at the side of the indoor pool with the paper, then went for a swim. They took a long walk in the forest in the late morning and had lunch at a pub, where they were accosted by another couple of roughly their own age who had recognized them from the hotel. In the afternoon Alan played golf with the man, Ray, and Carla stayed in her room, reading. She had no desire to pass the time chatting to Steph, Ray's wife. She found it hard to concentrate on her book. Ripples of terror spread through her body from time to time, like an inner hysteria. The words *I have to leave him* kept formulating themselves in her mind, a little ribbon of imaginary type-script.

Ray discovered from Alan over drinks after their golf game that he and Carla were having dinner at the hotel, and suggested that the four of them should dine together. Alan could not decently refuse. And so Carla had spent the evening smiling, and listening to Ray and Alan dis-cussing golf, and discussing with Steph mortgages, clothes, and the future of the Royal Family. She was relieved not to be alone with Alan. *I might have done it this evening*, she kept thinking. This panic, the fact of being in a different place with him, might just have brought everything to a head. And then where would she have been? Where would they have been? After dinner and a couple of brandies Alan had been feeling amorous. She found she had to steel herself to sex as she would to an injection at the dentist's. After it was over she felt the same relief. She did not think Alan had noticed. Like everything else that occurred between them, it was simply a matter of manu-facturing a façade, of going through the motions with the appropriate sounds and responses. *I cannot go on like this*, she thought as she lay awake listening to the sounds of Alan asleep.

I cannot go on like this. 'I'll have that piece of salmon, please. The one in the middle.' But not today. She was not going over the edge today. Nor tomorrow. As long as there were things to do, a frame to be made for the daily void of her life, she would get by. For the present. Just for the present.

When she returned from shopping, Alan had finished packing and preparing his notes for the headmaster's conference. His car was being serviced, so Carla ran him to the station.

'I enjoyed the weekend,' he remarked, turning to glance at her. Carla kept her eyes fastened on the road as she negotiated yet another of the endless roundabouts which the council seemed so fond of installing. 'We should do it more often.' Carla gave a little murmur that might have been agreement. After a pause Alan added, 'Ray and Steph were rather ghastly. I'm sorry about that. I mean, it was useful finding someone to play a round of golf with, but I didn't expect to get lumbered with them over dinner.'

'There wasn't much you could do about it,' said Carla. They crossed the hump-backed bridge above the railway line and pulled into the station car park.

'No. Still, I'd have preferred it if it had just been the two of us.'

He kissed her cheek and got out. She waited as he took his overnight bag and briefcase from the boot, then gave him a smile and a little wave, watching as he made his way to the platform. She sat for a few moments thinking about what he had just said. He meant it. He was happy in her company. This was more appalling than if they were in a state of mutual cold warfare, living on an emotional diet of bickering and unpleasantness, like so many foundering couples. At least people in that condition knew what lay ahead, the inevitability of a break-up, a situation where unhappiness was collective and guilt conjoint. Carla carried the burden herself. She couldn't leave him. He would be bewildered and empty; his job, which so burdened and frustrated him, would become impossible. He would be lonely. She thought back to those pictures of them in the beginning, the way in which she had leaned into him, her shelter, protector. All that had changed. It was she who moved with strength now – but with what direction or hope? Suddenly, without warning, the little tremors of terror began, emotion so physical that she had to grip the steering wheel hard.

After a few moments she drove home to prepare the pastry for tomorrow lunchtime's salmon en croute. Alan, watching from his departing train as she turned the car round in the car park, thought that she had waited to see him off, and lifted his hand in acknowledgement and farewell.

Olive had any number of long, dangling earrings, all silver – silver set with onyx, with jade, with amber, beryl, verdite, jasper – fashioned in romantic art-deco curlicues and pendants of intertwined leaves and stems. She kept them in a felt-lined box inlaid with sandalwood, which her father had brought back from India when she was a little girl. The faint fragrance every time she opened the box reminded her of him, of her childhood.

Her long fingers drifted through the heap of earrings. She held them up against her ears, one pair after another, and eventually chose two shaped like long silver teardrops, the ends studded with amber. They matched the clothes she was wearing, the sprigged skirt in black and brown, the blouse. She had ironed the blouse carefully that morning, and the neat frills of the collar sat stiff against the soft skin of her neck as she fastened the earrings on. She brushed her hair once more, and looked with a wry sigh at her reflection. Quite absurd, really, to try to make any impression on anyone twenty years younger than oneself, but still that girlish spirit of romance never quite died. Nice to make the effort. And it was good for the confidence, and therefore for the occasion itself. Taking pains over one's appearance was rejuvenating. Now she could look forward to the business of selecting clothes carefully each day, instead of throwing on much the same old assortments of cardigans and skirts. Not that anyone cared, least of all Peter Barrett. Still.

Silly, middle-aged woman, she told her reflection. She hadn't behaved or felt like this since the business with Mike Rayment ten years ago. She looked quickly away from the mirror. Any recollection of that time still brought a blotchy flush to her skin. She had actually thought that she had been caught up in a real romance. How quickly she had come to understand that it was nothing more than a grubby, adulterous liaison, shallow and meaningless on his part, just like the man himself. Silly middle-aged woman, then and now.

She went downstairs and picked up the little bunch of flowers which she had bought at the fruit shop to give to Carla. A sudden thresh of raindrops against the window made her look up. The sky was dark with the beginnings of a downpour. She had planned to walk the half mile across the park to the Tradescants' house, but this would now mean that she would arrive bedraggled, with her umbrella blown inside out. The possibility of driving crossed her mind, but only fleetingly, for once she was set on a course of action, Olive didn't like to abandon it. She buttoned and belted her raincoat, took her umbrella, and set off in the teeth of the wind and rain.

The business of preparing lunch was actively pleasurable to Carla. She enjoyed cooking. When she cooked she inhabited a guilt-free realm, one of soothing textures and smells, of innocent little tasks and processes. She rolled out the puff pastry to the right size, baked it until it was lightly brown and crisp, remembering to sprinkle it with a little semolina so that the salmon wouldn't make it soggy. Then she carefully laid the fillets of salmon on top and rolled out a further sheet of pastry, placed it on top and tucked it around underneath. She brushed it with beaten egg, marking the pastry with the end of a teaspoon to make fish scales, and put it in the oven. While it cooked she made the sauce, reflecting on the moral satisfaction that lay in having made her own fish stock, and not using a cube. In the background Jenni Murray discussed adoption reform, interviewed Maureen Lipman, and invited listeners to ring in with their experiences at the hands of traffic wardens. The rain pattered on the kitchen window.

She went through to the dining room and inspected the table, laid for three, dark-blue linen napkins matching the blue and white crockery, the silver prettily arranged, fresh flowers in a small vase in the centre, glasses for wine and water. Perhaps a little formal and perfect for lunch with a new junior teacher, but Carla scarcely knew how to give a breezy, informal lunch. It was not her style.

She went back to the kitchen, checked the fish, which was browning nicely, and began to prepare the salad. Carla reflected that, if she had had children, her whole existence would have been happily absorbed in these endless and ultimately pointless acts of domestic gratification. Wasn't that what life was all about? If a child had been born when she and Alan had intended, before they had learned that life was not as artless and easy as they had thought, he or she would now be – what? Twenty or so? She tried to visualize a young man or woman, the product of herself and Alan, but the concept was vague and elusive. The very idea made her feel old.

At that moment the doorbell rang, and when she opened it and saw the young man standing on the door-step, the connection with her reflections of a few seconds ago was a little startling.

He put out a hand. 'Mrs Tradescant? I'm Peter Barrett.'

They shook hands and Carla invited him in, taking his raincoat. As they exchanged pleasantries Carla discreetly studied the new member of staff. He was certainly very handsome, with dark, curling hair and lively brown eyes with an intent expression, and his colouring was clear, childlike, with a rosy flush. The effect of ingenuous youth was heightened by the old-fashioned clothes he was wearing, a tweed suit with a waistcoat, and brown brogues. He looked like someone from the 1930s, with all the candour and innocence she associated with that era.

'I do like your suit,' Carla said, and gave a little laugh.

This young man made her feel instantly maternal and able to say what she thought.

Peter Barrett pulled open his jacket and inspected the lining. 'Thanks. I got it at a second-hand shop in Greenwich. I think it was tailor-made for someone.'

You, thought Carla. 'Do come through. Olive isn't here yet. I expect she's still battling her way across the park. She walks everywhere. Did you drive here?'

'Yes. I've got a Morris Minor. Can't get it much above sixty, but it gets me around. I like old things.'

Carla showed him into the dining room. 'I'm just going to check that our lunch isn't burning to a cinder. I won't be a moment,' she said, and slipped through to the kitchen.

Peter glanced round the elegantly furnished room, and at the meticulously laid table. She seemed to have gone to a lot of trouble. Still, she was the headmaster's wife, and she probably had certain standards. She was certainly younger and much more attractive than he had expected. He went over to the French windows and stood with his hands in his pockets, gazing out at the rain falling on the garden.

That was how Olive found him, when she came into the dining room after divesting herself of her wet coat and scarf and handing the drooping little bunch of flowers to Carla. It was the way she would always remember him, when this was all over and in the past – in that pose, framed against the rainy windows, his hands in his trouser pockets, turning his head to smile at her as she came into the room.

'How d'you do again?' He crossed the room and shook her hand. He gestured to the window. 'I think it's clearing up.'

'I hope so,' replied Olive. 'I shouldn't like to have to walk back in that downpour.' She glanced round the room, then at the table, and sighed. 'How beautifully Mrs Tradescant always does things.'

By and large, the luncheon went smoothly. A faint note of restraint was struck by the manner in which Olive, even though she customarily called Carla by her first name, today seemed impelled by some notion of deference to refer indirectly to her as Mrs Tradescant. Clearly she thought that this was the proper way for young Mr Barrett to think of and address the headmaster's wife. At first Carla looked for an opportunity to say to Peter, 'Please, call me Carla,' but none presented itself. Then, after a while, the sense of his youthfulness and her own position as hostess made the formality feel perfectly natural. She let it pass.

Peter Barrett was a pleasant, entertaining young man – rather, Carla thought, like someone playing a part in a Terence Rattigan play, but fine all the same – and they had enough to talk about. Peter talked about himself, about his family in Winchester, and the few years he had spent in teaching. He had taken a degree in English at Bristol, then done a year's teacher training, and after that he had spent three years at a school in his home town before taking a post in Rome, where he had spent two years teaching English as a foreign language.

'Oh, so you speak Italian?' asked Olive, smiling. 'I adore Italy. I've spent many happy summers there.'

They talked for a while about Rome and Florence, then Carla asked, 'What brought you back to England?'

'I missed the climate. No, I really wanted to get back to

teaching literature on a broader scale. And I like teaching younger children. Tell me something about what you've been doing.'

Carla told him about the pupils she had been teaching, and the texts, and Olive talked about the other members of the faculty and the different syllabuses. The conversation, where not specifically concerned with the school, was unremarkable, with only one slightly jarring note. For some reason Olive brought up the matter of Chris Woodhead, and the question of his relationship with a sixth-former when he had been a teacher. It was topical at the time. Woodhead was the head of the schools inspectorate, and opinion was divided on his past conduct.

'Of course, he's an appalling man,' said Olive, 'but it does seem like something of a witch-hunt.'

'I agree,' said Carla. 'What he said about relationships between teachers and pupils was taken entirely out of context. I think they should leave him alone. I'm not sure why his ex-wife is making such a vendetta out of the whole thing, after all this time.'

There was the very slightest pause, and then Peter Barrett said, 'It's a bit embarrassing for the government, isn't it, given that they're trying to prevent abuse of trust in their age-of-consent legislation? I'm not sure that it's quite the unjust persecution that everyone's making out.'

Carla looked at him in faint surprise. 'You really think after all this time that people should dredge it up to try to discredit him?'

Peter shrugged. 'Well, it *is* to his discredit, isn't it? Teachers ought not to have relationships with their pupils. It's not on. You simply don't do it.'

'Oh, come on, teachers do it all the time,' retorted Carla. She felt mildly irritated and defensive, recollecting her own beginnings with Alan, yet recognizing that she had once held the opinions Peter was now expressing.

'That doesn't make it right.'

Conscious of the slight friction, Olive said quickly, 'Well, it's not even clear whether they had this relationship while she was still a pupil or not. Woodhead says one thing and his wife another. Who can say?' She gave Carla a smile. 'You know, this pudding really is very good.'

The conversation shifted tack, and half an hour later, after coffee, Peter took his leave.

'I'll see you next week,' he said to Olive. 'And thank you for lunch, Mrs Tradescant.'

It sounded too formal. It was her cue, but for some reason Carla did not take it. She shook his hand. 'I'm glad you could come. We'll be seeing a bit of one another during the term.'

'Of course, you're coaching the sixth-formers. Well, I'll see you in school. Thanks again.'

Carla closed the door and went back into the dining room. Olive was putting plates and coffee cups on to a tray.

'He's a nice young man, isn't he?' remarked Olive. It was a delightful, secret pleasure to use such scant words to describe her true feelings about such a glorious individual.

'Mmm. Quite the young fogey, though, with his tweed suit and his Morris Minor. I expect he looks just right in cricket flannels.' It was this old-fashionedness that appealed so much to Olive's romantic heart, but she couldn't explain this to Carla. She could never, ever tell anyone. She said nothing, heaping the napkins together. 'And I'm rather afraid,' went on Carla, 'that he's going to wreak a certain amount of havoc amongst the female population of Taft's.'

'I think you may be right,' sighed Olive. 'So it's just as well he's so principled, isn't it?'

But young Mr Barrett had no noticeable effect on the hearts and minds of the girls of Taft's. There may have been a slight flutter amongst one or two of the more impressionable members of year 8, but certainly no sign of the hysterical mass crush that might have been expected. Carla detected this during her regular visits to the school and to the staffroom, and brought the matter up one evening with Alan. She welcomed these impersonal areas of conversation for the semblance of sanity and amicability they created. She needed to see and hear herself as a normal being, even if it was a pretence. She sometimes wondered if she was going slowly mad.

'Peter Barrett's not creating the kind of stir you'd expected, is he?' She was on her third glass of wine, and could address and look at her husband without shuddering distaste.

Alan, yawning his way through *Newsnight*, murmured in agreement. 'Given the geriatric state of most of the male teaching staff, you'd have thought they'd go overboard for him. Seems not, however.'

'I suppose it might be different in an all girls' school. Here they're surrounded by boys, and Peter doesn't look much older than the average sixth-former. Besides, I imagine he doesn't exactly fit the desirable contemporary image – the way he dresses, and so forth. He's really quite peculiar.'

'I know what you mean. But he's a good teacher. He has a certain vitality. The sixth form like him.'

'I imagine they would.' She sighed and set down her glass. She felt she was coasting on an acceptable level of numbness. If only she could exist in a state of moderate inebriation permanently, dulled to the awfulness of her situation. She could talk in this normal way forever, the little waves of fear that normally lapped at her insides would be stilled. 'They're all much more level-headed and mature than we were. Mind you, I suppose in his position it helps to come armed with virtuous beliefs.'

Alan glanced at her. 'What might those be?'

'Oh, he made a very principled little statement when he was here for lunch. All about how teachers shouldn't screw around with their pupils. I made some objections along the lines of living with reality, but I quite admired him for what he said. I suppose he's right, really.'

'As I recall, that wasn't quite the line you took twenty-three years ago.' He stretched out an affectionate hand to touch her face. It was the hand with which he had just been scratching his chest through his unbuttoned shirt, and Carla flinched. Some things no amount of wine could improve.

'Haven't you ever thought that perhaps it was an abuse, the way you behaved?' She spoke rapidly, a slight uncontrollable tremor in her voice.

Alan stared at her, amazed at the volatility of her moods. Probably the amount of wine she drank most evenings. He had wondered recently if he should say something. He shrugged and looked away.

'I was young and randy. Anyway, as I recall, any students I did sleep with weren't exactly hard to persuade into bed. Including you.'

Carla felt a hard pulse beating in her head. She kept her voice level. 'Maybe if you'd been a bit more principled, everyone's story would be very different.'

Alan wondered what this meant exactly, then dismissed it, accepting the argument on a general level. 'Come on, it wasn't the same moral climate as today. And university students are more or less adults. It's not the same as between a teacher and a secondary-school pupil.' Carla fought to find words. This brief moment of friction, irrelevant in its source, drove her towards some sort of confrontation, an expression of everything she had felt these past months. Even though she knew the perils of attempting to elucidate truths after three glasses of wine, she felt she had to speak. But before she could, Alan added, 'Though try telling that to Mike Rayment.'

The sense of precipitation ebbed away. 'What?'

'No, nothing.' He was silent for a few seconds, then rubbed his chin. 'I don't think he's that bad. There was just some rumour drifting about – you know, when he's been giving lessons to a pupil after school hours.'

'You're joking!' Carla drank the remains of her wine. The brief incandescence of her emotions had died, but was now diverted and reignited. 'You can't allow that. You have to speak to him.'

'Speak to him?'

'Tell him he mustn't be alone with pupils. For God's sake, Alan, you know what a lech he is.' She faintly slurred the last three words. Looking at her, Alan realized she was a little drunk. 'I mean, chasing every young female teacher in sight is one thing, but pupils? You have to say something.'

'Nothing I can say. It's impracticable to suggest that he shouldn't ever be alone with female pupils. He has to see them on his own for all kinds of reasons — matters of discipline, discussions about folders, personal matters. He is a tutor, remember. Anyway, he'd see it as impugning his reputation. God, I can just see the shower of letters now, all the verbiage about teaching being a matter of professional trust —'

'You can't impugn Mike Rayment's reputation. It's beyond that.' Alan said nothing, and Carla added, 'Peter Barrett's right. Relations between teachers and their pupils should remain strictly platonic.'

Alan smiled and stretched out a hand, laid it gently on her thigh. 'Even when they're nineteen and beautiful and have the hots for you?'

It was as though he were describing a different world, people who had existed once, but had since ceased to be. Herself and Alan. She didn't look at him, stared into her empty wine glass. 'Was that how it was?'

'That's how it was.'

She looked up. 'Have you noticed how we're speaking in the past tense?' She rose from the sofa and wandered barefoot through to the kitchen. She put her glass in the dish-washer and went to bed.

Alan stared morosely at the television and wondered what was going wrong, and how he should tackle it. Carla wrapped the duvet tight around her shoulders and lay motionless in bed, wondering how she would get through the rest of this week, or this year.

It had not been a good afternoon for Katie. Smelly Jellicoe had had a go at her for not having handed in her French essay – she hadn't even started it yet – and Georgina had disappeared before lunchtime. Katie hadn't been able to find her anywhere round the school. So during lunchtime break she'd hung around with another couple of girls, but she brooded over Georgina's absence, feeling neglected. If Georgina had a doctor's appointment or something like that, why hadn't she told Katie? She kept things to herself, whereas Katie told Georgina just about everything. And the sight of Russell Tucker walking across the quad with Rosie Dobson didn't help. Clearly they were still an item.

Bea was coming out of school with two of her friends when she saw Katie up ahead, walking along morosely on her own, clutching her bag, head down. Bea felt a pang at the sight of the abject figure. Poor old Katie. She always seemed to be miserable about something these days, getting into arguments at home, being nagged about her schoolwork. Bea left her friends and caught up with Katie at the school gates.

'Hi,' said Bea.

Katie glanced up in vague surprise. She and her elder sister rarely went home together. Even if they got on the same bus, Bea sat with her friends and Katie with Georgina.

'Where's Georgina?'

Katie shrugged her shoulders.

The two sisters walked together in silence for a while.

'I've seen her hanging around with Hannah Keys now and again. Is that what's getting you down?' Katie said nothing, merely shot her sister a dark, pained look. Bea tried again. 'I know what it's like having a best friend who doesn't treat you very well. It's really hard to –'

'Oh, shut up, Bea!' retorted Katie hotly. 'I couldn't care less about Hannah, or who Georgina hangs around with. What's it to you, anyway?'

'Don't get so stressy! You just seem a bit fed up lately.'

It was an invitation to confide, and for the briefest of seconds Katie had an urge to tell her big sister everything. But she didn't know how to articulate 'everything' – the thoughts and emotions welled up in confusion in her head, beyond utterance. The impulse to share her unhappiness died away. All Katie could find to say was, 'It's all right for you. Everything goes right for you. Mummy and Daddy think you're perfect.'

Bea swung her bag over to her other shoulder and pushed her hair back from her face. 'No, they don't. Look at the way Dad gets when he gives me a driving lesson. God, the insults.'

After a few seconds' silence, Katie asked, apparently irrelevantly, 'Why did you dump Francis Bailey?'

'Francis? Because he was a waste of space. He has to be the most conceited guy I ever went out with.'

'He's really nice-looking.'

'So he thinks. Anyway, the average eighteen-year-old male isn't exactly what you'd call mature.'

They reached the bus stop and set their bags down. 'That's what Georgina says. She goes for the older type.'

Bea glanced at her sister. 'Does she now? Well, I know

she's your friend, but I wouldn't listen to everything she says. Stick to boys your own age.'

'Don't be so patronizing.' There followed a few seconds of silence, in which Katie struggled against temptation and then gave in. 'Actually, d'you know who I think's really nice? Russell Tucker.'

Bea smiled to herself and decided not to give Katie her own opinion of Russell Tucker, instead letting Katie talk happily about her hero until the bus came.

After tea, Katie went upstairs with her homework and tried to tackle her French essay. She had to have it by tomorrow or else. It was meant to be a description of a trip to a museum or art gallery. After ten dispirited minutes she heard the phone ring.

Her mother called up to her, 'Katie, it's Georgina.'

She went halfway downstairs and leaned over the banisters to take the phone. Back in her room she closed the door.

'Hi,' she said. 'Where were you today? I looked for you at lunchtime.'

'I bunked off,' said Georgina. Her tone was light.

'Where did you go?' As if she didn't know.

'Round to Ryan's.'

Katie wasn't sure how she felt about this new turn of events. She herself had only bunked off once, to get out of games, and she didn't think that really counted. She couldn't stand hockey. But missing a whole afternoon of lessons was different. She half admired Georgina's daring. She also felt mildly excluded.

'What did you do?'

'Sat around, had a bit of lunch, listened to music. I just didn't fancy being cooped up for double maths.'

'You could have told me.'

'Why? You wouldn't have wanted to come.'

'I might have.'

There was silence for a moment. Katie wondered if she had really meant that. She wasn't like Georgina, she was frightened of authority. But why not?

'I thought I might go round there again tomorrow,' said Georgina. 'You could come then.'

Katie glanced across at the French essay which she had hardly even begun. If she could miss French, then it wouldn't matter. Not till the following week. She could get it done over the weekend. But she felt scared. Still, agreeing now didn't necessarily commit her to anything. She could change her mind tomorrow.

'Yeah, I might. I'll see.'

And the conversation turned to other things.

6

Carla was coming to the end of a tutorial with Beatrice and another sixth-former, Colin Fowler, listening as they performed the final duologue from *A Doll's House*. Colin wasn't bad as Helmer. He'd quite captured the arrogant self-belief crumbling into bewilderment and incomprehension. Bea turned a little too theatrically towards Colin – or was it just her poise, and that cascade of red-gold hair that were themselves too beautiful and melodramatic? – and said, 'There. Now it's all over. Here are your keys. The servants know all about running the house – better than I did.'

Carla broke in. 'Hold on, Bea. That's good, but remember, whatever regrets Nora has, she's overcome them, she's being utterly practical, ruthlessly efficient. Perhaps she's behaving that way to prevent herself from changing her mind. So you must sound like that. Not regretful. Cold, absolutely calm. There's no going back for you now.' Bea listened, nodding. 'OK, just those lines again.'

Bea lifted her chin, and began again in her clear, light voice. Too light, thought Carla. The speeches really required a woman's voice, the tones of someone who had passed from girlhood into a life that would never be carefree again. And Bea – Bea was the epitome of girlish perfection, the thing that poets used to write about, at that flowering moment of unconscious loveliness. Carla smiled as she watched her act, enjoying the determination of her movements and voice as she strove to personify maturity and embittered disillusionment.

'. . . that our life together could be a real marriage.' Carla nodded on the pause. 'Goodbye.' Bea turned as Colin collapsed, rather gingerly, against one of the plastic stacking chairs, and called after her, 'Nora! Nora!' He got up again and looked forlornly round the room. 'Empty! She's not here any more –'

Carla interrupted him. 'OK, hold on, Colin.' She got up and came over. 'It's no good just sounding mildly surprised. This is a moment of awful realization. She hasn't just walked out of the room – she's walked out of your life. So maybe instead of looking round the room we want to do something else to convey –' The bell sounded. 'Anyway, that's something we can work on next time. Both of you have a think about it. And well done. I really think it's coming on very nicely indeed.'

Colin and Bea picked up their texts and the rest of their belongings.

'See you next week,' said Carla. As Bea and Colin left, Olive appeared in the doorway.

'Oh, I'm glad I caught you, Carla. I wanted a word. I don't know if you've read about it, but there's a new production of *Hamlet* at The Gielgud. It opened a week ago and the reviews are very good. Given that it's a set text, I thought it might be an idea if we took the upper-sixth students up one weekend to see it. It would be a nice break for them, and I'm sure we could get decent rates at a hotel as a party booking. I was thinking of the second weekend of November. Would you be interested in coming along?'

'Of course,' said Carla. 'It sounds like a good idea.' She would jump at any chance to spend a day or two away from Alan, especially over a weekend.

'There are eleven of them, but still I think that would be a manageable group. I'll go and see what I can book up, and let you know.'

'Fine.'

Carla went along to the staffroom for a quick coffee before going to her tennis game with Maeve. She was standing by the coffee maker when she was joined by Peter Barrett, looking a little gloomy.

'What's up?' asked Carla. 'You don't look very pleased with life.'

'I'm not, to be honest with you.'

'Let's sit down.' They took their coffee cups to a quiet corner of the staffroom.

'Tell me,' asked Peter as they sat down, 'is that man Michael Rayment normally an obstructive, unpleasant –' He hesitated over the word, his lips pressed together.

'Bastard?' supplied Carla. She sipped her coffee. 'On the whole, yes. Why, what's he done?'

'It's more a question of what he hasn't done. Or won't do. You know I'm doing a production of *The Snow Queen* with the year eights? Well, maybe I've got the etiquette wrong, but in my experience if you ask the head of art to help out with the set design, he or she is usually happy to help. But not Mike Rayment. He said he couldn't possibly spare the time, and his junior staff were all too busy. Not only that, but the way he spoke was downright unpleasant.

I mean, I've only just started here, so I can't see what I can have done to offend him.'

Carla gave Peter a considering look. 'Put it down to professional jealousy. Mike imagines he commands the attention and affection of all the females in this place. You're new, you're young. He probably sees you as a threat.'

'Good God.'

'Now, if you were *Miss* Barrett, I can assure you that he would be falling over himself to design your set, and trying to have cosy little private discussions about it. Anyway, what are you going to do?'

Peter sighed. 'I'll have a word with the design and technology people, I suppose, see if they can help out.'

'Bill Radcliffe's a very nice guy. I'm sure he'll be only too happy.' She glanced up and saw Mike Rayment heading towards them. 'Speak of the devil. This is my cue to leave,' murmured Carla. 'Bye.' She got up and made for the door, hoping to avoid Mike, but he loomed in her path.

'The very woman. I've found some props that might be useful for your A-level people. Why don't you come along and see what you think, if you've got a moment?' Mike had conveniently put the props in one of the small side rooms in his department, where he and Carla were unlikely to be disturbed during morning break. It was an erotic little scenario which he had much enjoyed putting together.

'That's very kind of you, Mike. Maybe another time. I've got to run.' Mike raised his eyebrows in regret. He hadn't actually thought he would bring it off, but it was worth a shot. He'd get his chance with her one of these days, of that he was convinced. He glanced across at Peter Barrett. She'd been sitting chatting to him. No doubt he fancied his chances, too, little snot. He'd taken an instinctive dislike to that young man the first time he'd met him. 'By the way,' added Carla, 'it's a pity you couldn't be as helpful to Peter Barrett. I mean, if you can go to so much trouble just to sort out some props for me, the least you could do is lend a hand with his set design.' She moved off before he had the chance to reply.

Mike stood for a moment, reflecting. So young Mr Barrett had been moaning to her about him? Not a very good idea, all things considered. Our new boy had no real idea just how difficult his life could be made. Mike shot Peter a chilly glance and went to pour himself some coffee.

Georgina and Katie were sitting on the radiator outside the art rooms during morning break.

'Did you get that French homework finished?' asked Georgina.

'No. I don't know what I'm going to tell Jellicoe. He's already been on at me about my course work.'

Georgina pulled her blonde hair over one shoulder and began to plait the ends. 'Tell you what,' she said after a moment, 'why don't we just bunk off? You said last night you wanted to.'

'I didn't say I wanted to. I said I might.'

'Well?' Georgina glanced up from plaiting her hair.

Katie felt that flutter of fear and excitement in her stomach. Jellicoe wasn't going to let her buy any more time over that essay. He might be quite a decent teacher, but when he got going with the withering sarcasm and how pathetic your prospects in the GCSEs were if you couldn't even get your work in on time, it wasn't very pleasant. She could do without it. If she skipped off, then she'd have the weekend to get the essay done, and it would be all right. She could catch up on whatever other prep he set them from someone else in the class. She thought of that strange, dingy flat where Ryan and his friends lived. It hung in her mind like a place of escape from the unhappy tangle of her life at school and at home.

She nodded. 'All right.' Then she hesitated. 'Won't someone notice?'

'Why should they? We're down in the morning register. Nobody notices if the odd face is missing from a class. We'll be fine. We'll get our stuff from the cloakroom and slip out the back way by the car park. The bell's going to go for the end of break in a minute, so if we wait till the teachers have all gone to their classes, no one'll catch us.'

Ten minutes later Katie and Georgina were hurrying to the bus stop, giggling. Katie was conscious of the thrill of a novel and illicit exhilaration. They sat on the top deck of the bus trying to look like they were out of school for a good reason, in case any adults were being especially nosey. It seemed strange to be out of school in the middle of the morning. She looked down at the drift of shoppers, the mums with the pushchairs and the old people, and thought about Jellicoe's French lesson proceeding without her. That thought made her happy.

A week later, Olive came to Carla just before the start of one of her tutorials.

'I've booked everything up for the theatre weekend.

Very nice seats in the circle, a good discount for going as a group, and we've got rooms at a hotel in Gloucester Road, very handy for the tube. It's called the Fairmount, Mr Perkins recommended it. The hockey team stayed there when they went up to a tournament last year.'

'Fine,' said Carla. 'I'm looking forward to it.'

'All the students are able to go, with the exception of Beatrice Rayment. Apparently she's attending some family thing that had already been arranged.'

'That's a pity.'

'Yes. Anyway, it's only a week away. I'll let you know more details about our travel arrangements nearer the time.'

But when Olive next spoke to Carla, a few days before the projected trip, she was distraught and unhappy. 'Carla, I'm so sorry to be letting you down. I really don't think there's anything I can do about it. My brother-in-law has died. It's dreadfully sudden, and my poor sister is in a very bad way. The funeral is on Saturday, and I have to be there. I'm simply not going to be able to come to London.'

'Oh. I see. That is bad news. About your brother-in-law, I mean. I'm so sorry.' Carla's concerns were less with Olive's family and more to do with the prospect of taking ten high-spirited sixth-formers up to London for the weekend on her own.

'I know what you're thinking. It's too much for you to handle on your own, isn't it? And I imagine the parents would prefer it if there was another member of staff.'

'I suppose I could find out if anyone else could come along . . .'

'Well, what about Peter Barrett? He's more likely to be

free, no family commitments and so forth. It is short notice, but it's worth asking.'

Carla considered this. She glanced at her watch. 'The thing is, I won't have a chance to speak to him today. I'm just off.'

'Oh, let me do that. It's my fault you're stuck like this, after all. I'll see him at lunchtime and let you know what he says. In the meantime, I'd better give you this.' She handed Carla a folder. 'It's all the tickets, and so forth. I do hope we'll be able to sort something out.'

That night Olive rang Carla and told her that Peter was very happy to take Olive's place on the trip. 'And it'll be nice for the students to have someone nearer their own age than two stuffy middle-aged women,' added Olive.

Carla wasn't quite sure, as she put the phone down, whether she liked being lumped together with Olive in that way. Still, she supposed there was some truth in what Olive said. Peter presumably would get along with them all fairly easily. It would make the trip more relaxing, even if it might also make her feel like a lone mother hen.

'Who was that?' asked Alan, coming into the room.

'Olive. She's asked Peter Barrett to come along on the theatre trip in place of her. She has to go to her brother-in-law's funeral.'

'Oh.' Alan nodded, not particularly interested. 'By the way, you know the Christmas raffle?'

'Mmm?' Now it was Carla's turn to evince a lack of interest. We bore each other rigid, she thought. Rigid was right. She felt spiritually frozen, immobile. Don't think about it. Not now.

'Well, Russell Tucker's father runs a travel agency, and

he's offered a weekend trip to Paris, including an overnight stay at the Ritz, as one of the prizes. First prize, I would say.'

'That's nice.'

'Very generous. The best we came up with last year was a portable colour TV. The trouble is, we'll have to find a second prize that's a bit nearer the mark. A case of wine rather than a couple of bottles, say. After all, if you're asking the parents to fork out a pound a ticket and sending home three books of the things . . .'

Carla had ceased to listen. She turned and glanced at the French windows, against which the rain was pattering. The curtains were not yet drawn. She wondered if she was going to get up to close them, but her body felt inert. No, she wasn't. What *did* she have the strength for? Enough to go upstairs, fill a suitcase, and just walk out? Out into the windy, rainy night . . . Where was she going to go, anyway?

She looked up at him. He had stopped talking and was staring down at her, bald patch shining, moustache drooping, his expression unreadable. 'I'm sorry – what were you saying?' she asked.

'It doesn't matter,' replied Alan. He sat down and picked up the TV remote control.

The next day, Friday, Katie and Georgina slipped out of school again, just before lunchtime. It was the fourth time they had done it so far, and it felt quite natural and easy. The fear had almost entirely evaporated, but not the sense of freedom. Katie had convinced herself she hated school, she'd go anywhere just to be away from it. She was probably going to fail her exams anyway, and no one at home cared. No one at home cared about anything she did, of that she had convinced herself.

They bought a packet of chips each and stood at the bus stop. 'What if one of the teachers sees us?' asked Katie suddenly. 'They sometimes come out at lunchtime.'

Georgina shrugged. 'We'll tell them we just fancied some chips for lunch. Let's stand against the wall so it doesn't look like we're waiting for a bus.' She gestured with a chip towards a very old, unwashed man standing at the other side of the road near a litter bin. 'That bloke's staring at you,' she said to Katie. 'He fancies you.' They both fell about like it was the funniest thing in the world.

The hours they spent at the flat had fallen into a pattern. They drank tea and smoked cigarettes, listened to music and chatted to Ryan and Phil and Des. Andy had a job at Tesco's. Katie had decided that there wasn't much going on between Georgina and Ryan. Not the kind of thing she had implied. Or maybe it was just they liked to keep it cool in front of other people. Georgina saw him on Saturdays, so Katie had no idea what they got up to then. That was the worst of it. Saturday nights on her own. Still, she and Georgina went out together on Fridays. Friday night was Ryan's night out drinking with the lads.

So they just talked, or watched television. The conversations weren't very interesting, Katie decided, but it didn't seem to matter. It was just time passing. It was doing something you weren't meant to. It was being free from school. That was good enough.

Today Katie remembered Phil's accordion. 'You know that accordion you showed me?'

'Yeah?'

'Why don't you get it out and play it?'

Phil laughed. 'No thanks. I get enough of that down the pub. I'm playing down there tonight.'

'Have a rehearsal, then.'

He laughed again and stubbed out his cigarette. 'All right.'

So Phil got out his accordion and played some tunes. They started to sing along, Katie and Georgina and Des and Ryan. They sang 'My Old Man Said Follow the Van', 'Yellow Submarine', 'Waltzing Matilda' and 'I'm Forever Blowing Bubbles'. It seemed like a good laugh, like they were really having a lot of fun.

Later, when she was walking up the path to her front door at the end of her day, Katie thought back to it, and it had changed to being empty and sad.

On Saturday, the sixth-form expedition embarked from Huntsbridge station on the journey to London. The students all aligned themselves in two rows of seats on the train, leaving no room for Carla and Peter, which Carla didn't mind at all. She sat in a seat behind them and idly watched as Peter stowed odds and ends in the luggage rack. He had his jacket off, and she could see the muscles of his shoulders working beneath his shirt. The direction of her thoughts faintly alarmed her. Finding Mike Rayment's proximity disturbing was bad enough, without starting to fantasize about someone half her age. She pulled a book of Raymond Carver short stories from her bag and began to read. Peter sat down next to her. She wondered if she appeared rude, and whether she should put her book away, but he had a paper, so perhaps he would just get on with reading it.

After a moment he said, 'What are we going to do about lunch when we get to London?'

She looked up. 'I hadn't really thought. McDonald's, something like that? It's got to be somewhere fairly fast. Even if the train's on time we won't have more than an hour and a half to get to the hotel, leave our belongings, and then get to the theatre. We should be there by two-fifteen at the latest.' Sitting so close to him, she noticed for the first time the precise colour of his eyes, dark brown flecked with green, and the fact that, despite his boyish colouring, his beard was quite heavy, a faint shadow on his skin where it was shaved very close.

He nodded. At that moment one of the students put her head round the side of the seat to ask Peter something and he leaned forward. Carla began to read again. After a few seconds he leaned back. Carla was aware that he glanced at her, but she kept her eyes fastened resolutely on her book. Talking to him at such close quarters made her strangely self-conscious. Besides, she didn't think they had very much to say to one another. To her relief, Peter unfolded his paper and began to read, and for the rest of the journey they scarcely spoke.

Despite their apparent maturity, the sixth-form contingent were just as boisterous as any other school outing, if slightly easier to keep track of. By the time they'd left their belongings at the hotel, had lunch, and reached the Gielgud, Carla felt weary. As the play got underway she welcomed the familiar, soothing embrace of a theatre in darkness. It was wonderful to be far away from Alan.

The distance itself helped her to regain a sense of her individuality. She settled back in her seat and felt, if not happiness, a sense of peace.

When the play was over they made their way back to Gloucester Road on the tube and assembled in the lobby of the hotel.

Carla addressed them. 'OK. Everyone can go off to their rooms and relax for a while. Mr Barrett has identified an Italian restaurant nearby where we might be able to have dinner. I'll pop in and see if they can reserve us some tables. So let's all meet down here at half seven. How does that sound?'

Everyone murmured in agreement and headed off to their rooms. They were all on the second floor, the students in five doubles, and Peter and Carla with rooms on their own. Olive had grumbled to Carla when making the bookings that single rooms didn't seem to exist any more, and that they would have to pay for doubles each, such a waste. Thank God for that, reflected Carla, as she kicked off her shoes and stretched herself out on her double bed. How wonderful to be in a space of one's own, a piece of artificial containment in which one could exist, just for a few hours, in complete detachment, belonging to nobody. She closed her eyes and wondered if she might sleep, but the noise of traffic crept up from the street below, and she found herself thinking about the play, then about Alan, then, unstoppably, about what might have happened if she had taken up Mike Rayment's blatant offer the other day and gone to his room to look at the props. This is no good, she decided. She fished her book out of her bag, propped up two pillows and lay back to read.

After twenty minutes she stopped. Wonderful though the stories were, those broken, bright fragments of other people's lives, there was something unsettling about the relationships they described. They were always fractured in some way, whether by an accident, or someone's alcohol problem, or a bizarre decision taken like a wrong street turning, or simply by life becoming too hard to bear, but they were never brittle or insubstantial. All the men and women in his stories were shored up by love, even when things had gone badly wrong. Even when they were divorced, these people seemed to cling to one another. Where was the boredom, the empty sadness, the vague disgust, the reality of not caring any more? She wanted to read the truth of her own life, find clues and answers, be reassured that someone else had felt what she was feeling and could supply a solution. No one could.

She closed the book, put on her shoes and left the hotel to check out the Italian restaurant at the end of the street. A waiter told her that he would reserve two tables of six for later on. She left the restaurant and decided to take a walk, but after a couple of blocks she began to feel cold. Anyway, it depressed her to be in London. It made her wish she had never left. She didn't want to be here as a mere visitor. She wanted to belong to it, to have a home nearby to go to, for the streets to mean something, be part of a pattern in her life. She had a sudden fantasy of a small flat somewhere, a daily routine all of her own, singular possessions, silence in the evenings, reclaimed territory. She stopped still on the pavement, astonished by the idea, wondering if she could really do it, if perhaps, when she got back home to Huntsbridge, she could make a proper attempt to start something new, find a job in London, a place to live, instead of just going over and over it in her mind. She had spent too long telling herself it wasn't possible. It had to be possible. Otherwise she would go mad. Abruptly she turned around and went back to the hotel. In her room she lay down once again on the bed. This time she did not attempt to read. Her brain felt like a clear, uncluttered space. She felt the lightness of hope, of possibility. She fell asleep and slept for an hour, waking up in time to have a quick bath and change before meeting the rest of them in the hotel lobby.

Without any prior agreement, Carla and Peter, as teachers will tend to, each sat with a group of students at either table. At first the students Carla was with talked to her politely about the play, then the conversation veered away to their own more immediate concerns, and she withdrew a little, pretending to listen. She noticed that Peter's table seemed to be enjoying themselves, that there was more talk and laughter, and that Peter was joining in. Unlike Carla, he clearly didn't feel in any way excluded. Quite the opposite. It was only to be expected. He looked like one of them. For the first time, he wasn't wearing one of his old-fashioned suits, but was dressed much as the students were. She vaguely wished that Olive could have come after all. At least it would have been someone to talk to. Or possibly not. Olive would have been on the other table, and in that case everything would have been much more sedate. Peter had ordered some wine, she noticed. On her table everyone was sticking to soft drinks, which she thought was more sensible. Perhaps she should say something, tell him that she thought wine wasn't appropriate . . . No, leave them alone. They were young. Peter glanced in her direction and caught her eye. She half-smiled, then found that he was holding her gaze for a little longer than was necessary. Her heart began to thud, an unfamiliar sensation, and she looked away. Why had he done that? Perhaps there had been something in her expression that told him that she didn't approve of him ordering wine. But there had been no hesitancy in his gaze. One of the students made a remark to her, trying to include her in the conversation, and Carla's attention was taken up once more.

At the end of the meal one of the students on Peter's table, Andrea, came over to Carla's table and began to talk in a low voice to another girl, Tracy. Tracy listened for a moment and then turned with an excited face to Carla. 'Mrs Tradescant, Andrea says that Mr Barrett thinks it would be OK if we went on somewhere, a club or something. Just for a couple of hours. It's still very early. Please?' The others joined in.

'Well, I don't know . . .' She really wasn't sure about it. She had no notion what kind of place they were thinking of, but wherever it was, Carla was pretty sure she wouldn't want to be there. Nor would the students want her there. The idea of ten teenagers on the loose in London, when they were supposed to be in her charge, wasn't to be contemplated.

Peter came over. 'I said I'd go with them. I'll make sure they don't get up to anything.'

Carla looked at him. He was barely eight years older than they were. Still, he was here with his teacher's hat on. It was a matter of trust. She couldn't keep them all cooped up in the hotel, where there was nothing for them to do.

'Very well,' she said. 'But you must all stick together, and I think it would be best if you were back by eleven at the latest.' This provoked a couple of groans, but Carla stuck to it. 'Eleven,' she repeated firmly. 'Let me know when you get back,' she added to Peter.

While Carla remained behind to settle the bill, the sixth-formers left with Peter. On a sudden impulse, she ordered a brandy and sat at the deserted table for a while. She felt faintly excited. Now that she had laid the mental foundations for her departure, she wished that there was something practical and immediate to be done. She itched to start looking for a place to live, combing the pages of the *TES* for a job. But all that must wait. First she must face the present, and Alan. Would she change her mind when she got back to Huntsbridge tomorrow? That thought made her afraid. She remembered how impossible departure had seemed just a few weeks ago. Why should it seem any more possible from a different perspective? It was the guilt that was the worst. He had done nothing wrong. How was she going to tell him? *What* was she going to tell him?

She paid for the drink and went back to the hotel. In her room she lay on the bed and watched a film about the fortunes of a Miami casino boss. She became completely engrossed, and it was only when the film ended that she glanced at her watch and realized that it was twenty past eleven. They still weren't back. Or maybe they were and Peter had forgotten to tell her. She rang his room, but there was no reply. Irritation stirred within her. The least he could do was get them back on time. No doubt they'd be back soon. She picked up her book and read for a while, glancing at her watch every now and then. Twice she rang Peter's room.

By midnight she was angry. She should never have agreed to let them go off on their own. Obviously Peter was too young to exercise any authority over them. God alone knew what they were up to. For want of anything better to do, she slipped on her shoes and went down to the lobby. It was deserted. She pushed open the swing doors of the hotel and looked up and down the street. A group of people were making their way down the pavement, and as they got nearer Carla recognized the students, and Peter. She went back into the lobby, a little tide of relief in her heart, and waited for them. As they came in she did an automatic head-count, a reflex teacher response. They were all there. Then she noticed that Colin was being supported by two of his friends, clearly drunk. They all seemed to be rather the worse for wear, giggling and talking loudly. She stepped forward.

'I frankly don't believe this,' she said icily. The group fell silent, and Colin groaned. She scanned their faces. Then she turned to Peter. 'I trusted you to make sure that they behaved responsibly and got back here at a decent time. Look at them. Look at the state of them. Do you imagine their parents would be happy to know that a teacher in charge of a school party has allowed this kind of carry-on?'

Peter regarded her. He was more than usually flushed, his dark eyes very bright. 'Loosen up,' he said mildly. 'Colin's not as bad as he looks. He's only had three pints at the most. He just can't hold his drink.' One of the girls sniggered, which set the others off.

Carla felt incensed. 'Is that your excuse? You let pupils in your charge get into this state and think it doesn't matter? I was a fool to let them go.' She turned to the students. 'You'd better get to bed now. I'll see you all in the morning. I don't want anyone down to breakfast later than nine. We have to get to the station for eleven.'

With a few murmurs of 'sorry' and explosions of giggling, they went to their rooms. Carla glanced at Peter. 'I don't think there's anything more to be said. Good night.'

She left him and went up to her room. She sat on the edge of the bed for a little while, feeling middle-aged and stroppy, and wishing she didn't have to be either of those things. Then with a sigh she rose, undressed and put on her nightdress. She picked up a towel and was about to head for the bathroom when she heard a knock at the door.

'Who is it?'

'Peter.'

She hesitated, then opened the door. 'I was just getting ready for bed.'

'Can I come in for a moment?' he asked.

She shrugged and let him come in, closing the door behind him. She felt a little foolish and precarious in her long cotton nightgown, divested of authority. He stood, hands on his hips, staring down at the carpet for a few seconds. Then he looked up at her. She felt faintly disturbed by the intensity of his gaze.

'You didn't give me the chance to apologize downstairs. I shouldn't have let them stay out a bit later than we'd agreed. But at the time it didn't seem to matter. Anyway, I acknowledge that I was in the wrong, but I don't think you should have spoken to me in front of the students in the way you did.'

Carla hardly heard him, simply gazed at him, allowing herself to be overwhelmed by the fact of him, his youth and proximity. She felt all her defences slipping away, her middle-aged authority melting into something totally fluid and ageless. She felt naked with need, the reality of the past months caught up in this moment. She could not, whatever the cost in humiliation, let it pass. He stared at her, waiting, frowning a little. Was he conscious, she wondered, of the current of her feelings? They felt to her radiant, intense.

Drawing a small, sharp breath she said, 'Peter, would you do something for me?' His eyes were fastened on hers. 'Would you kiss me?' The words were uttered before she could stop herself. She could hardly believe she had said them. She waited for his expression to change to one of helpless embarrassment. But it didn't alter. He simply stood, hands on hips, staring at her. Then he leaned forward and put his mouth gently to hers. She closed her eyes. It lasted for several seconds. When she opened her eyes, he was regarding her steadily, his expression unfathomable.

'Thank you,' she said. 'I had forgotten what that felt like.'

He put out a hand slowly and touched the lace at the neckline of her nightdress. 'All the little buttons done up, right to the top,' he said. She said nothing, feeling her insides dissolving, and he put out the other hand and unfastened the top button. Then the next, and the next, carefully and quite unhurriedly. He slid his hands beneath the flimsy cotton and cupped both of her breasts. He kissed her again as he had before, very gently. Then he began to unfasten the rest of the buttons, all the way down, and with each button he unfastened he kissed an inch of her skin, her breasts, stomach, thighs, until he was on his knees. She closed her eyes and ran her fingers through his hair. Then he rose, parted the unbuttoned nightdress and drew it from her body, letting it fall to the floor. He undressed while she watched and then lay her on the bed and made love to her. And all the while Carla felt as though her spirit was holding its breath, her body lost in pleasure.

Afterwards she lay very still, her mind a blank, while he traced lines with the tips of his fingers on the skin of her back.

'I didn't expect to be doing this,' she said at last. It was about the only thought she could summon up.

'Nor did I, exactly,' replied Peter. 'You have beautiful skin. In fact, you're beautiful all over.'

'No, I'm not. I'm forty-two.' As soon as she said it, she wished she hadn't.

'So?'

Her mind returned to what he had said before. 'What did you mean by "exactly"?'

'I meant, the thought *had* crossed my mind.'

'When?' She turned her head on the pillow to look at him and he smiled. The shadow of his beard was very dark. She put out a hand and lightly touched the faint bristles with her fingertips.

'On the train. I had a little fantasy about you. Having you.'

She gasped and laughed. 'I thought you were reading your newspaper.'

'That was just a front.' He rolled on to his back and clasped his hands behind his head. 'I liked you from that day I came to lunch at your house. I thought you were a challenge. All buttoned-up, just like your night-dress.'

'Thanks. Do you normally seduce middle-aged married women?' She wondered why she kept saying this kind of thing. Some sort of defence mechanism.

'I do, as a matter of fact. I like the combination of experience and non-exigence.'

She contemplated him. 'You're serious, aren't you?'

'Not really.' He turned to look at her. 'What about you? How many other young masters at Taft's have fallen prey to your charms?'

'I don't like this conversation. I mean it. I don't like you saying that.' She was silent for a moment. 'I don't do this kind of thing. I never have.'

'I believe you.' He touched her cheek . . . 'You're actually blushing. I just thought, the way Mike Rayment is, you know . . .'

She put her face in her hands. 'God, don't. No. He's just a pest. He fancies anything that's female and alive.'

'So tell me.'

She waited. 'What?'

His eyes travelled across her face. 'Is this of any significance to you at all?'

'Significance?' She stared at him in astonishment. 'Of course it is. Why on earth do you ask?'

'Insecurity.' He smiled. 'I just needed to know.'

The next morning Alan got up around ten, read the Sunday papers, smoked eight cigarettes, and stood by the French windows and contemplated the rainy garden. In his brief-case there were several letters from angry parents to be answered, all demanding to know when GCSE Photography was to be reinstated. He had to get a reply drafted by tomorrow. Well, it could wait until the afternoon, when Carla got back. Somehow, while she was away, he couldn't get started. *I can't get started.* Hearing these words in his head made him think of the song, and he hummed a little of it, tunelessly, sadly. Things were peculiar between himself and Carla these days. He couldn't put his finger on it, but she was distant. She didn't smile or laugh a lot. The menopause? Possibly. Then again, he wouldn't know because at some point, he couldn't say when, they seemed to have stopped communicating. The things they spoke about, the conversations they had, all seemed to lack any proper empathetic point of contact. Nothing met in the middle. Everything was devoid of feeling. The weekend in the New Forest had been all right, but it was as though she was on some other wavelength. He wondered if he had been wrong about her and Mike Rayment. Maybe they'd been having an affair for ages and Carla's behaviour was the only clue. He didn't think so. Maybe he should sit her down when she got back and have a talk with her. Explain that he thought something was wrong and try to find out what it was. Yes, he would do that. He loved her, he needed her, and it made him anxious to think that their steady, comfortable life wasn't giving her everything she wanted. He would talk to her and find out.

On the train Carla and Peter didn't sit together. It would have been impossible to be so proximate without betraying something, in their looks or manner. So Carla sat at a window seat among a group of students, her book in her lap unread, gazing out at the rain and trying to fathom the new feelings within her. All ideas of London and a job were gone. Living with Alan was neither here nor there, now. He and the house and Taft's were merely a backdrop to this new and unexpected scenario. She didn't care to look beyond the immediate future, or further than the next time she could be with Peter. She felt no guilt whatsoever.

When they got off the train at Huntsbridge, Peter handed Carla her overnight bag.

'I'll see you at lunchtime tomorrow,' he said.

It was said within everyone's hearing, and sounded perfectly matter-of-fact, innocent. She knew exactly what he meant. She had no tutorials at school tomorrow. She would be at home. And he would come. She felt filled with happiness, alive for the first time in a long time.

'Yes.' She glanced in the direction of the car park and saw Alan, standing beside the car. She took her bag and walked towards her husband, smiling.

7

The next morning was one of exquisite torment for Carla. Once Alan had left for school she tried to occupy her time and thoughts with the routine of shopping and housework. In the supermarket she dithered. He had said lunchtime. Should she make him some lunch? Or would he have already eaten at school? Were they meant to care about lunch? Such mundane considerations had a disfiguring effect on her state of desire. Housework, too, once past the hoovering and wiping stage, became a pointless exercise of refinement. She spent impossibly slow, stupid shifts of time moving vases of flowers, rearranging cushions, straightening mirrors. At each mirror she stood transfixed for a few moments, gazing at her reflection as if trying to fathom something, to see herself dispassionately. She traced the tips of her fingers softly across her unlined brow, down the skin of her throat. What was forty-two, after all? She didn't think she looked more than thirty-five. He had said she was beautiful. The self-doubt was agonizing. She longed to be just ten years younger again.

She glanced at her watch and saw that it was twenty past twelve. Her heart leapt in her throat. The lunch bell at Taft's would ring in ten minutes. She went upstairs and stood hesitating in front of her wardrobe. The skirt and top she had put on that morning had seemed fine. She looked good in them. But now she wasn't so sure. She pulled out a couple of dresses and spent long minutes considering them, holding them against her, reluctant to undress and try them on in case he arrived while she was changing. They were wrong for the time of year, the time of day, she decided. She put them back and closed the wardrobe. Then she opened it and took one of the dresses out again. Her brain felt numb. At that moment the doorbell rang and she went downstairs, trembling, moving quite slowly to contain her agitation.

In the event, what she was wearing didn't matter. He said nothing when he came in, just closed the door and leaned against it. His curling hair was touched with rain, his breathing rapid and his colour high, as though he had hurried. They fell into one another, kissing, pulling at clothing, totally immersed in the immediacy of their need. He took her at the foot of the stairs, his raincoat still on, his trousers round his ankles, she with her skirt around her thighs. It was only afterwards, as she half-sat and half-lay against the stairs, his face buried in her shoulder as he recovered his breath, that she felt how undignified it all was.

But that didn't matter either. He was totally beyond caring about that, and infected her with his feeling. They pulled their clothes together and went upstairs to the spare bedroom and made love again. Afterwards she made some sandwiches – which she didn't want but he did – and they lay on the bed and talked. Throughout half an hour of conversation, only two things of consequence were said.

The first was when Carla asked if anyone had seen him

coming to the front door. Peter said he didn't think so. It hadn't crossed his mind.

'It would be better if you came through the garden. There's a path that runs past the tennis courts at the end of the park to the lane at the back of the house.'

Peter nodded, and said he would do that. He kissed her throat. 'I'll come every day. Every day that I can.'

The second was when he was about to make love to her again, just fifteen minutes before he was due to be back at school. He suddenly said, with a faint embarrassment that reminded her of how young he was, 'I meant to ask you the other night. It seems stupid, but I don't need to take precautions, do I? I mean, you've got nothing to worry about – from me. It's just, you know . . .'

She felt as though briefly jolted by an electric current. Because of Alan, because of the faint, not-quite-dead hope which had always underlain sex between them, the issue of contraception had never arisen. The years of habit had meant that it hadn't even occurred to her with Peter. But that wasn't all he was talking about, was he? How different it all was from the carefree seventies. Long seconds passed. She touched his face and made a decision. It seemed the right one, born out of happiness and total confidence in this new love. For that was what it was, surely, for both of them.

'No,' she said, 'you don't need to worry.'

It was habit now. Monday mornings, bunk off at lunchtime, go round to the flat. She and Georgina varied it occasionally, going back for the last lesson every so often so that people wouldn't get too suspicious. Wednesdays and Fridays were the same, roughly. They had started to take food round, too, because there was never anything to eat at that place.

This Monday, today, there was someone new at the flat. He was sitting on the sofa with his legs crossed, an ankle on one knee, a Sun Valley tobacco tin balanced on it while he hand-rolled a cigarette. He had a thin face, blond hair which stuck out past his ears, a sparse blond moustache and a beard which was hardly there at all.

Georgina went and squashed herself down next to Ryan on the bean bag. He put an arm around her without taking his eyes off the television. Phil came out of the kitchen.

'Hi, girls,' he said. He gestured towards the boy on the sofa. 'This is Daniel,' he said. 'He's my cousin.'

Daniel glanced up and nodded at Katie. He had very round blue eyes with huge shadows beneath them. His clothes – a jacket, a waistcoat, a T-shirt and grubby blue jeans – looked very worn and slightly too small.

Georgina turned and gave Daniel an expressionless glance, said nothing. Daniel glanced at her too. Then he went back to rolling his cigarette. Katie sat down at the other end of the long, battered sofa and watched. His fingers were small, delicate, and very dirty at the ends.

Des came through from his bedroom, pulling on a jacket, and said hi to the girls. Then he and Phil left the flat.

Daniel finished rolling his cigarette. He held it out and looked at it, letting out a long sigh. He glanced at Katie, who by now had tucked her feet up beneath her and had turned her attention to the television and Jerry Springer.

She didn't take her coat off. It was cold in the flat. Aware of his gaze, she turned and looked at him.

'D'you want this one?' he asked.

Katie looked at the thin roll-up, little shreds of tobacco hanging out of the end of the Rizla paper. She shook her head. 'No, thanks.'

'Good. It took me ages to make it.' His voice was what her mother would have called polite. It was gentle and well-modulated, without the estuary twang which characterised the voices of the local youths. Its sound took Katie by surprise. She watched as he pushed back his shabby jacket and fished in the little pocket of his waistcoat for a lighter. The waistcoat was from a pinstripe suit.

Daniel flicked the lighter and lit his roll-up, then coughed. His eyes began to water, and he leaned forward, coughing even more. Katie thumped him on the back.

'Thanks,' he said and sat back, wiping his eyes.

'What's your second name?' asked Katie.

'Aha,' said Daniel. He narrowed his eyes and smiled through the smoke – not at her, but somewhere in the distance. They watched Jerry Springer for a while, then Ryan and Georgina began to snog. Katie could think of no other word for it. They had never done this before. They sat on the bean bag kissing. Katie felt horribly embarrassed. She tried not to look at them. When they got up from the bean bag and went through to Ryan's bedroom, she felt even more embarrassed. What would this young man think that she and Georgina came here for?

But Daniel didn't seem particularly concerned.

'Would you like a cup of tea?' he asked.

'Yes, thanks.'

They went through to the kitchen together, and Katie fished some mugs from the sink and washed them while Daniel put on the kettle. The kitchen never seemed to get any better. The sink always seemed to be full of dishes, the same black bag of washing propped up by the fridge. But there had to be some sort of rhythm to it somewhere, Katie supposed. Maybe they did it all at the weekend, and the cycle kicked in again on Monday.

'Bunking off school, are you?' asked Daniel conversationally, leaning by the cooker, smoking down the very last half-inch of his cigarette.

Katie nodded.

'I used to do that.' He spoke as though those days were far away. Katie regarded him. It was hard to tell, because of his straggly hair and moustache, how old he was, but he didn't look *that* old. Not as old as Des and Phil and the rest.

'How old are you?' she asked him.

He paused before replying, flicking his spent fag into the sink beside the dishes. 'Seventeen.' He tried to sound nonchalant.

They took their tea through to the living room and talked. Katie tried not to think about what Georgina and Ryan were doing. It was hard to tell from the things Daniel told her exactly who he was and where he came from. It seemed he had been living non-specifically somewhere in London, had then found himself without anywhere to stay, and had got in touch with Phil after spending one very unpleasant night sleeping rough. It was clear he thought a great deal of his cousin.

'What are you going to do now?' Katie asked.

Daniel looked around the room with his owlish blue eyes. 'I don't know,' he said at last.

Then he asked her about herself, and she told him about her family, about her father and what it was like having him teach at the same school. Daniel listened very attentively, she noticed, looking at her in a manner she could only describe as careful. She didn't think she had ever felt so listened to. His eyes never left her face. Their gaze was so gently intent that she began to wonder if he was on something.

'D'you do drugs?' she asked.

He looked a little startled. 'I haven't got any money,' he replied. He took out his tobacco tin and began to shred tobacco. Then he took out a paper and laid it on his knee, creasing it flat with a grimy thumb. 'If I had any, I might score some dope.'

She watched in silence as he painstakingly rolled another cigarette. Katie suddenly realized that she felt at peace sitting on the sofa with this odd young man. She felt better for having talked at length about everything to someone who seemed interested. The door to Ryan's bedroom opened and Georgina came out. She went through to the kitchen and made herself some tea. Ryan emerged a few moments later and took the tea which Georgina had made him. A faint pall of embarrassment hung in the air. Daniel smoked in silence. Katie glanced at him, wondering what he was thinking.

'We'd better be going,' said Georgina.

Katie took her mug through to the kitchen, rinsed it and set it on the draining board. She went back through and said goodbye to Daniel.

He raised a hand and smiled at her. It was the first time he had smiled, and his face looked nice, Katie thought. But not seventeen. Old and tired.

On the bus Katie said to Georgina, 'I didn't think it was very nice, you two going off like that.' Georgina shrugged and gazed out of the window. Katie longed to ask what they had done in Ryan's bedroom, whether they had gone the whole way, and what it was like. But she couldn't. She stared at her shoes and contemplated life. She always felt this way when they left the flat. For a couple of hours there she felt in an odd limbo of freedom, but the return to earth was depressing. There was still all the school work to be done. However much they bunked off, some of it still had to be faced. In fact, the more they skipped lessons, the more complex and burdensome everything connected with school seemed to become. Maybe she should give up this bunking-off lark. But she knew she wouldn't. There was something which drew her back to the flat. And she liked Daniel. But maybe he would be gone by the next time they went. He had an air of impermanence which made it highly probable. She hoped not. They had only talked for forty minutes or so, but he was like the closest thing to a friend she had met in a long time.

All that week Alan kept putting off his intended talk with Carla. On Monday he had to attend a PTA meeting, on Tuesday there was the inaugural hockey match on the new floodlit, Astroturf pitch, on Wednesday a parents' evening, on Thursday a fund-raising event for the new pavilion, and on Friday a meeting of heads of department followed by drinks at the pub. By the time the weekend came, he noticed that she seemed more cheerful. Still a little remote, but better. Maybe he had misinterpreted her moods. He decided to leave it, see how things went.

Carla told herself that now she knew what it was like to be fucked, properly, every day of your life. She liked thinking in those terms, relishing those words. She felt full, sated, replete with sex. Not tired, old, huffing-puffing sex either. Twenty-seven-year-old rampant, can't-get-enough-of-it stuff. She felt senseless with the pleasure of it. Even just kissing him was better than any sex she had ever had with anyone. Peter came to the house every day that week. He would cross the garden and tap on the French windows and come in, and she would be waiting there in the living room for him, giddy and soft with anticipation. It was like being nineteen again, only nothing at nineteen had ever been like this. She could actually scare herself by imagining what it would have been like if this hadn't happened, if she had drifted away into her fifties and never known this. Her sexuality untouched, everything lost, unknown. She felt as though she wanted to lay herself open to every pleasure imaginable.

Then the weekend arrived, sour and real. She faced the two days with Alan with something of her old dread, that insides-shrivelling sense of emptiness. But at least she could think of Peter and of being with him again, having him. She counted the hours.

On Monday she waited. At half past twelve she lay down on the sofa with a book and looked up every few minutes at the French windows, conjuring the sight and sound of him. But the garden beyond lay still. By the time ten to one came, nervous anxiety had set in. By one-fifteen she was desperate and bewildered. At half one she knew that he wouldn't come. She cried for an hour, and had to ring Maeve to cancel their three o'clock game of tennis. She hadn't the heart for it, for anything. What if that was it, if he had just got bored and decided a week of her was enough?

That evening Alan noticed her silence and suspected that he had been right, that Carla was on some kind of hormonal roller-coaster. He would see how things went over the next few days, and then suggest that she see someone. He was always seeing articles about things they could do these days, HRT, that kind of thing.

All day since lunchtime Carla had been conducting an internal dialogue with herself, futile and repetitive, in which she reasoned that it was only one day, he must have had some commitment at school. Then she would swing back to the conviction that he had realized over the weekend the folly of what they were doing, and had decided just to stop. She had never known such misery. The hollowness of her life for the past year or so could not compare to this. At least that had provided the impetus to leave Alan, which she had been on the brink of doing, and of making a new life for herself. Now she had begun an affair into which she had thrown herself whole, emotionally. Without it, without the fact of it and the reassurance of her lover's existence and reciprocated need, she was nothing, could do nothing, find no future.

When she went to bed, she actually clasped her hands and beseeched God to let Peter come the next day.

*

That evening Katie sat at the kitchen table, eating a pot of Sainsbury's Economy Chocolate Mousse, *Blue Peter* chattering in the background from the portable television on the breakfast bar.

Bea came into the kitchen to make a cup of tea. She glanced at her sister as she waited for the kettle to boil.

'Anna French said she saw you and Georgina in town at lunchtime.'

Katie flushed guiltily. Anna French was in the sixth form, and sixth-formers were allowed into town at lunchtime, but not the lower forms.

'We just went to a café. We didn't fancy any of the things in the school cafeteria.'

'You know you're not allowed to be in town in school hours. What if a member of staff had seen you?'

'Oh, get off my case, Bea! It was just the once.'

'Yes, well, think about it from Daddy's point of view. It doesn't exactly look good for him if you start bunking off and getting into trouble.'

'God, you're so supercilious! Why are you so concerned about *him*? He doesn't exactly care about embarrassing us, does he? Everybody knows about him and Paula Kennedy. I mean *everybody*! It's horrible. Sometimes I really hate him.'

'Shut up!' hissed Bea. 'Mummy might hear!'

'Sometimes I think it'd be better if she did know. And I'd rather be at the comprehensive than in the same school as him.'

Katie picked up her empty pot and dropped it in the bin, then left the kitchen. In the hallway she caught sight of her school bag lying at the foot of the stairs. It bulged reproachfully. She was behind on everything now. Most of her teachers had had a go at her, telling her that if she didn't pull her socks up she was going to do badly in the GCSEs. Much they cared. Not one of them had noticed her absence from their classes now and then. OK, she and Georgina had contrived it so that the absences were random rather than regular, but something in her wished that they'd cotton on. She felt powerless to end what had been started, as though it needed an outside agency to bring it to a halt. She thought about what Bea had just said, and wished in a way that it had been a teacher who'd seen them at lunchtime. Then there would have been a row, and it would have been over. Katie picked the bag up and went up to her room. She'd have to tackle some of it. Listlessly she sat down and pulled out her copy of *Macbeth* and began to make notes for an essay on guilt.

'I had a play rehearsal,' said Peter, mildly surprised by the forcefulness of Carla's reproach.

'Couldn't you have let me know, or something? I spent an awful hour, waiting for you.' Carla was not experienced or wise. Had she been, she would have known to greet Peter that Tuesday with a smile, and no mention of his absence the day before.

'Sorry. I don't see how I could have.'

Still she didn't let it go. The habit of marital sparring was dangerously easy to transpose. 'You might have rung.'

Peter sighed in exasperation and hung his long gabardine raincoat, the one that made him look like a pre-war journalist, on the end of the banister. The spontaneity of their rendezvous, which was one of the things he enjoyed most, as well as its clandestine nature, had evaporated. A mundane note had been struck. In an effort to make things better, he took her in his arms and kissed her. Carla, still absorbed in the rights and wrongs of the day before, returned the kiss briefly. She was distracted by the fact of Peter's raincoat hanging half-on, half-off the banister. She moved over to put it on the coat rack. 'There is a phone in the staffroom,' she added.

He was about to open his mouth and point out to her the impracticality of an English master ringing the headmaster's wife from the staffroom to tell her their lunchtime assignation was off, but didn't. This wasn't the kind of thing he wanted from their affair. Nor what he had expected. He thought of his past lover in Rome, his signora. Signora Isabella Ciurlo, forty, not particularly beautiful, but exotic, with clever, amused eyes, eyes that had seen it all, and a generous body. She had never once reproached Peter, took him or left him at her pleasure, made no demands, had no expectations. Sometimes, when they had arranged to meet at her apartment, she wouldn't be there. She would forget, or decide to go shopping. She had a son of about his age, who lived with his father, and she would take him on trips, spend lavish amounts of money on him, talk about him endlessly. She made it clear that she had no such feelings for Peter. She liked Peter, she made herself available to him, but she did not care. Or if she did, she was careful never to show it. How much easier Peter had found this than the claustrophobia of the few intense relationships he had had with girls of his age. What a relief to be free of guilt and blame, to be accepted and enjoyed without demands or conditions. He put Isabella's behaviour down to her maturity, and had resolved thereafter that all his lovers would be women over thirty, who would not stifle him with love. When he had first seen Carla, so composed and beautiful and detached in her manner, he had imagined she would be one of these, just like his signora.

He watched as she hung up his coat, then turned her troubled face to him.

'Smile,' he said, and kissed her. She frowned, then smiled. 'I might not be able to come every day,' he said. 'Things crop up. Besides, it might look odd. I'll come as often as I can.'

'But how will I know? How will I know if you're coming?'

Peter shrugged. He had had enough of this conversation. He was only here for one thing. 'Come upstairs,' he said.

It was late November now, and each time that Katie and Georgina went to the flat, Daniel was still there. He seemed always to be in the same spot, in the same clothes, busy with his tobacco tin. Once when Katie sat down on the sofa next to him she found a little book, green, clothbound. She picked it up and looked at the spine.

'*Pendennis*,' she read. 'Are you reading this?'

Daniel nodded. 'You've lost my place.'

'Sorry.' Katie flicked through the pages. It didn't look particularly interesting. The language was old-fashioned, like Dickens. 'What's it about, then?'

Daniel scratched his head. 'About a man. A young man, trying to make his way in the world. He doesn't know what he really wants, and it's a story about how he finds out what it is.'

'And what is it?'

'I don't know. I haven't finished it.'

'Oh, right.' She closed the book and looked at the spine again. 'Thackeray. I've got one of his books at home. *Vanity Fair*. My mother gave it to me last Christmas, but I haven't read it yet.'

'You ought to. That's his best.'

So Katie began to read *Vanity Fair*. It pleased her to be doing something deliberately to form a connection with another person. She became quite bound up in the book, reading it night after night, and looked forward to discussing the characters and story with Daniel the next time she went to the flat. Georgina, who spent her time at the flat either in front of the television or in Ryan's room, was bemused.

'I thought you bunked off to get away from all that rubbish? You're really strange.'

Implicit in this was Georgina's disdain for Daniel. To her he was totally unprepossessing, without any interesting or redeeming qualities. 'I don't know what you find so interesting in him,' she remarked to Katie on their way home on the bus one afternoon. 'He's really sad, if you ask me.'

'I like him.'

'Just imagine snogging him. Yuck.'

'I never said I fancied him. I just like talking to him.' In fact, he was about the only person she did talk to, properly. The members of her family seemed to have floated away to another time and space. She hardly seemed to make any connection with any of them.

*

One Saturday morning, three weeks before Christmas, Katie and Jenny had a blazing row. On the surface it was to do with how Katie wasn't helping round the house in the way she should, couldn't she see her mother was at her wits' end trying to cope, couldn't she just for once in her life try to act responsibly, grow up a bit? It had ended with her mother bursting into tears, and Katie grabbing her coat and slamming out of the house. In a confused and miserable way, Katie knew that her mother must have an inkling about what had been going on between her father and the photography assistant at school, but why did she have to take her unhappiness out on Katie? It wasn't the first time her father had done something like this, you'd think she'd be used to it. So why didn't she take it out on Max and Sam, too? Her mother said all those things about her growing up and acting responsibly, when she didn't understand that Katie didn't feel anything like grown up. Everyone said you should be mature at fifteen, there were people around her doing grown-up things and acting like they knew it all, like Georgina, but she just felt like a child. And nobody would treat her like a child. It was all she wanted. Just to be cuddled, or teased, or played with. Max seemed to be the only person who didn't expect her to behave as though she was as together as any twenty-year-old.

And Daniel. Thinking this, thinking about the peaceful neutrality of the flat, Katie walked into town and got a bus to the other side of Huntsbridge and walked to the flat. Ryan, who answered the door, hungover and wearing only boxer shorts, looked surprised to see her.

'Is Daniel in?' she asked.

'He's gone down the shops to get some milk.'

Katie hesitated. She didn't want to wait for him in the flat. She felt apprehensive, being there without Georgina. Besides, the air from the flat was filled with something densely masculine and foreign and early morning. She didn't want to be part of it. 'I'll go and see if I can find him,' she said.

She walked slowly past the Chinese takeaway, past the bookie's, down to the end of the street towards the newsagent's. She felt a little wave of relief when she saw Daniel standing outside the shop, bending down to talk to a dog tied up outside. He was patting the dog, scratching its head, when he looked up and saw Katie.

'Hi.' He didn't seem surprised. That was one of the things she liked about Daniel. He just accepted things. Georgina said it was because he was stupid, but Katie thought it was good. His mild, tolerant smile made her feel better already.

'I hope you don't mind me coming to see you. I need to talk to someone.'

Daniel nodded. 'I've just got to get some milk.' They went into the newsagent's and Katie huddled close to the feeble storage heater next to the magazines while Daniel bought his milk. 'I'll take this back to the fellows and then we can go for a walk.'

Katie smiled as they walked along. She liked his culti-vated voice, but the things he said could sound quite funny sometimes. He went up to the flat while Katie waited on the pavement, then they set off together.

'There's a park over the road,' he said.

'Aren't you cold?' asked Katie, glancing at him as they

crossed over. She had never seen him in anything but the same clothes, and he didn't seem to possess a coat.

'Not really.' He had his jacket pulled tight around him, though, and his eyes looked watery.

They walked around for an hour or so. Katie told him about the argument with her mother.

'She's fed up with my father. I sometimes wish they'd get divorced.' There was silence for a few seconds as they walked. 'No, I don't, really. But I wish she wouldn't go on at *me* all the time, when he's the one she should be shouting at.'

'Why doesn't she?'

Katie shrugged. 'She adores him. And she's a bit afraid of him. She never criticizes him. She puts up with everything he does. I don't know how she can stand it. All the staff and the people at school knowing . . . It makes me want to die, sometimes, when I come into a classroom and I know they've been gossiping about my father.'

Daniel dipped his hand in his pocket and pulled out a harmonica. He put it to his mouth and drew a few quivering notes, then burst into a melancholy version of 'Alfie'. The sobbing notes swooped and fell in the chilly air of the park. A woman walking her dog by the trees stared across. Katie stopped on the path, astonished. 'I didn't know you could play one of those. That's brilliant!'

Daniel took the harmonica from his mouth and smiled. 'It's not, actually.' He wiped the instrument on his sleeve. 'But it's not too bad. I jam with Phil in the evening sometimes. He asked the landlord at the Imperial if I could play with the band, but he said no.'

'Why not?'

'Said I'm too young. And I look too scruffy.'

Katie gazed sorrowfully at him. He was so sad and insubstantial, she felt he might vanish at any moment, leaving no trace. There was so little to Daniel, either behind him or ahead of him. That she knew of, at any rate.

'Play some more,' she begged.

So Daniel played 'Summertime', then 'Alfie' again, then a wistful version of 'Silent Night', which made Katie cry a little, secretly, her face turned away from Daniel. They walked all round the park until they were back at the gates. It was nearly lunchtime and Katie's stomach growled with hunger. 'I have to be getting back,' she said. She wanted the warmth and safety of home on a Saturday lunchtime. The argument would be forgotten. 'Thanks for listening to me. I love the way you play your mouth-organ thingie.'

'Harmonica.'

'Sorry, harmonica. I'll see you soon.'

Daniel raised a hand as Katie set off for the bus stop, then turned and walked off slowly in the other direction, without any particular purpose.

8

Every love affair needs context in which to shape itself, and grow to whatever its inevitable outcome will be. Carla was conscious, as the days passed, of how static her relationship with Peter was, bound by the dimensions of the school lunch-break and the four walls of the spare bedroom. They made love, they occasionally ate, and they talked. But like everything else, the conversation was curved, contained. There was nothing to explore. Thoughts came back on themselves. Carla knew as much about Peter's past as he cared to tell, and he about hers. This much lay between them. But they did not touch on anything external, for nothing of the real world touched their relationship. Beyond sex, and the dusty precincts of Taft's, they had no shared experiences. Carla knew from instinct and recollection, and from the pages of many novels, that a love affair should be like a voyage, that beyond the joyous embarkation there should be momentum and discovery, and a sense of destination, albeit unknown. Her affair with Peter lacked those elements.

'I want to do things with you,' she said one day. They were sitting at the kitchen table, she in her kimono of dark-blue sprigged silk, he in his clothes, but with buttons still to be fastened and tie to be tied. Carla had made him coffee and sandwiches.

'Things?'

'Share things. I mean go to plays, go for meals, for walks, see places and people. Do all the things with you that normal lovers do.'

He should have said, yes, he would like to share life with her in that way, too. But he didn't. Her heart shrank a little.

'We're all right as we are.' He didn't look at her as he spoke. 'Besides,' he added, putting down his coffee mug, 'all that's impossible. How could we, without everyone finding out?'

She put out a hand and touched his arm. 'You and your Italian woman did things together. You've told me.' Peter had told her about Signora Isabella. Both of them later wished he hadn't. Carla had felt an unhappy ache of jealousy, Peter an unexpected nostalgia and melancholy.

'She was divorced. It was different.'

How different. He had recollections of easy southern days, of sun and warmth, of space and serenity. The signora had made his heart ache with her casual unconcern at times, but even then he had known how shallow it was, and he had been largely happy. If only Carla could manufacture some indifference, make herself occasionally unavailable, laugh more and treat him with less intensity. He glanced now out of the kitchen window at the bleak garden and thought of the cold, hurried walk he would take back to the school and the fug of the classrooms, the noise of children. He felt around him the claustrophobia of Huntsbridge, and of this thing with Carla. No space or freedom here. The very touch of Carla's hand upon his arm had the feel of a restraint.

'I don't have to stay married, Peter.' Carla's voice was quiet.

He looked at her, not sure what to say. She was offering herself to him in a way which he had never intended or desired. He did not love her. He liked her, liked making love to her, though recently that had begun to pall slightly. He felt that a break was needed, a couple of weeks in which he could not see her, so that he could come back to her with a renewal of need, and keep alive the intensity of sexual feeling which had existed in the beginning. That was all it was about. She was a diversion, an excitement. He wished she could be as cool and dispassionate as he had once supposed her to be.

'Carla, that has nothing to do with me. I have never asked you to leave Alan. It's not what we're all about, you and I.'

'What are we about, Peter?' asked Carla, her voice a little wild. Something in his tone and manner made her feel suddenly alone, hollow inside with fear.

He stood up, took his tie from the back of his chair, and began to tie it. 'I don't know.' He looked at the expression on her face and was instantly filled with compassion. Easy to be compassionate when you were twenty-seven and not in love. He smiled at her. 'Yes, I do. Come here.' She rose and went gratefully to his arms. He parted the robe with one hand as he kissed her and slipped his fingers between her thighs. 'We're about this,' he murmured, moving his fingers inside her, feeling himself grow hard. He glanced at the hands of the kitchen clock as he kissed her. Twenty past. Just enough time to have her here, up against the kitchen sink, before he had to get back. He'd never made love to any one against a kitchen sink before.

Afterwards, as he was leaving, she broached it again. 'Just an evening. Maybe up in London, dinner or something. I just feel so – so *confined* like this. Boxed in. I need to be with you where there are other people, some space. Don't you feel that?'

'Yes, I do.' She echoed his own feelings so clearly that he couldn't help but agree. 'All right. We'll do something. I'll fix it up. I promise.'

A week later, early on Friday evening, Carla was getting ready to go out with Peter. He had booked a table for dinner at a restaurant up in London, and they were to meet there. It had been agreed that they couldn't travel together from Huntsbridge in case they met someone from Taft's or the local neighbourhood on the train. Carla had told Alan that she was going up to see a couple of her old girlfriends from the school in Herne Hill where she had taught a few years ago, just an all-girl get-together. If things went on too late, she might stay up there and come back in the morning. Although each and every act of her adultery with Peter had scarcely touched her conscience, this evening's deceit made Carla uneasy. It involved telling Alan a direct lie to his face, and the worst of it was that he smiled so readily, accepting what she said, saying fine and he hoped she would have a good time. Who was she seeing? Louise and Hilary? Well, give them his love.

She stood at the mirror, nervously putting the finishing touches to her make-up, standing back and surveying herself, almost unable to look herself in the eye. Still, she told herself, it was no good feeling sorry for Alan. If their marriage was over and he didn't see it, that was his problem. She was making a new future now with someone else. At this her mind faltered. She found it hard to give shape to the future. At the edges of her mind lurked shadows, obstacles and uncertainties which were not allowed any clear definition. She did not know if Peter loved her, but she told herself that he must, and that if he did, then nothing else mattered. They could be together. Tonight was just the first step in taking their relationship further, accepting it as something more than just sex.

Alan was sitting on the sofa going through the order of service for the school carol service next week. He glanced up as Carla came into the room and was struck by how lovely she looked. She always dressed well, but tonight she looked particularly pretty. Radiant.

'You look fantastic,' he said. 'You should wear that colour more often.' He reached out from where he sat on the sofa and smoothed the red silk down over her hip. She hoped he wasn't going to get amorous and pull her down next to him on the sofa. She didn't think she could bear that. She moved away as though to check her hair in the mirror.

'Right, I'd better be off.'

'OK,' replied Alan. 'Have a good time.'

Carla put on her coat, took the car keys from the hall table and drove to the station in time for the half-past-seven train.

Alan yawned, glanced at his watch, and wondered whether he should pop down to The Green Man for a drink. Nigel Sproke and Jeff Perkins went in for a couple of pints most Friday evenings around this time. But he knew how it would be. Friendly greetings, the conversation would appear relaxed, matey, but there would be an undercurrent, a restraint imposed by the fact of his being the headmaster. He found himself wishing on a fairly regular basis that he didn't have this particular position of authority. He didn't enjoy the remoteness that came with it. Come to that, he didn't really enjoy the job. He wasn't much good at it, he had begun to realize. He wasn't cut out to be an administrator, a paper-pusher, a people manipulator. He was a teacher. That was what he had started out as, and somehow it had got left behind. His mind drifted back through his teaching career to his early days as a university lecturer. He had enjoyed that. Good days to be an academic, the seventies.

He went through to the kitchen and investigated the fridge, and found that Carla had left him some cold chicken and a salad. Not really what he wanted on a December evening. He opened a can of oxtail soup and heated it up, and ate it with a hunk of French bread. Then he settled down with a large glass of whisky and the paper and consulted the TV listings. '8 o'clock. Three Terms. A drama about a struggling comprehensive whose fortunes are turned around by the arrival of a dynamic new head.' That should be good for a laugh. He switched it on and watched in mild disbelief for twenty minutes or so as staff and pupils conducted themselves towards one another with unnatural belligerence. Then the doorbell rang.

Alan turned down the sound and went to answer it. On the doorstep stood a girl. At first he assumed it was one of his sixth-formers, but on closer inspection realized that he didn't recognize her. She was dressed in a long black coat, and had blonde, curling hair, cut short, and a pale, small face. She wore glasses which magnified her blue eyes.

'Mr Tradescant?'

'Yes,' said Alan. 'Can I help you?'

'I'm Imogen Young,' said the girl.

Because there was something faintly familiar about her, he wondered whether she might be an old girl. 'Oh, I see,' said Alan uncertainly. 'I'm sorry, but my memory must be going. Were you in the '97 year? I don't think –'

'I'm your daughter,' said the girl. Her eyes seemed to grow even larger.

He stared at her blankly. 'What daughter?'

'How many have you got?'

'I haven't got any!' The night air was bitter, and Alan wanted this young woman to go away, very much. He didn't like this. He was cold.

'Yes, you have. My mother is Winifred Young. You're my father.' The girl seemed very certain about this, her voice firm.

Alan felt filled with exasperation and bewilderment. 'Jesus Christ,' he said, 'you'd better come in.' She stepped into the hall and he closed the door. 'Jesus Christ,' he said again. 'Look, what is all this about? Who? Winifred *who*?' He ran his fingers through his scant locks and glared at her.

'Winifred Young. She was one of your students at university. You taught her in 1977.' The girl regarded him, scanning his features and figure critically, then added, 'She said you might not remember her.'

There was a silence, and a picture of Winifred Young filled his mind, fading up from the past and into the present. If he hadn't seen her face in a photograph recently, one of the ones Carla had dragged out from the cupboard in the study, he doubted if he would have remembered her. But he did. Winifred, thin and blonde and moderately attractive. He had slept with her, he knew that much, but he couldn't recall anything about it. Was it on that trip to Paris? He stared at the girl. Yes, she looked like her mother, except that Winifred had had straight blonde hair, parted in the middle like every other girl in those days.

'I'm not your father,' he said. He sounded so sure of this that the girl's gaze wavered for a second.

'My mother says you are.'

Alan shook his head in bewilderment. 'I think we'd better have a talk about this. Take off your coat and come and sit down.'

She unwrapped herself from her large coat. She was quite a tall girl, Alan noticed. Had Winifred been tall? He couldn't remember. Imogen was dressed in baggy combat trousers, and a black T-shirt underneath a long blue cardigan. She wore trainers that made her feet look very big.

'Sit down,' said Alan, indicating an armchair. He glanced at his whisky glass sitting on the table. 'Would you like a drink?'

Imogen sat down, pushing her glasses a little way up her nose, and regarded Alan. She placed a small rucksack on the floor at her feet. 'Yes, please. Do you have any wine?'

'Yes, I imagine so. White or red?'

'White, please.'

He found a half-opened bottle in the fridge and poured out a glass, making a mental note to speak to Carla about the fact that she regularly seemed to be opening wine at lunchtime these days. He took the glass back through and handed it to the girl, then sat down on the sofa, cradling his glass of whisky. There was silence between them for several long seconds. Alan decided that he'd better adopt a strategic role, a mild offensive such as he used with Mike Rayment. Not that it ever worked.

'So, perhaps you should explain all this a little more clearly. I don't think I quite understand where you picked up your misapprehensions about me.'

Imogen didn't say anything for a moment, which gave Alan time to reflect on what he'd just said and how stupid it sounded. It was obvious where she'd picked up her misapprehensions. Her mother, Winifred. He tried to remember whether Winifred had been the kind of girl to sleep around or not, but couldn't. Everybody had seemed to be sleeping with everybody else back then.

'It's not a misapprehension,' replied Imogen. 'You even look like me.' She took a sip of her wine and glanced at his balding pate. 'Well, somewhat.'

He laughed, a short, unamused laugh. 'I don't know what your mother has told you, but I can assure you that there is scant likelihood of my being your father.'

Imogen set her wine glass down on the table and looked at him earnestly. 'I know it's a big shock for you. I thought of phoning first, or even writing. But when it came to it, I thought I'd better just come and – well, sort of confront you. Mum told me about you about twelve years ago. She told me how she'd been a third-year student when you came to the university, and how you went out with one another a bit towards the end of the year. It was just before her finals, she said. You all went on a trip to Paris. She didn't find out that she was pregnant till during the summer. She thought about telling you, but she didn't really want to be involved with you any more. Anyway, she'd left university by then, and she knew you were seeing someone else. She can't remember her name, but she thinks it's the person you married. So she had me, and her family helped out a bit, and when I was old enough she got a job teaching, and she managed to bring me up. When I was ten she got married to my stepdad, Colin. I've got two brothers, Ian and Douglas.'

Alan, who had listened patiently, said again, 'Imogen, I'm not your father.'

'Mum says you were the only person she slept with during her final year. I believe her. Why should she lie?'

Alan took a long slug of his whisky, waiting for its warmth to settle in his stomach and camouflage the embarrassment he felt at what he had to say. 'The thing is, I can't be anybody's father.'

He could see this was something she hadn't expected. 'How d'you mean – you can't be?'

'I don't have any children. I can't have.'

'What? Not at all?'

Alan felt annoyed at this persecution. This young woman was a complete stranger, sitting in his house with some fabricated nonsense about her parentage, putting him through the third degree. 'Well, it's extremely unlikely.' He took another long drink. 'I have a very low sperm count.' He could hardly believe he was sitting here discussing this with someone who had knocked on his door only five minutes ago.

'But you could be.'

'What?'

'My father. Having a low sperm count doesn't rule you out of anything.'

This was true. Alan had to acknowledge that this was true. A small prickle of doubt raised the hairs on the back of his neck. He looked at her more closely. She did look like him a bit. Curly hair, same smallish face, short-sighted gaze. He knew, with sudden clarity, that the way she was sitting in her armchair, leaning forward, peering slightly from behind her glasses, was the way he himself sat when talking intently with someone. Christ, he was doing it now. He leaned back, pushing his glasses up his nose, uncertain what to say.

'You are, you know,' she said at last. 'Mum's never had the slightest doubt.'

Alan looked at her, taking in the fact of her, the growing possibility that here, sitting in his living room, twenty – what? – twenty-three years old, was his own daughter. A bit of himself. He studied her hands, her nails, let his gaze travel all over her, earlobes, jawline, the lot. She was pretty.

'Christ,' he said at last. He met her gaze and nodded. 'I have to admit the possibility.' She nodded back. The last thing he expected to feel, an odd kind of ballooning joy, seemed to fill every bit of him. He had to wait for it to subside before he felt capable of speaking again. He had to struggle for something mundane and practical to say.

'Why did she never tell me?' he asked at last. 'Didn't she think I should know that I had a daughter?'

Imogen shrugged. 'Don't ask me. I don't know what your relationship was like. Maybe she didn't want you to feel she expected anything from you. She's a very independent sort of person. I take after her in that.'

Alan nodded thoughtfully. 'The thing is,' he said after a pause, 'say I am your father, why have you come to see me now?'

'That's a funny question. It's my identity. You're part of it. You grow up knowing that some person out there somewhere is your father, and you naturally want to see what he's like.'

'I suppose so.' This idea was going to need some adjusting to. To be someone's father. All this time, and not to have known. And what about Carla? What was she going to say when she found out about all this? He was unbelievably thankful that she was safely out of the way this evening. He could just imagine her sitting at the other end of the sofa, her face rigid as she listened to this girl. His daughter. His daughter.

'Mum has told me a lot about you. What you looked like, the kind of person you were.'

Alan couldn't keep his eyes off her, filled with a sense of revelation, examining every little thing about her. For some reason, thoughts of his mother, who had died only nine months ago, came crowding into his mind. What would she have thought of this young woman, her granddaughter? He asked her bemusedly, 'You're – what? Twenty-three? Didn't you want to find me before now?'

'Of course I did.' Imogen stared down at her hands. 'I

used to ask questions about you all the time. But when I was younger, when I thought about meeting you face to face, it scared me. I mean, a stranger . . . imagine meeting a stranger who's your father. I used to think – what if I didn't like you? What if you didn't like me? Anyway, you left London a few years back and Mum lost track of you. I thought I'd missed my chance of ever finding you. Then some months ago someone who used to know you when you lived in Dulwich came to work at the school where she teaches, and she found out you'd moved here. Mum was very surprised to find you were a headmaster.' Imogen picked up her wine again.

'Oh?'

'She said she couldn't imagine you in a fogeyish kind of job. You didn't have a respectable enough image.'

'Wasn't I respectable when she knew me? I thought university lecturers were fairly well regarded.'

Imogen laughed through a mouthful of wine. 'That's not the way she described you. She said you were completely different. Very off-the-wall. Quite outrageous in the things you said and did. She said she'd always expected you to finish up as some kind of liberal academic guru in an American university, surrounded by adoring neophytes.'

Alan felt a flicker of sudden sadness. He had once imagined something similar for himself. He sighed. 'And here you find me, a slack-bellied, balding man of declining years, with small horizons and no hopes left.' He laughed and drained the last of his whisky.

When he lowered his glass she was regarding him gravely. 'I like the way you said that. It sounded really good. The words, I mean.'

'I'm glad you liked it,' said Alan, rising from the sofa to replenish his glass. An evening full of astonishment. He felt giddy with it – that and the whisky. He noticed she had almost finished her wine. 'Another drink?'

She shook her head. 'No, thanks. I don't like too much alcohol. I'd rather have a smoke.' She leaned down and picked up her rucksack, taking from it some cigarette papers and a small foil parcel. Alan, from twenty years back, recognized instantly the makings of a joint. He gathered from certain of his students that they called them spliffs these days.

He watched for a few helpless seconds as she began to shred the tobacco, transported back through time to student rooms, dimly lit, Velvet Underground on the turntable. *Turntable*. Who had one of those nowadays? Well, he did, for a start. Not that he often used it. 'Imogen, I'm a headmaster. This is my house. You really can't do that here, you know.'

She stopped and looked up at him. How very much he liked those blue eyes behind the glasses. A trace of the little girl within the woman. 'Oh, I'm sorry. I won't if you don't want me to.'

He hesitated, hating himself for what he was, then said, 'Oh, bugger it – go on.'

He went into the kitchen to the cupboard where they kept the drinks. Something momentous had happened to him, he realized. He poured a generous measure of whisky and stared at it. It was as though this young woman had sprung some switch in him. His own perception of himself as a rather dull, preoccupied headmaster had fallen away. She touched chords within him that lifted him back to the kind of person he had once been, in the days when he had fathered her. He turned these words around in his mind, trying to recall Winifred, wanting to recollect this act of begetting. Bemused, he took his drink back into the living room and sat down, watching Imogen as she lit up her joint. She inhaled deeply, then let out the smoke. Wordlessly she offered it to Alan. He stared at it, then took it. He had forgotten the smell, the sweetness of the smoke, the way it puddled and expanded deliciously in your insides. God, this was strong stuff. Like riding a bicycle, you never forgot. Know your shit. His head felt lighter. He could feel his mind shifting up a gear. Oh, the forgotten sensation. Lucy in the Sky. He handed it back to her, rose and fetched an ashtray and laid it on the table between them.

They smoked and talked. She told him about her schooldays, college, her film studies, about how she was going to the States next summer to travel and see if she could pick up some work. That was why she had wanted to get in touch with him, before she went. Then they talked about him, working backwards, arriving at the point which fascinated them most – the time when she had been conceived. More smoke, more whisky, and it all slipped into a retrospective, Alan's memories of how he had been then, how *it* had been. He found himself laughing a lot, stupidly, the way dope made you, but she was doing it too, so that was all right. Hendrix. Joplin. Did they listen to any of that these days, people her age? Yes, but not really. She didn't really know much Hendrix. And then he was pulling out his old LPs and Hendrix was booming in ragged chords through the room, the speakers vibrating. Blue plaque for the man, too right. God, these sounds, hadn't listened in years. Where had it all gone? He stopped playing air guitar and sat back down, stunned by it all. This girl, this girl was his daughter. Expansive delight, the joys of Hendrix, drugs – YES! This was himself, this he knew and remembered.

She was hungry, they went into the kitchen and she ate the chicken and salad. They found a chocolate swiss roll and ate it between them. Back in the living room she rolled another joint, and they waded through it all. *Magical Mystery Tour*, some Stones, Led Zeppelin, Dylan. By the end of the evening he felt he knew her well, and himself even better. It was a quarter past midnight. Where was she staying? She was getting a train back to London, where she lived. No, she wasn't. The last one left at ten to. She would stay here. He took her rucksack up to the spare room and left her splashing water on her face in the bathroom.

He went back downstairs to the haze of smoke and the over-warm room. Fragments of music hung in his mind like echoes. He felt shot, exhausted, stoned, something he hadn't felt for years. And exhilarated. He picked up their glasses, went into the kitchen and put things in the dish-washer. Purple haze . . . 'Scuse me, while I kiss this guy . . . Or was it kick the sky? All these years and he still didn't know. Didn't want to.

He thought about Carla. Clearly she wasn't coming back tonight. What was she going to say when she returned tomorrow, met Imogen? Maybe he should make sure she got up early, left before Carla arrived. He closed the dish-washer. Ah, fuck it, he thought. He didn't care. Right at that moment, he didn't care.

*

To Peter's surprise, he and Carla had a very pleasant evening. Peter's feelings about the whole thing had been somewhat cagey beforehand. He had never intended to start this kind of affair with anyone. That first evening in the hotel room had been one of those impulsive things, more to do with sex than anything else. The clandestine assignations at her house had been the same. He wanted only the minimum amount of emotional input, just enough to drive the thing. But, as it turned out, dinner was good, the wine a great help, and gossip about the school had kept things light, amusing. Only now and again had Carla made tentative remarks which tried to strike a more serious note. Above all, he liked the way she looked, the way people glanced at her. She was very lovely. Womanly.

The bill came and Peter glanced at his watch. 'Do you realize what time it is?' he said. 'We're going to have to move if we're going to catch the last train.'

Carla shrugged and smiled. 'I told Alan I might not be back tonight, that I might stay up in town.' She watched as Peter scrutinized the bill, then opened her bag. 'Peter, let me pay.'

He looked up at her. 'Certainly not.'

'Please. I'm sure you can't afford it.'

He coloured slightly. 'I can afford to take you out. I wouldn't have booked a table here if I couldn't.'

'Sorry,' she said. How easily offended someone of his age could be. This note of disparity, this reminder of the difference in their ages, settled like a small depression on her. She sat brooding while he paid the bill, then looked up and smiled as he laid his hand over hers and gently pressed her fingers.

'I don't want to go back either,' he said. 'But I don't know where we could stay.'

'I do,' said Carla. 'There's a hotel in St James's that Maeve and I stay in sometimes when we come up to London.' She paused. 'It's not cheap.' He said nothing. 'So please let me pay.'

'All right,' said Peter.

He found checking into the hotel embarrassing. Carla seemed quite serene, handling it all with aplomb. Peter stood awkwardly in the lobby, feeling like somebody's son, while she handed over her credit card.

In the lift he kissed her, enjoying the new dimension of illicitness, and in the room he didn't wait to let her undress before making urgent love to her. He no longer worried that this first time didn't last long enough to satisfy her. There would be a second, and maybe even a third time before they slept.

Later they sprawled together in bed with drinks from the minibar. Carla lay in the crook of Peter's arm, enjoying the sensation of his muscle moving each time he pressed the buttons on the remote control, roving through the channels. She loved the firmness of him, the contours of his strong, young arms and the flatness of his stomach. She felt happy. They had moved forward. This evening they had taken a step towards making something else of their relationship, something larger.

'I wonder what Alan's doing right now,' she murmured sleepily.

Peter lowered his hand and set the remote on the covers. 'I wish you hadn't said that.'

She glanced at him quickly. 'What's wrong?'

He said nothing for a few seconds, staring blankly at the screen. 'The one thing I try to do in all of this is not to think of him.'

'Don't worry. I told you, I don't love him any more. There's nothing between us. There hasn't been for a long time. Don't feel guilty.'

He looked into her eyes. 'I like him. He's a really decent bloke. I don't think he knows any of those things you've just said, even if they're true. That's why I try never to think about him. I don't want him to be hurt.'

A flood of small, bitter truths and reproaches came to her mind and mouth, but she resisted the urge to utter any of them. She didn't care for the idea that Peter should have any fondness for Alan. It didn't have the right resonance. Alan should be the enemy.

After a moment she said, 'I can't stand the thought of the Christmas holidays. How are we going to see one another?' Peter said nothing. 'I suppose,' she added tentatively, 'I could always come to your flat. All I need to do is tell Alan I'm going shopping. That way –' she stroked his arm '– we could at least have a couple of hours together now and then.'

'Actually,' said Peter, 'I don't know that I'm going to be around over the holidays. Some married friends from university have invited me to their place in Durham for a week or so, then I'll be going to Winchester, to my parents, for Christmas.' His voice was indifferent, but the words he uttered filled Carla with a chilling sense of desolation. How would she get through three weeks alone with Alan? For that was what lay in prospect. In the past they'd spent Christmas either at Alan's parents, or her brother Patrick had come to stay. But since Alan's mother had died last March, his father had gone into a residential home, and Patrick had a job in Dubai. It would be just her and Alan, without even the knowledge that Peter was nearby.

'When will you be back?'

Peter shrugged. 'Don't know. Just after New Year, I suppose.' He turned and looked at her, then kissed her softly. 'Don't look so sad.'

'I'm not,' said Carla quickly. 'It's just – I mean, I'll miss you. Can't I come and see you when you get back? After all, I've never seen where you live.'

The idea of his absence had clearly upset her more than he'd expected. From Peter's point of view, it seemed that a couple of weeks away from one another would do them both some good. Still, if she wanted to see him before the start of term, why not? 'Yes, if you like.' Peter yawned behind his hand.

'Let's fix a time now. That way I'll have something to look forward to, and Christmas won't be too unbearable.'

Her words made Peter realize how barren her life was. He had his family and friends, and he was actively looking forward to going away. But for Carla, there was only her empty marriage. He felt sorry for her. It made him worry, too, that she might have expectations which he could never fulfil.

He smiled and shrugged. 'All right. Let's say the third. Sometime in the afternoon, around three.' She snuggled against him, fractionally happier. 'Anyway,' said Peter, 'I need to go to sleep. I've got a rugby match I'm supposed to be refereeing at ten-thirty tomorrow. I'll have to be up early.' He kissed her briefly on the forehead, slipped his arm from around her, switched off the light and turned over.

Carla lay in the darkness and pulled the unfamiliar covers up to her chin. She had thought he might hold her, that they might fall sleep in one another's arms. She glanced at him as he lay on the other side of the bed, his young form outlined by the dim light that crept beneath the door from the corridor. He looked very separate, and quite remote.

9

Alan woke the next morning with a dope hangover, a cloudy, depressed feeling with faintly neurotic edges. He thought immediately of Imogen. He lay there for a while taking stock of all that had happened the previous evening, this revelation of a daughter suddenly springing into his life. It had made more sense in the context of a couple of large whiskies and a joint than it did in the cold light of day. It wasn't that he any longer doubted who she was, it was more the question of what to do about her. They had got on well last night, in a rather ridiculous fashion, but were there obligations here, obligations of a material kind? Had Winifred-of-long-ago sent her here to exact some kind of dues? He didn't think so. Imogen was grown up, her own woman. If Winifred had wanted anything from him, she would have been in touch long ago. Twenty-three years ago, to be exact.

He heard sounds from downstairs and sprang out of bed in a manner unusual with him, his heart in his mouth. Carla. What if Carla was back? No, she couldn't be. It was too early. Still, Imogen mustn't be here when she arrived. He had to broach this subject with Carla in a delicate fashion, choosing his own time and method.

He pulled on a pair of trousers and a sweatshirt and went downstairs. Imogen was dressed and making herself coffee and toast. Her glasses lay on the worktop. She looked round at him, her eyes a little unfocused, and smiled. 'D'you want some coffee?'

'Yes, please. Good morning, by the way.'

'Morning.'

He didn't quite know what to say. She was a stranger, and yet she was not. He padded round the kitchen, picked up her glasses, took off his own, and put hers on. He could see through them. They weren't perfect, but they were close. More proof. Poor kid. What a thing to inherit, his short-sightedness.

They sat at the kitchen table and drank coffee together. Imogen glanced round. 'Your wife has very particular taste, hasn't she? Everything's so elegant, so spotless. What's she like?'

'The same. Far too refined for me. I think I annoy her. My smoking, my untidiness.' This revelation came to him out of the blue.

'What does she do?'

'Do? Well, she teaches part-time at the school where I work, and she does – well, I don't know. Bits and pieces, here and there.'

Imogen nodded. There was a brief silence. 'I'm really glad I came. I was terrified of what you might be like. But I'm really glad.'

'Good. I think I am, too.'

'Think?'

Alan shrugged. 'It's difficult. I don't know how Carla's going to react when I tell her.' He stared gloomily at his coffee cup. 'We always thought we'd have children, you see. Not that it was ever much of an issue. But still, finding out about you might create . . . problems.'

'I didn't come to find you just to say hello and goodbye. I want us to get to know one another, have a proper relationship.' She said this with such sweet earnestness that Alan smiled. 'She'll have to know about me, meet me.'

'Hmm.'

'Anyway –' She gathered up her rucksack. '– I have to get going.'

Alan followed her into the hall and watched as she put on her coat. 'Does your mother – does Winifred expect me to get in touch with her, d'you think?'

'Oh, God, I don't know. She might like to say hello. I think she quite liked the idea that I wanted to meet you. Why don't you call her some time?' She scribbled down her mother's name and number on the pad beside the telephone. Alan stood with his hands in his pockets, staring bleakly down at it. 'Don't worry – I don't think she'll care one way or the other if you don't ring. She doesn't expect it.'

Alan opened the front door and gave an involuntary shiver. 'Christ, it's freezing,' he said. 'Don't you want me to give you a lift?'

She shook her head. 'No, thanks. I like walking.' Her breath plumed in the cold air. She leaned forward and kissed him on one unshaven cheek. 'What do I call you?' she asked. 'Dad? Father?'

'Alan. Just call me Alan. That'll do.'

'All right. Alan. When will you be up in London? We can meet then and have lunch.'

'Not till after Christmas. Maybe towards the end of the holidays. But I will come. I will be in touch. I've got your

173

number. Don't worry.' He raised a hand and watched as she strode off down the utterly quiet road. What would any early-rising neighbours think, seeing a young woman leaving his house first thing on a Saturday morning? He didn't care. Last night had given something back to him. Loosened something in him. Or maybe Imogen had. He watched, musing, until she was out of sight.

When Carla returned later that morning, he decided against telling her about Imogen. She wouldn't believe him. And if he explained it to her, she'd still refuse to accept it. He knew she would. She would tell him that it was all highly unlikely, and the girl must be after something. So why had he accepted it so readily? Why had he not the slightest doubt in the world that his daughter was who she said she was? Because he knew. He just knew. He'd have to establish the relationship more firmly before Carla could be told, that was all.

'Have a good time?' he asked.

'Yes, not bad,' replied Carla, her voice non-committal. Alan thought she looked rather despondent. She must be tired. He made them both some coffee while Carla changed into trousers and a sweatshirt.

She came into the kitchen, brushing her dark hair. 'Alan, it's the end of term next week, and we still haven't thought about what we're going to be doing over Christmas.'

Alan handed her a cup of coffee. 'Stay here, I suppose. Be quite nice, just the two of us for a change. Though I thought we should pop down to see Dad on Boxing Day.'

'I don't want us just to be on our own.' The sudden edge in her voice caused him to glance at her. 'I mean,' she added apologetically, 'that it just strikes me as rather gloomy. Why don't we go down and see your father on Christmas Day, then have some people over for lunch on Boxing Day? Say, the Rayments, and Maeve and George.'

'Isn't that rather a lot of work for you?'

'I don't mind. I like entertaining. You know I do.' At least if she could fill the hours with planning and shopping, the time would seem less empty and terrifying. 'Fine by me,' said Alan.

'I'll give them a ring now,' said Carla. She went into the hall and picked up the phone, noticing as she did so the name and number scribbled down on the notepad. It wasn't in Alan's handwriting, and it hadn't been there yesterday. Winifred. Awful name. Perhaps Alan was seeing someone. Perhaps that someone had been here last night, while she was away. The idea filled her with amazement. She put the phone back down again, studying her feelings. One part of her told her that if he was, it was a good thing, that it eased the guilt and made things easier for her and Peter. Another part of her didn't like it. Not one little bit. She tore off the scrap of paper and stuffed it into her pocket, then picked up the phone again to ring Maeve.

Katie and Daniel sat on the sofa watching a video of *The Matrix* which Phil had rented the night before. Georgina and Ryan were, as usual, in Ryan's room with the door closed.

'This could be a really cool film,' said Daniel, 'if they didn't spoil it at the end. All the guns and stuff.'

'I like Keanu Reeves.'

After a few seconds Daniel glanced at her. 'It was good,

that Saturday you came to see me. It was nice to be with you away from here.'

Katie felt warmth spreading up her neck and across her cheeks. It was a simple remark, but it gave her a strange feeling to hear him say it. She nodded, returning his glance. 'I liked it, too.'

Daniel looked back at the television. 'Why don't we go out now? We could go and look round the shops. I like the shops at Christmas.'

It was only as he uttered the word that it occurred to Katie that Christmas, for Daniel, must mean spending it here, in this flat. No family, no presents, nothing any different from the way it usually was. It was a horrible, lonely idea. She felt a pang of unhappiness for him.

'I can't,' she replied. 'I might get seen by someone if we went round the shops. I told you how one of my sister's friends saw Georgina and me. It's too much of a risk.'

'Well, let's do something on Saturday. We could have lunch and just wander about. I'd like to take you out.'

This made Katie laugh. 'Take me out?'

Daniel looked at her mildly, a little hurt. 'Well, OK, I haven't any money. But I'd like to see you.'

Katie realized that things were moving imperceptibly on to a different level. She hesitated, then said, 'All right.'

Daniel nodded. 'Why don't we meet in the precinct around eleven, outside HMV?'

'Fine.'

Daniel nodded and turned his attention back to the film.

*

So they met on Saturday morning. As she walked through the precinct, Katie was aware of the sharp rise of pleasure she felt when she caught sight of Daniel, mixed with a strange pity at the figure he cut amongst the crowds of winter shoppers, standing there in his shabby clothes and battered trainers, the end of a roll-up pinched between his fingers. She didn't care how he looked, she realized. She was happy to be with him. They went into HMV and examined the racks of CDs, then they wandered out and into Woolworth's where they cruised the aisles, simply staring at anything and everything. After that they went to McDonald's and Katie paid for hamburgers and Cokes, and then they looked round Ottakar's bookshop. Daniel sat in one of the armchairs and read the best part of a biography of Keith Moon, while Katie went through all the teenage fiction without finding one thing that particularly interested her.

They wandered round town for the entire afternoon, talking, looking at things, perfectly happy in one another's company as dusk fell and the Christmas lights twinkled. At five o'clock Katie said she had to go home.

'We're going out tomorrow so I have to get my home-work done tonight. My mother's getting really stressed out about it.'

'I've had a good time,' said Daniel.

'So have I.'

They walked to the bus stop. As they stood waiting for Katie's bus, the first awkward silence of the afternoon descended. Today had been different from any other time they had spent together. Daniel hadn't so much as held her hand, but an intimacy had been created which seemed to demand something, now that she was about to go. She saw her bus looming through the winter darkness.

'Will you be round next week?' asked Daniel.

'I'll try,' said Katie. Daniel nodded. The bus pulled up.

'Right, well . . . see you soon.' She gave Daniel a glance and a smile and got on, digging in her pocket for her bus pass.

'Bye.' Daniel raised a hand, the doors closed, and the bus pulled away. Katie fell into a seat. He hadn't done anything. It was just like always. Well, what had she expected? It hadn't really been like going out with someone. They'd just spent the day together. Daniel wasn't someone you dated, like Russell Tucker. She thought of Russell Tucker and felt strangely unmoved. She was no longer interested in him, nor Rosie Dobson. She stared past her reflection at the darkness as the bus trundled her home, then realized that Daniel hadn't had any money, and was probably now walking all the way back to the flat. That sad thought prompted a sudden wish that he was still here, sitting next to her on the bus, and that they were both going somewhere together. Where? She had no idea. There wasn't anywhere to go.

'I think she's having an affair.' Maeve sat in Jenny Rayment's kitchen, drinking coffee. The Christmas holidays loomed, and Jenny's kitchen was snug with steam. She was in what she referred to as a domestic frenzy, cooking vast quantities of food for the freezer. She hated the business of cooking meals every day over the holidays. Far easier to capitalize on the occasional bouts of energy which overtook her and lay up stores against her more customary lethargy.

'You think everyone's having an affair.'

'No, I don't. But when I say I think someone is, I'm usually right. What about Alison Froggett and that chap from the Fiat dealership?'

Jenny poked at the batch of meat she was frying. 'I suppose so. Anyway, what makes you think Carla's got someone?'

'Well, for weeks now we haven't had lunch once. We used to have lunch together regularly, at least twice a week, after tennis. And that's another thing. She's moved our tennis times from the morning to the afternoon.'

'Well, that's hardly significant.'

'Not on its own, but taken together with everything else it is. This sudden switch in routine. It's lunchtime, you see. She gets up to something then.'

'Well, I don't think you should speculate and gossip about it.'

'You are joking, aren't you?' Maeve looked up at her friend with a tiny twinge of misgiving.

'Of course I am.' Jenny opened the fridge and took out a bottle of wine, then fished a corkscrew from a drawer. She handed them both to Maeve. 'Come on, let's have a drink. I don't care what time it is. I'll make us some lunch so we needn't feel guilty.' Maeve opened the wine and fetched some glasses, while Jenny went on with her cooking, adding in remote tones, 'Anyway, if she is having an affair, it's probably with my husband.'

Maeve wasn't quite sure how to respond to this, so she didn't. A silence fell. The meat hissed, Jenny stirred, Maeve sipped her wine. When she had tipped in some stock, Jenny left her stew to simmer and sat down at the kitchen table with a sigh and took a gulp of her wine. Maeve regarded her. She had known Jenny for almost twenty years now, shared with her the intimacies of pregnancy, childbirth, bringing up a family, but still she felt she couldn't tell her exactly what she thought. She couldn't tell Jenny that things might be different if she hadn't let herself go, if she hadn't piled on the weight and stopped bothering about her clothes. She was still so pretty, in a faded, fat way. The loveliness was there, tucked in amongst the plumpness. Her skin had always been radiant, her hair blonde and soft. But it was as though she didn't care any more. She wore layers of clothing, slightly hippyish, and now the blonde hair was greying, and invariably coming loose from a scarf or a hairband. A bit of a mess, in fact. Pretty, but still a mess. Over the years her resilience seemed to have been worn down, whether by Mike or by the demands of the children, Maeve couldn't be sure. As her weight increased, and the children grew, so Jenny's once bright, forceful personality seemed to have been diminished.

Jenny broke the silence. 'Do you think it's Mike?' The enquiry sounded almost casual. But Maeve could tell from the tension in her voice how desperately Jenny wanted to know.

'I don't think so,' she replied slowly, wondering how far honesty could be stretched in this conversation. It involved acknowledgement of Mike's philandering, something which, for all the closeness of their friendship, had never been addressed. Jenny knew, and Maeve knew, and

Jenny knew that Maeve and everybody else knew, but nothing was ever said. 'The way she talks about him, I don't think she – well, forgive me for saying it – but I don't think she especially likes Mike.'

'I'm not sure that's got a lot to do with it,' murmured Jenny. 'Not at our age.'

'Well, of course, most women fancy him,' said Maeve lightly, trying to steer the conversation, 'But I'm pretty sure it's not Mike.' Oh God, she thought. It was as good as coming right out and saying he was a front runner in the adultery stakes.

'But it could be.'

'It's not.'

'He does have affairs, you know.' Jenny drank some more of her wine. Her eyes were a little pink. 'Lots and lots of them. Maybe even with you.'

'Jenny,' said Maeve gently.

Jenny poured them both more wine. She shrugged. 'Sorry. But why not? He's had everyone else. And I know he fancies Carla. I know that for a fact.' Another large gulp of wine.

Maeve wished she hadn't started this conversation. She had only intended a bit of cosy speculation about Carla's possible affair, not an in-depth exposure of Mike's infidelities. 'If Carla's having an affair with anyone, it's not your husband.'

'That's all you know.' Jenny got up to give her vat of stew a stir.

'I think it's that new English teacher.'

'Peter Barrett?' Jenny turned, surprised. She let the matter of Mike slip away. She had seen from Maeve's face that now was not the time to air that particular piece of linen. Maeve felt uncomfortable talking about it, that was clear. Well, let it go. She turned her attention to this interesting speculation. 'But he's only twenty something.' She took a loaf from the bread bin and began to butter slices thickly. 'Ham or cheese? That's all I've got.'

'Ham, thanks. Well, he may be young, but what difference does that make? Carla's very attractive. Anyway, I think it's him because I've seen him coming up that path past the tennis courts two days running now, the one that leads to the back of Carla's house, always at lunchtime.'

'No!' Jenny put two plates of sandwiches on the table, then sat down and began to eat greedily, between drinks of wine, feeling happier. And so they gossiped on for another hour or so, sowing the seeds.

Olive heard the rumour from Fiona Mather, who taught Geography at Taft's. Fiona was a garrulous and excitable woman, close to Olive in age, and also unmarried. She took the view that this was a basis for friendship with Olive, and had regarded Olive as her best chum, as she put it, for the four years she had been at Taft's. Olive was moderately fond of Fiona, but she found her rather wearisome at times. Still, it was a lonely life outside school, and she was glad of someone to go to concerts and the cinema with, and on Saturday shopping expeditions. She drew the line, however, at too close a friendship, and had so far successfully scotched Fiona's suggestions of holidays together. She was always grateful for the silence of her own little flat after an evening spent listening to Fiona's rapid chatter, with its Morningside inflection, and she didn't think she could take it day after day for any protracted period of time.

It was a Saturday, and they had taken the train up to London to do some Christmas shopping. Now they were rounding the day off with tea at Fortnum's, to be followed by a film at one of the Leicester Square cinemas. They hadn't yet decided which. There was no circumlocution with Fiona. They had been talking about the forthcoming Christmas staff party, when suddenly Fiona leaned over and said in a low, confidential voice, 'By the way, have you heard about Carla Tradescant and Peter Barrett?'

Olive didn't hear the question in the way in which it was intended. Her cast of mind was such that she did not bracket Carla and Peter together in any sense. Instead, she wondered what external event or affliction had visited the two random individuals whom Fiona had named.

'Why, what's happened to them?'

Fiona took another bite of scone and raised her eyebrows. 'Nothing's *happened* to them. Well, I wouldn't put it like that, anyway. What I meant was, have you heard the rumours about them?'

It still took a couple of seconds for Olive to divine the sense of this. When she did, her heart sank, instantly, heavily, like a stone. 'No,' she replied. 'I haven't.' She almost added that she had no wish to, but a deadly curiosity prevented her. She waited, watching Fiona's long teeth as she bit into her scone again. How true it is, she thought, that we feel instant distaste for the bearer of tidings we would rather not hear.

'Apparently – mind you, this is all hearsay – *apparently* he goes up to the Tradescant's house every lunchtime.

The head's in school, in the lunch hall, but Carla's never there. Put two and two together, and what do you get? An affair. Can you imagine – the headmaster's wife and a twenty-seven-year-old teacher?' Fiona giggled, sputtering crumbs on to her lip. She licked them off and drank some tea. Her eyes were bright with pleasure. 'Mind you, he's very nice. I wouldn't say no myself.'

Olive felt a little tide of anger race through her. 'Well, if it is just hearsay, I don't think it's very responsible of you to repeat it, if you don't mind my saying so. It's exactly the kind of thing that causes mischief and wrecks people's lives. I'm frankly appalled that you should spread gossip of that sort.'

Olive's cheeks were red with anger, and Fiona sat back, bridling, somewhat startled by the apparent depth of feeling she had aroused. But it was not so much righteous indignation at malicious gossip that Olive felt – more a sense of agonizing loss at the thought of her beautiful paragon of young manhood involved in such a tawdry scenario. Dear Peter. Dear bright-eyed, handsome Peter – how could he disappoint her in such a way? To throw himself away on a woman almost old enough to be his mother, when he should be finding some creature, some maiden, as perfect and young as himself. The whole idea was detestable to Olive. It made Peter an adulterer, a liar, and something much cheaper and less fine than she had fondly imagined. Oh, she knew that she'd idealized him because of his looks, but it was an innocent indulgence of fancy that was entitled, surely, to possess some small basis in truth. He should be as he looked. As she sat digesting the bitter implications of Fiona's words, she

184

wondered if she herself were guilty of mere jealousy, if she weren't deluding herself that her emotions with regard to this young man were less than pure. But no — she could not honestly accuse herself of any libidinous feelings towards him. Far from it. She would be quite happy if he were to find himself an equal, a girl as radiant as he. It perfectly suited Olive's romantic inclinations that Peter the young prince should have his princess, but not someone more along the lines of Snow White's wicked stepmother. It was not difficult for her to cast Carla in this light. If the rumour was true, Carla was obviously to blame. She was older, worldly, quite capable of putting temptation in Peter's way. No doubt it was Carla who had manipulated Peter to gratify herself.

While all this was whirling through Olive's mind, Fiona was gathering together her own dented pride. 'Well, I don't see that you're entitled to take such a self-righteous line, Olive. You enjoy a piece of gossip as much as the rest of us. Wasn't it *you* who told *me* about Mike Rayment and that photography assistant?'

There was something in this, Olive knew. She shrugged, damping down her feelings. 'Perhaps I was a little sharp. It's just a little shocking to hear that kind of thing about the headmaster's wife. I'd prefer to think it isn't true.'

Mollified, Fiona poured them both more tea. 'Maybe you would, but facts have to be faced. They're both being very indiscreet. It would be a kindness if someone were to have a word with that young man before there's a nasty scandal.' She paused, then added, 'He's a member of your department, after all.'

'"After all"? What do you mean by that? You're not

185

suggesting *I* say something, are you? I couldn't possibly! There may be absolutely no substance to this rumour. How would I look then? No, no, quite absurd to even suggest it. Totally inappropriate.'

'Oh, don't go getting all het up again. I'm just saying.' Fiona licked her forefinger and pressed it into the crumbs on her plate. 'Anyway, let's think about what film we're going to see. What about *Notting Hill*? I know you liked that Hugh Grant in *Four Weddings and a Funeral*. A nice romantic comedy with some good-looking young people is just what we need to cheer us up.'

Jenny could not resist passing on Maeve's little gossiping speculation to her husband, partly out of relief that it was not Mike with whom Carla was having an affair, and partly out of morbid curiosity as to how he would react to the news. She had heard him bitching about this good-looking new English teacher on more than one occasion, and she knew that Mike himself had been sniffing around Carla for years now. It would do him good to have his nose put out of joint. She watched his face closely for signs of discomfiture as she told him.

He just laughed. 'What a load of bollocks Maeve talks. I happen to know that our Mr Barrett has something going with one of the upper sixth.'

Jenny was taken aback. 'How do you know?'

'I overheard a couple of students in my art group talking about it.'

'Well, what about when Maeve's seen him going up to the Tradescants' house?'

Mike shrugged. 'How do I know what trivia goes to

186

fuel Maeve's lurid imagination? I'd've thought you could find something better to do than sitting around gossiping and drinking wine. Like getting rid of some of that weight, for a start.'

He left the kitchen. Jenny stood there, quite still. He hurt her so much, so often, that she had thought she might have grown a thicker skin. But she hadn't. She had never been anything but totally raw and vulnerable where Mike was concerned. She still loved him with that painful kind of adoration which resisted every slight, every cruelty and infidelity. She had long ago learned to see him through other people's eyes, but nothing could alter her own feelings for him. She withstood everything, all the little affairs, his lies, his unkindness to her, because she was convinced that, in the end, he needed her. It wasn't something he would ever openly admit, he was probably contemptuous of himself for feeling it, but she knew she was necessary to his existence. She must be, or why hadn't he left her long ago, for any one of the women with whom he'd had his affairs? That was what Jenny told herself. It was simply something she had to believe in order to survive.

Mike went upstairs to his studio, which overlooked the back garden. He stood at the window, staring down. He'd made it up, that business about the sixth-former and Barrett. Well, not entirely. He'd heard a couple of sixth-form girls talking about him. That was all. But it had been enough to prevent Jenny having the satisfaction of seeing him in any way disturbed by her tittle tattle. That was what she wanted. It was pathetic, that she should need such means to get to him, to provoke feeling in him. But it had done the job. Mike knew that what Jenny had told him was probably true. Veteran bitches like Maeve Porter, ears and snouts to the ground, generally got these things right. Carla and that smooth prick, with his affected clothes and his Ford Anglia, or whatever the fuck he drove, were having an affair. The idea of Barrett succeeding where he had failed galled Mike immeasurably. He could just picture it. How flattered, how delighted Carla must be to have the attentions of someone like Peter. Getting it on a regular basis, too, from what Jenny had said. At least, he reflected, there was the happy thought that Alan, that soft turd, was being played for a complete fool. That was one element of satisfaction to be had from it all.

IO

I am a tragic figure, thought Alan, as he stood on the fire escape at the end of the science block, smoking a solitary cigarette. I am headmaster of a school whose place in the league tables slips lower every autumn, with a staff whose morale gets correspondingly worse, I don't much like my job, and I can't even have a fag in my own fucking study. He took a final drag, sucking the healing smoke deep into his lungs, and flicked the fag-end down into the shrubbery below. Then he went back through the empty lab and strolled down the corridor, taking stock of the events of the coming days. Already he could scent the mounting faint hysteria which marked an end of term, particularly the Christmas term. Tonight was the carol concert in the chapel, same old hymns, same old readings, same old cant, and the following day, Saturday, was the Christmas Fayre, God bless the PTA. Then in the evening, the staff party. They never did very much. Just drinks at The Green Man, then on to a local restaurant. He understood that Jeff Perkins, in charge of these extravaganzas, had booked a table at some Thai restaurant. As head, Alan always felt obliged to show up, though he found the business of pretending he was a bit pissed and that his defences were down somewhat trying. Maybe this year he *should* get pissed, and see what happened. He almost envied the three members of staff who'd been roped in to supervise

189

– if that was the word – the sixth-form disco, which was to take place in the school hall. They wouldn't miss a lot.

The bell for lunchtime break shrilled, and within fifteen seconds the quiet corridor was teeming with pupils. Peter Barrett came out of D2 on the heels of his year ten students, clearly in something of a hurry. He slowed down when he saw Alan.

'Play rehearsals going well?' asked Alan conversationally. He liked Peter Barrett, thought him a good teacher and a welcome breath of fresh air at Taft's. Whenever Alan spoke to him, however, Peter seemed rather reserved, even a little nervous. Maybe Alan could draw him out a bit more at the staff party.

'Yes, it's coming along nicely. They're an enthusiastic bunch, the year eights. The set's been a bit of a headache. Mike Rayment seems to be a bit too busy to help out, but Bill Radcliffe's come to our rescue.'

'Good. Speaking of Mike Rayment, there's a project I've been meaning to talk to you about. I can tell you're in a bit of a hurry now, so I won't keep you. Remind me to tell you about it tomorrow night.'

'Tomorrow night?' Peter looked confused.

'The staff party. Just a few drinks here, then we go on to a restaurant. Didn't the other members of staff mention it to you?'

'Oh, yes, yes, of course. Right. Yes . . . Well, I'll see you there.'

Alan smiled and continued along the corridor.

Peter hurried out of school and across the road to the phone box by the newsagent's. He had to ring Carla to tell her he couldn't come round that lunchtime. Events with the play had overtaken him, and they'd decided to have a dress rehearsal today, instead of Monday.

'Oh, Peter!' Carla's voice was desolate. 'How can you? That means I won't be able to see you before you go away!' It was true. There would be another dress rehearsal on Monday, then on Tuesday and Wednesday they were performing excerpts from the play at lunchtime to the Lower School, and in the evenings there would be performances of the play itself. Term ended on Thursday at lunchtime, and Peter was going away on Friday.

'Carla, I can't help it.'

'Peter, there must be something you can do! You have no idea what it means, not being able to see you for a month!' Her voice had the faintly hysterical note he dreaded.

He sighed. 'I was going to suggest that you come round to the flat tomorrow night, if you can get away. But I've just been reminded that there's the staff party.'

'But can't you skip that? People do.'

'Not really. Alan says he wants to talk to me about something in particular. But maybe I can slip away early, and you could come round then.'

'All right.' He could hear the relief in her voice.

'I'll ring you when I get away. Right now I've got to rush. Bye.'

He put the phone down and sped back across the road to school, hoping that he'd still have enough time for a quick lunch before the rehearsal.

Carla put the phone down and wandered into the living room. She lay down on the sofa and stared out through the French windows to the garden. Her imagination could almost create Peter, his figure crossing the lawn, raincoat flapping, dark head bent against the wind, hurrying to her. The garden was empty now. A day must come when it stayed empty forever, when he no longer came to her. Where would they be then? Would they be together, somewhere else? She had no idea, nor any hope. She put her hands over her eyes. She would see him tomorrow evening. That much she could hold on to. After that, it was just a question of waiting for time to pass, as it would. She would fill it somehow. One good thing about having a headmaster for a husband was that it meant plenty of socializing over Christmas.

Oh, well. There was no sense in lying here. She had intended to go shopping later. She might as well start now. She hadn't thought of a thing to buy Alan for Christmas. With Peter it was different. She could think of a hundred things she would like to buy for him. As it was, she knew that she must restrict herself to one gift. Instinct told her that. At least it would be one pleasurable piece of shopping amongst the rest, which was mere duty.

At the staff party, Peter decided not to remind Alan about whatever it was he had wanted to discuss. The more often he spoke to friendly, avuncular Alan, the worse he felt. But in the restaurant after the meal, just as Peter was about to slip away, Alan rose from his chair and came round to where Peter was sitting.

'Peter, that thing I wanted to discuss with you.'

'Oh, yes?' Peter picked up his drink and got up from his chair. The curry house was very busy, and they moved back against the wall to talk.

'The school magazine. I don't know if you know much about it, but it's an important mouthpiece for the school. We start preparing it around January for publication in the late summer, so that it goes out with prospectuses in the autumn, and people can pick up copies on the open day. The present format is all well and good, but the trouble is I think it's become somewhat lackadaisical, too formulaic. The way it's put together now, Mike Rayment is in charge of the art editing, Verity Roberts looks after the photo editing, and Fiona Mather is responsible for the text editing. I feel that the end product doesn't really have a spirit, an *essence*. It lacks vitality. Do you see what I'm driving at?'

Peter nodded intently, bemused.

'I feel it needs to be more a product of the pupils themselves. What I have in mind is that the children themselves should edit the magazine, and set up an editorial committee under the control and supervision of a single member of staff. Obviously Mike and Verity would still have an input, and I always take a close interest in the project, but the children themselves would collect and collate the material, and the editorial direction would be down to one person. I think it needs someone young, with a fresh approach, and that's why I thought you might be interested.'

'What? You'd like me to edit the school magazine?' Peter tried to sound pleased. His heart sank at the thought of the task, but there wasn't much you could do if the head indicated he wanted you to do something.

Alan nodded and sipped his lager. 'I think you'd be excellent. You're new to the school, you can inject some vigour into the magazine, make it more exciting.'

'Well . . . Yes, naturally, I'd be delighted. Thank you.'

'Excellent. I thought it would be the kind of thing to appeal to you. I just wanted to sound you out in principle. We'll have a more in-depth discussion at the start of the new term.'

Peter left the restaurant a few minutes later. The last thing he needed was a project which would bring him into closer and more frequent contact with Alan. Peter felt hellishly uncomfortable simply being with him, while all the time he was having an affair with his wife. He put the key in the lock of his Morris Minor and sighed. Wouldn't it just be great to drive away somewhere, anywhere, and start again. He had no idea how he had got himself into all this. Well, he did, but he had never meant to get in so deep.

He was about to get into the car when he saw a girl on the other side of the road, walking quickly. Not a particularly nice part of town to be on your own in, thought Peter, nor a nice time of night. A fierce wind blew ragged gusts of sleet along the deserted street. The girl passed beneath a street light, which picked up reddish glints from her long hair, and Peter suddenly realized that it was Beatrice Rayment. What on earth was she doing round here at this hour?

He locked the car again quickly and crossed the road at a gentle run, calling out to her. She turned quickly, a little fearfully, then saw who it was.

'Hello, Mr Barrett.'

'Beatrice. I saw you from the other side of the road. Where are you off to?'

'Home. I was at the school disco, but I was feeling really tired, so I thought I might as well just leave.'

Peter glanced up and down the dark street. 'Well, listen, I don't think you should be out on your own like this. There can be some unpleasant types round here at this time of night, like the dear creatures who regularly deface the school walls with graffiti.'

'I'm all right.' Her face was very pale and pretty, framed by the red hair which blew about it. 'There's a night bus that goes from outside the precinct.'

'No, that's not a good idea. Come on, I'll give you a lift.' He nodded his head in the direction of his car.

'Isn't it taking you out of your way?' They began to cross the road together.

'Not really. Anyway, it doesn't matter. I'd rather see you get home safely.'

He drove her the couple of miles to her house and pulled up outside. The windows were dark.

'I like your car,' said Bea. 'It suits you.'

He looked at her and smiled. 'Thank you. Old and worn out. I don't know if I should take that as a compliment or not.'

She laughed. 'Well, you know what I mean. It's like the way you dress and things, a bit old-fashioned. You're not exactly old.'

'I'm twenty-seven, to be precise.'

'Really?' There was a brief silence. By telling her his age, Peter realized that he had unintentionally broken through that teacher–pupil wall of glass. He probably shouldn't have said it. Anyway, to a seventeen-year-old it probably still sounded ancient.

'Well, anyway, thanks for the lift.' She opened the door and prepared to get out.

Peter glanced up at the house. 'It looks rather dark and empty. Will you be all right?'

'Of course I will,' she replied, with gentle, sixth-form contempt. 'My mother's out with my brothers and sister at the cinema, and Dad's at the staff thing.'

'Oh, yes, of course. Still, I'll see you to the door.' He got out and walked round to the other side to accompany her up to the house.

'Thanks, but you didn't have to,' said Beatrice, as they reached the door.

'It's the polite thing to do,' said Peter, 'and the safe thing.'

She put her key in the door. Peter was about to turn away when she said, 'Would you like to come in for some coffee? It seems rude just to send you off after you brought me all the way home.'

Peter said yes without knowing why. She went ahead of him, switching on lights. He followed her into the cosy, cluttered kitchen.

'I'd better not stay very long. I don't really want to be here when your father gets home.'

'Why ever not?' Beatrice turned her face to him in amazement as she filled the kettle. Her blue eyes were very large, and very clear. Quite beautiful, thought Peter.

'Well, he's not exactly keen on me.' Peter sat down on a kitchen chair, his hands in his coat pockets.

'Why? What have you done?'

'Oh, I don't know . . .' He told her, as she made the coffee, of his various unhappy run-ins with Mike. Then she sat down at the other side of the table, passing him his coffee, and talked about her father for a while, even touching on his reputation for womanizing, to Peter's surprise. From that they moved on to the rest of her family, and then to school matters, and in the end Peter stayed for far longer than he had intended. When he glanced at his watch, he saw that it was nearly ten o'clock. He had been so absorbed in their conversation that Carla had slipped his mind.

'God, is that the time? Listen, would you mind very much if I used your phone? I should be seeing someone, and I'm a bit late.'

'Of course not. The phone's over there.' Beatrice stood up and took the mugs to the sink to wash. She had her back turned to him, and as he listened to the phone ringing at the other end, Peter's gaze was fastened unconsciously on her slender figure, and the extraordinary cascade of hair which fell almost to her waist.

At the other end, Carla picked up the phone. 'Hi, it's me,' said Peter.

'Where on earth have you been? I've been waiting hours! I thought you'd have got away by half eight at least!'

'Yes, well, I got held up.' Beatrice turned around to pick up a tea towel, and Peter's gaze slid away. 'I had to give someone a lift. I'll be home in ten minutes.'

There was silence at the other end, and then Carla gave a little wail of despair. 'Oh, God, no! There's Alan now! He's getting out of a taxi. How can I possibly go out at this time? There's nowhere I could realistically be going!'

Peter didn't know what to say. 'Well, that's that, then, I'm afraid. I'm sorry.' He hesitated. 'We'll just have to wait till the third.'

'I suppose so.' Carla's voice was now soft with misery. 'I'll have to go.'

Peter put the phone down and turned to Beatrice, who was slipping the mugs on to hooks on the dresser. He gave a sigh. 'Right, well . . .'

'I hope it hasn't messed your evening up, you giving me a lift.'

'No, not at all. Don't worry.'

'Well, it was very kind of you.'

He made his way down the hall to the front door. Outside, a light snow had begun to fall. Bea shivered at the sudden touch of the cold air. Peter turned to her. 'I'll see you in school next week. Goodnight.'

''Night, Mr Barrett.' She stood framed in the doorway. 'I'm just going to stand here until you've got safely to your car.'

Peter chuckled as he walked down the path. In a way he was glad it had happened. It would be something of a relief not to see Carla for a few weeks.

For Christmas, Alan gave Carla an angora sweater of very pale blue, *The Oxford Book of Letters*, and the new Hilary Mantel novel. Carla in turn gave Alan a new edition of Halliwell, a copy of the *Encyclopaedia of Rock Music*, and some shirts. Carla liked the sweater very much, and felt a tremble of guilt as she slipped it on. The cowl neck suited her, and the wool was deliciously soft and sensuous against her skin. She wanted Peter to see her in it.

She thought about him as she worked throughout Boxing Day on preparations for the dinner party, and wondered if he was thinking of her. The expensive leather wallet which she had bought for him still lay upstairs in a drawer, carefully wrapped. She would give it to him on the third. It seemed an age away. She felt she wanted to be frozen, all animation suspended, between now and then, so that she would not have to endure the long days of companionship with Alan, the prickles of loathing every time he touched her, the pretence of smiles and intimate, casual conversation. The new term would bring a sea change, she told herself. During this spell of absence from one another, their feelings would crystallize, hers and Peter's. He would come back knowing that this was more than a casual affair, that issues had to be resolved. That would involve telling Alan, and then facing the consequences together. At least they would be together. This belief soothed Carla's spirit as she prepared the canapés and prowled round the carefully decorated dinner table, moving glasses, adjusting candles. This would soon come to an end, and she would be free.

'What a farce,' said Mike, as he and Jenny got ready to go out. 'I mean, what a complete bloody joke. There's poor old Alan, with no idea that his wife's humping young Mr Barrett and making an utter fool of him, and she has the nerve to invite us round to witness his unsuspecting humiliation.' He let Jenny adjust his tie, then they went downstairs together.

'She doesn't know we know,' said Jenny. 'Anyway, it may all be entirely untrue.'

'Come off it.' Mike poured himself a slug of Scotch and cast a glance at himself in the mirror over the drawing-room mantelpiece, smoothing back his thick red hair.

'You were the one that told me about Carla's little affair, remember. Don't start back-pedalling now.'

'I wish you wouldn't start on the Scotch. I don't want you getting drunk. You can be horribly indiscreet when you're drunk, and I don't want a scene at Carla's dinner table.'

Mike knocked back his drink. 'I don't make scenes. Mind you, it might be doing Alan a kindness to let him know what his wife's up to. Poor sod.'

'Mike!' exclaimed Jenny warningly.

'Oh, don't be a silly bitch. Come on, let's get going. I'll drive there, you can drive back.'

George Porter, as chairman of Taft's PTA, was bursting with news when he arrived at the Tradescants'.

'I'm here to tell you,' he informed Alan and Carla, as Alan handed him a glass of champagne, 'that you two have won first prize in the PTA raffle.'

'Oh, no!' groaned Alan.

'What do you mean, "Oh, no"?' asked Maeve. 'I wouldn't have minded winning a weekend break in Paris, a room at the Ritz.' She raised her glass. 'Merry Christmas.'

Everyone murmured in response. 'That's the Rayments' car,' said Carla, and went to open the front door.

'You should count yourself bloody lucky,' said George cheerfully. 'Not a bad prize at all. Someone's got to win it.'

'Yes, but preferably not the headmaster,' said Alan. 'It's a little embarrassing.'

'Well,' said George, 'that's what happens if you buy

eight books of tickets. Odds are you're bound to win something.'

'As head, I'm duty bound to buy a load of tickets, but I shouldn't *win* anything. What do you think, darling?' He turned to Carla as she came into the room with Mike and Jenny.

'What do I think of what?' Carla's smile was cool and careful.

'Winning a weekend for two in Paris,' said Maeve, her eyes on Carla's face.

George turned to Mike and Jenny. 'This pair only managed to win first prize in the PTA raffle.'

'How romantic,' said Mike. 'How very, very romantic. You must be thrilled, Carla.'

Oh, God, thought Jenny.

'I don't know,' said Carla. 'Perhaps we should turn it down. I mean, it doesn't look awfully good, does it?' Paris. With Alan. A romantic, interminable weekend. She remembered the New Forest and felt leaden inside.

Alan reflected for a moment, and then said firmly, 'No. Come to think of it, I've never won a raffle prize in my life, and I'm not about to turn this one down. It's just what Carla and I need, a weekend in Paris.'

'Oh, absolutely,' said Mike. He smiled at Carla, and she quailed slightly as she met his gaze. Why was he giving her that knowing look? Probably just his usual leer. She and Peter had been very careful. Mike Rayment couldn't know a thing, nor could Jenny. She gave Maeve a quick glance, but could read nothing. What if they did know? What if people knew, everyone but Alan? She suddenly felt horribly uncomfortable.

'I'll just fetch the canapés,' she said, and went through to the kitchen.

For Christmas Katie gave Georgina a soap bag containing shampoo and body lotion from the Body Shop, and Georgina gave Katie a set of five lipsticks from Marks & Spencer. Ryan was away for Christmas, so they didn't go round to the flat until after New Year. Katie wanted to see Daniel, but for some reason she couldn't bring herself to go there on her own. The day they had spent together, the way it had ended, had brought an odd feeling of constraint. Yet she thought about him every day, and there was a moment on Christmas Day when she imagined him in the flat and felt a sharp, desolate pain that almost made her cry.

They eventually went round on the third of January. It was freezing, bleak and raw, the sky white, the streets melancholy with the deadness of post-Christmas. As they walked past the shops to the flat, Katie became aware that she felt an odd tightness inside, a kind of scared happiness at the prospect of seeing Daniel. It was an entirely new sensation, and her mind dipped at the unexpectedness of it.

The flat was its usual spartan chaos, the television on, Daniel at his place on the sofa.

'Ryan's still in bed,' said Andy, who was on his way out to his afternoon shift at the supermarket. Georgina went into Ryan's room and closed the door. Katie sat down next to Daniel. She felt oddly self-conscious. She watched his fingers as he rolled his cigarette. She liked his fingers. She liked every part of him. He was warm and familiar.

She couldn't tell him any of these things. They were new, and marvellous.

He lit his cigarette, then suddenly said, 'I can't stand this place any more. Let's go out for a walk.' His tone of voice was strange, almost angry. She had never heard Daniel get angry.

She looked at his pathetically thin, shabby jacket, with only the T-shirt and waistcoat beneath. 'It's too cold. I mean, I'm all right, I've got my coat, but you'll be too cold.'

'I'm fine. Come on.'

They went to the park and walked around. A father with his little girl stood throwing lumps of bread at some despondent Canada geese by the pond. The water was scummy, littered at the edge with older bits of bread. Vandals had torn the planking from the wooden benches so no one could sit down.

'How was your Christmas?' asked Daniel.

'Fine,' said Katie. She didn't want to ask him about his. He stood staring out across the pond, smoking. Katie tried to think of something to say, but couldn't. She had never felt this awkwardness between them before.

Suddenly the pigeons which were milling among the geese at the pondside rose in a flurry and swooped low across the park. The little girl screamed and ran to her pushchair. Daniel turned to look at Katie, the wind blowing strands of blond hair across his face. 'I really missed you.' He said it intently, as though he had been thinking it over for a long time.

Something broke within Katie, and she felt a flooding sense of relief. She gazed back at him. 'I missed you, too. I thought about you every day.'

As though it were a perfectly natural thing to do, Daniel put his arms around Katie and held her. His arms felt cold, and the side of his face where her cheek touched his, but she could feel creeping warmth where his heart was beating. She hugged him tight. 'I hate my life,' he said softly, suddenly. 'These last two weeks I've kept thinking I wish I could just go into a coma and wake up somewhere further down the line. Things might be better then.'

'Don't. Don't wish that.' She took her head from his shoulder and looked up at him. She could not describe the way she felt about his face. She had never thought about whether he was good-looking, or handsome. All she knew was that his features were completely familiar, perfect, like a reflection of someone deep inside her that she had always known was there, but had never seen. He kissed her, his sparse beard and moustache tickling her face, and the warmth and sweetness of the kiss was a revelation. All kinds of sensations and thoughts welled up in her, from the pit of her stomach to the top of her brain, a million and one unresolved fragments of feeling, happiness, panic, desperation, loss, wonder. When the kiss ended, she wondered if she should try to say some of it, but nothing would come out. They just looked at one another. Katie felt as though the rest of the world were out there somewhere, separate, nothing to do with her and Daniel. Her and Daniel, that was all it was.

'You know what?' said Daniel, smoothing her forehead with his thumb, so that Katie could smell the scent of stale tobacco on his fingers.

'What?'

He looked into her eyes. 'I'm a mess. I'm a real mess.

I've cried my eyes out over Christmas because I miss my family and I don't know where I'm going or what I'm doing.' His voice broke slightly. 'And I thought about you all the time, how you've become my friend. The only thing about me that's not a mess is you.' He gave a sudden shudder, whether from cold or emotion, Katie didn't know, but she held him tight, tears rising in her eyes for him. She had never felt so much part of another person in her life. It was a very strange and wonderful feeling, pushing everything and everyone else away.

'Don't worry,' she said. 'It'll get better. It will.' And she wished she knew how, and that there was something she could do. But she was only fifteen, and she couldn't help at all.

She raised her face to his and he kissed her again, and this time she could feel the wetness of his tears on her face.

Carla drove to Peter's flat. It was on the edge of town, on the first floor of a large Victorian townhouse. As she parked the car and crossed the road, she felt a trembling of anticipation and longing. This is like being sixteen and in love for the first time, she told herself. She pressed the bell and went upstairs.

'God, I've missed you, Peter, I've missed you . . .' He was fumbling urgently with the zip of her skirt and kissing her almost before she had got through the door. She had thought it might be different, gentler, that he would want to tell her how much he had been thinking about her, that they might talk, take things slowly, intimately. But Peter was too hungry, too impatient, the way he had been that first lunchtime when he had come to the house. 'Have you missed me? Have you?' she asked. His hands were busy with the fastening of her bra.

He kissed her long and hard. 'Of course I have. God, I want you. Come here . . .'

'Peter –' She pulled away briefly. 'It's been a long four weeks. I want to look at you, talk to you –'

'And I want to make love to you. We can talk later.'

Some time later, lying on his bed, they talked. Carla told him how it had been over Christmas, the people they'd seen, the various social gatherings. 'I thought about you every minute.' She ran a hand over the dark hair on his chest. 'Did you think about me?'

Peter said nothing for a moment. Now that his passion was spent, he seemed oddly absent, distant, Carla noticed. 'Yes. Yes, I did.' He turned to look at her, his expression thoughtful. He hugged her quickly, his gaze taking on more warmth. 'Of course I did.'

'And?' Her hand strayed to his head. She brushed her fingers through his curling hair.

And? Again he said nothing for a moment. He couldn't tell her the truth. Distance had helped him to see that what they were doing was potentially dangerous, that it couldn't go on indefinitely without something happening, someone finding out. And that would be bad news, not just for him and for his career, but for poor old Alan. The Tradescants' marriage might be in trouble, perhaps on the point of breaking up, but he didn't want to be the catalyst. He knew he was guilty of more than a little cowardice in all this. If Alan and Carla broke up because of him, he would be left feeling a sort of responsibility for Carla. And that wasn't something he had ever wanted or intended. Responsibility was something he had shied away from in every relationship he had ever had. He had sometimes wondered if he wasn't emotionally bereft, incapable of falling in love. He knew he had never loved anybody, not in that obsessive, hopeless and unconditional way that other people seemed to. Girls had loved him like that, but it was always unreciprocated. If he could only fall in love with someone, then perhaps he could find that perfect balance, one where he wanted to give as much as take. Then again, perhaps it was destined never to happen to him.

Carla's hand moved down to his own, covering it. She twined her fingers in his, lifted them, laid his hand on her breast, moving it gently, then leaning over to kiss him. Even as he returned her kiss he knew that this affair couldn't go on much longer, that soon the risk would no longer be worth taking.

11

January passed, and with it the flurry of entrance examinations. Alan noted dismally that the number of applications was down yet again. With numbers falling, Taft's couldn't even afford to operate a policy of only allowing the most able students to sit A-levels, the way some schools did, and thereby boost their ratings.

Eight years before I retire, thought Alan. My God.

February came, and with it a severe cold snap, so that the boiler broke down, several pipes froze, and Taft's had to close for two days. It was always a depressing time of year, but for Alan it was even more so than usual. He felt strangely alone as he waded through the reams of administration. Carla seemed preoccupied and remote, as though in some world of her own. Alan found himself thinking a lot about Imogen. He spoke to her a few times on the phone, but work made it impossible for him to get up to London to see her. Next month he would, he promised himself.

Through the winter weeks Carla and Peter saw one another as often as Peter chose. Carla did not admit this to herself. She never liked to acknowledge the balance of their relationship. The trouble with that was that, instead of slipping into an easier, gentler phase, the intensity of their affair had increased. For her, at any rate. Uncertainty and hope made her hungrier, and each time he came to her she seemed to need him more. Some instinct told her that she should make a little distance, relax, make an effort to be cooler. But it was impossible. Being in love was a force which drove itself, contradicting every wise impulse.

Katie sat, propped up against the headboard of her bed, and wrote in her diary.

WEDNESDAY. Georgina and I had a HUGE row today. We bunked off before lunch instead of after, so we went into town to a café to get something to eat. This man started talking to Georgina, and she was smiling and talking back and I really didn't like it. I made her leave by saying I was going and things like that, so she had to come. Things like that happen because she looks much older than she is. Even with my tie stuffed in my pocket I look like I'm still at school, but she doesn't. We were going to get the bus to the flat but we went into Boot's first to have a look at stuff. Georgina was looking at this lipstick and the woman came over and said can I help you? in that snotty way they do. Georgina said no we're just looking thank you, and then when the woman turned away Georgina made as if she was putting the lipstick back, and then she put it in her pocket. She grabbed my sleeve and we went out, I thought I was going to die. There was a security guard at the doors and he looked at us and I was sure he was going to stop us, but he didn't. I was so, so scared. I said why did you do that? She just said oh, it wasn't a big deal, she'd been out with Hannah Keys last Saturday and they'd nicked a scarf from Littlewoods and two pairs of tights out of M&S. I know she's started going around with Hannah sometimes but I'm not jealous. I don't like Hannah. I told Georgina I thought it was really stupid, shoplifting, but she just laughed and said it was a good buzz and anyway I was just jealous that she had been into town with Hannah. I said I wasn't, don't be stupid, but I must have been upset about something because then I said I bet you stole those lipsticks you gave me for Christmas. She went really mad, and we had a huge row right at the bus stop. The bus came and she got on it and I did too, but because she got on first it was like I was following her or something, when I wasn't. And the argument went on, and then she started having a go at Daniel and saying how pathetic he was, and Ryan and the others only put up with him because he's Phil's cousin. I couldn't stand that. I really couldn't. I started telling her she was wrong and how really nice he is, and then I ended up wondering why I was bothering. It cooled down a bit but when we got to the flat we still weren't really speaking. And I hate the way that because Georgina always does things first, gets in first, like going up the stairs in front of me and ringing the bell, it's like I'm tagging behind. I hate that. I sometimes think I hate her. Then afterwards when we were going home she took the lipstick out of her pocket and said I don't really want this, you have it. So now I've got this lipstick that she stole. I'll probably throw it away.

Katie rolled on to her back and bit the end of her pen. She wanted to write about Daniel, but she couldn't. Everything she felt about him was impossible to put into words. Most of all, it was sad. They had this nice thing, it was so special, and so good having someone to kiss and go for walks with and hold you, but it was like it didn't exist, really. Not in the real world. Daniel didn't have a real world. Whatever odd limbo he existed in did not properly touch her realm of school and home and family. He was floating out there somewhere, with only a vague past that she hardly knew about, a fragile present, and no future. In Katie's imagination a boyfriend, someone that you felt really serious about, had always been someone like yourself, from the same background, maybe at the same school. A Russell Tucker type. Someone on the same trajectory, someone your friends and family knew about. You became an item, went out to the pictures and so on, moved in the same circle of friends, and the thing either went somewhere, or it didn't, according to the rules and conventions governing boy–girl relationships.

But this was nothing like that. She couldn't imagine saying to her parents, 'I've got a boyfriend,' and presenting them with Daniel. They would look at him and think he was . . . Katie's mind failed her. Well, what was he? She had only ever cared about who he was, but that wouldn't be enough for other people. It wasn't enough for Georgina, who despised him. Not that Ryan was anything to write home about. He kept talking about getting himself a job, but he never did. He was a waste of space. But Daniel wasn't. Katie knew he wasn't.

There was a light tap at the door, and her mother came in.

'Come on, now,' said Jenny, bending down to kiss her. 'Time your light was out.'

Katie dropped her diary and her pen and impulsively put her arms up to hug her mother as she bent over her. Jenny smiled at her in surprise. She gazed at Katie, trying to fathom her. She had seemed happier over the last few weeks, but still had her bouts of black sulkiness. They held one another tight for a few seconds, then Jenny straightened up.

'See you in the morning.' She left the room, closing the door behind her. Katie lay back on her pillow and tried to imagine the future, wondering what she and Daniel were going to do, ever.

For over two months Alan had been trying to work out the best way of telling Carla about Imogen. A moment's spare space in the day would find him devising strategies for introducing the subject, working out ways of saying it, but he always finished up at a loss. At the end of one long and involved curriculum meeting between himself and Olive Draycott, he had looked up at Olive, at those kind, muddy eyes, and wondered whether he could put the problem to her in a hypothetical fashion. She was good at sorting out things, advising people how to handle matters. But his courage failed him. What if she guessed? What if she realized that he was talking about himself? She probably would. Women had a way of divining these things.

One evening, after a glass of whisky, Alan resolved that he would do it, that he would sit Carla down, say that he had something important to tell her, and just come out with it. But when she came into the room, and Alan said, 'Have you got a minute?' she merely picked up the car keys and said, 'I'm going to my aerobics class with Maeve, and I'm already late. Can it wait till I get back?' She lied casually and easily these days, not much caring if Maeve were to ring up in the next hour, uncovering her deception. She would do anything to snatch just forty-five stolen minutes with Peter.

The front door slammed. Alan went to the window and parted the curtains, watching as Carla ran down the path to the car. She was always moving in that brisk, light way these days. She had lost the brooding air she had had a few months ago, but she seemed no less remote. More cheerful, but still on another plane. Alan couldn't work out the vagaries of her moods. She seemed to have completely lost interest in sex, was always making excuses. That was another thing he felt they should discuss. That and Imogen. Alan sighed and glanced at his watch. This aerobics class seemed to be a regular thing, once a week. As though she needed it on top of all the tennis she played. She wouldn't be back now until half seven. He wondered whether she'd left him anything to eat.

In the fridge he found a microwaveable tuna and pasta bake from Sainsbury's. He stabbed the plastic film with a fork, shoved it in the oven on the correct setting, and thought about Imogen. All right, he still hadn't told Carla, but that was no reason why he shouldn't go up to town and see Imogen, take her to lunch. He'd only spoken to her twice on the phone since the strange night she had come to call, and they should be getting to know one another. She would be going to America in June. Funny how easy it had been, talking to her on the phone. When he'd called her the first time, just after the holidays, he had felt some trepidation. The glow of that boozy, dope-laden evening together had faded. In retrospect it had an air of unreality. She was, in theory, a stranger. But she didn't feel like one. It wasn't as though those twenty-three years of absence didn't exist, nothing like that, but talking to her was so simple, so natural. He supposed the answer was that they liked one another, they wanted to know one another. He felt a strange, creeping sense of warmth at this thought. The microwave beeped and broke his reverie, and he found that he was smiling.

His mind made up, he went into the hall. He fished his address book from the pocket of his jacket, hanging on the hall stand, and rang her number. Her flatmate answered. When Imogen came on the line she sounded pleased to hear his voice. They talked for a little while, and then she asked, 'When are you coming up to London to see me?'

'Funnily enough,' replied Alan, 'that's why I'm ringing. I thought I might come up next Saturday. How does that sound?'

'It sounds excellent.' He could hear in her voice that she was smiling.

They made their arrangements, and then Imogen asked, 'Have you told Carla about me?'

Alan hesitated. 'No, not yet. I know I should have, but somehow there never seems to be a right time. I was going to talk to her this evening. I'd given myself some Dutch courage –'

'Yes, I have seen what a bit of whisky does for you.'

He liked that, the faint reproof, jokey, daughterly. It made him smile. He felt like someone's father. That was what she made him feel. That was what was so good.

'– but she was on her way out. So the moment passed. As all my moments seem to, somehow.'

'Well, I suppose it's up to you, all that. I'm just glad I'll be seeing you at the weekend.'

When he hung up, Alan wondered what excuse he was going to make to Carla about going up to London. Perhaps that would push him to it. He didn't like being evasive at the best of times, so perhaps the business of having to make an excuse would force him to explain to her. He would see. He would come to that. He went back into the kitchen to eat his tuna and pasta bake.

Carla stood at the window of Peter's flat and looked down on to the dark street. Peter came through from the kitchen in a pair of baggy cords and a T-shirt, his feet bare, carrying a glass of red wine and a beer. He put them down on the table and settled himself on the sofa.

'Come and have your drink.'

Carla didn't turn round. She continued to stare at the cars hissing through the rain. 'Do you ever wonder,' she asked, 'what lies in the future?'

He knew where this was going. She didn't often go off on this tack, but when she did, he had to be on his guard. Perhaps being flippant would steer her away from a serious course.

'Only up to a point. Only up to next Wednesday, say.'

'Why?' She turned and looked at him. 'Why next Wednesday? What's happening?'

He frowned for a second, then realized that he had managed to divert her, but not in the way he had intended. 'Nothing. It was a joke. Well, not a joke as such –'

'Oh.' She came and sat down next to him, nestling against him. 'I thought maybe you were going away somewhere.' He said nothing, drank some of his beer. 'I dread that, you know. That's what I meant about the future.' There was silence for a few seconds. 'I mean, I suppose you will have to go away at some time.' There was emptiness in her voice.

She stroked the back of his hand, watching the way the tendons and muscles slipped and moved beneath his young skin. She loved the smell of him, especially after they had made love. Say it, please, her mind beseeched. Say not without me.

But all Peter said was, 'I suppose so.' He glanced at his watch. Twenty past seven. Manchester United were playing Barcelona in the European Champions League that night, and the kick-off was at half seven.

'When? When do you think you'll ever go away?' She sat up and reached for her glass, turning to look at him.

Peter felt suddenly exasperated. He ran a hand through his curling hair. 'God, I don't know. I've only been here five months. And I'm not likely to last much longer if anyone gets wind of us.'

'Does it worry you?'

'Worry me? Of course it does!' He took another swig of his beer. 'If you want to know, Carla, it's something of a preoccupation. The longer we go on, the more likely it is people are going to find out. People can't carry on affairs in a place like Huntsbridge without *someone* finding out.'

'And what happens then?'

He looked directly at her and said nothing for a long moment. Then his gaze softened. 'I don't know.' He leaned forward and kissed her gently, briefly. As an answer, it would do. If they started exploring the truth now, he would miss the kick-off.

She smiled at him. The way he had said that gave her some hope. It was as though he were saying that they would face it together, whatever happened. It was enough to keep her hoping.

'Listen,' said Peter, rising from the sofa, 'do you mind very much if I switch on the television? There's something I really want to watch.'

She swallowed her disappointment. She so much wanted to talk about *them*, to resolve possibilities, to see more clearly what lay ahead. She wanted to be rid of this sour taste of fear. Above all, she wanted to be able to put a space between Peter and herself, on one side, and Alan on the other. Peter wouldn't let her do that. Everything he said bracketed her with Alan, himself the guilty outsider. She knew that was the wrong balance. I want to belong to him, she thought, gazing at his profile as he concentrated on Des Lynam.

She rose and picked up her coat. 'I have to be going, anyway.'

He glanced at her, then got to his feet. 'Sorry. It's just I really want to watch this –'

She stopped his mouth gently with her hand, then took it away and kissed him.

'When can you come to the house?'

'I don't know. Friday, maybe.'

'Maybe?'

'Jeff Perkins has been off with flu. I may have to take over the lunchtime rugby practice.'

'I'll be at school for a tutorial on Friday morning. Tell me then whether you can make it or not.'

He nodded, and went with her to the front door, where he kissed her again before she left.

Carla went downstairs and walked to her car. She paused

and glanced up at the window of his flat, where, she knew, he would probably be back on the sofa, watching the match, not giving her a thought. She lifted her head and let the rain feather her face for a few seconds, then she drew a deep, shuddering breath, and got into the car.

'Beatrice?'

The year thirteen English class were leaving the room when Olive called Beatrice's name. Bea turned. 'Yes, Miss Draycott?'

'I shouldn't have to remind you, but your *Room with a View* essay is a week overdue. I really must have work handed in on time.' It was unusual to have to pull Bea Rayment up on anything, and Olive found it an effort to take a stern line with one possessed of such ethereal prettiness and gentleness.

'I'm really sorry. I don't know what it is, but I'm having a lot of trouble with it. I think I've got some sort of mental block.'

'A mental block? In what sense? The essay's just about the development of Lucy's character. Now, what kind of a mental block could you develop in relation to that?'

'I don't know. It just seems to be a very hard essay to write. I'm not really sure what's wanted.'

Olive sighed. Beatrice was a competent enough student, but not especially perceptive when it came to character analysis. Perhaps she had simply developed a blind spot in relation to the novel. It happened. 'Well, it's essential that you get to grips with this aspect of the book for A-level. A question is almost bound to come up. Maybe you need some help with the text. What do you think?'

'I think that would be useful.'

'Mmm. The trouble is, I don't know that I have any available time to give you. Mrs Tradescant's timetable is full, and she's not available after school.' She pondered for a few seconds. 'Leave it with me. I'll have a word with Mr Barrett, and see if he can help out.'

She mentioned it to Peter at morning break. 'I suspect she's been struggling with the text since last term, but she's going to have to get the hang of it before summer. She needs someone to go over it with her, but I haven't any free time. I'm too busy as it is. I wondered if you could help.'

Peter hesitated. 'Um – lunchtimes are a bit tricky . . .'

Olive suddenly remembered the conversation with Fiona Mather just before Christmas, how she said Peter had been seen going to the Tradescants' house at lunchtimes. She had never been able to believe it was true, but . . . She thought he coloured faintly as he added, 'I sometimes have to help out with the rugby coaching, and so on.'

'I see. Well, that's a pity.'

'But I could give her some extra tuition after school. I don't know what after-school clubs she's involved in, but I could do – let's see . . . I could see her after school on Tuesdays.'

Olive brightened. 'Oh, well, that would be ideal. It's just a question of taking her right through the text and discussing it with her, make sure she's got the hang of it. It'll probably require no more than two or three sessions. I'll tell her she needn't hurry with the essay. Will you see Beatrice and sort it out with her yourself? Excellent.'

*

Peter caught up with Beatrice ten minutes later, just before her Economics class.

'Miss Draycott says you're struggling a bit with the Forster.'

Beatrice made a face. 'I really don't like it. To be honest, I think it's awful.'

'Well, that's not quite the point, I'm afraid. It's your A-level text. You don't have to like it, but you've got to be able to answer questions on it. Anyway, I can give you some extra help after school, if you want. What about Tuesday afternoons?'

Beatrice nodded reluctantly. Extra work after school was always a drag. Still, it was nice of him to offer. 'Yes, that would be fine. Thank you very much.'

'Right. Pop along to my room next Tuesday about ten past.'

She nodded and moved off, flicking the mass of her red hair behind her shoulder in a characteristic movement. Peter stood for a few seconds, watching her go.

On Friday evening, Carla was lying on the sofa with her legs curled up, sipping her customary glass of wine, watching television. Alan came in with the evening paper and sat down near to her. They sat in silence for a little while, then Alan reached across and caressed one of her legs in the way he often did. It had occurred to him that it might be a good idea to soften her up, so to speak, perhaps kill two birds with one stone – their lack of a sex life, and Imogen. He wasn't sure how he was going to weave the two together, but he would see. Something had to be said before he went up to town tomorrow.

Carla moved her leg away restlessly. 'Alan, I'm not in the mood.'

The predictability of the rebuff irritated him. He just wanted to be close to her. 'I was only stroking your leg, not jumping on top of you. Anyway, you're never in the mood for anything these days. We must be the only couple in Britain who has sex once every three months. If that.'

She sighed. 'I'm sorry. I can't explain it.'

'Hormones.'

'Very possibly.' She hadn't taken her eyes off the television.

Alan sighed inwardly. He'd gone about this in entirely the wrong way. But how was he supposed to talk to her about the fact that they hardly ever made love? Whatever he said, she'd just say she didn't want to talk about it, or that she couldn't explain it. Clearly it didn't matter to her one way or another whether they had a sex life. The omens for discussing anything didn't look very good, and after that little exchange he couldn't see how he was going to introduce the subject of Imogen.

'There's something I want to tell you.' He found himself saying it so suddenly that he surprised even himself.

'What?' She glanced at him with a frown, her voice irritable. The fact was, she was in a foul mood. When Peter had told her that morning that he couldn't see her at lunchtime because Jeff Perkins was still off, she shouldn't have reacted petulantly. She knew it annoyed Peter. But she couldn't help it. She needed him so much that every bit of time he could spare was precious. Now she had a whole weekend ahead of her, without even the assurance that he would come on Monday. Added to which, Mike Rayment had seen her stalking crossly away from Peter, and had murmured to her as she passed, 'Finding the younger members of staff difficult to cope with?' Bastard. She wished she could have slapped his face. His remark had given her a prickle of misgiving, rather like his behaviour at Christmas. Insinuating, knowing, more than just his usual line in lechery. Could anybody know about her and Peter? She didn't see how. Anyhow, the day had been wretched, and she certainly didn't want in-depth conversations with Alan now.

Her response signalled to Alan that this wasn't the time for the great revelation. He hesitated, then merely said, 'I was thinking of going up to London tomorrow. Thought I might have a look at the sales. I still need a new suit.'

'Is that all? From the way you spoke, I thought it was going to be something earth-shattering.' She sipped her wine. For a frightening moment Alan thought she might be considering whether or not to come with him, since he'd mentioned the sales. But she said nothing more, so he flicked the paper open again, feeling both relief and a slight weight of guilt.

The next day, Alan took the train up to London. He met Imogen for lunch in a health-food restaurant near her Notting Hill flat.

'You didn't tell me you were a vegetarian,' said Alan, scanning the menu warily.

'I became one when I was fourteen. It drove Mum crackers. She never knew what to cook for me.'

Alan gazed at her. Fourteen. What had she been like

then? Or at any other age, for that matter? The sudden sense of loss which struck him expanded in a sad, empty space somewhere near his heart. He had missed so much. The knowledge of his daughter was entirely different from any of the theoretical notions he had had when he and Carla had first begun to try for a family, and he now realized, in the person she had become, how much he would have liked to have contributed. Not, he reflected, that he could have made her much better. He loved the upright independence of her, the short-sighted stare from behind her glasses, the messy blonde curls.

They ordered some food. 'Mum used to buy me veggie burgers and revolting things like that, so when I was fifteen I bought a vegetarian cookbook and learned to cook for myself. I'm not bad now, though I say so myself. In fact, I would have made you lunch at the flat, but Ewan, my flatmate, has his boyfriend staying for the weekend, and the place is a mess.'

'I thought gay men were supposed to be tremendously fastidious and houseproud,' remarked Alan. He dug into his artichoke-and-sweet-potato pie and found it much better than he had expected. The thick chunks of poppy-seed bread were quite delicious, too. It was a change from bland school food, and the endless ready-prepared meals that Carla seemed to go in for these days. She hardly ever did any proper cooking now, unless they had people round.

'Huh. That's a myth. When Ewan and I first decided to share, I made the same assumption, thought that he'd like to keep the place clean, and so on. Nothing could be further from the truth. Beer cans and empty curry trays, dirty dishes in the sink, all the stereotypical male mess. Still, it's only for another four months.'

'You're look forward to going to the States, aren't you?' Alan hoped he didn't sound too wistful.

'Yes, I am.' She glanced up at him. 'I will keep in touch, I promise.'

He nodded. 'It just seems rather sad, finding out about you, and then – well, off you go.'

Imogen speared a piece of okra and chewed reflectively. 'You could come and visit me.'

'I might.' He tried to picture himself and Carla flying to the States to visit his daughter. Somehow it didn't work. Not at all. Not in the slightest. He shook his head. 'God, a future. How I envy you. What I wouldn't give to have one of those.'

'Come on, you've got a future. You've got your position as a headmaster, there must still be things you want to achieve.'

Alan finished his pie, wiped his mouth with his napkin and sat back. 'I have eight years ahead of me until I retire. Eight years of pushing paper and pacing round corridors, watching things slip out of my control.' He regarded her frankly. 'I don't want to be what I am. And when I look ahead, my heart sinks. Even when I look beyond that, to when I retire, the whole thing is a blank. I can't see myself. I have no notion of any future for myself.' He raised his eyebrows and sighed. 'The whole thing is quite frightening. One minute you're young and everything is before you, and then suddenly you wake up and find the years have sped by, and you're looking backwards instead of forwards.'

Imogen put down her fork and looked at him crossly. 'That's pathetic. If you don't like what you're doing, find something else to do. You can't just sit there sighing and say that there's nothing left for you. Remember that night I came to your house? You weren't like this. When you told me all about yourself, you weren't talking about some sad old failure.'

'I was drunk. Or stoned. Both.'

'So? Whatever you once were, you still can be. Just because you've turned yourself into a headmaster doesn't mean you have to go on being one. Think back to when you were a young man, about my age, try recapturing some of what you felt then.'

'Ah, but that was then. I'm not the same person. You'll find out someday, how age changes you.'

She shrugged. 'It's your life. You only get the one. As for chances, I believe they're what you make for yourself.'

There was a brief silence. Alan made an effort to smile. 'Well, let's not depress one another. I'd much rather talk about you. Tell me everything you're going to do when you get to the States, where you're going to live, and so on. I want to hear it all. If I can't do it myself, at least I can enjoy it vicariously.'

Carla did her housework, went shopping, dropped in to see Maeve and George, and then came back to the empty house. She made herself a sandwich and some coffee and stood gazing out of the French windows. Thank God Alan had gone up to London for the day. With any luck he might not come back until late evening, if he decided to look up some old friends. He probably would. She knew him inside out, almost knew the very moment in the day when the notion would creep into his mind. The deadly predictability was stifling. How could two people know one another so intimately and still find one another interesting?

She turned to take her empty cup into the kitchen, and as she did so, recollection and realization struck her. Her mind flew back to the piece of paper on the notepad by the phone in the hall, the one she had found after coming back from spending the night with Peter. The woman whose name had been written down in strange handwriting, with a phone number. That was where he had gone. That was whom he was seeing. She had thought the notion of Alan wandering around the sales rather unlikely. She went upstairs and went to the wardrobe. The trousers she had been wearing were hanging there with other clothes waiting to go to the dry cleaner's. She fished in the pocket and pulled out the piece of paper and uncrumpled it. There was the name, Winifred, and a London number. How could she have forgotten about this?

She sat down on the bed and brooded for a while, contemplating the number and wondered whether to ring it. No, that would achieve nothing. But who on earth could this Winifred woman be, and how could Alan have met her? Probably at one of those headmasters' conferences. That was his only opportunity. But if that was so, and she lived in London, when on earth were they seeing one another? There was that night that she and Peter had gone away together, but Carla couldn't think of any other opportunities he might have had. And why on earth had she left her number scribbled on the pad in the hall?

Surely, if he was having an affair, Alan already knew it?

She struggled with the idea of Alan and another woman. It seemed impossible, distasteful. It made her angry. She knew how utterly unreasonable such an emotion was, when she herself was having an affair with a man fifteen years her junior, but reason didn't come into it. Anger was what she felt. She rose from the bed, ravelling up her thoughts, this new knowledge, tucking it all away against the day when it would be useful, when she could do something with it. She didn't know yet what that might be, but she had a fair idea that the moment would present itself.

As she went back downstairs she realized that the thought of Alan's affair had, in some strange way, faintly excited her. She wanted Peter. As the idea grew, she began to feel weak with desire. It was Saturday afternoon, he would long since have finished with the school rugby matches. She would go round, surprise him. He would be pleased to see her, of course he would. She slipped on her coat and left the house. As she reached the car, she hesitated. It was one thing to go to him in the evening, once a week, when it was dark, but in broad daylight, when anyone might recognize her car parked near his flat . . . ? The hesitation lasted only a few seconds. She got in, pulling the door behind her and switching on the ignition. The idea of Alan's infidelity seemed to have precipitated something inside her, like setting a roller coaster in motion. She felt slightly reckless. If the momentum drove them all towards discovery and everything that that might entail, Carla decided that she would welcome it.

But when she reached Peter's flat and pressed the bell, there was no answer. She went slowly back to the car, filled with a sour sense of disappointment. He might be anywhere. When he was away from her, what did she know about him, after all? It was that she hated most, the slipping feeling of despair, lack of control. He might need her physically, but it was her own emotional need of him that was most damning, condemning her to pain.

She drove back home, conscious of how alone she felt.

Alan caught the last train out of Charing Cross and arrived home at midnight. He was surprised to find Carla still up, curled up on the sofa in her nightdress and blue silk robe.

She looked up at him as he came into the living room and he saw from her faintly blurred gaze that she was a little drunk. In her lap she cradled a glass of brandy. She didn't often drink brandy.

'Find anything nice in the sales?'

Alan glanced aside, throwing his keys on to the shelf, covering his guilt. 'They're finished. I don't know why I thought I'd find anything.' He sat down on the sofa near to her, loosening his tie.

'So, what else did you do after the shops closed?' She lifted her chin, her dark hair brushing her jaw, blue eyes narrowed. Her smile was challenging. He wondered how much she'd drunk while he was out.

'I looked up David Martin. Remember David? Head of Languages at Plumstead Comp.'

Carla nodded too vehemently and looked back at the television. 'Oh, David, yes. How was he?'

Alan shrugged. 'Good. He's remarried. Very nice girl

with a strange name. She was only around for a few minutes. Anastasia, something like that . . .' He had meant to tell her all about the conversation he'd had with David, how he'd unburdened himself, told David how disillusioned he was with his job and his life, but he had the feeling Carla wasn't in the mood to pay proper attention. So instead he asked, 'How was your day?' He stretched out his hand, as he had last night, and stroked her bare foot. She didn't pull away. He slid his hand beneath the hem of her nightdress.

'The usual.' She looked at him, assessing him over the rim of her brandy glass, trying to see him through the eyes of another woman. It was oddly arousing, the touch of his hand, knowing that he had betrayed her just hours before. She was drunk, she knew. It made a difference. His hand crept higher, his other arm moved to embrace her, and she allowed it, suffering his kiss without even feeling it. She tried to think about Peter, but couldn't. She let everything that was familiar happen to her, the usual detestation distanced by alcohol. They would make love, and she would suffer it, because at least it would put a stop to his complaining. And besides, there was something in the knowledge that he could come to her from another woman and still want her. Even though it didn't matter in the slightest.

12

At ten past four the following Tuesday, Beatrice went to Mr Barrett for her extra tuition, dutifully taking along her copy of *A Room with a View*. She had tried to re-read it over the weekend, but it was a bore. More than that, it annoyed her, though she couldn't say why. It wasn't that she didn't like Forster; she had read *Maurice* and *Howard's End* and enjoyed them, but something about the character of Lucy Honeychurch got on her wick.

'So,' said Peter, 'where shall we start? What about this essay that you haven't been able to get to grips with? Let's have a talk about that.'

Bea sat there in her drab Taft's uniform, knee-length skirt, dark tights, baggy blue sweatshirt over a white blouse, listening to Mr Barrett and taking down notes, talking over aspects of the book. At the end of half an hour, Peter felt they'd covered the main points.

'Do you think you understand enough to give the essay another shot? Just remember, Lucy's development is fundamental to the book. She starts off as something of a child, and by the end she has acquired a degree of wisdom and maturity. Do you see how Forster uses George and his father, and sets their social position against that of Cecil and his mother, to illustrate how she grows?'

Beatrice nodded, finishing off her notes. Peter paused, contemplating the light in her hair, the slender quickness of her hand as she wrote. She looked up, and he was struck then by the realization that he had been waiting for her to do that, to glance up at him with her clear blue eyes. It washed over him, a very pleasant sensation. Then he saw that she was gazing at him, waiting.

Disconcerted, he looked back at his books and papers. 'Right, then – tackle that essay for Miss Draycott, and for next week . . . let's see –' He scanned the Associated Examining Board's specimen questions '– OK . . . here's one. "To what extent is snobbery a key element in the novel?" Have a think about that for next Tuesday.'

'OK.' She closed her book and gathered up her belongings, then rose. 'Bye. And thanks.'

Her departure was swift and casual. Peter found himself standing in the middle of the room, strangely bereft. He had no idea why he felt so odd, quite unlike himself. He hoped he wasn't catching Jeff Perkin's flu. He strolled to the window and watched Bea as she crossed the quad, thinking of nothing much.

Bea's thoughts, however, were more particular. Throughout the tutorial she'd found that she had had to make a deliberate effort to listen to Mr Barrett, rather than just look at him and think about him. It had begun that night when he had given her a lift home. Pupils weren't meant to feel that way about teachers. But since that evening, and their long, effortless conversation, the invisible barriers that normally existed between a student and a member of staff seemed to have been removed. Her perception of him was altered. She had realized for the first time today that she felt an attraction for him that went beyond the mere fact of his good looks. She liked his sense of humour, the way he laughed, the habit he had of raising his eyebrows when he was about to say something dry, the sound of his voice – it was hard to think of anything that she didn't find pleasing. Apart from that, she had become aware of a connection between them, a warmth and affinity. The simple fact was – and she knew he felt this, too – they liked being with one another.

'You should be going home,' said Daniel. He and Katie sat, or rather lay together on the battered sofa. The flat was empty. Georgina had gone an hour ago, when Ryan had had to leave for the afternoon shift of his new job at the petrol station. The others were out.

'I don't want to. I like lying here with you. I want the rest of the world to go away.'

He shifted his position, put one hand behind his head. 'I know.'

There was silence for a while, then Daniel said, 'It's all going to be different soon. It has to be. I can't stay here for ever. When I came, Phil told the others it was only going to be temporary, and I've been here four months. He hasn't said anything, but I know I'm going to have to go.'

'Where will you go?'

'I don't know. If I could get a job, then . . .' He shrugged.

Katie thought about Daniel getting a job, and couldn't. She tried to imagine him gone, her life going on without him. Everything that lay ahead seemed dark and shadowy. GCSEs in four months. That was real. No getting away from that. She felt cold at the thought. She was struggling to keep up with the work, and most of her teachers were so useless they hardly noticed.

She hugged him suddenly, then put her mouth up to be kissed. She loved kissing him, the sweetness, the softness of it, the way it made her feel. When they lay together like this he would touch her breasts through her school jumper, and it sent giddy warmth throughout her limbs. This was sex, this was the thing beyond all the mechanical stuff they taught you at school about boys and girls. This was the feeling. They stopped kissing and she looked at him. She felt scared about what she was going to ask him, but she needed to.

'Do you ever think about – doing it? Sleeping with me?'

Daniel nodded. 'Yes. A lot.'

She felt excited and afraid, deep in her stomach. 'We could, you know. I mean, if you wanted.' She added, 'I haven't ever done it before.'

'Neither have I.' He looked at her gravely, said nothing for a while. Then he shook his head. 'It would have to be different. It would have to be right. The time, everything. I would want it to be somewhere else, with things being happy. Not when it's all such a mess like this. Me.'

She understood, and felt oddly relieved, yet sad. If there was to be a first time, she knew she wanted it to be Daniel. 'I do love you, you know.' They said this to each other often. They never tired of saying it, or hearing it, bound together by the warmth and joy of the words, the comforting words.

'I know.' He nodded. 'And I love you. It's nothing to do with that.'

'I know.'

They held one another for a few silent moments.

'You have to go,' he said.

Katie sat up. 'I'd better not bunk off on Friday. I think my French teacher is getting a bit funny. I'll come on Saturday.'

'OK.'

When Katie had gone, Daniel rolled himself a cigarette. He should think about making Phil some tea. He'd be home soon. Five o'clock. The picture came into his mind, unbidden. It kept coming around this time of day. His mother in the kitchen. Radio Two in the background, calling to him and asking if he'd had a good day, what would he like for tea.

No, that was when he was younger. It didn't happen now. Wouldn't. They didn't care about him. He'd left home, that was that. He squeezed his eyes tight shut against the tears. After a second he shook his head, as though clearing it, and took another deep drag of his flimsy cigarette. He got up and went into the kitchen to put on the kettle. Soon he would have to start thinking about where he was going next.

On Friday morning, Mike Rayment was unloading some materials from the boot of his relatively new Ford Galaxy when Peter Barrett, arriving late, drove too quickly into the staff car park and crunched the rear lights of Mike's car. It was annoying for both of them. Mike's reaction was to call Peter an effing idiot, followed by a few other insulting epithets, to which Peter responded warmly. The exchange escalated. Only a sense of the indignity of the spectacle of two teachers shoving and punching one another in the car park prevented things from going further.

Weary of the altercation, Peter reached into his car for his books and said, 'I don't want to listen to any more of this. I'll give you a note of my insurers later in the staff room when you've cooled down a bit. You're behaving like an overgrown schoolboy.'

Mike's face reddened even more. 'Jesus, that's rich, coming from a little snot who's banging someone his mother's age.' Peter closed the car door and stood stock still. 'Did you think it was some kind of secret?' Mike was gratified by Peter's unguarded reaction. 'Half the school knows about it. I wouldn't count on keeping this job, if I were you. Not going to look too good on the old C V, is it? Being asked to leave for screwing the headmaster's wife.' Mike slammed the boot of his car closed and walked off across the car park.

Peter glanced round to see if anyone might have over-heard. The car park was empty, there were no faces at any windows. But that didn't matter. If Mike Rayment knew about his affair with Carla, then presumably everyone else did. He locked his car, pausing to examine the crumpled front wing and broken headlight, then made his way into school. And he thought they'd been so discreet. He pushed through the swing doors and walked down the corridor towards the staffroom. A group of pupils barged past him, but he was too lost in thought to notice or reprimand them. Had someone seen him at lunchtime going up the path to the Tradescants' house? It wasn't overlooked, he'd never seen anyone, not once. Had Carla told someone?

From the very first, this affair had been a much bigger thing for her than for him, emotionally. He could just imagine her longing to confide in someone. He groaned inwardly at the thought.

At that moment, by unpleasant coincidence, the door to the headmaster's room opened just as Peter was passing, and Alan stepped out into the corridor. It was a singularly nasty moment for Peter. He stopped, staring at the head.

Alan's expression was troubled. 'I saw you coming in from the car park. Just wanted to have a quick word with you about something. Have you got a moment before assembly?'

Peter nodded, and followed Alan through to his room. Alan closed the door. Peter was aware of his heart thudding.

'Do take a seat.' Alan moved behind his desk, frowning as if searching for a way to say what he had to say. Peter sat down, his books still clutched to his chest.

'Mike Rayment came to see me on Friday evening.' Alan sat down, moved a couple of things around his desk, then looked up directly at Peter. 'He tells me you'd planned to take the fifth-formers to a play in the first week of the summer term, something that involves missing art lessons. The thing is, he's not very happy about it, says too many of them are falling behind with their course work, and it's too close to the mocks.'

Relief flooded Peter, so much so that his limbs relaxed slightly, and two books slid to the floor. Retrieving them, he said, 'Why didn't he come and speak to me about it? The thing's not finalized.' As he spoke, his eyes were scanning Alan's face. No, he couldn't know. He couldn't possibly know, and be sitting here talking in a normal way about the fifth form and some play.

'Well, Mike has his ways of dealing with things. Likes to get matters sorted out from the top, as it were. Is there any way of rearranging the play, finding another date that doesn't clash with art?'

Peter shrugged. 'I'll have to look into it. Possibly.'

Alan nodded. 'Right.' There was silence for a few seconds. 'Everything going all right?' asked Alan. 'Feel you've settled in well?'

'Yes, everything's going pretty nicely, thanks.'

'Good. I hope you've managed to make some sort of social life for yourself. Huntsbridge isn't exactly a lively sort of place.'

'No, no, it's fine.'

Alan nodded some more, then glanced at his watch. 'Time for assembly. I'll let you get off.'

Peter left Alan's room without another word, wondering why he hadn't felt this wretched before. Guilt was easy to stifle – up to a point. And that point was when one was about to be found out. In a school the size of Taft's, if Mike Rayment knew he'd been seeing Carla, then it was only a matter of time until it trickled back, somehow, to Alan.

Olive had been in the ladies' washing her hands when Peter had inadvertently driven into Mike's car. Through the frosted window she had heard the crunch of metal and glass, and then the altercation between Mike and Peter which followed. Every word had been perfectly clear. When it was over she stood by the basin, waiting, not wishing to go out into the corridor in case she should bump into Peter on his way in from the car park. She let a little time slip by, then went to her form room to take the register before assembly.

The ugliness of the phrase Mike had used made it stick in her mind. *Screwing the headmaster's wife.* Ever since that conversation with Fiona, she had hoped that it wasn't true. She had wanted Peter to live up to his image, to be above such casual immorality. Was it because she now looked back on her own pathetic dalliance with Mike Rayment that she viewed such behaviour with repugnance? She earnestly wanted the best for beautiful Peter, not for him to do wanton damage to himself and others by betrayal and deceit. Now she had to accept that Fiona's piece of gossip was true. Mike Rayment had put it bluntly to Peter and she, standing frozen by the window, had heard not one word of denial, just the slamming of car doors and feet walking away. That which had been a rumour was a stark fact.

All through assembly she agonized over it. She glanced around at the faces of the members of staff, wondering who knew and who didn't. Her gaze rested finally on Alan's face as he addressed the school, going through the items of the day. He couldn't know. Those to whom the greatest damage was being done were always the last to know. Perhaps it wasn't too late, maybe she could do something to avert potential disaster. Hadn't Fiona Mather suggested that she should say something to Peter? She was his head of department, after all. But the thought of confronting him was too appalling. Maybe she could just hint at it, indicate to him that his behaviour was being scrutinized, that as a friend she was giving him a friendly warning of the malicious gossip. But even doing that struck her as extremely embarrassing.

Her thoughts turned to Carla. She preferred to think of Carla as taking the devil's part in all this. She was older than Peter, after all. She knew what she was doing. She had probably effectively seduced the poor boy. As a married woman, she should have been able to resist any such temptation. If anybody should be spoken to about this, it should be Carla.

'. . . and finally, could I ask year eight boys who have rugby practice on Tuesdays *not* to leave bags at the entrance to the sports hall, as they get in everybody's way. Thank you.' With these words of dismissal from Alan, the school rose from their seats in a murmuring mass. Olive glanced over at Peter. His normally cheerful, unconcerned expression was replaced by one of dark preoccupation. Perhaps what Mike had said to him would have some effect. He might have the sense to end it by himself. Maybe there was no need for her to speak to either of them. There were those who would say that it wasn't her business, in any event. But these things could be so complex. Perhaps Peter was caught up in something that he couldn't resolve. He was so young. Olive sighed inwardly. Really, as the older and wiser party, it was up to Carla to put an end to this nonsense. Whatever sorry state her marriage might be in, this kind of thing was pure selfishness. Couldn't she see the harm that it was likely to do to Peter's teaching career, to say nothing of Alan's position?

Olive steeled her resolve. As a friend of Carla's it was her duty to say something, to alert Carla to the rumours and the damage that was being done. She would speak to Carla later that morning when she came in to tutor the sixth-formers.

Carla walked the mile and a half to Taft's, absorbed in her thoughts. She knew that she was not happy, she knew the difference between cheerful contentment and the troughs of anxiety mixed with peaks of exhilaration that composed her moods these days. But anything was better than the way she had felt before Peter. Now she lived from day to day. She closed her eyes to the future. She no longer sought purpose or direction in their relationship. She couldn't afford to. The here and now would have to do. She had seen him only once this week, for an all-too-brief and erotic half an hour at lunchtime on Monday. All the rest of this week his free time during the day had been taken up.

She turned in at the gate by the pavilion and walked past the playing fields towards the school. Even from this distance her eyes sought out the familiar lines of Peter's little car in the car park. As she came into school, she met Alan in the corridor.

'Carla, I'm glad I bumped into you.' He grasped her arm lightly, familiarly, above the elbow. She resisted the desire to shake his hand off. 'I won't be in this evening. There's a meeting of department heads, and I'll probably go for a drink afterwards. So don't go to any trouble over supper.' Not that she ever did these days. 'I'll probably grab something at the pub.'

She nodded. 'Fine. I'll see you later.' As she walked away, her heart rose. She would have the evening free for

Peter. She would go and tell him as soon as she'd finished her lesson with the sixth form.

At the end of her tutorial, Carla hurried down the corridor towards C5, where Peter taught the year nines on a Friday, hoping to catch him before he went to lunch. She stood in the corridor until all the pupils had filed out, then slipped into the classroom. Peter was rubbing the blackboard. He turned to look at her, and his heart fell a little. This had to be the beginning of the end. He hadn't rationalized this – lessons had taken up all his attention throughout the morning – but the sight of her now brought it home to him.

Carla closed the door, smiling. 'I wanted to see you on your own for a few minutes.'

Peter glanced at his watch. Pointlessly. He knew the time. It was a gesture, probably the first in a line of prevarications and excuses. 'I've got a departmental meeting in fifteen minutes. I have to get some lunch.'

She shook her head. 'This will only take a few seconds. Alan's going to some seminar this evening. I can come round for an hour or so.'

Peter said nothing for a few seconds. He put down the blackboard duster. 'There's nothing I'd like more, believe me. But we've got some problems, and they have to be faced.'

The tone of his voice caused chilly fingers of fear to pluck at Carla's insides. Her smile faded. 'What do you mean?'

He sighed and leaned against his desk. 'I had a run-in – literally – with Mike Rayment in the car park. I pranged his car and we had an argument. Anyway, the upshot was that he knows about us. Says half the school does. He really enjoyed letting me know, vindictive bastard.' Peter waited, his eyes on Carla's face.

She looked away from him, trying slowly to comprehend this news, to make sense of its implications. Her eyes ranged across the rows of desks and round the walls of the room. So Mike knew. That explained a lot. It took some moments for her turbulent feelings to identify themselves. She realized, to her surprise, that her paramount emotion was one of relief. She was glad that the thing was open and acknowledged, whatever scandal might ensue. But behind that she felt the coldness of fear. What would Peter do? What was he thinking at this minute?

Her eyes met his. 'Good,' she said.

'Good?' Peter stared.

Carla came towards him. 'I'm glad. It means things have to change.' She was close against him, her hands on either side of his face, her breath warm against his skin. He loved the way her breath always smelt of clover, like a child's. 'It couldn't go on the way it has been. Now we find out just how much we really matter to one another.' She kissed him, and he returned it hungrily, helplessly, giving way for a few fervent moments to the strength of his desire. He was so used to having her whenever he wanted, mostly more than once, that he could hardly contain himself. He pulled her blouse apart and thrust his hands inside her bra, almost ripping at it, groping for the softness of her breasts. He felt dizzy with lust.

Then a sudden jolt of clear sense hit him and he pulled

away, breathing hard. 'This is the last place we should be doing this.' He heard feet in the corridor outside and took a few steps away from Carla. 'Quick, do up your blouse.' He put up a hand to push back the curling locks of hair that had fallen over his forehead. He took two deep breaths to try to steady himself, horribly aware of the tell-tale flush on his face.

The door opened and Olive stood in the doorway. She glanced rapidly from Carla to Peter, her face expressionless. Peter looked across at Carla, taking in the evidence of her rumpled blouse, her normally smooth hair slightly fluffed. It was a ridiculous scenario. He felt humiliated by Olive's presence. Everything must be clear to her, if she didn't know already. Her attitude towards him had always been one of maternal kindness and solicitude, and the idea of this dissolving into contempt for him, as it must, was not pleasant.

When Olive spoke, her voice was cool. The fact that she had found them together like this, so evidently *in flagrante*, made her all the more determined to put an end to it, if she could. 'Do excuse me. I just wanted a few words with Mrs Tradescant. Or is this an inconvenient moment?'

Carla began to gather up her books from the desk where she had dropped them.

'Not at all,' replied Peter. 'I was just going to lunch.' He left the room quickly, without glancing at Carla.

Olive closed the door behind him. Carla passed a hand down either side of her hair, as though trying to smooth away her embarrassment. She did not meet Olive's eye. 'Is it going to take very long, Olive? I have a few things

243

to attend to.' Her voice was stiff. She felt acutely the mortification of being chanced upon with Peter in such a way. Whatever she might have said about being glad their affair was out in the open, the immediate situation was not comfortable.

Olive sat down on the edge of one of the desks. 'You needn't look embarrassed, Carla. I know all about what's going on.' There was nothing challenging in Olive's tone. If anything, she sounded a little sad.

Carla muttered something which Olive couldn't hear, then turned and walked to the window, staring out.

'I heard the rumour a couple of months ago, and of course I didn't want to believe it. I didn't want to think that either of you could be so stupid, so reckless.' Olive sighed. 'I came to look for you because I wanted to tell you about the rumours, to warn you, and I find you – well . . . together. Don't you think it's all really very silly, Carla, and cruel, what you're doing?'

There was silence for a few seconds, then Carla turned to look at Olive. 'Cruel? What on earth do you mean by that?'

'To Alan. He hasn't faintest idea, so far as I can tell, and long may it remain that way.'

'Leave Alan out of it. Anyway, what business is it of yours, you interfering old hen?' Carla's anger at the situation which was erupting slipped out of control. Far from being relieved, she now felt a helpless fury that her affair with Peter was no longer their own private domain. How dare Olive lecture her like this?

Olive felt her own temper rise a degree. 'Not only is it cruel to Alan, it's cruel to Peter Barrett. Can't you see the harm you're doing him, and his career? You've taken advantage of his youth and inexperience –'

Carla interrupted this with a derisive laugh. 'His inexperience? Oh, my dear Olive, wouldn't *you* just like to know about that! He's far from inexperienced, believe me. And as for anyone taking advantage, it was really rather the other way around. Peter knows exactly what he's doing. Both of us do.' Carla hesitated fractionally before adding, 'Do you think his career is really more important to him than what we have together?'

Olive caught the hesitation. She looked back at Carla and glimpsed the uncertainty lurking behind the anger in her eyes. She said nothing for several seconds, letting the silence develop, adding weight to what she had to say. 'What do you think?' she asked quietly. 'He's twenty-seven, Carla. Everything has just begun for him. Whatever he feels for you, he knows that. So do you. You're . . . what? – forty-two, forty-three? Where do you imagine he's going to be in ten, fifteen years' time? With you?'

Carla felt the bare truth of this, and tried to defend herself from it with another storm of anger. 'What do you know about our feelings for one another? Do you have the first idea of what real love is like? Of course not! I imagine the nearest you've ever come to it is a bit of a fling with Mike Rayment.' Olive stared at Carla, horrified. 'Did you think I didn't know about that? He's not a great one for discretion, is our Michael, especially when he's had a few drinks. He told me about you and him three years ago. Must have had the mistaken idea that jokes about his past sexual conquests would add to his appeal. Far from it, I can assure you. So you're not exactly blameless, are you? Don't come giving me moral lectures, Olive! Just stay out of it!'

Carla left the room in a passion. Olive remained where she was, seated on the edge of a desk. So now she knew. Mike had joked about her to Carla, probably to others. Their brief intimacy, in spite of the guilt and the faint sordidness, had always been pathetically precious to Olive. No man had ever made her feel physically desired the way he did, even in the confines of a paint store. Of course, she had known that Mike Rayment would physically desire anything in a skirt, but she had never had to confront that truth so baldly until now. Perhaps Carla was right. She was in no position to judge others. And maybe whatever Peter and Carla's affair consisted of was more than she imagined, strong enough to endure the storm which, inevitably, was brewing.

It seemed to be Olive's day for heart-to-heart talks. That afternoon she kept Katie behind after double English to speak to her about her work. She told her that, as her form mistress, she'd noticed a slipping in standards, and that her subject teachers were concerned about the state of her course work.

'It's not as though you've found things a struggle in the past. You're a very bright girl, Katie, so I simply don't understand why you're letting things go like this, particularly in your GCSE year. Is there anything troubling you that you'd like to tell me about?'

Katie shook her head and bit her lip. When she had conversations like this with her mum, the same thing happened. A million and one thoughts would be whirling around in her head, but she could voice none of them. All she could do was stand mute and apologetic, longing to get away, painfully aware of the disappointment she caused, helpless to explain.

'Would some extra tuition help, do you think? If you're having problems with your English course work, maybe Mr Barrett could find you some free time. He's helped a few people after school hours.'

Katie shrugged. 'Maybe. I don't know.' She knew that Miss Draycott expected more of a response in return for her concern, so she gave her a contrite look and added, 'I'm really sorry, Miss Draycott. I know I haven't been doing my best. I promise I'll try to do better.' It was simply a matter of saying what the old dear wanted to hear. Katie just wished Miss Draycott wasn't so sympathetic and mumsy. If she carried on being this nice, looking at her with those big, concerned eyes, Katie had the feeling she might easily burst into tears and tell her everything. Only it wasn't that easy at all. Nothing was.

'Well, let's hope that we see an improvement in things. You have it in you to do very well, dear. Don't throw it away, especially not in such an important year.'

'No. All right. Thank you.'

Katie took her books and left the classroom, just glad to be away, stuffing the guilt and worry to the back of her mind, and went in search of Georgina. Olive watched her go, musing on the apparently mutually satisfactory conclusion of their conversation, knowing in despair that they hadn't even touched upon the truth, whatever it was. These teenage girls were impenetrable, their woes and preoccupations hidden deep within them, far behind the sullen expressions and mouthed platitudes of obedience. She would simply have to try and keep a closer eye on the girl, try to see if she could help her pull her socks up a little. If there was one thing that Olive hated, it was the waste of a good mind.

Carla arrived at Peter's flat a little after seven. All day Peter had been trying to formulate ways of telling her that their affair should end, dreading the idea of a scene, unable to imagine any way of avoiding it. He half hoped that she might have come to the same conclusion, that her own realization of the inevitable would help to let her down lightly. What alternative had they but to bring things to a halt, now that people were starting to talk? It was disarming, therefore, to find that she came to him, smiling, warm, as though the events of the day had changed nothing. She embraced him, kissing him for a long moment. 'God, I've been wanting you all day . . .'

He pushed her gently from him. 'Carla, listen, we have to talk. Come on, sit down. I'll get us both a drink.'

He returned with two glasses of wine and handed one to Carla, who had taken her coat off and was sitting on the sofa. Her eyes looked very large, her expression nervous. Peter sat down at the other end of the sofa, keeping a distance between them. She waited for him to speak, but he said nothing, merely ran his fingers through his hair and stared at his glass.

'What is it you want to talk about?' asked Carla at last.

Peter looked up abruptly. 'I've done nothing all day but go over and over what Mike Rayment said. That, and

Olive coming in and finding us together. God.' He closed his eyes briefly. 'What did she say after I left?'

'That she knew – that she'd heard gossip from Fiona Mather as long ago as Christmas . . . oh, do we have to talk about this?' Carla's voice was tight, impatient.

'Of course we do,' said Peter sharply. 'It matters. It matters very much to both of us.' He paused. This was the moment. It had to be said. 'In fact, Carla, I don't see how we can go on.'

She stared at him, a horrid sick, sinking feeling inside her. She struggled against it. 'Peter, don't say that. I don't want us to end. Please.' She put out a hand and laid it over his, her voice intent. 'Remember what I said earlier – this is where we find out just what we mean to one another.'

There was a long silence. 'Well, that's just it, isn't it?' said Peter at last.

'What do you mean?' She heard her own voice coming as though from a distance, dry and thin. Her eyes were fastened on his, but he would not look at her. He raised his shoulders and spread his hands in the juvenile cop-out gesture. She had never seen him do anything that made him look so young.

'It doesn't matter that much to me. I don't want to hurt you, Carla, but I never wanted anything more than a casual affair. I thought you were the same. If we go on, Alan is bound to find out, and I don't want that. I like the guy. I don't want him to be hurt, and I don't want to get myself and my career into a hellish mess. I know that sounds selfish, but there are priorities for both of us. If it stops now, then there's nothing for people to talk about. No substance. No pain for anyone.'

No pain. Carla could hardly believe he had said that. The sense of panic that gripped her was so physical that she actually felt herself begin to tremble. He couldn't end it. She couldn't bear it if she didn't have him. Her life would be empty, black. Her mind was racing, frantic, and she had to swallow hard, willing herself to be calm. Gently, gently, there was a way of handling this, there must be. It meant more to him than he was admitting. Even if it was only about sex for him, she knew that must be true.

Now he turned to look at her, his expression fixed. 'It's the best thing to do, Carla. I just think we should call it a day now, before things get out of hand. It's been good. We've had a great time.'

What children said when they'd been to the pictures and McDonald's, thought Carla. Her hand was still on his; she clasped the unresponsive fingers. Their inertness chilled her. 'Please, Peter. Don't make it so final.' Her voice was low as she struggled to keep her words calm. 'If you end it now, I don't think I can bear it. I can see why you're afraid –'

'It's not that –'

'Please – let me finish. I can see why you're afraid of gossip. I don't want a scandal either. Believe me.'

'Look, Carla, you said today that you were *glad* people knew. You said it meant things have to change. Well, that's true. They have changed. Surely you must see that we can't go on seeing each other. If you don't want a scandal, then there's no alternative.'

'Yes, yes, I see that – for the present. I just can't bear the thought of ending it completely.' Her words were rapid, anxious; her eyes scanned his face with hope. He read their desperate expression. 'Let's give it a month – two months, if you like. We won't see one another, won't give anyone grounds for speculation. The gossip will die away, believe me. But please, please –' Her hand clasped his insistently. '– let's not make it so final.' He stared at the floor, saying nothing. 'Please, Peter.'

He shook his head. 'I don't know.' But he wondered whether it much mattered. He hated seeing the rawness of her need, hearing the desperation in her voice. He had never meant to make her love him – that had never been the deal. But she did. He knew that. It mattered to her in a way he had never intended. He could have seen it coming months ago. He should have ended it then. Would it hurt her if he pretended to compromise? He had already decided, this very afternoon, that he was packing this job in at the end of the summer term. He was only on a temporary contract, anyway. In just three months he would say goodbye to Taft's, Huntsbridge, Carla – the lot. Why put her through agony if he could postpone it?

He sighed. 'All right. Let's see how things go. We'll just cool it for the time being. But as of tonight, we don't see one another. Right? No phone calls, nothing.'

She nodded. Reprieve. The pain that had tightened around her heart loosened a little. The idea of not seeing him for weeks on end was wretched, but at least it wasn't final. There was even the possibility that not seeing her for two months would change things in her favour, that . . . Her mind slowed, stopped. There was no point in any of that. She must just live with the situation.

The silence stretched between them. At last, wishing

she was strong enough not to ask, feeling naked, pathetic in her need, Carla said, 'Do you want me to stay?'

'I don't think so,' replied Peter. 'I couldn't. I'm not in the mood. Not after what happened today. It's made me see how stupid –'

'OK, OK,' said Carla gently, stopping him, afraid that if he said any more he might persuade himself out of the delicate compromise she had just engineered. She set down her glass and stood up, picking up her coat. She bent down and kissed Peter softly on the lips. 'Call me when you can.'

He heard the door close, and her feet on the stair, and sat back against the sofa, closing his eyes in guilt and relief. It didn't matter what she believed. Let her. As far as he was concerned, it was over.

13

Three weeks later the weather suddenly lifted, the rawness of March was transformed by an earthy lightness gladdening the air, bringing promise of better things. On Tuesday morning, Peter walked from the flat to his car and felt the faint, fresh warmth kindle his spirits. He noticed for the first time that the lawn next to the playing fields was dotted with crocuses, and found himself remembering, with pleasure, that he had a tutorial with Beatrice at ten past four that afternoon. All day he was in an unnaturally good mood.

Beatrice arrived five minutes late, apologetic. While she sat and read out her essay to him, Peter found himself incapable of sitting still, but paced round the room, listening, pausing to watch her occasionally. Outside, the air was filled with clear, dewy sunshine.

When she had finished he perched on the edge of a desk, one foot swinging. 'Very good. That remark of Mrs Vyse's about Lucy becoming wonderful, one of us – did you pick that up yourself, or was it something I mentioned last week?'

She shook her head. 'You didn't mention it.'

'In that case, well done. I think you could have said more about Mr Beebe, but he's a big subject, and we'll tackle him separately. Now, we were going to discuss Cecil this week, weren't we? I've forgotten what the essay title was.'

'It was about whether as a reader you developed any sympathy for Cecil.'

'That's it.' Peter stood up, still restless, and paced to the window. 'Well, did you?'

She turned her head to follow him, chin on one hand, and gazed at him as he leaned against the window ledge, hands in his pockets. The sunshine touched his hair, the curve of his cheek. She was happy simply being here in this room with him, talking. 'Yes, I did. I mean, you really dislike him as a character, compared to George, say, or Freddie, but you can't help feeling sorry for him. I think it's when Lucy tells him she doesn't want to marry him that he suddenly becomes sympathetic.'

'Yes, he comes out of that well, doesn't he? You suddenly see him in a much better light than before.'

'I thought it was rather noble, the way he accepted his own shortcomings, and a bit sad. But I can't help feeling –' Beatrice stopped.

'What?'

'I know this sounds stupid, and it's only a book, but don't you feel that, well, things might have been different if only Cecil hadn't messed up the business of kissing her?'

'In what way?' At the mention of kissing, Peter found that his eyes had moved to Bea's lips, parted in the framing of her question.

'I mean, if he had kissed her properly.' He noticed that she had blushed slightly.

'Why do you think he didn't? They were engaged, after all.'

She shrugged. 'He didn't know how. No – I mean, he

couldn't. That thing that Lucy said about Cecil not being able to know anyone intimately.'

'That's right.'

'Whereas with George it was completely different –' She broke off, smiling. 'Actually, I think that's my favourite passage in the book.'

'Which?' He still leaned against the window, eyes fastened on her face, thinking that when she smiled, it was as miraculous as the March sun breaking through the spring clouds.

'The part where she falls into the field and he kisses her.'

'Why don't you read it out?'

She flipped through the pages and found the passage, and began with mild self-consciousness to read. He gazed at her bent head, and in that moment, in a rush to his senses, came the idea of what it would be like to kiss this girl, to take her in his arms. He felt heat touch his limbs. He pushed himself away from the window ledge and began to walk round the room again. She was still reading, but he could hardly hear. When he looked back at her, it happened again, a delirious sensation filling him.

'. . . *the silence of life had been broken by Miss Bartlett, who stood brown against the view.*' Bea stopped reading and closed the book, and looked up at him.

For a few long seconds they simply regarded one another in complete silence. Then Peter nodded, and spoke to restore the equilibrium. 'It's very good, isn't it?' His mouth felt dry. He had no idea what to make of his feelings. He wondered what she was thinking, and whether he was mistaken in the expression of her eyes, and the faint colour in her cheeks. He shouldn't be thinking this, he told himself. He shouldn't even allow the idea to enter his head. But he couldn't help it. He raked his mind for a few apposite remarks on the subject of sympathy for Cecil, made them, succeeded in expanding upon them, and so brought his mind back down to earth.

'OK . . .' He glanced at his watch. 'So for next week, have a think about Mr Beebe . . . Where did I put that question sheet?'

Beatrice reached out to the pile of papers next to her. 'It's here.' She handed it to Peter and her fingers brushed his. The effect of it, the significance, astonished and appalled him.

'Thank you.' He looked down quickly at the sheet. 'Right, here we are . . . "*What do you think about Forster's presentation of Mr Beebe? Consider: Mr Beebe's reactions to some key events in the novel, Mr Beebe's attitude to people and ideas, and whether he is just a stereotype of a clergyman.*" That's enough to be going on with.' He watched as Bea scribbled this down, and found himself imagining what it would be like to touch her hair with his fingers, draw them slowly down through the long curls, picturing the way it would bring her chin up, her eyes to his . . . 'Don't do an essay, just some notes.'

She nodded, gathered her things together and stood up. He crossed to the door and held it open for her, waiting for her to pass through just so that he could feel her proximity for the briefest of seconds.

'Thanks, Mr Barrett. Goodnight.' She went out.

'Beatrice –' Bea stopped in the corridor and turned.

He had been about to ask her to call him Peter. He very much wanted her to. But he didn't. It wasn't appropriate.

'Nothing.' He shook his head. 'Forget it.'

She said goodnight again. He closed the door and walked over to the window, waiting for her to appear from the main door and cross the quad. He followed her with his eyes, knowing exactly now what it was he felt.

All evening, Peter thought about Beatrice, reliving those moments of being with her, until the recollection of her very features became frustratingly indistinct. In assembly the next morning he sought her out, and kept glancing at her face now and then throughout those fifteen minutes just to savour the extraordinary rush of feeling. Each glimpse he caught of her during the day, through the window of the IT room, or strolling from the lunch hall with friends, was an electric moment. That pale profile, the way her mouth moved, framed words and curved in occasional smiles, her hand lifting to push back her hair. He could hardly think of her as a schoolgirl. She would soon be eighteen, after all, and she was exceptional. How was it that he had never seen it before?

For Beatrice, much the same thing had happened. But she had no idea what to make of the situation. On the morning of the tutorial, she had heard her father indulging in some mild rant against Peter, and had been surprised by the sense of antagonism and protection it kindled in her. She knew that she more than liked Peter Barrett. That was easy enough. He was young and good-looking, and everyone got crushes on teachers now and again. But to have those feelings reciprocated, to meet his eye and feel the shock of their complete unity of feeling was something she didn't know how to handle.

The week passed, and in the consciousness of each the significance of next Tuesday began to grow. Beatrice was studious in avoiding Peter's eye whenever they passed in the corridor, though she could feel his gaze as though it were a kind of warmth. She felt an extraordinary gladness when he was nearby, whether in the brief quarter-hour of morning assembly, or emerging from a classroom just when she came out of another. The rest of the day, those long spaces between glimpses of him, seemed empty and monotonous. The way these feelings had grown in her both excited and unnerved her. She spent hours in the library taking down notes, trying to frame sensible answers to the questions he had set her.

When Tuesday came, the hours leading up to four o'clock possessed little significance for Peter. He taught lessons mechanically, could eat scarcely anything at lunch-time, and wanted to talk to no one. The strength of his infatuation bewildered him. He had never felt so strongly about anyone. It was, he told himself, simply because of the unnaturalness, the impossibility of the situation. The allure of the unattainable. Besides, he didn't know her properly. It was easy to be in love with someone when you didn't know them, and could still weave all kinds of romance about them. All week he had tried to focus on the reality of his position, to suppress his feelings by telling himself that she was merely a sixth-form student whom he happened to find remarkably attractive. He was a teacher, she was a pupil, and that trust shouldn't be broken. He was determined to contain the situation. Crossing the quad just after lunch, he glimpsed Carla coming along the path by the playing fields and had to double back behind the science block to avoid her. He had spent the last few weeks keeping well out of her way, dreading any encounter and the guilt it would produce. But the mere sight of her was enough. It reinforced his determination. After his affair with Carla, and the way he had misled her, there was something faintly indecent in allowing himself to indulge his feelings for a sixth-former. And what about that day back in October, when he had sat at lunch in the Tradescants' house, roundly condemning relationships between teachers and pupils? He must be mad even to let himself think this way.

Beatrice found Peter sitting at the desk in his form room, marking exercise books at the end of afternoon lessons. The day had been as long for her as it had been for him, and her heart was thudding as she sat down. He glanced up briefly, and she felt immediately conscious of the remoteness of his mood. She had no idea of the reason for it, and was aware of a sense of flatness and disappointment.

'I'll just finish these. Won't be a moment.' He wrote for a few seconds, closed the last book and placed it on top of the pile. 'OK. Let's get going. Tell me all about Mr Beebe.'

The tutorial, thus begun, carried on in a brisk, business-like manner. Peter asked questions, Bea answered them. The animation and interest of the previous week had entirely fled. Each avoided the other's gaze, and the space between them seemed infinite. She felt he longed to be elsewhere, and to him it seemed that her participation in the tutorial was wooden and unenthusiastic. Peter felt puzzled and depressed. At one point he walked to the window while she talked in response to some question of his, and as he looked out he suddenly realized the source of his dissatisfaction. He didn't want to be doing this. Perhaps she didn't either. In ten minutes the tutorial would be over, the last hour he would spend alone with her before the end of term on Friday, and here they were, slogging away at some wretched book, squandering the moments with bald literary discussions. But what else could they do? What did he expect? He struggled to revive his earlier feelings of self-condemnation. He shouldn't want her to return his feelings. But he did. And he knew she did. As she stopped speaking, he turned from the window. When their eyes met, he had that extraordinary sensation of their thoughts being carried on some common current. It was bewildering, exhilarating. He couldn't take his eyes from hers. It was the first time this afternoon that they had actually allowed themselves just to look at one another without speaking, without avoidance or mild embarrassment. He thought of all the things it was possible to do and say within the space of this moment, alone with her. It was as though she was waiting.

I can't do this, thought Peter.

He took his eyes from hers and walked to his desk. 'OK, that's good. I think we'd better call it a day now.' He put together the papers on his desk and picked up the pile of exercise books. When he looked up again she was putting on her coat. He resisted the temptation to help her. He mustn't go near her, mustn't touch her. As if to confirm and remind himself of the professional nature of the relationship, he added, 'How do you feel about the book now? D'you think the tutorials have been a help?'

She nodded, and he wondered if her eyes didn't look unnaturally bright. She said nothing as she put her books in her bag. Then she smiled and said, 'It's been a great help. Really. Thanks very much, Mr Barrett.'

As she moved towards the door, Peter stayed by his desk, pretending to look for something. When he looked up she was gone. The room, the very air, felt dead and blank. As did Peter. So much for principles.

He put out the lights and went out, walking along the echoing corridor past the science block towards the side door to the car park. He said goodnight to the groundsman as he made his way to his car. He chucked his books into the back seat, got in and put the key in the ignition. Then he sat there, doing nothing. He stared straight ahead. All he could think was that he should be with her. She was somewhere, maybe walking to the bus stop, and she was on her own, and that was not how it was meant to be. He thought of her eyes as she looked at him, the moment he had wasted. For the first time in his life he was in love, and he was doing nothing about it. God, he was a fool. He sat for a few more numb seconds, then took the key from the ignition and got out. He walked across the car park towards the gate, his pace quickening, his raincoat flapping in the March wind. He saw her walking out of the gate and he broke into a run. As he came up to her and she turned, he was suddenly conscious of the way the wind rocked the tree tops and the high call of the rooks across the playing fields. He didn't care what he was at that moment. Being a teacher meant nothing.

They faced one another, and for a few seconds his mind was lost in confusion. 'I'm sorry,' he said at last. 'I'm sorry for letting you go like that. I haven't said anything I wanted to say. You know why.'

'Yes.' He marvelled at the expression in her eyes. It wasn't enquiring, or expectant, but totally pacific and accepting.

'The thing is, I can't not tell you. I mean, I have to – I have to –' He stopped, and looked up at the trees in despair. 'God, I don't know what to tell you.' He looked back at her. She gave a tentative smile, and suddenly he felt entirely certain, and could say it. 'I'm in love with you. It's as simple as that.'

She nodded. Something rose in her throat that prevented her from speaking. All she could do was nod, wondering why this didn't seem peculiar, why it wasn't anything like a teacher coming on to you. It was him, and he felt the same way, and she felt frightened and happy.

He gave a little laugh. 'Right. OK. I've said that.' He looked at her helplessly. 'Do you want to go somewhere? Talk?'

She nodded again. 'All right.'

He glanced up and down the road. 'I'll go and get my car. Walk up to the next block and I'll pick you up.'

He hurried back to his car, feelings in turmoil. This was exactly what he had promised himself he would never do. It was more than inappropriate. It was wrong. Just as his affair with Carla had been. Carla. That had been the beginning of his unprofessional career at Taft's. But that affair was dead and gone. Compared to what he felt about Beatrice, it was nothing. It was all in the past. His footsteps slowed. Christ, what was he thinking of? How could he even think of starting something with this girl, when just three weeks ago he had been conducting an adulterous affair with the headmaster's wife? Some ideas of unworthiness crept into his mind. He got into the car and drove slowly to the gate. What he had done had been bad enough. This was worse, far worse. He stopped at the gate. He could easily drive away now, stick to his principles. He glanced to his left and saw her, still walking in the other direction. Go on, he thought to himself, go right, drive home and forget this. But he turned the wheel slowly left and drove to meet her.

She got in and closed the door. He gave her a quick smile and set off. He didn't speak. After a while she asked, 'Where are we going?'

'I don't know.' Peter glanced out absently at the bleak outlines of a retail park, a housing estate beyond. It was a depressing scenario, but at least they were away from town, and from Taft's. He stopped the car. There was silence, just the slow sound of the engine ticking as it cooled.

Peter turned to her. 'I had to tell you how I felt. I couldn't just let you go without knowing. Somehow it seemed important.' He leaned his head back and sighed. 'Maybe I shouldn't have.'

'Why?' She turned her candid, blue gaze on him. He felt lost. How he loved her. Without even knowing her properly, he loved her.

'Because it's no good. Because I'm your teacher, and teachers don't do these things. That's why it would have been better if I'd stuck to my principles and said nothing.'

He paused. 'I nearly drove off in the other direction when I got to the school gate.'

There was silence for a few seconds, then Beatrice said, 'Can you imagine how I would have felt if you had done that?'

He looked at her quickly and saw that her eyes were bright, the way they had been in the classroom. 'How?' He felt he scarcely dared breathe.

'Lost. Completely lost.'

He leaned across and kissed her, and felt that it was as wonderful as though he'd never kissed anyone in his life before. He touched her hair, stroked it, gazed into her eyes, then kissed her again. They sat, holding one another for a while. And then they began to talk. They talked for a long while, till the light in the sky was ebbing, and the looming shadows of the retail park deepening, utterly absorbed in one another.

The time crept towards half past six.

'I don't want to let you go,' said Peter.

'I know.'

'I wish –' He stopped and looked out at the gathering dusk. 'There's no point in wishing that.' Silence for a while. 'There are some things I have to tell you. Not now. It's too late. Anyway, I don't want to spoil this. What I have to tell you may change your mind about me.'

'It couldn't.'

He thought of Carla. They couldn't go on without her knowing about that. 'Don't be too sure.' Then he looked back at her and smiled, touching her hair, then her face. '"Then there was a star danced, and under that were you born." A slight misquotation, but apt. And if you don't know where that's from, you should. Look it up. Come on, I'll drive you home.' Home. He thought of Mike Rayment, and what he would say if he knew about this.

They drove back and Peter parked round the corner from Bea's house. He kissed her again, and then said, 'We can't meet until the Easter break. I'll call you.'

'Four days.'

'Four days. Not so long as from last Tuesday until today. That was when I knew – last Tuesday. When did you?'

'Then.'

They smiled at one another in young and perfect happiness.

'I've worked it out,' said Alan. 'We'll park in Ashford and catch the train there. Makes more sense than going all the way into Waterloo.'

He and Carla were having supper in the kitchen. Coq au vin. Carla had started cooking again, he'd noticed. Her enthusiasm seemed to come and go, for some reason – possibly temperamental. She had seemed a bit tired and run-down recently, but maybe this weekend break in Paris would cheer her up. It would be an opportunity for them to discuss some important things – Imogen, for a start. He couldn't leave it any longer to tell her. He saw this Parisian holiday as a kind of watershed. He hoped things would be discussed between himself and Carla which would bring about a kind of rejuvenation. Of everything. He had already begun to form vague ideas of a change in career, and he hoped that discussing it with Carla would help solidify things. Not that he had any clear ideas of

265

what that change might be. He had toyed with the idea of becoming a schools inspector, but the thought of having anything more to do with schools was stultifying. He wanted a complete change of direction. Not that that was easy at fifty-two. Maybe Carla would help him think of something.

These musings caused him to glance across at her hopefully, thoughtfully. Carla met his gaze.

'What?'

'I was just thinking that we might try to use this holiday as – oh, I don't know . . . a base from which to work out new plans for ourselves. I don't think you've been happy in Huntsbridge this last year or so. I'm not exactly enchanted with it. We should start thinking about the future.'

'Yes.' Carla spoke blankly. She prodded her food with her fork, ate some, then drank off her wine and refilled her glass and Alan's. She could not even bear to think about the trip to Paris, which loomed two days ahead, the day after the end of term. She'd been feeling off-colour for the past week, and half-hoped she might be coming down with something, so that the trip would have to be cancelled. But nothing specific had manifested itself, just a vague malaise. The worst of it was that each aspect of the trip – the first-class tickets on Eurostar, a room at the Ritz, the beauty of Paris in springtime – would have been quite wonderful if she could have shared it with Peter. Instead, the prospect was stale and wearisome. Time together.

It was just twelve days – almost to the exact moment of the hour – since she and Peter had parted. All she could do was measure out the days. It wasn't as though she could even look forward to a time when they could be together again. It was too remote, too tentative for that. In that interval she had wept secretly and often, paced the empty house, and wondered how and why their affair had been discovered, and by whom. She loathed Mike Rayment more than ever, saw him as the destructive engine, and wondered how she could ever have been glad that whispers had begun.

She ate a little more, drank a little more, and gazed speculatively at Alan, as he devoured his coq au vin. In between mouthfuls he was describing the outcome of some school meeting, but she didn't bother to listen. She could see why women poisoned their husbands. If it weren't for Alan, if Peter hadn't been so uneasy about him finding out, there would have been no problem. It was that which concerned Peter. She set down her glass. If she were to leave Alan, then it wouldn't matter what people said or thought. If she were free, then she and Peter could do exactly as they pleased. No need to wait for two or three months. She could do it. Hadn't she been on the brink of leaving Alan on the very day that she and Peter had become lovers? Why hadn't she? If she had done it then, it would have spared her this torment. And there was the business of this Winifred woman. Admittedly Alan hadn't been behaving as though he were having an affair – he was never away from home, had neither the time nor the opportunity that Carla could see – but still, it was a possibility. More ammunition, some justification. Alan had said he wanted to make plans for the future while they were in Paris. Very well. Time for some heart-to-heart discussions. They wouldn't exactly be the kind of plans Alan had in mind, but she was tired of feeling sorry for Alan. It was time she thought about herself.

On Saturday morning they drove to Ashford and caught the Eurostar. Ever since coming to her decision, Carla had been filled with a mixture of impatience and trepidation. She both longed for and dreaded the moment when she would tell Alan. This made her restless and more animated than usual, so that she found it easy to talk. She even felt a kind of happiness as they sat together on the train to Paris. The prospect of the freedom which lay ahead infected her with a holiday mood, reflecting Alan's own good humour. He was pleased to see her apparently cheerful, and this touched her with faint guilt. Maybe it was unfair to wait until this weekend to do it, but why not let him enjoy as much of the trip as he could before she told him she was leaving him?

Paris basked in brilliant spring sunshine. Their room at the Ritz overlooked a small square of garden, with high plane trees in young leaf. Carla opened the windows and stepped out on to the balcony, drinking in the quiet air. She felt as though she were on the brink of a new chapter in her life. She was only forty-two, still young and vital. Everything was about to change.

In the room behind her, Alan finished unpacking his overnight bag. He came on to the balcony and put his hands on her shoulders and kissed her neck, then slipped his hands down across the swell of her breasts. She closed her eyes and pretended it was Peter.

'What would you like to do? Lunch, and then a walk?'

'Yes, I'm hungry.'

They had a late lunch in the brasserie, then walked in the Tuileries, looking at the flowers, watching the children. There was a snaking queue stretching from the entrance to the Louvre.

'We should come tomorrow morning,' said Alan. 'We probably won't have to wait if we come early. I haven't been to the Louvre since '77. It was on a trip with some students from King's.'

'I know,' said Carla. 'I was on the same trip.'

'Good God, so you were. I'd forgotten.' He turned to her in surprise, and she glanced at his face, taking in the fluffy, greying hair, the glasses, the moustache and kind, pouchy face, remembering him as he had been then. Skinny, outrageously cool, clever, always somebody else's. She felt an odd pang, a real sense of loss at the thought of their beginnings. If only she could recapture some sense of what he had been, and how much she had loved and admired him back in those days. Impossible. Utterly impossible. She would have to tell him tonight. It was no good pretending any more, talking about going to the Louvre together in the morning. If she didn't tell him tonight, he would want to make love when they got back to the hotel, and Carla knew that she couldn't bear it. She had to tell him tonight.

They went out for dinner, took a taxi to a small restaurant near the Palais Royal which Mike Rayment had recommended to Alan. Alan, knowing Carla's opinion of Mike, didn't mention this fact. It was intimate and very pretty, and Alan wondered, as they sat down, whether

Mike had brought Jenny here, or some other woman.

Alan ordered a glass of champagne each, and they studied the menu. When they had ordered, they chatted about Taft's, as usual, and the people there. As they talked, Carla felt oddly calm and detached, thinking about what she planned to tell him. Or would she? Little shafts of uncertainty and fear kept striking her. Yes, yes, she would. She had to. It couldn't go on any longer. She would wait until they'd eaten. Fortified by the champagne and half a glass of Sancerre, Alan decided just before the main course to tell Carla about Imogen. They had to deal with that before he could go on to talk about his tentative plans for the future.

He pleated his napkin for a few seconds, then said, 'I have something I want to tell you.'

Carla could tell from his voice that this was something important. She wondered if it was about the woman he had been seeing, and felt afraid. Why afraid? But she was. She waited.

'Someone came to see me just before Christmas. It was when you were up in London seeing Louise and Hilary.' The night she and Peter had spent in London. Was that what it was about? Did he know? And if so, why now? But she realized, a second later, that it was nothing to do with that. 'A girl came to see me. Her name was – is – Imogen. She's twenty-three. And she happens to be – well, that is to say . . . she told me that she's my daughter.'

There was silence. Alan had been staring down at the napkin with which he was fiddling while he spoke, and now he looked up. Carla's expression was incredulous.

'Your daughter? You're telling me you have a daughter?'

Alan nodded. 'It was before you and I met. I knew nothing about it – not until Imogen came to see me. I had a brief fling with her mother when I came to teach at King's, and Imogen was apparently the result.'

Carla sat in silence for several seconds. At first she felt nothing but disbelief. Yet why should it be untrue? Hadn't she spent enough years half-hoping that she might conceive, knowing that there was an outside chance? Only the outside chance had been someone else's, a long time ago. She watched him, sipping his wine as though nothing important had occurred. How matter-of-factly he had spoken, delivering this shattering, momentous news in a voice of calm. She could not identify the emotion which welled up within her. It wasn't as though he had deceived her. It had been before they married. He hadn't known. As she stared at him, it came to her. She felt envious, horribly jealous, and consumed with a wild sense of injustice. As long as a child had been something neither of them could have, it had been bearable. It hadn't ever mattered that much, because for so long she had been happy just to have Alan, content with what they shared. Not having children was one of those things. And now he sat there, not meaning to be smug, but happily informing her that it wasn't as they had always thought. He had a child. She didn't – *they* didn't. But he did. And he had known since before Christmas and told her nothing. He had a child. Anger at the unfairness of it prompted her instantly, spitefully, to be glad that she could tell him about Peter – not just that she was leaving him, but everything, the whole affair. She had something with which to strike back. She tried to subdue herself, to remain composed until the moment was right. She swallowed and spoke as calmly as she could. 'Tell me about her.'

Alan told her about Imogen, everything he knew. Their food arrived halfway through, and Carla ate while he talked. She could tell from the way he spoke that he enjoyed talking about her. Clearly he and his new-found daughter got on well. They spoke on the phone, and had had lunch together. The knife twisted in the wound. All this had been happening while she knew nothing about it.

'Why didn't you tell me before?'

Alan picked up his knife and fork and began to eat. 'I kept meaning to, but there never seemed to be a right moment. I thought you might be – oh, I don't know . . . I mean, I knew it would come as something of a shock.' He glanced at her and smiled. 'You seem to be taking it very well. Better than I did.'

'You still haven't told me who Imogen's mother is.'

'Winifred Young. Well, she's McNair now. You probably don't remember her.'

'Yes. Yes, I do.' Carla thought of the old photos which she had looked out a few months ago, the one she had found of them on the trip to Paris. Alan with his arm round some blonde in the back row. Winifred. The name written on the piece of paper. Alan hadn't been having an affair with anyone. A small, hysterical laugh escaped her. She put her napkin to her mouth.

'What's funny?' asked Alan, looking up from his wood pigeon with truffle sauce. He was relieved that Carla had received his news with such equanimity, felt lightened, as though a burden had been lifted. He had been afraid she would be resentful and upset, but she didn't appear to be.

She stared back at him. He had no idea, no idea at all of how all this had affected her. He expected her just to accept it, that he had a new dimension to his life from which she must be forever excluded. It didn't seem to occur to him that it had destroyed one of the basic assumptions of their relationship – that they were together in their childlessness. Well, she thought bitterly, in a way it made things better. He had someone else in his life, she wouldn't be leaving him entirely high and dry.

She lowered her napkin to answer his question. 'I thought you'd been having an affair. I found Winifred's name and number on the pad by the phone. I assumed it was someone you were seeing.' She could feel herself holding back momentarily, like someone with a knife poised, ready to strike.

Alan laughed. 'An affair? Of course I haven't been having an affair. Oh, poor you, thinking that.'

'I have.'

'Sorry?' Alan cut another chunk of pigeon.

He hadn't caught it, hadn't understood. She could pretend she had meant something different. It wasn't too late. But she brought the knife down. 'I have. Been having an affair.' She said it quite clearly. There was no one near to overhear.

He stopped, blinked. Carla couldn't look at him. Her face felt cold, bloodless.

'Jesus. Carla.' He put his knife and fork together, then leaned his elbows on the table and put his head between his hands. It made sense. It made sense of a lot of things. It made sense of the way she had been for many months.

The pain of this realization, the knowledge of her deception, stunned him. Why had she suddenly come out with this now? Why now, at this moment? After a few seconds he looked up at her. 'With Mike Rayment?'

'God, no,' replied Carla, blankly realizing that there was no going back. He would ask and she must answer. It felt as though the whole world was collapsing, crumbling. Strange how little it took. Just a couple of words, one minute things were one way, and the next they were quite another.

'Who, then?' The waiter glided to their table and asked if they had finished. Alan said nothing, continuing to stare at his wife, and Carla nodded for both of them. The waiter took the plates.

'Peter Barrett.' For some reason she had to look away.

'Jesus. How long?'

'It doesn't matter.'

'It matters.'

'Since November.'

'Jesus.' Alan shook his head. 'He's half your age. What on earth do you think you're doing?' He felt like crying.

The cold pleasure of hurting him melted away. She felt tired, tired in anticipation of all the pain and recrimination which must now come. 'What does it matter?' She shrugged. 'You were ready enough to assume that I would have an affair with Mike Rayment.'

'I just thought that if it had to be anybody, it would be him. But Peter Barrett? He's hardly more than a boy. Oh, God, Carla.'

'The point is, I have to tell you that I'm leaving you. I'm sorry to do it now, this way, but these things don't have a right moment, do they? It's like not being able to tell me about Imogen until now.'

So that was it, thought Alan. Twenty years of being together, and it could all be over in a second. I'm in shock, he thought. Peter Barrett. That boy.

He let out a little breath, half laugh, half expression of disbelief. 'Let me get this right . . . You've been having an affair behind my back for four months with a member of my teaching staff. For four bloody months! And you're leaving me. For him.'

'I would have left anyway, Alan. I don't want to live with you any more. Whether or not I live with Peter doesn't matter.' This touched a small fear which dwelt in her mind, unexplored. What would Peter say when she went to him? She had no idea, she was not prepared to think about that now. 'I don't think there's anything left to keep us together.'

'I see.' He motioned to a passing waiter and asked for the bill. They left together in silence, caught a taxi in silence, went back to the hotel in silence. She could think of nothing to say, felt numbed by what she had done. It was remarkable how instantly and utterly it had opened up a huge and irretrievable space between them. Alan, familiar and predictable, was in a world of his own now. She glanced at him in the lift, his expressionless face, and, for the first time in a long time, had no idea of what he was thinking.

In the room he poured himself a drink from the minibar. Carla sat on the edge of the bed, uncertain of what came next. She felt oddly without control over the situation, even though it was she who had engineered it.

Alan spoke at last. 'Are you still seeing him?'

'No. Not for the present. We agreed to – to let things rest for a while. He was worried that people were beginning to talk.'

'People? What people?'

'I don't know. Other members of staff.'

'Dear God in heaven . . .' Alan began to pace the room. 'I can't believe all this. Tell me, are we so desperately unhappy together? Have we been?'

She shrugged. 'What's happy? I'm just not in love with you any more, Alan.'

'So why now? Why pick this evening to do it? Why didn't you tell me before we left? Before starting this *farce* of a weekend!' He hurled the glass he had been drinking from across the room. It fell harmlessly into the heavy folds of the curtain and dropped to the carpet, dribbling some drops of whisky. As a gesture, it was pathetic.

Carla rounded on him in fury. 'Why did *I* choose this evening? You ask me *that*, when you'd been saving up your own little bombshell to drop? Jesus! Out of the blue comes your long-lost daughter, and I'm expected to take it as a matter of course!'

Alan blustered. 'It's not the same thing. It was something I'd been trying to get round to telling you. I wanted the right moment –'

'Alan, we've been married for twenty years! And all that time I thought we couldn't have children, and then you calmly announce that you've got a ready-made little family of your own! How do you think it feels to sit and listen while you tell me how wonderful she is, how much like

276

you, and how well you get on together?' Tears of anger and self-pity came to her eyes.

'Don't talk as though I've denied you something! We went over all this years ago. You always said no – no, you weren't interested in AID, no, you didn't want to look into adoption, no, no, no, every time. You said you were happy as you were. So what is all this about? Would you rather I hadn't told you?'

'Yes! Yes, that way at least I wouldn't have to feel cut out, like you have something private, something that's nothing to do with me! I hate that!'

'*You* hate that? Christ, Carla, think what you're saying! How do you think I feel about your affair with Peter Barrett? Isn't that something private, something that's nothing to do with me?' His voice ground out the sarcasm as they faced one another over the bed. 'At least I haven't betrayed anyone! At least I haven't taken twenty years of marriage and just chucked it away –'

'Haven't you? Haven't you? Are you so sure you can just calmly announce the existence of some long-lost daughter and not expect it to do some damage?'

'Don't pretend it makes any difference! You've spent the last four months lying and cheating, sleeping with someone else behind my back! By the time I told you about Imogen this evening, any damage there was to be done had already been done by you!'

Carla put her hands against her ears, screwing her eyes shut. 'Don't say her name! I don't want to hear her bloody name!'

Alan stood breathing heavily, arms at his sides, anger draining away. Through his own pain he actually felt a flash of pity for her. He had been stupid not to see how hard it might hit her. She had always said throughout their marriage that she hadn't minded being childless, but to find out that he had a child, but not one she could share . . . He sighed, trying to inject a note of reasonableness. He hated rows. 'Carla, there is a difference here. I didn't set out to hurt you, whereas you most certainly intended to hurt me. Or at least, you didn't care if you hurt me, or destroyed our marriage. You've already told me you're leaving me. None of this has anything to do with –' he nearly said Imogen's name, and stopped, '– with my daughter.'

'And don't call her that either!'

Alan's anger flared up again. 'Why not? That's what she is! And it has nothing to do with her! Nothing!'

'Yes, it has! If you hadn't told me –' Carla stopped.

'If I hadn't told you – what?'

'I might not –' Carla broke off again, her voice dropping. 'I might not have told you about Peter. You made me want to. I wanted to hurt you back.'

Alan stared at her for a long moment, trying to comprehend this. She had taken his news about Imogen as some form of personal attack.

'You're saying that this is my fault? That if I hadn't been honest with you about something that had happened in my life, that you would have carried on lying? That would have been fine, wouldn't it? Me none the wiser, you with your little affair . . . It's just as well I did tell you, then, isn't it? At least now we all know where we stand.'

He said nothing after that. In a way she wished he would. He got undressed, put on his nightshirt, went to the bathroom, and then got into bed. Carla could think of nothing to say. She had not expected to feel so wretched, so shaken by what had happened between them. Yet it had been what she had wanted. She, too, got undressed. They lay back to back on their respective sides of the bed, waiting for sleep, waiting for tomorrow. Carla had never felt so far away from Alan in her life, and she had not expected to dislike the feeling so much.

14

They went back to Huntsbridge the next day. Carla said she would go alone if Alan wanted, but he pointed out that there was nothing to keep him in Paris. Their wretched weekend, which should never have begun, was over.

When they arrived back at the house, Alan asked her, 'Where will you go?'

'What?' She was hanging her coat up. The question surprised her. She had given no real thought to the matter.

'Where will you go? Surely you've thought this out?'

'I don't know.' It was true. Leaving Alan had been a metaphorical thing, but he clearly took it at face value. Where *would* she go? She could hardly just pack a bag and go to Peter's. That would be a mistake, she knew.

'And what about money? Why haven't you been busy clearing out the joint account? You really aren't being very practical about this, Carla.'

She didn't like him like this. 'I'm going to make some tea,' she said.

He followed her through to the kitchen. All right, drop the hard act, he told himself. It was just a front for the pain he felt. Throughout the journey home he had had time to reflect on the practicalities of their wretched situation. 'Look,' he said, his tone weary but reasonable, 'I don't want you to go. I can't forgive you for what you've done, but I don't want you to go.'

'How can I stay? You hate me, there's nothing left.' Carla felt utterly wrung out. It was no easy thing severing intimate ties – how could she ever have imagined it would be? She had thought freedom would just come with words.

'I don't hate you. I hate what you've done – to me, to us. But it's stupid for you to leave. You've got nowhere to go. Anyway, we have to see if we can't sort this out . . .' What did he mean? he wondered. This thing had shattered him, he had no idea how he was going to face school and his colleagues next term, but at the end of it all he didn't want to lose his marriage. Carla was his life. Whatever she had done, he wanted to think it could be repaired.

'Alan, I don't want to sort it out. Even before the thing with Peter began, I was going to leave. Just face it – we don't belong together any more.' Her mind clouded with pain as she said this. Being with him had become intolerable, but she wasn't sure how it would be without him. They had been together for so long. Yet what was begun must be finished.

He rested his tired head in his hands. 'We'll get a divorce, if that's what you want. I don't know that it has to come to that. But until then, there's no point in you leaving. This is your home. Everything you need and want is here. Apart from me. But we're civilized adults. We can cooperate until something is sorted out. Money, possessions. It all takes time.'

She sat at the other end of the kitchen table, hands clasped between her knees, miserable and dispirited. Funny how she had thought that Peter was the important thing in all this. He was nothing to do with it. This was her and Alan. She hadn't known that mutual unhappiness could lock people in so closely. At last she looked up. 'All right. Until something's sorted out.'

During the first week of the Easter break, Peter arranged to meet Beatrice. He picked her up outside the library near her home and they drove out to the countryside. They parked near a river and walked along the bank, deserted except for the occasional fisherman.

'What's this dreadful secret you've got to tell me?' asked Beatrice.

Peter stopped. 'Let me kiss you first. In case it's the last time. It really is that bad.'

She laughed, and they kissed for a long moment, standing beneath the boughs of a chestnut tree. She looked into his eyes. 'Nothing can be that bad.' The wind lifted her hair, blowing the red-gold curls about her face.

Peter smoothed them down. 'You're beautiful. And I love you. I don't want to tell you what I have to tell you.'

His voice sounded so serious and wistful that she felt a little afraid. 'Go on.'

He leaned back against the tree and put his hands into the pockets of his coat. There was no gentle way of leading up to this. 'Until a few weeks ago, I was having an affair with a married woman.' Bea's smile faded. She said nothing. Peter scuffed at the ground with his foot. 'I wasn't in love with her. I didn't much like her, in some ways.'

'Why did you, then?' She sounded genuinely curious.

He hesitated. He hadn't expected to be asked this. Still, he had resolved to be honest. 'Sex. It was about sex.'

She turned slowly and began to walk along the bank. Peter pushed himself away from the tree and followed her. He had no idea what to say next. After a moment he took her sleeve, and she stopped.

'What are you – angry? Disappointed? I told you it was bad.' He shrugged. 'I'm not a particularly good person. A lot of the time I don't like myself. If it changes the way you feel about me, it's what I deserve. But whatever happens, I had to be honest with you.'

'You can't help what happened in the past. I'm just a bit – I don't know . . . How can I be hurt? What's it to do with me? But I do feel hurt. That's stupid, isn't it?'

'No, it's not. Come here.' He held her close, then kissed her. 'I don't want to hurt you. All that's over. It never mattered. You matter.'

After a moment she said, 'It must have been very good with her, if sex was what it was all about.' He said nothing. She could tell he wasn't going to respond to this. 'I want it to be better with me.'

'Don't talk in that way. I feel bad enough about seeing you.'

'I'm not a child. Don't you want me? Don't you want to make love to me?'

'Beatrice, this is only the second time we've met like this. Yes, of course I want to. God, do I want to. But –'

'Then let's go back to yours. Now. I want to get rid of that other woman from your mind in every way.' When she kissed him, he wondered how he could ever have wanted anyone else in his life before.

Katie and Georgina were in town, cruising the shops, bored with the Easter break already. Georgina was moody. She and Ryan weren't getting along particularly well together, and she had a suspicion that he was rather fed up with her. She didn't like this. If anyone was going to get fed up first, she should. So that Tuesday she was irritable, and when Georgina was irritable she took it out on Katie.

'God, this is boring. I get really sick of going round the shops. Why can't you ever think of something interesting to do?'

'Me? Why should it be down to me? Anyway, name one interesting thing that there is to do in Huntsbridge.'

'At least when I'm out with Hannah we have a bit of a laugh. You never *do* anything.'

'Like do what?'

'Nothing daring. You're never on for a dare.'

'Oh, really? Dare me to do what?'

'Nick something.'

'Oh, that's just stupid. If Hannah's so interesting and daring, why don't you just go and be her friend, instead of mine?'

'I might. I really might. Sometimes I get sick of being with you.'

'Thanks.' But Katie was a little frightened. She didn't want to be friendless. Georgina saw a lot of Hannah, and she might just carry out her threat. And if Georgina decided not to be her friend, what might she become instead?

Suddenly Georgina's mood changed. 'Oh, come on, don't look such a misery-guts. I don't mean it. It's just you're never up for anything good. It's not such a big deal, pinching stuff. It's a laugh. It's not really stealing. It's like redistribution of wealth. These big shops make too much money, they rip people off.' Katie stared at her friend. Sometimes she couldn't make Georgina out. She struck all these poses about vegetarianism and animal experimentation, she'd even taken part in a school debate about human rights, and yet she could cheerfully go around shoplifting and not think there was anything bad about it.

'I don't want to.'

Georgina shrugged. 'Suit yourself. Come on, let's go into Debenham's.'

They were looking at scarves. Katie got bored. She turned away, while Georgina carried on inspecting the velvet scarves, and scanned the rest of the ground floor idly.

'Come on, let's go,' she said at last. 'I'm hungry. Let's go to Burger King.'

Georgina joined her, and they walked to the door. Out on the street, a hand fell on the shoulder of each girl.

'OK, back inside, girls. Let's go to the manager's office, shall we?'

Katie felt as though her knees had turned to water as the security guard walked them back through the store to the lift.

'We haven't done anything!' she kept saying, trying not to cry. She stared at Georgina, who was white-faced, seeking her support. 'We haven't done anything!'

As they got out of the lift, the guard said, 'What's this, then?' He pulled aside Georgina's coat, and drew from an inside pocket one of the velvet scarves.

'But I didn't take it!' gasped Katie.

Then they were inside an office, two women at computer screens looking up and staring, then through another door, into another office. A man, talking to the guard, coming over to them.

'. . . the dark-haired one put a block in, and this one took the scarf,' the guard was saying.

The man scrutinized them. 'Right, better ring the police. Come on, girls, come and sit over here.'

Katie sat next to Georgina in terrified silence, trying to comprehend what was happening. After a while a policeman arrived, filling the office with his dark presence, and spoke to the manager, then to the girls. Katie could hardly take in what he was saying to them. The words 'arrested on suspicion of shoplifting' stood out, and then she realized that they were being cautioned. She was a criminal. She began to weep and protest to the policeman, but he was unsympathetic and matter-of-fact.

'Better save all that till we get to the station. Come on.'

The hours that followed were a confusion of fear and misery. At the station the custody officer said everything the first policeman had said, and read them their rights. Then she and Georgina were put into separate detention rooms and told to wait until their parents arrived. It was the longest wait of Katie's life. She couldn't drink the cup of tea which was brought for her. Terror filled her, numbing her thoughts. The only thing she held on to was that she hadn't done anything. Georgina had, but just because Katie had been with her didn't mean she was guilty as well. Did it?

At last the door opened, and the policewoman who had brought the cup of tea said, 'Come on. Mum's here.'

A new tide of fear washed through Katie. She got up and went out to face her mother. She was standing there with Mrs Lister. When she saw Katie she said nothing. Katie didn't think she would ever forget the expression on her mother's face. She began to cry again. Nobody comforted her.

'OK, come on, this way . . .' Katie watched as Georgina was led off with her mother to an interview room. She sat with her mother, waiting, wondering what Georgina was saying. Jenny tried to talk to her in a low voice about what had been going on, but Katie just wept and said over and over, 'I didn't do anything.'

At last Georgina and Mrs Lister emerged. Mrs Lister's face was like stone, and Georgina's eyes were pink with crying. She didn't look at Katie.

'Come along,' said the police officer. 'We'd like to talk to you now.' Katie and her mother followed him into the interview room. As Katie watched the police officer setting up the tape machine and reciting the date and time, she felt a bleak relief. At least now they would all listen, and she could tell them how she hadn't done anything.

She sat at a table next to Jenny and faced the police officer.

'Right, now, Katie,' said the police officer. 'You know we arrested you and your friend at Debenham's on suspicion of shoplifting today – the fact is, your mate's just admitted to us that she stole the scarf.' Katie nodded, waiting. 'She also says that you were involved in the offence, that you acted as a lookout.' Katie's face burned crimson. She was aware of her mother's eyes fastened on her face. She just shook her head. For a horrible moment no words would come out. She couldn't believe Georgina had said that. She was so stunned that for a moment she let her mind race back, wondering if at the time something had been said or done to implicate her, something she had missed. 'Would you like to talk us through it, tell us exactly what happened?'

Katie shook her head. 'It's not true. I didn't know anything about it!'

'The security guard says he watched you looking around while your friend was at the scarf counter, checking no one was watching. He says you stood between your friend and the assistant at the pay point, so that no one could see what was going on.'

'I didn't! I didn't do anything like that!' Katie began to cry again.

'Well, it seems very strange to me, two girls out together in the shops, one there with the intention of stealing things, and the other knowing nothing about it. What's more usual is for one to be acting as a lookout, and it sounds to me as though that's exactly what you were doing, Katie.'

It went on and on. Katie refused to admit she had done anything. At length the police officer said, 'It would really be much better for you if you admitted that what you were doing was wrong, Katie.'

'I didn't *do* anything!' wailed Katie.

'Katie, the policeman's right. If you did this with Georgina, best to just come out and say so.'

Even her mother didn't believe her, thought Katie in despair.

At length they were taken back out to the custody area. Georgina was there with her mother. Katie looked at her, but Georgina didn't look back. The officer who had interviewed Katie and Georgina went away for a while.

He came back looking grim and had a brief confabulation with the desk sergeant. Then the sergeant came over and addressed Georgina and her mother. 'The inspector's decided that since this is Georgina's first offence, and she's never been in trouble before, we'll administer a caution.' He went on to explain what it meant. Katie had heard of being given a caution. It sounded like a kindly warning. She hadn't realized that it meant being photographed as well, exactly like a criminal, then having your fingerprints taken and a DNA sample. When he had finished, Georgina was led away by the police officer to receive her caution from the inspector. The sergeant turned to Katie.

'As for you, young lady, we've considered what the security guard told us about the events in the store, and we've decided that there's insufficient evidence to charge you with this offence. Just count yourself lucky that the evidence turned out in your favour – and be careful who you associate with in future.'

Katie felt dazed as she and her mother left the police station. She had no idea what time it was. The only thing she could think of was that Georgina had lied, and had done so merely to get Katie into trouble. She could have told the truth to help her friend, but she hadn't. She wasn't any kind of friend at all.

Katie and her mother drove home. All the way she had to listen to her mother's harangue, how ashamed, how could she, what would her father say, did she realize exactly how bad it could have been . . . On and on.

'And that's not the end of your troubles, my girl,' said Jenny, as they pulled up outside the house. 'A letter came from the school this morning.' Katie started to feel afraid all over again. 'Apparently they've noticed a spell of unexplained absences from certain lessons over the past term. Now, how do you account for that?'

Katie said nothing as they got out of the car. They went into the house.

'Come on. Upstairs to your room. You're going to tell me just exactly what's been going on.'

And Katie did. She sat next to her mother on the bed and with something like relief she told her how it had begun. She told her how she and Georgina had slipped out on a regular basis, and where they had gone. Jenny was appalled.

'You spent the time at the flat of some men you didn't even know?'

'We didn't do anything, mum. We just went there and talked and listened to music. Honestly. Nothing happened. And we did know them. Well, one was someone Georgina knew.'

'How are we going to explain this to the school? Do you realize how bad it looks for your father?'

'I'm sorry,' mumbled Katie miserably.

Jenny regarded her child sadly. It was partly her fault, she knew. She hadn't paid enough attention. Having four children wasn't easy, and Max and Sam took up so much of her time. It was wrong to assume that just because Katie was fifteen she could handle her own life. She had expected Katie to cope with adolescence as easily as Bea seemed to have. But she and Bea were very different. She should have talked to Katie more, tried to find out how she was. But Katie was usually so hard to reach. Not now, though. At this moment she was lost and frightened, and Jenny thought she had heard everything there was to hear.

'Well, you certainly won't be going near that flat again. I can't believe you've done this! And what you've put everyone through today! Oh, Katie . . .'

It was the worst, hearing despair and disappointment in her mother's voice. She fell against her and wept, told her over and over how sorry she was. At least it was finished. At least it was all out in the open now and would stop. Eventually Jenny got up.

'Where are you going?'

'To ring Mrs Lister. I don't know if the school has written to her, but if they haven't, she has to know what you and Georgina have been getting up to. I want this friendship to end, Katie.'

'Don't worry,' murmured Katie miserably.

'I never much cared for Georgina. I think she's been a bad influence on you. For the next few weeks you're grounded, and that includes weekends. Your father and I will decide when we feel you can be trusted again. I want you straight home from school every night, and I'm going to make sure that each of your subject teachers keeps a check on your attendance at every lesson. How could you do this in your GCSE year, Katie? Don't you realize how badly it must have affected your work?'

'We didn't do it all that often. It wasn't like every day. I've kept up my course work. And I'll make up for it, Mummy. I really will.'

'I don't see how you can. And I don't know what the school's going to say about you bunking off. Still, that's something you'll have to face.' Jenny sighed. 'I'd better go and ring Georgina's mother.'

She reached the door, and Katie said, 'Mummy, I'm telling the truth about today, really I am. I didn't know that Georgina had stolen anything. She's done it before, but I haven't ever. I promise. She lied about me. I know she's my best friend, but it's true. She must have lied.'

Her mother paused in the doorway, and in her face Katie could read doubt.

'We'll talk about it later, when I've had a word with your father. In the meantime, I think you should just stay in your room and have a think about the trouble you've caused everyone.'

She left, and Katie lay back against her pillow. She couldn't cry any more. All she could do was wait for the worst thing of all, the row that her father was going to create when he heard about what had been going on. She could imagine what he'd say. It would mostly be about the appalling position it put him in, as a senior member of staff, to have his daughter arrested by the police, to say nothing of her playing truant on a regular basis. It would all be about him. How wonderful it would be, thought Katie miserably, if she could just summon up the nerve and say a few things back to him, tell him how humiliating it was for her to have a father who did the things he did, and thought no one knew, when everyone in the school whispered about it. But she wouldn't. That wasn't the way it went. She wouldn't say anything of the kind, ever.

Jenny went slowly downstairs and into the kitchen. She sat down at the table. Mike was out with the boys at rugby. Like Katie, Jenny thought she could predict Mike's immediate reaction to the day's events. But beyond that, would it occur to him to go to Katie, to find out what was troubling her enough to make her want to play truant? Would he sit down with Jenny later tonight, arm around her, talking it through? The first of those, possibly, once he had vented his wrath and spelled out to everyone just what a difficult position he had been put in by Katie's behaviour. But the second . . . she very much doubted that. He rarely showed her any physical affection now. There was sex, yes, because someone like Mike needed it, but it wasn't the same as occasional hugs, or curling up together just to talk. Even talking came low down his list of priorities. Oh, of course they would discuss the business of Katie, but it wouldn't feel like a shared thing. In fact, she wondered when she had last felt like a real part of a couple. Sometimes it seemed to Jenny that she merely existed within this family as a handmaid, a useful adjunct to their frantically busy, important lives. Someone who, if she didn't exactly keep the ship afloat, at least kept it hoovered and ironed and cooked for, with crisps and biscuits in the cupboard and clean clothes folded in the drawers. Beyond that, she might as well be invisible. She didn't mind that so much with the children. She imagined that most children simply regarded their mother as some-one to service their lives, and provide affection and reassurance and new trainers. That was as it should be. But Mike – Christ, the least he could do was *see* her, think about her, feel how things were for her. His ego was too massive for that. It hadn't mattered in the beginning, because he had loved her then, and passion took the place of things as simple as sympathy and affection. But when the passion melted away after the first few years, she missed those things. She felt entitled to them.

She rose with a sigh to fill the kettle, glancing at the clock. They would be home soon, and she must prepare herself for telling Mike about Katie. Maybe, just maybe, this minor drama would bring them together for a little while, and maybe they really would sit together later in the evening, alone, and talk about things the way they used to. She could always hope.

The remainder of the Easter break passed numbly for Carla. She had had no idea of how dreadful, how isolating it would be, living in the same house as Alan, but both of them as far apart as it was possible to be. He slept in the spare room. He went into school much of the time and busied himself there. At the Easter weekend he went to see his father, alone. He mentioned it to Carla, asked if she wanted to come, but she could tell he didn't want her to. There were occasional meals together, and bleak, difficult conversations. That easy, idle inconsequentiality of his affection had quite vanished, and she was surprised how much difference it made. All these months she had accustomed herself to detesting him, hating the harmless-ness, the niceness of him, wanting so much to be free. Now life was chilled. She had made strangers of them. Yet wasn't this what she had wanted? A break, an end to everything, so that she could be free? Free to do – what? To be with Peter. Her lover.

But with each day that passed Carla couldn't find the courage to go to see Peter, to tell him what had happened.

Several times, during those empty days, she went to pick up the phone to call him. But she was afraid of what he might say in response when she told him. She recalled only too clearly that last conversation, that way he had shrugged and spread his hands. *It doesn't matter that much to me.* The clean, clear indifference in his voice. No, she would have to let some time pass. Time to make him miss her, to see that she was what he really wanted. When she thought back to the passion they had shared, she could convince herself that this would – this must come about. She knew Peter. She knew he needed her too much to let it go completely. And when he did come round at last, she would be able to walk away from Alan. At least the worst of that had already been done. With this painful hope she shored up the days.

Understanding unfolded gradually in Alan's mind. It was only very slowly that he came to a realization of his true feelings. His initial reaction to Carla's confession of her infidelity had been anger and grief. The first few days had found him wanting to recover ground. Carla had said the affair was over for the moment. Maybe they could salvage things. He was so used to Carla being part of his life that his immediate instincts were to repair that life, make it whole again. He spent long, sad hours brooding over the matter. But instead of coming to a sense of forgiveness, he found himself questioning everything on which their life together had been based. As the days passed he reckoned up the instances of deceit, the hours she had spent with that boy, and the carelessness with which she had destroyed their marriage. From this he fell to pondering the substance of that marriage, and he came to the reluctant conclusion that she cared very little for him. He knew now, not just from the fact of her infidelity, but from every recollected slight, every contemptuous remark or instance of impatient indifference, that she had merely tolerated him for some time now. She did not love him.

The moment when he properly realized this came as he was sitting in his office in the empty school, towards the very end of the holiday, affecting to go through paperwork. He felt pain curl round his heart at the true understanding of how things had changed for Carla and himself. The fact was, there was nothing between them worth repairing. He stood up and went to the window and gazed across the empty playing fields. He thought about Carla, her present manner in this worst of times. He couldn't read her well, but he knew that there was not the slightest sign of regret, or any desire to apologize or be forgiven. She might be miserable, but she hadn't made any gesture of contrition. There was no way forward. He might as well go home right now and tell her so.

He drove back to the house and went through to the kitchen. From the window he could see her in the garden, in jeans, a long cardigan over a T-shirt, wearing gardening gloves and cutting back the straggling overgrown tendrils of some rambling rose. It was such a careless, domestic picture. To an outside observer, she looked like a woman who had done nothing – nothing that mattered. Something hardened in his heart, making him want to weep, or to kill her. He held on to this feeling for some moments, watching her, until he was sure that he knew, truthfully and finally, that he no longer loved her.

He went out into the garden. 'I want to talk. Come inside.'

She looked at him carefully, put down the secateurs and drew off her gloves, then followed him into the house.

'I want this farce to end. I've been going over it all in my mind this past week or so, and I think we should just call it a day.' The tired matter-of-factness of his voice startled her. If anything, she had been expecting him to attempt some kind of reconciliation. Not that she wanted it, but it was what she had anticipated. 'You've made it pretty clear that there's nothing left for you in this marriage, so you might as well go. I don't know why I asked you to stay in the first place.'

There was a silence, in which Carla turned away, folding her arms and pacing the kitchen.

'The thing is, I don't want to leave. As you said, I have nowhere to go.'

'What about your lover? What about young Mr Barrett? Won't he have you?'

'Leave Peter out of this. He's the only good thing left in my life.' Alan felt this, the knife twisting in the wound. For how long had he been so unimportant, living in a guileless state of betrayed affection? 'The fact is, Alan, my life is here. This house. All the things in it. I don't want to go.'

He regarded her steadily for a few seconds. 'Then I can't stay here with you. I don't want to be in this house with you, Carla. I don't want to be anywhere near you.' He left the kitchen, and she heard him go out through the front door.

She felt a little shocked and unsteady. It really was over.

The coldness in his voice told her that. She filled the kettle and made some coffee. After ten minutes she heard him come back into the house, then go upstairs to the study.

An hour passed, and Alan came downstairs. His face looked agitated, his person rumpled, the way he usually did when he'd been in a difficult staff meeting. How familiar, she thought fleetingly, and soon to be out of her life for good. She felt a pang at the oddness of this.

'I got the paper and I've rung around, and I've found somewhere over the other side of town. I'll pack a few things and come back later when I know what the place needs, get some bits and pieces.'

He went to make himself some coffee. He felt exhilarated, buoyed up by a sense of achievement. He had thought the business of finding somewhere to live might take days, but provided he could come up with the necessary deposits for rent and electricity, the agency would give him the keys this afternoon. Admittedly it wasn't much of a place, but it was worth it simply to be able to transport his existence elsewhere as soon as he could, to keep up the momentum of departure from Carla.

Carla was slightly stunned by the suddenness of it all. Her accustomed sense of involvement in Alan's doings made her immediately wonder what kind of place it was he was moving to, and what sort of things he might need. She let it fade away. It was nothing to her. They were to be nothing to one another from now on. The dull knowledge pressed home. Well, let him go. How many times she had wished she could be on her own, without his irritating ways and cheerful heedlessness of her true feelings. Let him go.

He packed a suitcase and took it to the car, and drove away. After an hour he came back with a couple of cardboard boxes. She imagined him stopping at the supermarket to fetch them. He packed quite a lot of books. She knew he would be careful to take only his. Then he went upstairs and came back down with the portable TV from their bedroom. She said nothing as he took it out to the car. What could she say? He looked – not cheerful, but animated, busy.

'I'll have to spend the afternoon getting odds and ends. A kettle, things for the kitchen. It's got basic furniture, but – oh, that reminds me.' He snapped his fingers and went upstairs. He came back down with the duvet from the spare room and some sheets and pillowcases from the airing cupboard. 'I'll have to get used to using a launderette again,' he remarked as he carried them out to the car.

The things he was taking were not large or significant. Just little things. Just sheets and books. Yet she knew that fragments of their life together were being broken off and carried away forever. The thing that had been Carla and Alan for so long was being disassembled. Carla found herself struggling with this realization, and the sense of exclusion she felt. She wanted to know what his flat was like, or bedsit, or whatever. She wanted to be able to suggest things he might need, where to put things. He would, she knew, be fairly hopeless on his own. But this was his adventure. She was no longer part of anything he did. His words on parting drove this home to her.

'We'll sort the rest out with the divorce, I suppose.' He drove off.

She went back into the kitchen to contemplate the long

afternoon that stretched ahead, and the empty days that would follow.

It wasn't Jenny's habit to ask her elder daughter where she was going when she went out over the holidays. Beatrice was almost eighteen, after all, and had never given her parents particular cause for concern. Jenny trusted her. She noticed that Bea went out more often than usual, but she was never home late in the evenings, and Jenny thought nothing of it. It wasn't until the end of the holidays that she began to get an idea of what was going on in her daughter's life.

She had been collecting Max from a football party, and was stopped at the traffic lights just down the road from home. Glancing idly to her left, she saw a Morris Minor parked in a side street. She recognized Beatrice immediately, but it took her some seconds to identify the young man who was kissing her. When she realized who it was, she was astonished. That young man, Barrett, the one who had supposedly been having an affair with Carla. The car behind her began to sound his horn, and she pulled away, anxious and dismayed.

'That was Bea,' remarked Max.

'Was it?'

'And that looked like Mr Barrett from school.' Max looked at his mother, watching for her reaction with interest. Jenny said nothing, her mouth in a tight line.

When she got home, Jenny went upstairs to Mike's studio, where he was painting. She paused on the landing halfway up, wondering whether she should speak to Beatrice first before telling Mike. She decided it made no difference one way or the other. Beatrice simply shouldn't be seeing someone of that age, let alone one of her teachers. What on earth was this young man playing at?

She reached the studio at the top of the house and paused to get her breath. She went into the studio cautiously; it irritated Mike to be disturbed.

'Have you got a moment?'

He glanced at her impatiently. 'Is it important?' If she'd come all the way up here, instead of just shouting at him from the foot of the stairs, he supposed it must be.

'It is, rather. I was driving Max home, and I saw Beatrice sitting in a parked car with a man, just round the corner.'

'A man?'

'It was Peter Barrett.'

Mike laid down his brush and wiped paint-stained hands on his shirt. 'Bea? With that little shit?'

Jenny sighed and shrugged. 'They were sitting in his car, kissing. I thought she'd been going out rather a lot over the holidays. She's obviously been seeing him.' From below came the sound of the front door opening and then closing. 'That must be her now. We'll have to speak to her. I know he's only young, but he's one of her teachers. It's really not on.'

Mike raked his fingers through his hair, rage boiling in him. 'Not on? That's putting it fucking mildly! You do realize he's been screwing Carla Tradescant for the past few months? And now he thinks he can move in on my daughter! You're damn right I'm going to speak to her. Christ, first Katie, and now Bea! What is this family playing at?'

He left the studio and went downstairs, Jenny following

fearfully and breathlessly in his wake. Bea was in the kitchen at the fridge. She looked up as her father came in, saw his expression, and was instantly on her guard. She closed the fridge door.

Jenny began to wish she hadn't told Mike – not yet, not without preparing Beatrice first. His temper was one of the worst things about him. He was incapable of handling crises with the children in a calm and rational manner, and if ever something had to be dealt with sensitively, this was it, she knew.

'Mike –' she began.

Mike ignored her and fixed Beatrice with an angry gaze. 'I want to know exactly what's been going on between you and Peter Barrett.'

Bea hesitated, wanting to respond in an adult fashion, but feeling like a guilty child. 'I've just seen him a few times.'

'Have you been sleeping with him? I demand to know! Tell me!'

From her room upstairs, Katie could hear the sound of raised voices in the kitchen below. She left the French prep she was trying to finish and went out on to the landing, leaning over the banisters to listen. Bea and her father were having an argument. Katie didn't think she could remember the last time her father had raised his voice to Bea. Tingling with curiosity, she crept down to the bottom of the stairs and sat, listening.

'Well, have you?' demanded Mike again.

'Mike!' protested Jenny.

'Shut up, Jenny. I'm not afraid to ask her, even if you are.'

Bea's face was burning with anger and embarrassment. 'Daddy, it has nothing to do with you.'

'Oh, yes it has! In the first place, he is a teacher at your school. Do you understand all that that implies?'

'I don't care. Neither does he.'

'Mike,' interrupted Jenny, trying to placate everyone, 'maybe this isn't the best way of going about things. It may not be as bad as you're making out –'

'Jesus Christ!' roared Mike in exasperation. 'It's an abuse of trust! He can't just go around seducing sixth-form pupils! Don't you understand that?'

Still perched at the foot of the stairs, Katie listened, comprehension dawning. Bea had been seeing that young English teacher! How extraordinary! And all the time Katie had thought of Bea as someone who never did anything wrong. Fascinated, thrilled, she got up and went slowly down the hall towards the kitchen. She saw her mother trying to calm Mike, who was in a furious temper, and Bea, her eyes bright with anger, shouting at their father.

'You're not really in a position to talk about abusing people's trust, Dad, are you?' Bea was astonished at her own daring as soon as the words were spoken.

'What? How dare you speak to me like that?' He slapped her face before he could stop himself. Bea stared at him, appalled. Her face glowed crimson where he had hit her.

'Oh, Mike . . .' Jenny's voice was trembling, both hands on Mike's arm. Katie looked on, aghast. Nobody paid her any attention.

'It's true,' said Bea in a low voice, her eyes fixed on her father's. 'I don't care if you hit me again – I'll just say it again. Everybody at school knows about you, the things you do, the way you try to grope people, all your stupid little affairs. So don't you start going on about Peter abusing people's trust. It's not like that. It's nothing like that.'

Oh, go on, brilliant! thought Katie. She wanted to say it out loud. Her eyes were fixed on her sister's face.

'Oh, really?' Mike's fist clenched and unclenched at his side, his fury scarcely contained. 'So I take it that Mr Barrett has told you all about himself, has he? All about the little affair he's been conducting over the past few months? You didn't think you were the only one to be taken in by his boyish good looks and old-fashioned charm, surely.'

Bea hated her father's grinding sarcasm more than anything else. 'Yes, he told me about it. And it's over, so it doesn't matter.'

'I wonder if that's what Mrs Tradescant thinks.'

'What's she go to do with it?'

Mike smiled and Jenny felt his muscles slacken beneath his shirt, where she still held his arm. Her protective instinct was suddenly aroused. She didn't want Mike to tell Bea that. Whatever the rights and wrongs, she didn't want Bea to know that. She glanced at Katie, suddenly noticing her presence.

'Katie, go up to your room,' said Jenny. Katie didn't move. She wanted to hear all of this.

'You mean to say he didn't tell you? Dear me. Very remiss.' Jenny tried to interrupt, to prevent Mike from saying anything more in front of Katie, but Mike was unstoppable. 'He's been having an affair with Carla

Tradescant, wife of our venerated headmaster, for some months now. I'm surprised it's not the talk of the sixth-form common room. So maybe you begin to see why I'm not exactly keen on you having anything to do with him.' Bea said nothing, her face aghast. Then she turned and left the kitchen. Mike went after her and stopped her at the foot of the stairs. 'He's a worthless little shit, and I don't want you to see him again – understand?' His tone was low and threatening. Bea didn't respond, didn't even look at him. Then she went upstairs to her room.

Katie stood there, ignored by her parents as they carried on the row between them, digesting all she had just heard. In one of those small, defining moments of adolescence, her perceptions of the infallibility and security of the adult world had been altered for ever. For a few moments she watched Mike and Jenny bickering, Mike pacing the kitchen, Jenny following, reproaching, pleading. She felt quite separate, shut out. She went back upstairs. For a few seconds she stood hesitantly outside her sister's room, wondering whether there was anything she could say to make things better. She knew there wasn't. She wasn't meant to understand these things, and the truth was, she didn't. So she went back to her room and carried on with her French prep.

15

Bea was to ring Peter next day, so that they could arrange to meet. Peter waited all day. His nonchalant mood of the morning dwindled as time trickled past, and apprehension grew in him. The very air seemed chilled by the silence of the telephone. He thought of calling her house, but the strong possibility of the phone being answered by Mike Rayment deterred him. There was an explanation. Perhaps she'd had to go out unexpectedly, do something with her parents. She would call. He did some work, put on the radio, tried to read, but as the afternoon crawled by he rose and went to the window, conscious of the ache in his heart. On the radio Mick Hucknall sang 'Every Time We Say Goodbye', and Peter felt his heart tighten. Even the cheesiest love song could get to him. He had never known anything like this. He pressed his forehead against the cold glass and waited, unable to do anything more.

By the time evening came, his fear and anxiety seemed to have solidified within him, constricting his mind, rendering him almost incapable of rational thought. What could have changed? What reason could there be for her not to call? Bea had been here only yesterday, his lover of two weeks now, and the tenderness, the understanding of one another which had grown between them seemed to him to be the logical perfection of love itself. He adored her, every particle and aspect of her. Until this time, he had told himself then, he hadn't known what being in love was. How wrong. Today he knew. Twisted up in these endless hours, he really knew. It wasn't the heaven of it that brought it home to you, but the hell. He wanted to go out – he *had* to go out, if he wanted to buy food and eat – but couldn't bring himself to. She might call in that space.

At last he did go out, hurried to the late shop two blocks away, and bought some groceries. Back at the flat, he realized that he had no appetite for food until this uncertainty was resolved. He picked up the phone and keyed in her number, praying that she would answer. It was Mike's voice he heard at the other end, and he instantly cut off, thankful that he had remembered to withhold his own number.

When at last he went to bed, wretched and sick at heart, he thought he had worked through every possibility. The clearest one seemed to be that Mike or his wife had found out, that they had confronted Bea and had told her she had to end the relationship. But that didn't explain why she hadn't called. He lay in the darkness, wanting her, wondering if she was thinking about him. In two days time the summer term would start, and at least then he would see her and be able to talk to her. That was, if she didn't call tomorrow. He was certain she would. Even if Mike Rayment . . . His mind stopped. Cold realization clutched at him. What if Mike had told her about Carla? The one thing Peter hadn't brought himself to do was to tell Bea exactly who it was he'd been having an affair with. He would have told her if she'd asked – at least, that was what he imagined. But she hadn't asked. Peter had begun to think it didn't matter any more. Past. Forgotten. But it did matter. For reasons he could not explore, he knew it did.

For a long, hopeless time he lay awake, certain now of the reason for her silence, desperately wishing for time to pass until school began, when he could see her again and try to sort it all out.

Alan drove into the school car park on the first day of the summer term, and parked his car next to Olive's Fiat. The day was bright, promising warmth. He sat there for a few moments, waiting to be assailed by the apprehensive melancholy which usually characterized a return to Taft's at the start of a new term. It didn't happen. He felt nothing. For four days now he had been living in the small flat near the Superbowl, and in that short space of time he felt as though he had changed his identity. The flat consisted of two rooms, a living room fifteen feet by twelve, with a sort of kitchenette in one corner, separated from the rest of the living area by a shabby breakfast bar, and a bedroom of somewhat smaller dimensions, plus a tiny bathroom with a loo and a shower which didn't work properly. He hadn't lived anywhere so pitiful since his days as a student. Some young men lived on the floor below, and the noise of their comings and goings, their music, the smell of their takeaways, made him feel singularly isolated. He didn't even have the consolation of being young any more. It wouldn't be for ever, of course, only until he and Carla were divorced and the money was sorted out. Even now it would be possible to find something more salubrious. This flat had been a spur-of-the-moment thing, a way to get out of the house and away from Carla. But he didn't much care to find anything else. There was something about the seediness of this existence which was almost invigorating. At nights, at chucking-out time at the pub on the corner, the air was filled with a babble of voices, occasional shouts, and cars and motorbikes droned along the street even in the small hours. The red neon sign of the 24-hour minicab place opposite pulsed eternally. The boys below talked, doors slammed. Sleep was difficult, but sleep would have been, anyway. The suburbs, the natural home of any respectable headmaster of an independent school, were blessedly far away. As he sat in the evenings in the shabby armchair with his supermarket ready-meal on a tray before him, the little portable TV for company, he discerned glimmerings of a self he had forgotten. Away from domesticity, his mind grew clearer, and his thoughts random and surprising.

So now he sat in the car park, struggling into his headmasterly identity. What would the teachers and pupils of Taft's know of recent events? How many knew about Carla and Peter Barrett? What was he going to do or say if and when he encountered Barrett?

'All these questions and more . . .' muttered Alan to himself. He took the key from the ignition and got out of the car.

Olive greeted him with her usual calm smile, and ran through a list of things she wanted to discuss. He tried to translate her manner, her look, gauging whether or not she was privy to the recent details of his domestic life. He could read nothing.

On his way to the hall to take assembly, Alan encountered Peter at a corridor junction. Buffered by a swarm of pupils, he scarcely scanned the other man's face. Peter did not meet his eye, merely carried on his conversation with one of the year sevens trotting by his side. That hadn't been hard, thought Alan, surprised by how little he felt now about Carla's infidelity. What was intolerable was the thought of other people's knowledge, and he had yet to discover how far that went, and to what effect.

Nobody looked at him any differently, it seemed, neither with scorn nor sympathy. Everyone's behaviour was blindingly normal. He got on with the routine of assembly, welcoming the school back, determination to make this summer term one of hard work and enjoyment, those with exams having a chance to demonstrate their abilities, events to look forward to include Founder's Day, school sports, last but not least . . . Yet there was a difference. He felt detached, as though some veil hung between him and the rest of them, as though his voice and actions came from far away, from a place quite unconnected to his real thoughts.

At morning break Mrs Prosser tapped on Alan's door and peeped round. 'Mr Rayment would like a word, Headmaster.'

That much was normal, too – it was almost a relief to know that Mike was running true to form with a complaint on the first day of term, like a greyhound out of the slips. He couldn't help wondering, as Mike's leonine form filled the doorway, whether Mike knew, and what he thought. Pity. Contempt, probably.

'Come in, Mike. How can I help?'

Instead of ranging around the room as he usually did, Mike slumped into a chair opposite Alan's desk.

He sat in grim silence for a few seconds, picking paint from the end of his thumb. 'I want to talk to you about Barrett.'

'Ah, the school magazine. I'd heard there was a problem there. I've had a word with Verity –'

'I'm not here about the school magazine, Alan. Did you know that Barrett has been seeing my daughter?'

Given the recent revelation of Carla's affair with Peter, Alan found this turn of events somewhat astonishing. He blinked at Mike, speechless for a few seconds. 'Beatrice?'

'Well, I don't mean Katie, do I? Mind you, given his track record, I wouldn't be surprised if he started going for fifteen-year-olds. The point is, Alan, I want you to warn the little prick off. Jenny and I have spoken to Bea, told her not to see him again, but as headmaster I want you to make it perfectly clear to him that the school doesn't tolerate that kind of behaviour from the teaching staff.'

Still trying to take this in, Alan wondered bemusedly whether to raise the small matter of Paula Kennedy, the photography assistant. There was no point, he decided. Mike probably didn't have time for moral equivalence, not where his daughter was concerned. He said nothing for a few moments, fiddling with his letter-opener.

'Well?' demanded Mike. 'Are you going to speak to him? Because if you don't, I intend to take matters into my own hands, and give him the message in my own way. And that'll be a damn sight worse than any letter from the school governors.'

Oh God, thought Alan, this meant having to call Barrett in, talk to him face to face. The guy who'd been screwing his wife for a couple of terms. He couldn't do it. How could he? What was the etiquette for such occasions? He sighed. 'All right. I'll say something to him.'

'Good.'

Mike was about to rise from the chair, when Alan suddenly looked up and said in a different voice, his headmasterly tone quite gone, 'Why didn't you tell me about Carla and Peter Barrett, Mike?' His voice was naked, curious.

Mike sat down again, taken aback. He ran his hands through his hair. 'Christ, Alan, it was hardly my affair.'

'Interestingly put. You'd probably have liked it to be. Leaving that aside, I should tell you that I've moved out. Carla and I have separated.' He regarded Mike. 'Or did you know already?'

'Yes. Jenny said something. I'm sorry. You can see why I don't want the bastard anywhere near Beatrice. In fact, I'd like to see him off the teaching staff.'

Alan smiled, musing. 'He certainly gets about a bit, doesn't he?'

'You're taking it in remarkably good part, considering he's managed to break up your marriage.' Mike hesitated, looking uncomfortable, something Alan didn't think he'd ever seen before. 'Look, Alan, I hadn't really given it proper thought. Don't want to make things embarrassing for you. If you'd rather not –'

Alan stopped him. 'No, don't worry. Anything rather than you taking the matter into your own hands. I'll speak to him. We're professionals, aren't we?'

'If you say so.' Mike nodded, rose, and left the room.

Alan sighed, and pulled towards him the pile of correspondence which Mrs Prosser had left on his desk. First Carla, now Beatrice Rayment. Poor Carla, her erstwhile lover had found someone else. Well, well . . . It astonished him how unmoved he now felt by what had happened with Carla. As for Beatrice, that was for Mike to worry about. The top letter on the pile was in a blue airmail envelope, which he opened with interest. As he read the contents he began to smile. How extraordinary. It was from that American fellow he had met up in London last October, at that conference on cultural divisions. They'd both attended a workshop on dominance and deference in urban literature. Amusing bloke. And here he was, offering Alan a post as visiting lecturer for a year at the college where he taught in New Jersey. Lecturing on the urban narrative. God, the things the Americans dreamed up. Nice thought, but not one he could realistically entertain. He folded the letter up and put it in his tray to reply to later. Then he moved on to the next letter, from a parent wanting to know whether speed bumps shouldn't be installed at the entrance to the school car park.

Peter knew, with a leaden sinking of his heart, that something had gone seriously wrong. Beatrice wouldn't even meet his eye in assembly. He glimpsed her throughout the day, but it was impossible to get her attention, to make her speak to him, without causing some kind of minor scene. He waited until the afternoon, watched the pupils streaming out across the quad at ten to four, trying to spot Bea among them. He knew she sometimes went home with her father, and on other days, when Mike was busy after school, walked to the bus stop. No point in driving past there and trying to speak to her. The pavement was always thronged with Taft's pupils.

Peter slipped on his jacket and went to his car, and drove to Bea's home. He parked round the corner from the bus stop and waited. When she eventually got off the bus, she was alone, and with relief Peter drove round the corner and pulled up. When she saw him, Bea stopped, hesitating.

Peter wound down the window. 'Please. I need to talk to you. I think I know what it is, and I have to explain.'

She glanced towards her house, then got in beside him. Peter drove out to the deserted road by the industrial estate.

After they'd been driving for a minute or so, Bea asked, 'Why didn't you tell me who it was?'

'Why does it make any difference? I told you I'd been seeing someone, that it was over.'

'Yes, but Mrs Tradescant! God, Peter . . .'

He said nothing, then stopped the car and looked at her. 'Is that it, then? Despite all the things we've said to one another, does such a little thing make that much difference?'

'It's not a little thing. It makes you seem . . . I don't know . . . Maybe it's because I know her, because I hate the thought of you being with her . . . I mean, the headmaster's wife!' She shook her head and looked out of the window. 'It makes you seem so devious, just after what you can get. How am I to know it's not that way with me? Did you tell her you loved her, tell her how wonderful she is? The same lies?'

'No!' The depth of feeling, the sense of despair at what

he stood to lose brought unexpected tears to Peter's eyes. 'No! I didn't love her! I have never loved anyone but you. What existed between Carla and myself was purely physical. You have to understand how unimportant it was.'

'But what about her marriage? What about Mr Tradescant? Didn't you ever think that what you were doing was wrong?'

Peter passed a hand across his face. 'Why does all this matter to you now? When I told you I'd been having an affair with a married woman, you didn't react like this. Why should her identity matter so much?'

'I thought you meant someone on her own, someone separated, or something like that. But *her* . . .'

'Bea, please.' He took her by the shoulders and turned her to face him. 'The thing just happened. I meant it be a one-off, but it just carried on. I didn't mean any harm. I certainly didn't want to hurt Alan Tradescant. I hope I haven't. The way she talked about him, I don't think she cared that much about him. If I could have known then that there would be you, that I would feel this way, I would never have begun it. But I can't change the past. It's over, please try to forget it. Just love me.'

She regarded him for a long time. 'I do. I can't help it. But knowing you could do that – it makes me afraid.'

'Oh, come here.' He held her and kissed her.

'There's more than just that,' said Bea at last.

He smoothed her hair and gazed at her. 'What?'

'My father knows I've been seeing you. He went completely berserk, going on about you abusing your position, how I'm never to see you again.'

'None of that matters. I told you. The fact that I'm a

teacher is an accident. We have to look at it that way. You'll be eighteen soon. We love one another, and nobody can change that or tell us what to do.'

'Yes, well – try telling my father that. You don't have to live in the same house as him.'

There was silence for a few seconds. 'Neither do you. I mean it. You don't have to stay there. Come and live with me.'

'But we can't do that . . . What about the school? What would people say?'

'I don't care. I'm not staying at Taft's after this term. You'll have done your exams, we can do exactly as we please. Why not start now? I don't intend to spend the next two months not being able to see you, just because of your father.'

Bea thought this over wonderingly. It was true. She wasn't a child. If she and Peter wanted to be together, they could be. But not as long as she lived at home. She felt a euphoric thrill at the thought of living with Peter, of being with him, not having to feel that hollow deadness on parting. The last three days had been bad enough. It didn't matter what people at school thought or said. In a way, it would be rather fun. And in a couple of months it would all be behind her, anyway. She looked at him and smiled. 'All right. It's going to cause absolute hell at home, but at least it'll be short-lived.'

'My only worry is that your father may decide to try and break my neck. But I'm not sure that I care.'

The next day Beatrice went home after school and began to pack her clothes. She took her bags downstairs to the hall and went through to the kitchen, where Jenny was preparing supper.

'Mummy, I've got something to tell you. Don't get all stressed out and upset when you hear it.' Jenny turned and looked at her daughter in puzzlement. 'I'm going to go and live with Peter.'

Jenny stared in astonishment. 'Don't be ridiculous.'

'It's not ridiculous. I've packed, and Peter's picking me up in ten minutes. I want to do it before Daddy gets home. We just want to be together. I know all the things Daddy said about him abusing his position and everything, but it's not true. Anyway, none of that's important.'

Jenny realized she was serious. She wiped her hands on a towel. 'Bea, I think we need to have a talk. Sit down.' She moved around the kitchen, trying to gather her wits about her. She wasn't going to lose her cool, the way Mike had. Bea had clearly got some very daft notions about Peter Barrett, and it was just a question of talking some sense into her. She sat down next to her daughter. 'Look, darling, I have some idea of how you're feeling. Maybe Daddy didn't go about things the right way the other day. He only has your well-being at heart. We both do. I know Peter Barrett's a very attractive young man, and you obviously feel quite strongly about him, but you have to see that he's taken advantage of his position. After all, you're a pupil at the school, and he's a teacher. It's really not at all appropriate, this relationship.'

'Oh, Mummy, don't use words like "appropriate"! I love him. We're in love.'

Jenny weighed this. 'Bea, he had an affair with Carla Tradescant for four months. With a married woman,

317

someone else's wife. What kind of person does that make him? How can you trust your feelings for him, or his for you? Don't you think you should be a bit more measured, take things more slowly?' Bea's eyes slid away from hers, and sensing a slight ascendancy, Jenny pressed on. 'You've got your A-levels coming up this term, for goodness' sake. They're vitally important. Surely the sensible thing to do would be to wait until those are out of the way, and then see how you feel. If he's so fond of you, he should have your best interests at heart, not suggest that you run off to live with him. How do you think it would look for the school if you were to do that? What kind of a position would it put Daddy in? Have you thought about that?'

Bea looked at her mother with candid, patient eyes. 'You don't understand. I love him. Every minute, every hour that I'm away from him is awful. He feels the same way. You talk as though I'm a fourteen-year-old with a crush on someone. I'm old enough to know what I'm doing. After all, you were eighteen when you married Daddy.' She paused, and Bea thought her mother was about to say something. But Jenny merely looked away, and Bea could not read the expression in her eyes. 'This is serious. We want to be together. I'm sorry if it makes things awkward for Daddy at school, but he should be used to living with awkward situations at that place by now. He's created enough of them himself. As for my exams, I've got a better chance of passing them if I'm happy than if I stay here fighting with Daddy all the time. Because that's what'll happen. I intend to carry on seeing Peter, no matter what he says.'

'And what about the business with Mrs Tradescant?'

asked Jenny quietly. 'You do know that the Tradescants have separated, don't you? All because of Peter Barrett.' Bea said nothing. She hadn't known that. 'You're nearly grown up, Bea. I can't stop you doing what you want. I'm only asking you to give it a little more thought.'

The clock ticked. Jenny waited, hoping. Suddenly the silence was broken by the sound of Mike's key in the front door. Go upstairs, Mike, prayed Jenny. Go up to your studio.

Mike came into the kitchen. 'Whose bags are those in the hall?'

Bea looked up. 'Mine.'

'Mike,' said Jenny quickly, 'Bea and I are just talking something through. D'you think –'

'Oh, really? And what are they doing there?'

'I've just told Mummy. I'm going to live with Peter Barrett.' She swallowed, waiting for the outburst. She wasn't going to back down now.

'Like hell you are,' said Mike calmly, but with murder in his eyes. He went to the sink and began to fill the kettle. From outside came the sound of a car horn. Bea rose.

'Sit down!' Mike spoke with the thunderous and instant authority of years of teaching, and for a moment Bea's reflexes made her hesitate. Then she went to the door. 'I said, sit down!'

'I'm not one of your classes, Daddy,' said Bea calmly. Mike made a grab for her, but she pulled her arm away, and he gripped her by her hair. Jenny rose, numb, appalled.

'Stop it! Let her go!' She gripped Mike's hand and prised his fingers from Bea's long, curling hair. Bea cried out in pain as she tugged away. She reached the hall and picked

319

up her bags, moving away quickly from her father, who was being pulled back by Jenny. He struggled against his wife, jerking back his elbow and catching Jenny underneath her chin so that her mouth snapped shut, catching her lower lip and making it bleed. She sat down heavily in a chair from the force of the blow, dizzy, aware of Mike lunging out into the hallway. Bea sped down the path and into Peter's car, and they were gone before Mike got past the front door. He stood raging and shouting on the path. Jenny sat in the chair, nursing her mouth, listening to his futile tirade. It was like a scene from some awful soap. She had to admit she had some sympathy with her daughter. She knew what it was like to love that way. She only hoped that Peter didn't turn out to be as big a bastard as Mike. She rather suspected he might.

Katie was in her room, lying on the bed reading a magazine, when she heard the sound of shouting from downstairs. Not again, she thought. Apprehensive but excited, she swung her legs off the bed, about to go and investigate. She heard the sound of the front door opening, and went to the window. Max and Sam came into her room, eyes wide.

'What's happening?' asked Sam. 'Dad's shouting his head off downstairs!'

'I don't know,' said Katie. The three of them hurried to the window and peered out, just in time to see Bea getting into Peter's car, dragging a couple of bags in with her. They watched as the Morris Minor roared off down the street, and their father appeared on the path below, still shouting.

'Wow,' said Katie under her breath.

*

Carla was stranded. Never had she felt so alone in her life. Maeve came round, and Carla told her everything. It helped, like a process of emptying and cleansing, to pour the whole story out to Maeve. She needed witnesses. She needed friends. She wept, and Maeve comforted her.

'We did know, you know – well, we guessed.'

'How?'

'People just get to know. It's hard to keep things secret in a community like this, with the school and everything.'

'I don't know where I go from here.' Carla dabbed her eyes.

'Maybe Alan will come back. It must be pretty hard for him to take, Peter being a member of staff, and so on. But after a while, he might –'

'I don't want him back. Anyway, there is no "back" – there's nothing for either of us to return to. That's the funny thing about marriage. I didn't know it until all this happened. It's not just two people. It's a thing you make, with a life of its own. I remember reading something a few months ago. Some American saying that people are wrong to talk about a marriage breaking down, as though it has an independent organic existence. But it does. All that shared past. The thing you are together. And when it's not there any more – well, it's just gone. You can't recreate it. At least, Alan and I can't. Anyway, I don't want to. Things had gone wrong long before Peter came on the scene. For me, at any rate.' She sighed and crumpled the damp tissue she held. 'I just want to know where I go from here.'

'What about Peter?' asked Maeve gently. She didn't imagine for one moment that the affair between Carla and

Peter had any future, but she was curious to know how things stood. Ever since she had first guessed the truth about Carla's affair, Maeve had been secretly envious. She only wished she could find out from Carla just what kind of lover Peter Barrett was, but it wasn't really the kind of thing one could bring up.

'I don't know,' said Carla. She suddenly felt defensive, afraid. Had he heard that Alan had left? If so, why had he not rung? 'I haven't seen him recently. We agreed to – to . . . give one another some space. Just for the time being.'

'Oh. Oh, well . . .'

'I suppose one just gets swept along by events. Alan's seen a solicitor, and I imagine I'll have to, as well. There's the house and money to sort out . . .' She gazed past Maeve at the French windows, which stood open now to the fresh spring air, and thought about Peter coming across the lawn in the rain, his head down, and how long ago it seemed.

On Friday morning of the first week of term, Carla was scheduled to rehearse Beatrice Rayment and Colin Fowler, polishing up their *Doll's House* duologue before the exams in a few weeks' time. She sat over her breakfast coffee, dreading the thought of going up to the school. Maeve had assured her that not many people knew about her and Peter, or even that Alan had moved out, but she wasn't sure that she could face the thought of looks and whispers.

A gust of nausea swept through her, and she put down her coffee cup. Well, she wasn't just going to retire into the background, like someone disgraced and ashamed.

That was the last thing she wanted people to think of her. She would tough this out. It happened to people all the time, and they just rode out scandal, lived their lives. For the present, this was her life, and she was going to get on with it.

She walked the mile and a half to the school, trying to enjoy the spring sunshine, but filled with a dragging lassitude. She put it down to apprehension. What if she saw Peter? Part of her longed to see him, another part was afraid. She realized now that with every day which had passed, a gulf had opened up between them, filled with deep and foreboding silence.

At Taft's the lesson bell had just gone, and the corridor was filled with pupils. No sign of Peter. She had to walk past his classroom to reach room C23, where the tutorials took place, but when she glanced in it was empty.

Beatrice and Colin were waiting for her. Carla said good morning, and they murmured in reply. As the lesson progressed, Carla noticed that Bea's normally pliant and friendly manner towards her was somehow altered. She didn't meet Carla's eye very often, and when she did, there was something searching in her expression. Maybe it was just part and parcel of the coldness with which she was trying to infuse the character she was playing. Or maybe she had heard something from her father of all that had been going on. Was it disapproval she read? No doubt. That was the censorious sixth form for you. She looked back to the text, and suddenly it began to dance before her eyes. Her head felt feathery, and the nausea she had experienced earlier filled her again. She closed her eyes briefly. She must be coming down with something. She swallowed and looked at her watch. Still fifteen minutes to the end of the lesson.

'Beatrice, Colin – I'm afraid I'll have to stop you. I'm feeling rather unwell.' She got up from the chair and reached for her coat. 'Just carry on without me . . .'

She went out into the corridor, wondering if she was going to be sick. She leaned against the wall, listening to the dim chant of children in a nearby classroom reciting something. After a few seconds she walked to the side entrance and out across the car park. She drew in deep breaths, telling herself she felt better. Yet the prospect of the walk back home was daunting, feeling as she did. She saw Peter's Morris Minor, and a few spaces away Alan's car. Blank, motionless, their owners busy elsewhere, just the sight of them made her feel horribly alone. No one to help her, no one to drive her home, or put her to bed, make her cups of tea, behave solicitously. Alan, not so long ago, would have done all that – and she would have accepted it, telling herself she didn't want it, loathing his kindness and attention, yet expecting it. Wouldn't she?

She made her way home and called the surgery, and was able to make an appointment for that afternoon. She went to bed and slept for two hours.

At the surgery, the doctor on duty was a young, plump woman, brisk and efficient. Carla hadn't seen her before. She rarely had any cause to visit the surgery. She explained her symptoms, the nausea and lassitude.

'Mhmm. Pop up on the table, and I'll examine you.' Carla lay on the table and stared at the ceiling while the doctor probed and pressed, giving herself up to the faintly enjoyable sensation of the young woman's cool fingers. Then she sat up while the doctor listened to her breathing and heart.

'Your uterus is rather full,' said the doctor. Carla buttoned her blouse, wondering what this meant. 'I wonder if you might be pregnant.'

Carla's fingers froze. 'No,' she said quickly. 'I really don't think that's possible.'

'Oh? How have your periods been?'

'Well, they've always been erratic . . . That is, I haven't had one in a while, but that's not unusual with me.' It was true. Over the last couple of years they'd become very irregular, sometimes with gaps as long as three months. All right, perhaps she had been careless where Peter was concerned, but it hadn't seemed to matter then. Not in the beginning, when everything had been so wonderful. Now, though . . . Now. Oh God.

'Well, let's just do a quick test anyway, shall we?' The doctor sent Carla off to give a urine sample. She came back in and handed it to the doctor, who did the test. Carla sat with her hands clasped, clenched, between her knees, watching the doctor's calm, quick movements, her dispassionate expression.

She held up the little wand. 'There we are, Mrs Tradescant. Clear as anything.' Carla stared at the wand, momentarily confused by the words the doctor had used, expecting to see nothing, but seeing instead, in one of its windows, a definite blue line. She glanced at the doctor's cheerful expression, which perplexed her even more.

'You mean it's all right?' She had no experience of the mysteries of pregnancy-testing kits.

'It means you're pregnant.'

Emotions settled upon her, one after the other, with the lightness of small, swift birds. Astonishment, a disbelieving delight at the mere fact of becoming pregnant when she had never, ever . . . Their pleasure was quickly eclipsed by icy reality, the understanding of what this meant. She let out a long breath. 'I see.'

'Now, you say your periods are erratic – can you remember the date of your last one?' Carla shook her head, her mind blank. The doctor was writing now, still talking, but Carla couldn't take in what she was saying. Pregnant. It had to be Peter's baby. For a moment her mind teetered on the truth. He would want none of this, had said he wanted only a casual affair, he hadn't called her and he didn't mean to. But then her mind rocked away from this, denying it. No. Their affair wasn't over. They were just giving things a rest, giving each other some space, the way she had told Maeve. This would make things different. He had probably been about to call her, anyway. She knew him, she loved him. There was still hope for both of them. This was going to be all right. '. . . but of course a scan will give us a more accurate picture. I'll arrange for you to attend the antenatal clinic at Greenford. Let's see, they have their clinics on Mondays and Fridays . . .' What would he say? She wouldn't think about that yet. No point in looking ahead too far. She would take this step by step, the way she had learned to with Peter. At least, she thought wryly, this evened things up with Alan. How bizarre.

16

'I know my father's going to be out this evening. If I go round now, I'll be back by seven. I have to talk to her, Peter. It's not the same on the phone. And there are one or two things I need.'

'OK. I'll cook supper while you're out.' He watched Bea as she pulled on her jacket, loving the way she put up a hand to lift her hair away from her collar. Small things. 'Come here,' he said. The way she came into his arms, her smile unfolding, was so familiar now. He would never grow tired of it, nor of the touch of her mouth, the graceful quickness of her movements, and the hundred and one mysteries she had brought into his life. He could not imagine being without her now. The temperature at school was still uncertain. Bea had sworn her closest friends to secrecy, and Mike Rayment had clearly decided that discretion was the best policy at present, but it could only be a matter of time before talk began. Peter fervently wished for the end of term, to be able to close this chapter of his life, leaving Huntsbridge behind to make a fresh start with Bea.

'Do you want me to drive you?'

'No, it's OK. I'll walk. It's only a mile or so, and it's a nice evening.'

She left the flat, and Peter watched from the window as she crossed the road and turned the corner. He sat down and began to mark a pile of year eight essays. After half an hour he went into the kitchen and began to prepare supper, thinking as he did so how much more of a pleasure it was, and less of a chore, to cook for someone else as well. It was Friday evening, and they had the whole weekend together. In his mind he built a picture of the kind of life he and Bea would make with one another, far away from this small-town claustrophobia, maybe in London. . . .

The sound of the doorbell surprised him. Mike Rayment, planning on horsewhipping him? He half-expected something of the kind any day now, but Bea had said he was busy this evening. He didn't exactly know many people in Huntsbridge, and the only person who had ever called round was Jeff Perkins, inviting him out for the odd drink. . . .

And Carla. This thought flashed through his mind at the very second he opened the door. The sight of her standing there filled him with a dull dismay.

'Hello, Peter,' she said. She spoke brightly, quickly, as though to counter the awful blankness of his expression. What it told her made her heart quail.

'Hello.'

'Can I come in? I need to talk to you.' He said nothing, but stepped aside to let her pass through. 'Oh, are you cooking? Smells nice.'

He wondered what lay behind this edgy cheerfulness of hers. Her face looked drawn and tired.

'Just a minute. I'll turn it off.' He went through to the little kitchen and switched off the gas beneath the pasta sauce he was cooking, then stood there, giving himself time. Why the hell was she here? Maybe she knew about

Beatrice. He didn't think so. That wouldn't bring her round here. Damn, damn. He should have made it clear last time that it was utterly, completely over. He didn't want to see her. They had nothing to say to one another. He just wanted to get rid of her before Bea got back. He went back through. Carla was standing by the window, looking out, still in her coat. Well, he wasn't going to suggest she take it off, nor was he about to offer her a drink. She had come here, she could make the running. But as the seconds passed, it seemed Carla could stand there for ever, staring out at the road.

'Carla, why have you come round? I don't think there's anything left to say. Not after last time.'

She turned to look at him. Her eyes seemed to have lost all life. The words he had just spoken, the cold impatience of his voice, told her all she needed to know. Still, she had to tell him.

'I came to tell you that I'm pregnant.'

Silence filled the room. Peter lifted a hand and ran his fingers slowly through his hair. At last he said, 'You told me there was nothing to worry about. Right at the very beginning, you told me that.'

How young and afraid he sounded, thought Carla. She had come here without any plan, unable to calculate what she would say in the light of the unpredictability of his reaction. Now she knew what that was, and she might as well tell the truth. Nothing to lose. 'I think perhaps I wanted it to happen. I was very much in love with you. I thought it didn't matter what happened. I thought we loved one another.'

'You lied to me? You've been waiting for this to

happen?' He was stunned, angry, incredulous. He knew all about Alan's low sperm count, Carla had told him months ago, but he couldn't believe she wouldn't take precautions with their own lovemaking.

'No. Nothing like that. I didn't plan . . . I didn't think it would all be like this.' Her eyes filled with tears. 'Oh, God . . .' There was a catch in her voice. 'You really don't want me at all, do you?' She imagined he must see her as she saw herself, a pathetic, middle-aged woman from whom all control was slipping away. The idea was horrible.

'No, Carla, I don't.' Peter's voice was dead level. She had planned this. Or if not that, she had recklessly let it happen.

'But what about the baby? Our baby?'

'Carla!' He couldn't stand this melodrama. 'Carla –' He put his hands on her shoulders, as much to steady his own temper as to comfort her, and she leaned her head against one of his arms and wept. This was awful, he thought. Awful and unreal. If he'd known in the beginning, he would never have gone near her. He had thought her cool, contained, able to fulfil his desires without threat or obligation. How far from the truth.

'Come on. Sit down.' He guided her to a chair and waited as she struggled to subdue her tears, working out what he must say. When at last she had recovered a little, he sat down opposite her. 'Carla, I don't want any part of this. You can't talk about "our baby". I never wanted this. I wouldn't have slept with you if I'd known there was the slightest risk.'

'What about the first time? You didn't care then.'

It was true. He could say nothing in the face of this, couldn't defend himself by recalling how unstoppable, how helplessly erotic that first time had been. He remained silent.

'Whatever you say Peter, it involves both of us.' Her voice was a little unsteady. He shook his head, stared down at the carpet, still saying nothing. 'Alan's left me.' At this, Peter looked up. 'I told him about us. He wants a divorce.'

They stared at one another. In her reddened eyes he could read so much – fear and love and hopelessness. And pain. For the first time, he felt true shame. So much so that he had to look away.

'I'm sorry.' He was struggling to take in this appalling situation, holding on to the fact that he had meant for none of this to happen. 'Look . . . How can you be sure? How can you be sure that it's mine? It could be Alan's. There's an outside chance.'

'After all these years? It's hardly likely.' She shook her head, wiping her eyes with a tissue. 'Peter, what are we going to do?'

'I told you, Carla, this is of your making. I never wanted anything like this. What happens is up to you.'

'Don't you care? Don't you even care about your own child?' Her voice shook.

Peter stood up, filled with rage and helplessness. 'No! No, I don't! Don't you understand that this has nothing to do with me? For God's sake, Carla, I'm only twenty-seven! Did you really think that something like this was going to change things between us? That it would make our affair into something it never was? Because if you did, then it was underhand, and calculating, and I'm not going to let you trap me!'

'Trap you?' She got up and went to him, hands on his, touching, clasping, conciliatory. He moved away. 'Trap you? Peter, it wasn't like that. It was nothing like that.'

'No? Well, by God, that's what it feels like. I'll give you money for an abortion, if you need it, but that's as far as I intend to get involved.'

Her hands went to her stomach in a swift, involuntary movement. 'You think I would get rid of it? You really think that?'

'It seems to me that it would be best for everyone.'

'Best for everyone? Best for you, you mean! No responsibility, no mess! Then you can just walk away from me with a clear conscience?' Anger born of fear brought a hysterical edge to Carla's voice. She saw very clearly now how little there had ever been between herself and Peter. She had been someone to while away dull hours in a strange town, a way of bringing some small thrill to his life. She should have admitted this to herself months ago, but love and hope and a longing to find something more than the mundane rut of her marriage had made it easy to deceive herself.

'You brought this on yourself, Carla. All of it. I've told you what I'm prepared to do, and that's where it ends.'

It was true, all he said. It hadn't been his fault. The part he had played had been entirely unintentional. But in her fear and isolation, she could not let him escape so easily. If there could not be love, then there must be recrimination, and suffering, some way of making him share her misery. Her voice shook again with suppressed anger and tears. 'Oh, no, Peter. It doesn't work like that. If I decide to keep this baby, your part in it has only just begun. You can't just walk away. There are ways of making sure you don't.'

His expression exposed the rawness of his fears. For a few seconds he could say nothing. Then he shook his head, young and beaten. 'Do what you want. Wreck both of our lives.'

The desire to hurt him trickled away. There was no way back, and no way forward, Carla knew. She had never had his love. There was no point in trying to make him pay for the wrongs she had done herself. All she would do was damage him. She still loved him enough not to wish that.

'I only want you to care.' Her voice was low, frayed into little more than a whisper by weeping and despair.

There was silence between them for a few long seconds, then the sound of feet on the stair, a key being inserted in the lock of the front door. Just before the door opened, in an instant of immediate and exquisitely painful revelation, Carla knew that it must be a girl, that Peter had someone else, someone about whom she had known nothing until this moment. When she saw Bea, saw the girl's expression, happiness melting into startled dismay, eyes flashing to Peter's face, she felt fully and finally defeated. This had all been so much of a game, right from the beginning, and she hadn't played by the rules. She had been too old, unwise and inexperienced, hoping for all the wrong things.

She thrust her hands into the pockets of her coat, and fled from the flat, from the sight of them both.

*

That evening Alan sat over his solitary supper and realized that he couldn't face another weekend alone in the flat. He went out to the nearest call box, rang Imogen, and told her he was coming up to London for the weekend.

'The thing is – can you put me up for the night?'

Imogen hesitated. 'Tomorrow? Saturday?'

'I mean, if it's too much trouble –'

'No, no – nothing like that. I'll make up the spare bed. It was just a bit of a surprise.' There was a pause. 'Is everything all right?'

'Well, no. Not exactly. Carla and I have separated.'

'Oh. Oh, I see. I'm really sorry.' She paused, not wishing to sound daft and self-centred, but said anyway, 'Nothing to do with me, I hope.'

'No, no . . . I'll tell you all about it. It's just that I'm living in this place that's little more than a bedsit, and there's a danger that I'll finish up listening to Leonard Cohen and cutting my throat if I have to stay here all weekend.'

She laughed. 'Sorry. It's not funny.'

'It is. It's about as hilarious as living in a hall of residence. Anyway, I'll be up some time after lunch. Say two.'

'OK.'

He pressed the button and took out his phone card. He stood there for a few seconds, gazing down at it, thinking of the little flat that didn't even have a phone, wondering why he didn't feel more depressed than he did. This should be the worst of times. Instead, it felt more real than anything he had known in ages, more vital and surprising. Certainly not happy, but authentic, genuine, actual. If anything, the hours spent at Taft's began to seem more and more superfluous to the new inner world he had discovered, where thoughts and ideas surfaced and broke like bubbles, astonishing him. It was a long, long time since he had been his own self. It was like floating free from . . . from something to which Carla had kept him anchored. So many years.

He wandered back to the flat, and went slowly upstairs, past the first floor where the young men lived. He didn't know their names. Their separate identities weren't even clear. Tonight a middle-aged man — about his own age, thinning blond hair, dressed in an expensive suit of the kind not generally seen in this part of town — was standing on the landing. The door to the flat was open, and voices came from within. The man glanced at Alan. He nodded, looking faintly embarrassed. 'Evening.'

'Evening,' replied Alan. He passed on up the stairs and into his flat. He watched television and drank a couple of whiskies. Not something he did on weekdays, but this was Friday night, after all, and the rest of the single world was out there doing stuff. He was single, but not out there, thank God. Good luck to them. All the bars and clubs and pubs and chip shops, all the wanting and watching, hoping and daring and faking . . . He toasted himself, his single state, feet up on the cheap coffee table, glass resting on his paunch. After a while the music began from below. Alan didn't mind it much. It wasn't especially loud, but it made him wish he could counter it with something of his own. He thought back to the night Imogen had first come into his life, and the stuff he'd played then. He wished he had it here. It would be good, it would be right, in this situation, to get a bit of Led Zeppelin blasting out. Some

Tull, Pink Floyd. *Dark Side of the Moon*. That was something he should have played to Imogen. The turntable was with Carla. She had no use for it. She never listened to the old music, wasn't true to the past. Their past. His past. He would go round and get it. That, and all his albums. Yes, he would. Next week. The music they listened to nowadays was nothing compared to what they had had back then. Ah, the things his pupils didn't know about him. Just another old geezer, a headmaster, an old fart. You wait, he thought. Wait for what? He sighed. To turn into old farts yourselves. We all turn into old farts in the end. But that life in the mind, that spark that never dies – people should live by it, do right by it, not slip, slip, slip, as he was doing, into the twilight world of being past it. Past it. Honour it, Alan. Be true to yourself. He had no idea what was himself any more. He'd spent twenty years thinking it had everything to do with Carla, but that had turned out to be an illusion.

He lay in his chair, somnolent, thinking about Carla and Peter Barrett. His initial hatred of the whole situation, all the jealousy, bitterness and humiliation, had turned into something more apathetic, touched with curiosity and envy. When he had been Peter's age, would he have turned down someone like Carla? No chance, married or not. But he'd have left it at a one-night stand, wouldn't have taken it any further. Stupid boy. He drank some more whisky. If Peter, why not Mike Rayment? She'd probably had him as well. Oh, God . . . He rubbed his forehead. This thing would hurt for a long time. Looking back, though, he should have seen how much was wrong, how little she wanted him. Well, she was free now. No going back. He closed his eyes and hummed a bit of Springsteen. *'Everybody's got a hungry heart . . . everybody's got a hungry heart . . .'* He wondered if he was too old to go to a Bruce Springsteen concert, or if the Boss even did tours any more.

The following afternoon, around three o'clock, Alan arrived at Imogen's. He sat down on the sofa, dropping his overnight bag on the floor, and sighed. Imogen inspected him. 'You do look a bit . . . careworn.'

'What a word. You are the very soul of tact. Mildly hungover would do, vaguely depressed, and completely knackered. I had to wait ages for the tube. I wish I'd known Chelsea were playing at home.'

'Sorry, I tend not to know about these things. Tea?'

Imogen made tea and they sat comfortably together. The sash windows were wide open to the warm May air, and the sound of traffic drifted up from the street. 'Sorry about the mess,' said Imogen, nodding in the direction of a stack of boxes beside the door. 'Ewan's moving out next week. He's got the chance of a flatshare in Vauxhall, so it seemed sensible for him to take it while he could, rather than wait till July.'

'Is that when the lease is up?' asked Alan. Imogen nodded, sipping her tea. 'What about the rent?'

She shrugged. 'I'll find it somehow. It's only for a couple of months.'

'Let me help. I'd like to. It's what fathers are for.'

She smiled. 'If you like. Thanks.' There was companionable silence for a while, then Imogen asked, 'Do you want to tell me about you and Carla?'

337

Alan told her all about it. Imogen said nothing, waiting until he seemed to have finished.

'So, moving out – was that a spur-of-the-moment thing, a kind of instant emotional reaction?'

'As in a major fit of pique?' Alan shook his head. 'No, it wasn't like that. In the beginning she talked about leaving me, but there wasn't really any place for her to go. She has friends in Huntsbridge, but not that kind. Anyway, the house is her home. Her domain. It became clear she wasn't going to go to this Peter guy, so we just stayed there, together, for something like a couple of weeks.'

'Unpleasant. Difficult.'

'I think I had some idea that we could put the pieces back together again. That when the pain lessened, we could go back to being the way we were before. So far as I could tell, the affair with Barrett had come to an end. But as the days went by, and I really thought about it, I realized I hadn't really known Carla well at all. She had turned into someone quite different from the girl I married. I've changed, too. She doesn't love me. Not as I am. She wanted – wants – something else. Not me. And when I saw all this, and weighed up the way she had behaved, not even caring about us, I decided I didn't want to fix things. Even if they could be fixed, I didn't want to. I didn't like her for what she had done, and I didn't want to stay. So I found a flat to rent, and moved out.'

'Do you still love her?'

Alan spread his hands. 'You tell me what love is. Familiarity and affection? Being used to someone? Needing them around? I don't think it fits her definition.'

'Do people at work know?'

'Some must. I don't care. I have to see Barrett every day, and it's become a matter of indifference. There's pride, of course. Humiliation, authority undermined, all that stuff.' He let out a long sigh. 'It's looking ahead that's the hard part. I feel like I'm completely cut adrift. I know the people I work with, they're friends of a kind, but nobody I can talk to. Nobody that matters.' He glanced at Imogen. 'It's funny how I've known you for just a few months, and I can talk to you in a way I could never talk to any of them. It's not even like talking to a daughter. Not that I would know, mind.'

'I'm glad you can talk to me. I wish I could help. With the future, I mean. Do you have to stay in Huntsbridge? Can't you just cut your ties, move away?'

Alan shook his head. 'It's not that easy. I could look for another job, but headmasterships don't come up that often. It could be years. Anyway, I'm probably too old.' He smiled. 'This fellow from the States that I met at a conference wrote to me the other day, offering me a job lecturing at his college in New Jersey.'

'Why don't you take it? That could be brilliant! You could come and see me in New York.'

'Not that easy. I have to give the school governors a year's notice under my contract. Anyway, it's only a visiting lectureship, just for a year. And there's the divorce to sort out. I've never done one of those before. They should sell self-help manuals – you know, *Divorce for Dummies*. So I'm afraid it's not on.'

'No, I suppose not.'

They talked through the afternoon. At six they took a bus to Hammersmith and walked down to a riverside pub.

They had a couple of drinks and some food, and then went back to the flat and watched a video of *Sliding Doors* with a bottle of wine. Ewan came and went. Alan stayed the night, and the next day, as Imogen was lunching with friends, he travelled back to Huntsbridge with a sheaf of Sunday newspapers. The dead hours he might have spent in his flat were taken care of, at any rate. But what about next weekend, and all the others? He couldn't contemplate those.

He unlocked his car in the station car park and chucked in his belongings. He remembered his resolve of Friday night. The turntable. His records. Yes. He would go and get them now. He should make some kind of contact with Carla, anyway, see how she was getting on. He drove the familiar route home and parked outside the house. It was mid-afternoon, and her car was there, so he supposed she was in. He walked up the path, took out his key, hesitated, then rang the bell.

Carla came to the door. When she saw him, she seemed startled and confused, running her hands through her hair, straightening her shirt over her jeans. 'I was having a nap. Come in.'

He followed her through to the kitchen, where she began to fill the kettle. 'Coffee?'

'I won't stop,' said Alan diffidently. 'I just came to collect some records. Listen – d'you mind if I take the deck and the speakers? You can keep the rest of the system.'

He half-expected her to protest that the sound system wasn't much use without the speakers, but she didn't seem to have been listening. Her eyes had an absorbed, intense expression. 'Please, Alan – stay and have some coffee. I want us to talk.'

He nodded and wandered through to the living room, where he crouched down by the shelf full of LPs and began to riffle through them.

In the kitchen Carla carefully spooned coffee into the cafetière, then poured in the boiling water. How strange that he should have come round this afternoon. How unexpected, the shock and relief of seeing him. All weekend she had been alone, churning the mill of thought and emotion. It seemed logical that he should come now, to help her. He would help her. They had always seen things through together. He would forgive and forget, and it would be all right. The sight of him, all the things she had detested – his moustache, his very bearing, the creased folds of his jacket, the smell of tobacco – she now found safe and familiar. Of course he had come.

She had no idea of how weakened and vulnerable the hours had left her. She could not view her thought processes with dispassion, or she would have understood that she was seeking now to protect herself, ready to turn truth and logic askew to her own ends. She took the coffee through and sat down on the sofa. Alan got up and came to sit down near her.

'You do the plunger thing. You always liked that,' said Carla.

He pushed the plunger down slowly and glanced at her. 'How are you getting on?' He genuinely wanted to know. It had been unusual over the past few weeks, being without her, not having to consider her. She looked tired and upset.

She breathed deeply in and out for a few seconds. He looked at her sharply, about to say something, when she suddenly said, 'I'm pregnant.'

He sat back slowly, absorbing, analysing. In an instant, the anger and pain that he had felt on learning about Peter flooded him again, then ebbed, slopping at the back of his mind. 'I see.' He studied the backs of his hands. 'I see.'

There was a long, painful silence. Carla did not move to pour the coffee. She was entirely still. Alan looked up at last, remembering what Mike had told him about Peter and Beatrice, wondering if Carla knew about that. 'What does young Mr Barrett have to say about it?'

'He's – he's not really prepared to get involved.' Carla spoke with difficulty.

This hurting just went on and on, thought Alan. You thought you were done with it, and then more came. 'It's his child, though, I take it.' He spoke it as a flat statement, not a question.

The look she gave him was almost supplicating. 'It might be. It might be yours.'

Alan got up and paced the room. 'Oh, please. Give me some credit.'

'It might be! Who's to say it isn't?'

Alan stopped and looked down at her. 'Carla, you're pregnant with someone else's child, and you want to pretend that it might be mine. Why?'

She began to weep, her shoulders shaking. 'Because I need you! Because I need someone to look after me!' The sound of her sobs tore at him. He sat down next to her and put his arms round her, listening to her as she wept and talked. 'I'm so, so sorry about everything that has

342

happened! I'm sorry I've hurt you! I'm sorry about what I've done to our marriage! Oh, God, Alan. I'm sorry . . .' She wept and wept.

'Carla, you're saying all this because you're in a mess. That's the only reason.'

She looked up at him through her tears. 'You can think that if you want. Maybe it's true. But I am sorry, truly sorry.'

'About what? Sorry that you slept with Peter Barrett? Sorry that you're pregnant?'

She managed to control her tears, wiping her eyes and nose on the cuff of her shirt. 'About us. About throwing away what we had. I thought I was bored, I thought everything was passing me by without ever knowing what it was like to be loved –'

'Loved? Didn't I love you?' He took her by her shoulders and gazed into her face.

'I didn't mean . . . Oh, Christ, I don't want to start crying again. It was nothing to do with you. Not in that way. But it's happened, and now I'm pregnant, and the thing is . . . I need you. Alan, I really and truly and dreadfully need you.' She clutched with damp, twisting fingers at the sleeves of his jacket. 'I want back what we had, what we had in the beginning. I want us to start again. We can, you know.' The expression in her eyes was beseeching. 'With a baby, it can be the way we always wanted it to be.'

Barefaced, he thought. But he didn't blame her. 'Carla, it's not my baby.' His voice was quiet, reasonable.

'But it might be! It could be! Alan, don't let's throw away all our years together! It's not just me you'd be rejecting. It's me and a child. Even if it's not yours, you could make it yours. I know I behaved badly about Imogen – I shouldn't have been so jealous. But I couldn't help it! If you had a daughter, I wanted it to be ours. We could make this baby ours.'

Something in this moved him. An outside chance said it could be his child. Look at Imogen. He knew it wasn't, but still . . . When Carla talked about how they were in the beginning, it touched him in a way he hadn't expected. Maybe he had been wrong to think that things had been irreparably damaged. Maybe there were ways of putting it all back together, the thing they once had. Make do and mend. Plod on. She was asking him to be a father to her child. She was appealing not for love, but for support.

Alan took his hands from her shoulders and stood up. 'Christ, Carla, you expect so much. You think you can just . . .' He shook his head, lost for words. She watched him, tearful, hopeful, without any clue of what she wanted from him beyond protection. 'I have to think about it all. I can't just sit here and say, fine, forget the divorce, we go on from here. I can't. Look, I'm sorry about the coffee. I have to go away and think. I'll speak to you – maybe tomorrow.'

He went. She heard the car start and sat inertly, staring at the coffee pot.

'You told her my final ultimatum?'

'Yes, Mike. When she came on Friday night she said it was a relief you hadn't kicked up a row at school, made things difficult for her and Peter. I told her that you were giving her until the weekend, that if she came back,

344

promised to stop seeing him, then you wouldn't do anything.'

'And?'

'She said, well, what could you do? So I told her that you were prepared to go to the governors and so on, and get Peter kicked out. That it would be very embarrassing for everyone, her especially.' Jenny shrugged. 'She says she doesn't care. She won't be threatened. She says she loves him, and that if anyone is going to be embarrassed, it'll be you.'

Mike strode round the room. 'How can she talk about *loving* him? She hasn't the first idea what she's talking about. She's shacked up with some bloody philanderer without any morals, and thinks it's love! Her own English teacher – and to top it all, someone who's been screwing the headmaster's wife rigid for four months! Does she have any idea how fucking humiliating the whole business is for this family, especially for me?'

'Keep your voice down. The children will hear you.'

'Peter Barrett is going to regret the day he ever set foot in that school. I knew from the beginning that he was trouble.'

'You're sounding extremely hackneyed, Mike. Anyway, don't you think this has more to do with your ego than Bea's happiness?'

'Meaning?'

She paused, meeting her husband's eye. 'First of all it's Carla Tradescant, whom you've wanted to get into bed for years. Oh, don't deny it. She's just about the only one you haven't had. We may not talk about it, Mike, but I'm tired of turning a blind eye to your bits on the side. You couldn't bear the fact that Peter Barrett did something you've always wanted to. And now your daughter. That really gets your goat, doesn't it?'

'Keep it down, for God's sake! You were the one who didn't want the kids to hear!'

Jenny got up from her chair, trembling slightly, surprised that she should be saying any of this at all. But it was a relief to find herself doing it. The events of the last two weeks had given her the nerve. She would no longer let herself be bullied. 'You think, because I'm fat and past it in your eyes, that you can do what you like, have whom you like! Well, I'm not going to take it any more, Mike. You're weak. You're so weak that you hate the idea of someone half your age getting the better of you. In fact, you can't stand it! Well, do you know what? It seems to me that Bea might have had the right idea, getting out of here and away from you. I'm beginning to wish I'd thought of it myself!'

'Jenny!'

She had slammed the door, leaving Mike standing, uncertain for once, in the middle of the room.

Alan couldn't get that Springsteen song out of his mind. He hummed it all the way into school in the car. '*Got a wife and kid in Baltimore, Jack, I went out for a ride and I never went back. Like the river that don't know where it's goin', I took a wrong turn and I just kept goin'* . . .' Some odd elation, some undercurrent of the song, was still with him when he went into school. He had tried to sort out his thoughts in relation to Carla, but that issue hung suspended, unresolved in his mind. He had slept badly, his brain restless

346

and light, and he wondered if he were becoming somehow unhinged by everything that was happening around him. He kept thinking back to Carla and yesterday, how that revelation and her plea to him should have grounded, stalled him. He even tried to feel the force of it, willing himself into a state of responsibility, of accepting events, faults on both sides, and pressing ahead with a shared future. The image, the resolution came no closer.

The morning passed by, a drift of meetings and documents. The lunchtime bell went. He sat contemplating the events of the coming month. A meeting of the school governors was to take place in two weeks' time. He had the minutes of the last one in front of him. He picked up his pen, preparing to enter the date in his diary.

Mrs Prosser tapped on the door and put her head round. 'Mr Rayment would like a word, Headmaster.'

Mike came in and closed the door. Alan looked at him interrogatively. He could tell he was incandescent about something. 'Mike?'

'It's about that bastard Barrett.'

'Look, I haven't had the chance to speak to him –'

'It's gone beyond that. I want you to take up the matter with the school governors.'

'Mike, I know she's your daughter, but you have to admit that this kind of thing does happen from time to time. It's not unknown. I mean, it's not a sackable offence, or anything like that –'

'I don't care!' snarled Mike. He leaned down and banged Alan's desk so suddenly that Alan jumped. 'I want to hurt the bastard! He's had your wife, he's on his way to wrecking my daughter's future! Do you realize she's moved out and gone to live with Barrett? I want him fixed! You can put it to the governors in such a way that he's forced to go, without references, and without much hope of getting a job elsewhere. Not in a hurry, at any rate. Given what he's done to you, I would have thought you'd be happy to help. You haven't so much as squeaked at him . . .'

The rant went on. Alan didn't listen. He was suddenly remembering a conversation he had had with Imogen a while ago, one in which he had said, *I don't want to be what I am. And when I look ahead, my heart sinks. Even when I look beyond that, to when I retire, the whole thing is a blank. I can't see myself. I have no notion of any future for myself.* And what was it she had said? He nodded to himself, recalling. She really had perspective, that kid.

He looked down at his diary. He suddenly realized he had no intention whatsoever of putting in the date of the next governors' meeting. Or any other date. He closed the diary. He capped his pen and put it in his jacket pocket. He stood up. Mike stopped talking. Alan took his cigarettes from his pocket and lit one.

'I wouldn't jeopardize young Mr Barrett's prospects, if I were you, Mike. He's going to need as much money as he can lay his hands on, believe you me. I'm afraid I can't take up the matter on your behalf at the meeting of the school governors, as I shan't be there.' He leaned over and fished around in his in-tray for a letter, which he tucked into his pocket. Then he moved out from behind his desk, smiling at Mike. 'Do you know where I'm going?'

Mike stared at him. 'Lunch?'

'Fuck lunch. I'm off, Mike. I don't like being a head-master any more. Why don't you apply for my job? You'd be much better at it than me.' He took the office keys from his pocket, opened a drawer, chucked them inside, and closed it. He walked past Mike to the door, through the office, down the corridor, across the car park. He got into his car and turned the engine, and reversed his car out of his parking space. He flicked his cigarette butt out of the window and drove off. He would never, ever come back to this place again. He felt wonderful.

Katie had her heart in her mouth as she slipped out of the school gates. It was the only chance she would get. There was a netball tournament going on all afternoon, with four visiting schools. Loads of spectators. Everyone who wasn't any good at netball, including Katie, was a mere spectator. She wouldn't be missed. Though after being hauled over the coals by everyone for skipping lessons, she knew she was taking a risk slipping out in the lunch hour. Still, it was the only opportunity. She was still grounded at weekends, and she had to be back home straight after school every day. Ever since Bea left her parents had become paranoid. What other chance had she of seeing Daniel?

For weeks she had been utterly miserable, in the worst state of helpless uncertainty. It wasn't just her own unhappiness she had agonized over, but Daniel's state of mind. What had he thought when she had just vanished from his life? She had told him she loved him, they loved each other, and then she had just disappeared. That was what it must seem like to him. He was so alone – the alonest person she knew – that she couldn't bear to think of how he must feel. She had wept over it at nights. He didn't have her phone number, had never rung her at home. He didn't know where she lived. Each day at lunchtime she had wandered down to the railings by the road which bordered the playing fields, hoping he might come there. He knew which school she went to. He might come. But he didn't, ever. He no longer believed in her. She had let him down, failed him. She had to see him.

She waited nervously at the bus stop, one eye on the school gates, just the way she had with Georgina a few weeks ago. She and Georgina didn't speak to one another now. Georgina hung around with Hannah. Katie no longer cared. In the first days after the shoplifting incident, she longed to have it out with her, to demand to know why she had done what she had done, but the remainder of the holidays dragged past, and by the time the new term started, it no longer mattered. It was something of a relief to be back in the mainstream, not exclusively Georgina's property any more. And doing more work at school actually helped, made her feel better. Why, she didn't know, but it did.

She stood alone, waiting for the bus.

Alan drove to his home. Carla's home. Her car was there, she was in. He got out and rang the doorbell.

The tense expression on Carla's face seemed to clear when she saw him standing there. 'Alan – I thought you might come round tonight. I didn't expect you in the middle of the day.' It struck him that this was a cue to ask who she was expecting, but he was making no cheap shots. 'Come in. Coffee?'

He followed her through to the kitchen. 'No, thanks.

Once again, can't stop. I just came by to tell you that I'm going away.'

She stared at him. 'Going away?'

'To the States. As of July. From Huntsbridge, as of tomorrow.'

She sat down. 'Alan, have you completely lost it?' She studied him, conscious of something febrile about him, his hair a little wild, his eyes bright.

'No, Carla. Quite the opposite, I hope. I've had as much as I can take of everything, and I'm packing it all in.'

He must be having some kind of breakdown, thought Carla. It must have been coming on for weeks. This wasn't what she had expected to have to cope with. After he had gone yesterday, she had been pretty sure that he would be persuaded that a reconciliation was for the best. That they could put it all behind them, and start afresh. It was what she needed. She could tolerate anything, so long as she wasn't left alone. Besides, she realized now how much about their relationship she had undervalued. That was what she had told herself. But clearly recent events had taken their toll on him.

'Come on, sit down,' she said calmly. 'Tell me what's happened.'

'What's happened? Let me see . . . Well, let's take you first. You've screwed up our marriage, you're pregnant by another man, and you're hoping I'll stick around to support you. Now, as for myself, I have just walked out of my job, I intend to leave you, this place, this country, and I also want all my records.'

This shook her, but she kept her voice steady and reasonable. 'Alan, don't be silly. You can't just walk out of your job. You're a headmaster. Headmasters don't just walk out!'

He shook his head. 'Carla, I'm leaving. I've had it. I'll be writing to the governors tomorrow, and then I'm history.'

The calm tone of his voice unnerved her. He wasn't talking like a man having a breakdown. 'Alan, this is stupid. Whatever's gone wrong in the past months, you know it is. You have a contract! If you walk out now, you'll be risking your pension!'

'Yes, I thought that might be your first consideration, what with the divorce and so forth. Well, I couldn't give a toss. I've been offered a visiting lectureship in New Jersey, and I'm going to take it. In the meantime, I think I'll stay with my daughter, if she'll have me.'

Panic and disbelief filled Carla. She had expected nothing like this. 'But Alan! What about everything we talked about yesterday? What about me?' Tears sprang to her eyes.

'What about you? You're nothing to do with me any more.'

The chill in his voice frightened her, turning her anguish to rage. 'How can you be so bloody irresponsible?' Her voice rose hysterically. Alan left the kitchen, went through to the living room, and began to pull his records from the shelf. 'This is entirely childish! You can't just leave your job like that! What do you think's going to happen? You'll never get a post as a headmaster anywhere else! Probably not even as a teacher – not at an HMC school! Have you thought about that?'

He stacked the records together on the table and picked

them up, a large unwieldy, slithering bundle against his chest. An echo of some dream came to him, then passed. 'Carla, I have entirely had it with other people's notions of being responsible. I'm actually not a very responsible kind of guy. I never was. I think I'll be true to myself for a change. You should try it. Or maybe you already have.'

He moved towards the door. She suddenly, senselessly, recalled lying in bed with him at the hall of residence that first afternoon years ago. She had said to him he could lose his job if he were found out, didn't he care? He hadn't cared. She had spent years with him, thinking he had turned into someone else. He hadn't.

Alan made it to the hall with his records, managed to open the front door with his chin on top of the pile. *Ziggy Stardust* slipped off and landed on the floor. Oh well, sod Bowie, he could stay there. He walked carefully down the path, knees bent, balancing his pile of records. He got the car door open and chucked them all on the back seat.

Carla had followed him down the path. She was weeping. For herself, he knew. 'Alan, don't do anything rash. Wait out the term. There are other ways of doing this. You can get yourself dismissed, make sure you don't lose everything –'

He laughed. 'You really don't know me at all, do you? Here's your ring back. And the house keys. I'll give you an address to send things to. In the meantime, our solicitors can chat away to one another.'

Carla stood on the pavement, watching as he drove away.

*

Katie climbed the steps to the first-floor flat and rang the bell. She waited a long time. When the door opened, it was Andy.

'Hello,' he said. 'Haven't seen you for a long time.'

'Is Daniel in?'

'No. He's gone.'

Something within her dropped like a stone, leaving a cold space. 'When?'

Andy shrugged. 'Couple of days ago. His mum and dad came and fetched him. I don't know what it was all about. They were really mad at Phil for not letting on he was here. Funny little guy. Sad, really. He didn't want any of his family to know where he was. I suppose Phil thought he was protecting him. He'd have been on the streets otherwise. But in the end Phil had to tell them.'

She swallowed hard. 'Is Phil in?' Phil must have an address, she would at least be able to write to Daniel and explain to him what had happened. Please, please, she prayed.

'Nope. He left yesterday. The lease is up soon. Everyone's off. Don't know where Phil went. Said something about a job up north.'

It sank in slowly. Daniel was gone. She had no means of finding out where he was. She would never see him again. The sense of loss that blossomed inside her was so painful that she thought she would never experience anything so desolating in her life again. She was only fifteen, so it didn't count. She knew that. It was what any sensible problem page would tell her.

'O K. Thanks.'

'Bye.' Andy closed the door. As Katie slowly descended

the stairs, she heard the hurried sound of footsteps approaching from below. She froze in disbelief. It was the head, Mr Tradescant. He was coming upstairs! Oh God, they knew, and he had come to find her . . .

Alan reached the landing where she stood, and stared at Katie in a puzzled, preoccupied way. What on earth was Katie Rayment doing in this part of town during school hours? Katie hesitated in momentary terror, then fled downstairs to the street. Instinctively Alan made a mental note to speak to her, and to her form teacher. Then he remembered – it was nothing to do with him any more. A glad lightness seemed to spread within him, expanding his heart, filling his whole being. He felt suddenly thirty years younger. He carried on upstairs to the flat, turned the key in the lock, and went to pack his few belongings.